W9-CZZ-882

She should fight doggedly on or risk dire, far-reaching consequences.

But at the moment she didn't want to listen to reason or warnings. She didn't want to think. She wanted only to feel. Finally, Mary Ellen sighed softly in acquiescence, wrapped her weak, weary arms around his neck and dissolved in his embrace.

The experienced Captain Knight knew the exact second of her surrender. And it *was* surrender. She didn't know it yet, but he did. He knew as well that this surrender was total.

She was now his.

Nan Ryan is the author of more than twenty sizzling historical romances. Readers love her trademark style—American historical stories brimming with fiery passion and fast-paced action.

When not writing, Nan can usually be found at the local library, researching her next novel.

She and her husband, Joe, currently live at the edge of Arizona's ruggedly beautiful Sonoran desert.

NAN RYAN

You Belong to My Heart

HARLEQUIN®

TORONTO • NEW YORK • LONDON
AMSTERDAM • PARIS • SYDNEY • HAMBURG
STOCKHOLM • ATHENS • TOKYO • MILAN • MADRID
PRAGUE • WARSAW • BUDAPEST • AUCKLAND

ISBN 0-373-81106-3

YOU BELONG TO MY HEART

Copyright © 1996 by Nan Ryan.

This edition published by arrangement with Harlequin Books S.A.

® and TM are trademarks of the publisher. Trademarks indicated with
® are registered in the United States Patent and Trademark Office, the
Canadian Trade Marks Office and in other countries.

www.eHarlequin.com

Printed in U.S.A.

For Lori Copeland and Heather Graham
Old, new, or ex—
you'll always be two of my best friends.

Part One

One

The summer sun had finally gone down on the longest day of the year. But the sticky, stifling heat remained even after night had fallen. As bedtime approached not a breath of air stirred the damask curtains framing the wide, ceiling-high windows. No cooling breeze blew in off the river below. The unending hours of darkness stretching before her promised little relief from the wretched, muggy, unbearable heat.

Mary Ellen Preble felt as if she could stand it no longer.

Not for one more minute.

She stopped pacing in the shadowy gloom of the silent, sweltering drawing room. She whirled about, crossed the large airless parlor, rushed anxiously into the marble floored corridor, and hurried headlong out the double fan-lighted front doors.

The miserable mistress of Longwood lifted her hot, heavy skirts, eagerly crossed the wide gallery, and fled down the front steps of the old family mansion, which sat high on the Chickasaw Bluffs overlooking the Mis-

sissippi River. The restless thirty-one-year-old divorcée was well aware that she shouldn't be venturing out
alone in this now Union-occupied city. But the sultry
June heat and the crushing loneliness of the big empty
house made her uncharacteristically reckless.

At the waist-high hedge bordering the terraced riverfront lawn, Mary Ellen paused, drew a deep, long
breath of the heavy night air, and gazed wistfully down
on the river far below.

In a flash she was through the gate and outside the
safety of Longwood's vast private grounds, heading
determinedly down to the giant waterway.

A full white moon on its ascendancy lighted her
way as she picked her careful path down the soaring
bluffs to the silvered Mississippi. At the river Mary
Ellen paused on the banks. She stepped out of her slippers, took off her stockings, and stuffed them neatly
into the toes of her shoes. Then she raised her skirts to
her knees and stepped barefoot onto a long, wide sandbar.

Mary Ellen Preble sighed.

The smooth wet sand felt incredibly good to her bare,
burning toes. She smiled at the simple pleasure of it. The
water, she knew, would feel even better. She would, she
decided, stroll to the very tip of the long soft sandbar, step
into the river, and wade out into the placid water. Splash
about and cool off for a few brief minutes before returning to the prison of her hot and lonely home high above.

Mary Ellen never made it to the water.

She had gone but a few steps when she spotted a bill
blowing across the sand. Squinting, supposing it was
useless Confederate currency, Mary Ellen moved forward, picked it up, and saw that it was a crisp fifty-dol-
lar greenback. Real money!

Curious, she glanced up. Another bill tumbled toward her. And another. Gripping the fifty in her hand, Mary Ellen released her skirts, allowing them to fall back around her bare feet. She followed the money trail, gathering up the bills eagerly.

Abruptly, she stopped short and stared.

A saber, moonlight glinting on its long sharp blade, stood upright, its tip embedded in the soft damp sand. Beside the saber, tall black boots, neatly polished and gleaming, sat upon the sand. Draped casually over the boots' toes, a tunic of unmistakable Union blue—with yellow naval Captain's eagles—billowed in the rising night breezes. A pair of matching navy trousers peeked from underneath the blouse.

Mary Ellen was immediately uneasy. She felt the wispy hair stand up on the back of her neck, felt her chest tighten in growing alarm.

She spun about anxiously, searching for the owner of the uniform and the money. She saw no one. She heard nothing. She was tempted to take the money and run as fast as she could back up the cliffs to the house. Lord knows they could use it.

After looking all around, she stooped and gingerly lifted the blue trousers. And saw, lying on the sand, a small black leather purse.

Now Mary Ellen Preble was no thief. She was a young woman of impeccable character whose illustrious family name was one of the most respected in all Tennessee and throughout the South. When she was but a child she had learned the importance of honor and honesty from her proud patrician father. Before the war she would never have considered taking something that didn't belong to her. Back then she wouldn't have dared take a look inside the black leather wallet.

Mary Ellen dropped the blue trousers, again looked cautiously about. Then slowly she sank onto her bare heels, lifted the small purse from the sand, peered inside and saw many bills. A neat, thick stack of spendable United States currency.

On a quick intake of breath, Mary Ellen did the human thing. She snatched all the bills from the wallet, dropped the empty purse back to the sand, and shot to her feet. Eagerly she wadded the bills and started to stuff them inside the low bodice of her dress.

A lean, dark hand, wet from the river, suddenly reached out and covered Mary Ellen's, the strong male fingers imprisoning her slender wrist.

Too stunned even to scream, Mary Ellen instinctively jerked her head up to confront her captor. She saw a dark man with midnight black hair dripping water and gleaming wet lips fashioned into an evil grin. An ominous challenging sparkle flashed from his luminous light eyes before he shifted slightly and his wide, glistening shoulders blocked out the day-bright moonlight.

Frozen with fear, Mary Ellen was unable to make a sound. Heart beating furiously, she lowered her gaze from the menacing eyes impaling her and saw a broad, powerful chest covered with wet, curling black hair. Spellbound, she continued to slide her gaze downward, following the tiny rivulets of water dripping from the crisp chest hair onto corded ribs and a flat abdomen. The hair thinned to a heavy black line going down his belly. When its wiry darkness blossomed again below his navel, Mary Ellen gasped in mortified shock and her blond head snapped up.

The river-wet stranger was stark naked!

Horrified, she blinked blindly at the chiseled face now fully concealed in deep shadow.

A low, masculine voice, which was strangely familiar, said, "The penalty for stealing from the occupying forces is death."

Heart slamming painfully against her ribs, Mary Ellen swayed in a step closer to cover the dark stranger's nakedness with her full, swirling skirts. The shielding gesture brought a soft, derisive chuckle from the shameless naked man.

He yanked her closer still, so close she could feel the moisture from his chest saturating the bodice of her cotton summer dress. "Are you embarrassed, ma'am?" he asked.

Mary Ellen finally found her tongue. Looking up into the pale eyes flashing at her in the darkness, she snapped, "Yes! Yes, of course, I'm embarrassed. You have no clothes on…. You are naked!"

"So I am," he said calmly in a low, soft baritone, "but then you've seen me like this before. Many times." His long, lean fingers continuing to grip her wrist as he slowly turned his dark head so that the bright moonlight struck him full in the face. "Have you forgotten all those hours we spent naked together?" A long pause. Then, "Have you forgotten…Mary?"

She trembled involuntarily. He called her Mary. Everyone she knew or had ever known called her Mary Ellen. Everyone but…

"Dear God," she choked, staring in disbelief at the well-remembered features. The high, intelligent forehead beneath the shimmering night-black hair. The magnificent opaque eyes under heavily arched black brows. The high, slanting cheekbones. The straight, narrow-bridged nose. The wide, full-lipped mouth. The firm, beautifully chiseled chin. "Cl…Clay. Clay Knight!"

Two

"Clay? Clay Knight!"

Pale white-blond hair and colorful pinafore skirts flying, nine-year-old Mary Ellen Preble raced excitedly down the stairs. She burst out the front doors of Longwood, calling to her favorite playmate, the quiet, dark-haired Clayton Knight.

"Clay, where are you?"

Mary Ellen had spotted Clayton Knight from her upstairs bedroom window as he came up the pebbled driveway, carrying a large flat box under his arm. She was supposed to be asleep at this hour, taking her afternoon nap. But naps were for babies and old people. She never took naps anymore.

No one knew that except Clay. Each afternoon at three she yawned dramatically and dutifully went up to her room for the hour and a half of total rest her parents insisted she needed.

But once inside the privacy of her enormous yellow-and-white bedroom, Mary Ellen never closed her eyes.

Instead she read from her favorite storybooks or

played with her huge collection of dolls or amused herself by turning somersaults atop her high featherbed.

Or she sat, arms wrapped around her bony knees, in one of the ceiling-high windows. There she spun lovely daydreams while looking out on the lush green manicured grounds of Longwood and the meandering Mississippi River below.

She was seated there in the open window today when she spotted Clay walking up the drive. She hadn't known he was coming. She waved madly to him, but he didn't see her. She couldn't shout from here lest she disturb her mother, who was resting down the hall in the master suite.

So Mary Ellen leapt down from the window, hastily threw on a fresh white blouse and bright blue pinafore over her chemise, and rushed downstairs. Ignoring the whispered warnings and reprimands of the servants, she flew out the front door.

But now that she was outside on the sunny gallery, there was no sign of Clay. She called out to him and got no response. Mary Ellen's small hands went to her narrow hips, and her dark eyes flashed with rising annoyance. Her voice lifting almost to a screech, she again shouted to the youthful companion she knew was probably hiding from her.

"Clayton Knight, so help me, if you don't answer me this very minute, I shall never speak to you again!"

No answer.

Frowning now and squinting in the brilliant August sunlight, Mary Ellen skipped impatiently down the front steps. She reached the bottom step and looked about, then squealed with childish delight when a sunburned arm shot out from behind a bushy magnolia and slim, tanned fingers snagged a flyaway lock of her white-blond hair.

A laughing Clay Knight stepped into her path, his pale gray eyes twinkling.

"You looking for somebody, Mary?" He gave her hair a gentle tug, then released it.

"Oh, you! You love to torment me." She made a mean face and hit at him, feigning anger. "Why didn't you tell me you were coming today?"

Clayton Knight shrugged narrow shoulders, bent from the waist, and picked up the long, flat·box he'd placed beside the sheltering magnolia. "Didn't know I was." He indicated the big box. "Mother finished this one sooner than expected. She said Mrs. Preble was anxious to have it, so she sent me over."

Her quick flash of anger now gone, Mary Ellen smiled up at him. "Good. Momma's asleep. Come on." She spun around and started back up the steps. "We'll leave the box inside by the tall petticoat mirror in the foyer." Her smile widened. "Then we can go out and play."

Clayton nodded and followed her.

The two children were good friends, had been friends since the day the shy six-year-old Clayton Knight first saw the rambunctious five-year-old Mary Ellen Preble. He had come alone to the Preble mansion to deliver an exquisite ball gown that his seamstress mother had made for the beautiful Julie Preble.

That very day—four years ago—Clay and Mary Ellen became friends and playmates, despite the difference in their backgrounds.

And there was quite a difference.

Young Mary Ellen was the adored only child of John Thomas Preble, one of Tennessee's richest, most powerful gentlemen. In an era when cotton was king and Memphis was the cotton capital of the world, the sharp-witted, deal-making John Thomas Preble became a millionaire cotton factor well before he had reached the ripe old age of thirty.

He had ordered construction of the stately home on the cliffs overlooking the muddy Mississippi a full year before meeting a dazzlingly beautiful young lady at a summertime ball in Charleston. Preble knew the moment he saw the slender blond charmer that he would make her his own.

So the big formal mansion became a wedding present to John Thomas Preble's blond eighteen-year-old bride, the beautiful South Carolina aristocrat, Miss Julie Caroline Dunwoody. After an extended honeymoon on the Continent, the wealthy groom carried his radiant, impressionable young bride across the marble threshold of her new home, Longwood.

Julie Dunwoody Preble was genuinely awed by the grandeur of Longwood.

Fronted by tall Corinthian columns, the palatial white mansion was named for John Thomas Preble's old boyhood home. No expense had been spared on this present Longwood's construction and decoration. Preble had sent to Europe for the best and costliest materials and ornaments. Silver doorknobs and hinges from England. Mantels of white Carrara marble. Mirrors from France. Sparkling chandeliers from Vienna.

The huge dwelling was grandly furnished with careful attention to detail. A twenty-five-piece rosewood parlor suite was created especially for Longwood. A gold-leaf harp and a piano graced the white-and-gold music room. Rich damask curtains and upholstery. Reed and Barton silver and fragile Sèvres porcelain. And upstairs in the spacious master suite, an imposing mahogany four-poster bed that measured seven and a half feet wide was reflected from every angle in gigantic gold-leafed mirrors.

The spacious grounds were kept perfectly manicured by a pair of talented gardeners. In season the well-tended flower gardens provided both color and fragrance. Eye-pleasing gardenias, hydrangeas, azaleas, and roses sweetened the moist summer air.

Down the terraced green lawn to the north was a marble sundial with shining brass gnomon on whose stone face was the inscription "I read only sunshine."

A few yards from the sundial a hexagonal white latticed summerhouse was shaded by an old walnut tree and covered with honeysuckle and ivy. Beyond the gazebo a roomy carriage house sheltered a one horse gig, a gleaming navy victoria, and a gold-crested black brougham. On the far side of the carriage house, an enclosed, heated stable was home to a dozen blooded horses.

John Thomas Preble had it all.

He was an influential, respected young man with a lovely, starry-eyed wife, a stately white mansion on the bluffs of the Mississippi, a dozen house servants, and a legion of slaves who worked the vast outlying Preble plantations.

It was into this kind of wealth and luxury that Mary Ellen—slightly less than a year after her parents had wed—was born on a warm beautiful June afternoon in 1831. Within hours of the birth, Mary Ellen's twenty-eight-year-old father threw a champagne-and-caviar feast on the manicured grounds of Longwood to celebrate the blessed event.

His exhausted wife and sleeping child safely sequestered behind closed curtains upstairs and cared for by a competent, hovering staff, the beaming father accepted congratulations from the city's blue bloods and businessmen. And he promised to introduce his perfect infant daughter to the world at an even more extravagant gala just as soon as his adored wife regained both her strength and her girlish figure.

There had been no such celebration the day Clayton Knight had come into the world. In May of 1830, the year before Mary Ellen Preble opened her eyes to great fanfare, Clayton Terrell Knight was delivered to a pain-gripped, sweat-soaked young woman in a hot, airless back room of a small, shotgun house on the mud flats four miles south of Memphis.

There were no soirees out on the front lawn. No gala parties to announce Clayton's birth. No guests coming by to congratulate the proud father. Actually, the father was neither proud nor present.

No one was present for the birth of Clayton Terrell Knight, save his frail, suffering mother and a half-blind midwife. The father would not learn of his son's birth until, tired and broke, he wandered back home after three days' absence in need of a shave and a hot meal.

Clay Knight's father was a darkly handsome, charming, uneducated man with little passion for home and hearth. Family and responsibility held little appeal for the lackadaisical, happy-go-lucky Jackson Knight. Nor, for that matter, did honest labor.

He had a propensity for the more exciting pursuits life had to offer. Like drinking. And gambling. And women.

There were occasions when Jackson Knight devoted his full and undivided attention to one of that trio of favorite vices. Other times he indulged in all three at once. Acquaintances agreed that nobody had more

fun than the silver-eyed, black-haired Jackson Knight
when he was seated at a green baize poker table with
a bourbon in one hand, glassine cards in the other, and
a buxom beauty on his knee.

Life was not so much fun for his neglected wife,
Anna. She had married beneath her, against the wishes
of her widowed father, the naval hero of 1812, Admiral Clayton L. Tigart. The aging commodore hadn't approved of the match. But he loved his only daughter,
so he gave the young couple his modest life's savings
as a wedding present.

The money hadn't gone toward building a home
for Anna, as the admiral had intended. The hedonistic
Jackson Knight had squandered the entire sum in less
than a year, with nothing to show for it. Anna never saw
a penny of the money.

The love she'd had for Jackson Knight had waned
and died in the long, lonely hours she'd spent waiting
alone in the darkness for him to come staggering home,
the scent of another woman's cheap perfume on his
clothes and on his lean body.

For the disillusioned Anna, her precious baby son,
Clayton, was the only good thing to come out of the
unhappy union with his handsome, worthless father. It
didn't matter, she told herself, that her son's father
was of the lower classes and considered white trash by
the gentry. Clayton could boast of at least one distinguished forebear, his maternal grandfather.

One morning just before dawn, when Clay was still
an infant, word came that Jackson Knight had been
knifed to death in a saloon brawl.

For young Anna Knight, it was no great shock or
loss. The only real change his death would make in her
hard life would be the extra money she'd now have to

buy food and necessities. No longer would Jackson Knight be there to take her meager earnings to fritter away on liquor, gambling, and women.

After her husband's death, Anna Knight was able to save enough to move with her baby son into a modest frame house in Germantown less than a mile from the city. Proud of the new place, Anna fixed it up happily, transforming the plain house into a warm, cozy home. The finishing touches were added when she carefully hung a framed picture of her father, the commodore, directly above the fireplace in the parlor.

With freedom from constant worry, Anna had a chance to catch her breath. She had the time and the energy to develop her innate talent for designing and making beautiful women's clothing.

Her reputation started to build. Word of mouth began to spread, reaching all the way to Memphis's wealthy elite. In time, Anna's flair for fashion caused her services to be vied for by the upper crust of the river city. She supported herself and her son by making elegant clothes for the city's gentry.

It was Anna's abundant talent that brought her to the attention of the young, wealthy mistress of Longwood. At a society ball honoring a visiting European count, Julie Preble's discerning eye fell upon one of Anna Knight's gorgeous creations. It was worn by a thin, graying Memphis matron who was more than happy to share the name and address of its maker.

Anna Knight was summoned to Longwood and her services engaged. Soon she had completed the first of what would be many exquisite ball gowns for her distinguished young client. With orders for her work growing rapidly and many more gowns to be made, Anna Knight was pressed for time.

So she was forced to call on her young son to help out.

A bright, dependable child, Clayton acted older than his six years. Of necessity he'd had to grow up quickly, to accept responsibilities other children his age never faced.

Anna Knight was a very smart and sensitive woman. Never had she said a derogatory word about Clayton's dead father. She had, in fact, bent over backward to tell the son who'd never known his father what a charming, likeable man Jackson Knight had been.

At the same time, she cleverly guided the impressionable little boy toward a path in life never sought by his father. In subtle, simple ways she demonstrated to Clayton the value of honesty and commitment and honest work. She taught him the meaning of respect, showed him the satisfaction that came from seeing a job well done.

She pointed often to the portrait of the white-haired, grim-faced admiral above the fireplace. She told Clayton of his grandfather's valor and how he should be proud to be the grandson of the commodore.

A shy, sweet-natured little boy, Clayton was happy, healthy, and well adjusted. Eagerly he said yes—just as always—when his busy mother asked if he would run a very important errand for her.

Clayton listened attentively as Anna Knight gave him clear, easy-to-understand instructions on how to get to Longwood. Cautioning him—just as always— not to speak to strangers or to stray off the path she had laid out for him, she sent her only child to the stately white mansion on the bluffs of the Mississippi to deliver a ball gown she'd just completed.

Pale gray eyes alert in his tanned face, short arms

wrapped around the big flat box, Clayton obediently walked straight to Longwood. Once there he climbed the front steps of the mansion. Before he reached the tall front doors, a little girl with white-blond hair dashed onto the shaded gallery.

She smiled at him.

He smiled back.

His was a snaggle-toothed smile. His two front teeth were missing. The little girl thought that was very funny, so she laughed. He laughed, too.

Clayton Knight had just met Mary Ellen Preble.

Three

Mary Ellen and Clay instantly became friends.

As the years went by they spent many an hour playing together and no one paid much attention. They were, after all, only children. Their close friendship went mostly unheeded by the grown-ups. No one saw any reason to worry about their childish devotion to each other.

Clay was frequently at Longwood, as was his mother. Anna Knight now sewed for only a handful of lucky ladies. One of those privileged few was Julie Preble, so it was necessary for Anna to spend a great deal of time with the mistress of Longwood for consultations and fittings.

Julie Preble was so delighted to be one of Anna's select clients, she treated the gifted seamstress more like an honored guest than a hired dressmaker. At Longwood Anna was not expected to use the servants' entrance as she was at the mansions of her other clients. Julie Preble had instructed the servants that Anna Knight was always to be admitted through the fanlighted front doors and ushered into the opulent front parlor.

Both John Thomas and Julie Preble liked the uncomplaining Anna Knight and felt sorry for her, that though she'd been born a respectable Tigart, with her marriage she had sunk to a much lower station in life.

The Prebles also liked Anna's well-behaved, mannerly young son. No one objected as the energetic youngsters romped freely about, unchaperoned and unwatched. The pair, everyone agreed, got along famously, and wasn't that wonderful? The Prebles knew they needn't worry when their only daughter was with Clay. Clayton Knight was a responsible young boy; he'd look out for Mary Ellen.

Mary Ellen was, from the minute she learned how to walk, a spirited tomboy. She liked to run and shout and play chase and climb trees as much as any boy. She liked to roam the lush Tennessee countryside, to venture deep into the woods with Clay and pretend that they were bold adventurers exploring a new, uncharted land.

Mary Ellen loved the river and was allowed to go down to the levee as long as she was with Clay. It was such fun to see the mighty steamers ferry passengers up and down the waterway and to watch the giant bales of cotton being loaded onto huge cargo craft. Enchanted by all the activity going on at the landing, Mary Ellen once asked Clay if he'd like to work on the river when he finished school. Maybe be a riverboat pilot?

"No," he was quick to set her straight. His silver-gray eyes flashing with excitement, he said, "You know very well that I want go to the Naval Academy."

She did know. Clay talked incessantly of going to the Naval Academy. He collected sea charts and atlases and books about faraway places. He pored over maps and books for hours at a time. He talked often of his grandfather, repeating to Mary Ellen the stories his mother had told him of Admiral Tigart's bravery. His aging grandfather was one of his heroes; the other was a young naval officer who'd been born right there in Tennessee, over in Knoxville. David Glasgow Farragut was, Clay believed, destined for greatness. He hoped that the day might come when he would serve under the brilliant Farragut.

"Yes, sir, it's the deep-water navy for me," Clay said. "Brave the Cape of Good Hope and then on to sail the seven seas." He paused, sighed dreamily, then added, "You can be the riverboat pilot."

"Me?" Mary Ellen made a face. "I can't. I'm a girl, silly."

"Really?" Dark eyebrows shot up as if he were surprised. He looked pointedly at her dirty face, her tangled blond hair. "You could sure have fooled me."

He laughed and threw shielding arms up before his face when she stuck out her tongue and slapped at him. Clay never really thought of Mary as a girl; she was his friend. It was the same for her. Clay was her pal, her playmate, her confidant.

Through the years they attended school together, they studied together, they played together as if they were the same sex. Finally, however, the day came— first for Clay, later for Mary Ellen—when they realized fully that they were indeed of opposite sexes.

The revelation came unexpectedly for Clay one bitter New Year's Day when he'd walked from his house in the cold to welcome Mary Ellen back from a long holiday trip she'd taken with her parents.

The Prebles had gone to South Carolina to spend the Christmas season with Julie Preble's family. They were to arrive back at Longwood sometime that Monday afternoon, the first day of the brand-new year, 1845.

When their carriage rolled up the pebbled drive before Longwood, Clay rushed out to meet it.

Mary Ellen, her blond curls gleaming in the weak winter sunshine, was the first one out of the big brougham. She bounced eagerly from the carriage, rushed the few short steps to him, and, as she'd done a thousand times before, threw her arms around Clay's neck and gave his tanned jaw a big kiss.

She squeezed him tightly and said, "Miss me?"

Outwardly Clay reacted just as he always had when the impulsive Mary Ellen displayed affection for him. He pulled a sour face, raised his hand, and made a big show of wiping her kiss from his cheek.

"Not really," he told her. "Been pretty busy myself."

But his heart misbehaved, skipping a couple of beats.

Mary Ellen giggled happily, wrapped both her arms around his right one, and drew him with her toward the house, saying, "No use pretending, Clay. I know very well that you missed me just as I missed you. Tell me you did. Say it or I'll pinch you."

He finally grinned. "A little, maybe."

That night, long after he had left Longwood and Mary Ellen, Clay couldn't get the memory of that unsettling moment out of his mind. He was puzzled by what had happened to him. Mary had kissed and hugged him a jillion times and he'd never been the least bit affected. Now here he was, wide awake in his bed long past midnight, remembering the touch of her soft warm lips against his cold cheek, recalling the fresh, clean scent of her glorious golden-white hair.

By the time Clay turned fifteen, he was already head over heels in love with Mary. But he didn't tell her. He didn't tell anyone. He carefully kept it to himself—would keep it to himself until Mary was older and came to realize she loved him, too. If she ever did.

If not, then he'd keep it to himself forever.

The days and weeks that followed were sweet agony for Clay. He and Mary were still together all the time—but it was different now.

At least for him.

Each time she smiled at him, said his name, touched him, he felt weak in the knees and it was all he could do not to gather her into his frightened arms and hold her close against his wildly beating heart.

Summertime came and with it new torture.

"Let's go swimming," Mary Ellen said the first really warm day Clay visited Longwood.

"Ahhh, no, I… I don't think we should, Mary."

"Why, Clayton Terrell Knight, why ever not?" Mary Ellen asked. She couldn't believe what she'd heard. Her lovely, childlike face turned up to his, she said, "Don't we go swimming every year as soon as it's warm enough?"

"Well, sure, but…" He fell silent.

"But what?"

He looked into her dark, arresting eyes, shook his head. "You wouldn't understand."

"I'm no dunce. Try me."

He laughed nervously. He wasn't about to admit the real reason. He said, "Look, Mary, I don't want to go swimming and that's that."

"Then be a big sissy," she said flippantly. "*I* am going down to the river for a refreshing swim."

She started to flounce away. He caught her arm, drew her back. "You know very well you're not allowed to go swimming alone."

"I know"—she flashed him her most persuasive smile— "so you'll *have* to come with me. Please. Please, Clay."

They went swimming.

They went down to their favorite spot on the river. Five summers before, they had discovered the secluded inlet around a bend in the winding waterway, three-quarters of a mile downstream from the busy Memphis port. They looked on it as their own private, tree-shaded lagoon, the secret cove that was theirs alone. It was shielded by a narrow, jutting rise of the Chickasaw Cliffs marching almost entirely across its entrance, so that once inside its narrow, underbrush-concealed opening, they could neither see nor be seen from the main Mississippi riverbed.

Her fair face flushed with rising excitement, Mary was kicking off her shoes the minute they got inside the bay. Unselfconsciously she yanked her dress over her head, stepped out of her lacy petticoats, and stood on the narrow banks in her camisole and pantalets.

"Last one in's a rotten egg," she shouted, and, pinching her nose together with thumb and forefinger, eagerly leapt into the cool, clear water.

Clay didn't move a muscle to get undressed. He stood on the banks, hip cocked, weight supported on his right foot, reluctant to strip down to his white linen underwear. Even more reluctant to get too close to the beautiful girl who *had* stripped down to her underwear.

He knew Mary too well. If he jumped in, she'd want to play, to duck him and ride on his back and horse around just as they'd always done. He wasn't sure he could stand it.

Slowly he sank to a crouching position on his heels. "I believe I'll pass this time."

"Whew, it's soooo cold!" Mary Ellen shouted, teeth

chattering as she treaded water anxiously. "Why did you have to go and force me to jump in?" she teased him. "It's not hot enough yet for swimming!"

Clay grinned, said nothing.

"Cl...Clay, I'm fr...freezing."

Clay picked up one of the big bath towels they'd brought from the house, rose to his feet, stepped down to the very edge of the water. "Maybe you ought to get out now."

"Ooooh, I think you're right," she said, and swam toward him.

He leaned over, reached for her hand. Mary Ellen took it and allowed him to pull her onto the bank. Even with the sun directly overhead, she was shivering from head to toe. Clay looked at her, and suddenly he was as hot as she was cold.

His sweet, beautiful Mary stood there directly before him in her childish innocence, thoughtlessly displaying her budding feminine charms. Her arms raised above her head, hands twisting the long rope of white-blond hair to wring out the excess water, she was totally oblivious of the fact that her wet white underwear clung seductively to her slender body.

But Clay wasn't.

His dark face burned like fire while he stared helplessly at the tight nipples of her small breasts pushing against the soggy, clinging fabric. He could no longer breathe when his treacherous silver gaze slid downward to the hint of downy blond growth between her pale, slim thighs.

He stared openly only for a split second, then hastily swirled the large, covering towel around Mary Ellen's shivering shoulders, shielding her from the hot eyes that longed to stay on her forever.

"Dry me off," she said, snuggling into the warmth of the towel.

"Dry yourself off," he said, sounding unfamiliarly gruff.

He turned around quickly, stepped away from her.

To his back Mary Ellen said, "Is something wrong? Are you mad at me about something?"

His eyes now closed in misery, his hands balled into tight fists at his sides, he managed, "No. No, nothing's wrong, Mary. Please…get dressed and let's go."

Mary Ellen was more impetuous and impulsive than Clay. So when the day came she realized she loved him, she felt compelled to tell him the minute it dawned on her. Only trouble was, it happened at school one morning during English class.

The teacher, Miss Zachary, a thin, bookish woman who wore wire-rimmed spectacles and drab, shapeless dresses, taught English literature to two classes at once. Although Mary Ellen was a year behind Clay in school, they shared the same class for this particular subject.

It was the middle of the morning on a cold bleak February day, and Mary Ellen was beginning to feel very sleepy in the stuffy, overheated classroom. Miss Zachary had been calling on students to take turns getting up before the class to read aloud their favorite short essay or poem or sonnet. Too drowsy to pay close attention, Mary Ellen was glad she sat in the last row at the very back of the room.

Vaguely she heard Miss Zachary call Clay's name. But she put her chin in her hand and allowed her heavy eyelids to shut fully before he stood up.

Half asleep, she heard Clay's calm, familiar voice as he began to read one of his favorite poems, a son-

net about the sea. His enunciation flawless, his in-
flection dramatic, he was spellbinding. The whispering among the restless students stopped immediately.
The rustling of clothes ceased as pupils quit squirm-
ing on the seats. There was no sound in the room save
the soft, yet clear, commanding voice of Clay
Knight.

Mary Ellen's eyes opened in wonder. She stared
fixedly at Clay. He stood at the front of the room,
framed by the powdery blackboard. His face was
deeply tanned even in the cold of this Tennessee winter. His hair, slightly rumpled, was as black as the
darkest moonless midnight. His eyes, beneath the longest lashes she'd ever seen on a boy, were a startling
silver gray, almost opaque. He was tall—taller than the
other boys his age—and he was slim, almost too thin,
but his shoulders were quite wide.

He wore a neatly pressed shirt of freshly laundered
white cotton and trousers of dark brown corduroy. He
stood with his feet slightly apart, his right arm bent,
hand raised, long tapered fingers holding the dog-
eared, well-worn book as if it were a priceless first edition. As he spoke the words, he glanced up frequently,
as though he knew the Lord Byron work by heart.

"Roll on, thou dark and deep blue ocean. Roll on…"

Mary Ellen Preble trembled.

She looked on the handsome face of the boy she had
known for almost as long as she could remember. She
saw him now as if for the very first time. Right then
and there she knew. She was in love with Clay Knight!
Further, she knew that she would love him until she
drew her last breath.

And she could hardly wait to tell him.

Soon as the last bell rang that afternoon and noisy

children poured out of the old red schoolhouse, Mary Ellen dashed out the front door, looking anxiously about for Clay. He was, as usual, waiting for her.

He was leaning against the exterior of the schoolhouse, his shoulders pressed against the rough red brick. He stood there in the cold, his black hair ruffling in the winter wind, his arms crossed over his chest.

His pale eyes immediately lighted when he caught sight of Mary. He smiled and pushed away from the building. His smile slipped a little when he saw the solemn expression on Mary's perfect features.

"What is it?" he asked, stepping close, searching her serious face for clues. "Something's happened," he said, and felt his chest tighten with worry.

"Yes," Mary Ellen confirmed, nodding, "something's happened. There's something I must tell you."

"So tell me," he said, trying to sound calm, to keep his tone level. "What? What is it?"

Mary Ellen shook her blond head forcefully. "No. Not here. I can't tell you in a crowd." She indicated the pupils swarming down the steps around them.

"Then where? And when?" he asked. "You know I have to go straight to the cotton office." Clay now worked after classes to save money for his preparatory school education.

"I know." Mary Ellen glanced at the street, saw the big black brougham with the Preble crest on the door. "Sam's here waiting with the carriage to collect me. We'll drive you to the cotton office. I can tell you on the way."

Once inside the roomy carriage, Clay leaned comfortably back against the smooth claret velvet seat, attempting to conceal his growing nervousness. "Now what is it?" he said. "What's troubling you, Mary?"

The carriage wheels began to turn. The big black brougham pulled out onto the busy thoroughfare.

Mary Ellen's dark, expressive eyes met Clay's squarely. She took hold of his right hand in both of her own and said in a clear, girlish voice, "I love you, Clay."

His breath caught in his chest, but only for a second. Certain she meant that she loved him just as she had always loved him—as a friend—he replied evenly, "I know you do, Mary. And I love you."

"No, no, you don't understand." Excitedly she squeezed the tanned hand she held, then drew it up to clasp it to her bosom. "I mean I am *in* love with you. I want to be your sweetheart, I want you to love me back. Will you?"

It was the moment he'd been waiting for for more than a year. Now it had finally happened, and he was so dumbstruck, he couldn't react. For a long moment he stared at this beautiful young girl who had just confessed her love for him and wondered if he were dreaming. Had she really said it? Did she really mean it?

"Mary," he said finally, his gray eyes soft and warm, "you *are* my sweetheart. My very own precious sweetheart. I have loved you for as long as I've known you. I've been *in* love with you since that January day last winter you came back from South Carolina and kissed me."

"Since I came… But, Clay," she said, incredulous, "that was more than a year ago."

"I know."

Mary Ellen giggled happily then, just like the very young girl she was. "Why didn't you tell me?"

Clay lifted his free hand, touched the silky pale hair

at her temple. "I was afraid. Afraid you might not feel the same way. Afraid you were too young and—"

"Too young?" she scoffed. "Too young! Why, I'm fifteen years old."

"I know," he said, smiling, so totally charmed, so much in love with this pretty child-woman, it was all he could do to keep fr(wrapping his arms around her and squeezing the very life out of her. "I know, sweetheart."

"My goodness, my mother married my father when she was eighteen," Mary Ellen told him, "and she had me when she was nineteen and…and… Why, I have an unmarried cousin in South Carolina who is twenty-one and everyone says she's an old maid. So don't you dare go thinking that I'm still a child, because I certainly am not." She paused, smiled, and told him, "I'd kiss you, but I don't know how. Will you teach me how?"

"I don't know how, either," Clay admitted.

"Okay, let's learn," she said, closed her eyes, puckered her lips, and leaned eagerly to him.

"Mary, I can't kiss you here. There are people all over the street."

Her dark eyes opened. "Oh! You're right, of course." She laughed then with the sheer joy of being young and happy and in love. She pressed Clay's hand more closely to her bosom. "Feel my heart, Clay. I may die any minute, it's pounding so hard and so fast."

His hand opened directly below her left breast. He felt her heart beating strongly, rapidly, against his palm. It thrilled him so, his own heart started to race.

He looked into her dark, flashing eyes and said, "Promise me, Mary, that your heart will never beat this way for anyone but me."

"How could it when it belongs to you?"

Four

For almost a year, their sweet innocent romance remained just that: a sweet innocent romance. Hand holding and chaste, awkward kisses. They made no attempt to hide their feelings for each other. And since they didn't, Mary Ellen's parents didn't worry too much about them. The Prebles, specifically John Thomas Preble, felt sure that if anything were actually going on between the two youngsters, Mary Ellen's and Clay's behavior would reveal it. Neither child acted the least bit guilty. They were as free and open with each other as they had been when they were little.

John Thomas Preble reasoned that it was entirely natural for Clay to be Mary Ellen's first real or imagined beau. The two had grown up together. Clay had watched after Mary Ellen, had been her best friend and fierce protector. She looked up to Clay, depended on him, trusted him. So now, anxious to be all grown up and have a beau like some of her more mature girlfriends, Mary Ellen had chosen Clay to step into the role.

Temporarily.

"She *will* outgrow him, won't she, darling?" Julie Preble asked.

"Yes, of course she will, my sweet," said John Thomas Preble.

It was bedtime.

Julie Preble, wearing a flowing sky blue negligee, sat at her vanity table, brushing her long silken hair.

Suave and handsome in a maroon satin smoking jacket and dark trousers, the master of Longwood crushed out his newly lit cigar, closed the book he was reading, and rose from his easy chair. He walked directly to his seated wife, went down on his knees behind her, and cupped her milky white shoulders with his strong hands. He leaned close, pressed his warm lips to the nape of her neck, then kissed a slow, wet path around to the side of her throat. At last he raised his head and his dark eyes met his wife's in the mirror.

"Mary Ellen thinks she's a woman," he said, half amused. "But she isn't. She's only a child, and she'll fancy herself in love a dozen times before she grows up." He smiled reassuringly at Julie. "Soon there'll be so many eager young suitors coming to call at Longwood, we'll have trouble keeping track of them."

Julie Preble nodded thoughtfully.

Concerned with their only daughter's happiness, they had discussed Clay Knight's relationship with Mary Ellen before. While they had nothing against the boy personally, he would hardly be an acceptable candidate for the role of future son-in-law. Both agreed that while they thought the world of Anna Knight and were certainly fond of Clay, the Knights were of a decidedly different class. A lower class. Cruel as it was, the Knights were considered "poor white trash" by the Prebles and their elite circle of patrician friends. A blue-blooded Preble could not consider marrying the son of a shiftless drunk and a common seamstress. It simply was not done.

John Thomas Preble said, "Give Mary Ellen a little time. She'll forget Clay Knight exists."

Convinced, Julie Preble laid the gold-handled brush on the vanity and leaned comfortably back against her husband's supporting chest.

She smiled then and said, "You're right, John. You're always right. Mary Ellen's such a pretty, bright, and curious child. I imagine she'll set many a young man's head to spinning in the next few years."

"She will indeed," agreed John Thomas Preble. Then he added gallantly, "Just as her beautiful mother makes my head spin."

His dark, penetrating gaze holding his wife's blue eyes in the mirror, he slowly, provocatively peeled the gossamer negligee and matching nightgown from her pale shoulders. He languidly slipped the frothy fabric down her arms and over her full breasts. He didn't stop until her slim white arms were freed and the gauzy garments were pooled around her flared hips.

"Ah, yes, my love," he murmured hoarsely, "just the sight of you sets my head to spinning."

Julie Preble drew a shallow breath and began to tingle with building anticipation. She knew what her husband was going to do to her—with her—and she could hardly wait. She purred and stretched her bared upper body like a seductive feline. Her husband rose to his feet behind her. His hands gently clasping either side of her head, he bent and kissed her shimmering blond hair.

Then he reached for her, lifted her easily into his arms. He carried her across the room to their giant four-poster, the half-off, half-on nightclothes encircling her hips spilling over his arms.

Julie Preble sighed softly and watched in the room's many gold reflecting mirrors as her husband gently lowered her to her feet, stepped back, and allowed her blue negligee and gown to slither to the plush carpet. Fire leapt into his dark eyes as he openly admired her nude female form. When she reached out, tugged the sash of his maroon smoking jacket, then pushed the rich fabric apart over his naked chest, he shuddered deeply.

Everything and everyone outside that suite was forgotten for the next glorious hour as the married lovers leisurely, expertly pleasured each other in their big four-poster bed.

"Kiss me," Clay murmured anxiously, "kiss me again, sweetheart. Never stop kissing me."

Mary Ellen kissed him again, her lips opening eagerly beneath his, her tongue seeking his.

They had learned a great deal about kissing since the first time they'd kissed. Together they had experimented, tested, researched the wonder and the ecstasy of it. Instinct had led them to discover that kissing was more—much more—than simply the blending of two pairs of lips. While they were still not fully skilled in the finer arts of kissing, they had come a long way since the first time they'd kissed.

Their very first kiss had come on a raw February afternoon a week after Mary Ellen's confession that she was in love with Clay. The delay was through no fault of their own. Circumstances beyond their control made it impossible for them to find the privacy they so longed for. As fate would have it, they weren't left by themselves for a minute, much to their mutual disappointment.

Finally, after the longest, most agonizing week either had ever spent, they were able to seize the unexpected chance to be alone. They stole a few quick moments of privacy in the summerhouse on the lower terrace of Longwood's winter-browned lawn.

There Clay guided Mary Ellen into the vine-covered, latticed gazebo and down onto one of the pair of matching white settees. He took the other directly across from her. For a time nothing happened. Nervous now that this opportunity had presented itself, Clay tried to work up his courage. His breath was coming fast, his palms perspiring despite the coldness of the February day.

He said again, as if he needed to fully explain his ineptness, "Mary, I don't know how to kiss. I've never kissed a girl."

She leaned forward on the settee, reached for his hand. "I'm glad," she told him honestly. "Nobody ever kissed me. We can learn together. Can't we?"

"Yes," he said, "we can. We will."

His heart hammering in his chest, Clay scooted forward to the edge of the white settee. Mary Ellen did the same. Their knees touched. Their faces were only inches apart. Mary Ellen held her breath when Clay's cold, tanned hands gently framed her face. He looked into her eyes.

Mary Ellen shivered, then said with childlike frankness, "I…I…don't know where to put my hands, Clay."

He smiled at her. "Anywhere you want to, sweetheart."

She swallowed hard and tentatively placed her hands on Clay's knees. Her sensitive fingertips felt the hardness of muscle and bone beneath the rough cor-

duroy fabric of his trousers. Clay's somber silver eyes
turned warm and tender. He gently tilted Mary Ellen's
chin up, lowered his tanned face, and kissed her. Mary
Ellen's fingers tightened their grip on his knees when
his mouth, smooth and warm and soft, touched her own
trembling lips.

It was a brief, totally innocent kiss. Two shy pairs
of lips meeting, touching, retreating. But it was thrilling to the naive young pair engaging in the sweet,
chaste kiss.

When Clay's lips left Mary Ellen's, he pulled back
a little, looked at her glowing young face, and was
filled with so much love for her, he felt his heart would
surely explode. He was suddenly very possessive, half
jealous.

He said, "Don't *ever* kiss anybody else, Mary."

"I won't," she told him happily.

"I couldn't stand it if you did. You're mine, for now
and for always. You belong to my heart. No other lips
must kiss you but mine, no other arms must hold you
but mine. Do you understand?"

"I do," she murmured dreamily. "Oh, I do. Now,
please, Clay. Kiss me again."

Their kisses, their touches, their need for each other,
had changed dramatically since that cold winter day.

Now Clay had passed his seventeenth birthday in
May and Mary Ellen's birthday was less than a week
away. On Saturday, the twenty-seventh of June, she
would turn sixteen.

More than a year had gone by since that initial shy
kiss in the summerhouse. Their kisses were now
deeply stirring, so hot and intense that no matter how
much they kissed and no matter how tightly they held

each other, it wasn't completely satisfying. Kissing was no longer enough.

They loved each other.

They wanted each other.

Each time they were together their kisses grew more heated, more passionate, more dangerous. The deep yearning, the acute frustration, grew steadily for them both. But it was even worse for Clay than it was for Mary Ellen. He wanted her so badly that he could hardly bear it, yet he felt obligated to keep her safe, even from himself. He was older than she, and he was responsible for her. He had always taken care of her, kept her from harm. He promised himself he would not take advantage of her.

But, Lord, he wanted her so much, it hurt!

Clay wasn't sure how much longer he could endure the pain. He couldn't sleep for thinking about her. Night after night he tossed in his narrow bed, miserable, unable to rest, tortured by his all-consuming passion for Mary. He blamed himself, not Mary. And manfully he fought against the demons of his dark sexuality, which were compelling him ever nearer to the irreversible act of seducing his fair angel.

Clay fought it, but he wasn't convinced he could win the battle much longer.

Five

The big day arrived.

Saturday, June 27.

Mary Ellen Preble's sixteenth birthday.

Gold engraved invitations had gone out a full month before the big event. The menu was planned weeks in advance, and a pair of noted chefs were summoned from New Orleans to oversee a staff of hand-picked cooks. Late Saturday afternoon a gigantic white birthday cake arrived fresh from the oven of Gambill's Bakery. The huge cake was to be but one of a dozen sweet confections that would top off the evening's feast.

Magnums of champagne chilled in ice filled silver buckets and bottle after bottle of Madeira, port, sauterne, and sherry had been brought up from the wine cellar. Hard liquor would be available for the gentlemen, peach and blackberry brandy for the ladies. And, of course, there would be a delicious fruit punch for the younger set.

Garlands of white roses and sweet peas were delivered late in the afternoon and artfully arranged through the lower rooms of the mansion. Japanese lanterns, strung from sparkling silver ropes, criss-crossed the vast backyard, where square white-clothed tables and

matching chairs were set up around a temporary par-
quet dance floor specially constructed for the evening.

It was a young girl's dream of magnificence.

As the sun began to set on the River City, a cortege
of carriages rolled up the circular pebbled drive of
Longwood. Upstairs in her white-and-yellow bedroom, an excited Mary Ellen sucked in her breath
while her personal maid, the ever-placid Letty, hooked
up the back of the snowy white organza dress.

Music was already playing. The sound of the coro-
nets and violins drifted up through the open, ceiling-
high windows of Mary Ellen's bedroom. She could
hardly stand still, she was so anxious to get downstairs. Letty left her, and Mary Ellen took one last minute to examine herself in the free-standing mirror.

What she saw disappointed her.

She looked no different from the way she had
looked last week. Or last year.

She had so hoped that by her sixteenth birthday she
would be a real woman, would look more like the
grown-up Brandy Templeton. The Templetons were
the Prebles' closest neighbors. They lived in an imposing red-brick mansion a quarter of a mile down River
Road from Longwood.

Brandy Templeton was tall, dark haired, and glamorous. She was eighteen but looked like a woman of
twenty-one. And she acted like it as well. Although the
Templeton mansion was near, Brandy never came to
Longwood. Her parents visited often, but Brandy never
did. Brandy had attended the snooty St. Agnes Academy for Young Ladies for the past two years, and everyone said she had become so cultured, so elegant, she
was very likely to nab Memphis's most eligible bachelor, the blond, patrician college man, Daniel Lawton.

The girls Mary Ellen's own age whispered that Brandy was also shockingly bold and flirtatious. Gossip had spread through Mary Ellen's circle last winter that a respected Tennessee congressman, married and the father of four, had shared a secret afternoon tryst with the gorgeous Brandy and had fallen madly in love with her.

Mary Ellen wasn't sure just what "tryst" meant. And she didn't want to ask anyone and show her ignorance. So she decided that the tryst had been nothing more sinful than Brandy sharing a bottle of champagne with the distinguished congressman in some romantic out-of-the-way restaurant. Urbane, broad-minded people did that sort of thing, Mary Ellen supposed.

Mary Ellen made a face at herself in the mirror.

She would never have the smoldering beauty and poise of Brandy Templeton and there was nothing she could do about it.

Frowning, she gave the bodice of her white dress a firm downward tug, causing the rounded, ruffled neckline to slip lower on the pale swell of her bosom. She drew in her breath to get the full effect of her breasts pressing against the tight, low bodice.

She smiled at herself. Maybe she *did* look sixteen. Maybe she looked almost as grown up as Brandy Templeton.

She whirled away from the mirror, flew across the room, and yanked open the door. When she stepped into the wide, upstairs corridor, she smoothed back her long, carefully brushed white-blond hair, pinched her cheeks, bit her lips, lifted her full white skirts, and headed for the grand staircase.

In the marble-floored foyer below, a nervous Clay Knight waited. He was afraid he was going to feel uncomfortable and out of place in this glittering gathering of the city's wealthiest citizens.

Mary had warned him that her father intended to make her sixteenth birthday the social event of the summer season. The guest list was all-encompassing. The governor of Tennessee was to be there.

Clay dreaded the long evening stretching before him. He knew very few of the elegantly clad people he'd seen arriving. If Mary left his side—which she would surely have to do since it was her birthday party—what was he supposed to do with himself?

"Clay."

The sweet, clear voice snapped him out of his worrisome reverie. Clay looked up and saw her on the landing above. She wore a dress he'd never seen before, a new dress for this very special occasion. It was white and it was lovely. Tier after tier of ruffles went from her narrow waist to the floor. The dress's bodice was very tight, and the neckline was quite daring. A wide ruffle clung to her pale, luminous shoulders and dipped provocatively low over her swelling breasts. Her gleaming white-blond hair fell around her flawless face and bare ivory shoulders. Her dark eyes were alive with excitement.

She was the most beautiful thing he had ever seen in his life. The virginal white dress, the magnolia white skin, the golden-white hair; she was a glorious vision that would stay with him forever. She was that totally irresistible combination of unspoiled angelic innocence and unashamed natural sensuality.

Clay was awestruck.

No more so than Mary Ellen.
With her first glimpse of Clay she made a misstep

and had to reach out and clutch the well-polished banister.

He was standing in a late afternoon sun shaft at the base of the staircase, looking up. His gleaming midnight hair was carefully brushed back off his high forehead and temples. His handsome, boyish face had a healthy, scrubbed-clean glow, and his beautiful silver-gray eyes looked startlingly pale against the darkness of his smooth olive skin. His shoulders appeared broader in an immaculate white dinner jacket, which was open, one side pushed back, his hand thrust into the pocket of his black dress trousers. A scarlet rose bloomed from the wide lapel of the dinner jacket. A white pleated shirt pulled appealingly across his chest. One knee was bent, a black patent-leather-shod foot resting on the bottom step of the stairs.

He was the most beautiful thing she had ever seen in her life. The jet-black hair, the silver eyes, the tall, slim frame: He was a living dream, and Mary Ellen knew she would never forget how he looked at this moment. He was an incredibly appealing combination of shy, little-boy charm and powerful, mature masculinity.

Mary Ellen was mesmerized.

For the longest moment they simply stared at each other.

Then Mary Ellen broke the spell. She smiled nervously and descended the stairs.

She reached him. She laid a hand on his pleated shirtfront and felt a wonderful wave of dizziness surge through her when his heart pounded strongly against her fingertips.

Laughing, she said, "Does this mean you think I look pretty?"

"You look beautiful," he told her honestly. "So beautiful I'm not sure I deserve you."

Mary Ellen glanced around; there was no one presently in the foyer. She leaned down, gave his full lips a quick kiss, and said, "I love you, Clay. Never forget that."

He grinned then, relaxed a little. "I won't."

"Is everyone here? Are they all outside?" He nodded. She swept down the last two steps and said, "It's time to make our entrance." She took his arm. Together they moved through the mansion's long, wide corridor and went outdoors to join the celebration just as the last of the dying June sun disappeared.

It was eight-thirty sharp.

Midnight.

Mary Ellen was turning about on the makeshift dance floor in the long arms of the tall, blond Daniel Lawton. Again. It was the third or fourth time she had danced with him. She would have much rather danced every dance with Clay, but John Thomas Preble had mildly scolded his daughter earlier in the evening, reminding her that she was the hostess. The party was in her honor; she couldn't allow one guest to totally dominate her time.

"You must circulate, Mary Ellen, dear," John Thomas had warned when he claimed his daughter for a waltz. "It's rude not to pay attention to your guests. Dance with some of the young men. Trade gossip with the young ladies. This is a party, for heaven's sake."

"I'm sorry, Papa. I'll be more sociable."

"That's my good girl."

So now she again danced with Daniel Lawton. Distracted, she attempted to make pleasant small talk with the handsome, golden-haired man who next year would complete his college education at Loyola. But she had a hard time paying attention. She couldn't locate Clay. She didn't see him on the dance floor or seated at their table.

"…and perhaps a pleasant ride in the country," her dance partner was saying.

"What? …I…I'm sorry, I didn't hear you." Mary Ellen forced herself to turn her attention to Daniel Lawton.

He squeezed her hand and smiled down at her. "I said I'd like permission to call you some evening soon. Take you to the opera or perhaps for a ride in the country."

"That's most kind, Mr. Lawton, but I—"

"Please. Call me Daniel."

"Daniel, that's most thoughtful, but I really couldn't say yes."

"No? Why ever not?" His smile showed his surprise; he was not used to a female turning down an invitation from him.

"I don't like the opera, and my father doesn't allow me to go for rides in the country with strange gentlemen."

"Strange gentlemen," he said, and laughed, amused. "Why, Mary Ellen, there's nothing strange about me." His encircling arm drew her closer, and his green-eyed gaze lowered pointedly to the pale expanse of flesh exposed by her low ruffled bodice. "Give me the opportunity to prove what a regular fellow I am."

At a table ringing the dance floor, John Thomas Preble, brandy snifter and lighted cigar in hand, smiled with pleasure as he watched his daughter being spun about the floor in the arms of young Daniel Lawton.

He was pleased to see Lawton laughing, as if Mary Ellen had said something clever to charm him.

John Thomas touched his wife's bare arm. She turned to him. He leaned close, whispered, "Young Lawton's dancing with our Mary Ellen again."

Julie Preble shook her head. "So I see. I'm surprised. Daniel is Brandy Templeton's escort this evening; I can't imagine him paying so much attention to Mary Ellen."

"Mmm," John Thomas mused. "I'm sure Pres Templeton's hoping his daughter'll snare young Lawton and put an end to the recent gossip. I hear Brandy's as wild as a March hare."

"Shhh, John," his wife cautioned, looked anxiously about.

His gaze lingering on Mary Ellen and Daniel, he said thoughtfully, "Lawton deserves better than the likes of Brandy Templeton. A gentleman wants a young lady with impeccable morals when he chooses a wife. A sweet, innocent girl like Mary Ellen." He smiled again and added, "He'd sure make a fine son-in-law."

"Indeed he would," agreed Julie Preble.

Mary Ellen's pleased parents were not the only ones closely observing the handsome, dancing couple.

His eyes like silver ice in his dark, unsmiling face, Clay was just beyond the lantern-lighted party's perimeter. Alone and apart from the crowd, he stood in the shadows and watched every move Mary made. Every move Daniel Lawton made.

His cold eyes never leaving the white-skinned girl in the ruffled white dress, Clay was utterly miserable. For the first time in his life he experienced the immeasurable agony and frustration of jealousy. His heart squeezed painfully in his chest. His entire body was rigid with tension. His hands clenched into fists inside his trouser pockets, he imagined all kinds of horrible things.

Mary would forget him; she would forget he existed, and there was nothing he could do about it. He was no match for a rich, older college man. He couldn't possibly compete with Daniel Lawton.

Mary was charmed and thrilled; he could tell. She would laugh and dance and flirt for the rest of the evening with Lawton. And when the evening ended, when the party was over, it would be Lawton who held her in his arms. It would be Lawton's mouth capturing Mary's lips for sweet kisses. Lawton's hands on Mary's pale flesh. Lawton's body pressing against her....

"Are you pouting or are you just bored?"

Coming out of his tortured trance with a jerk, Clay turned to see the dark-haired Brandy Templeton standing beside him.

He smiled. "Neither," he lied. "Just taking a breather."

"Mmmm." She swayed a half step closer, plucked the red rose from his lapel, lifted it to his face, and drew the fragrant blossom slowly along the rigid line of his jaw. "A good idea. There's a summerhouse down on the lower terrace. Why don't we walk down there and"—she paused, smiled wickedly—"rest."

"Ah...no, I...thanks all the same, but..."

"Why not?" she said, smiling seductively. "No one would miss us. See for yourself." She inclined her dark head toward the crowded dance floor.

Clay glanced again at the spinning couple. Just then

Daniel Lawton bent his golden head and whispered something against Mary's ear. She nodded and laughed with delight.

Clay ground his even white teeth.

Brandy smiled, wrapped long, red-nailed fingers around Clay's biceps, and squeezed. "Come with me."

Six

The rapidly wilting red rose plucked from Daniel's lapel lay forgotten on the seat of the long white settee. Near the rose was a pair of kid leather dancing slippers, sheer silk stockings tucked into the toes. Draped over the settee's high back was the most intimate of ladies' apparel: delicate lace-trimmed underpants.

Thrown carelessly over the settee's wooden arm was a pair of finely tailored dark trousers. White linen underwear tossed hurriedly after the trousers had missed and lay on the ground between the facing white settees.

"Oh, God, my...God." His hoarse voice hissed through clenched teeth, and the veins bulged on his neck. "Yes...oh, yes..."

Knees spread wide, shirt and jacket unbuttoned and open, he sat there bare-assed on the white wooden settee, his long fingers clasping the gleaming head bent to him, his heart hammering in his chest, the tendons pulling on the insides of his bare hair-dusted thighs.

Mindless of the music and laughter and people less than a hundred yards away up the terraced lawn, he surrendered completely to the building erotic pleasure. He'd never experienced anything like this. Never dreamed such wild ecstasy was possible. Couldn't believe his unexpected good fortune.

This incredibly beautiful young woman had kissed him until he was putty in her hands. Then she had opened his trousers and touched him and teased him until he was so totally aroused, he was throbbing and surging and so impressively huge that it surprised even him. He was immensely proud of his erection.

And rightly so.

She admired it as though she'd never seen anything to match, praising him for being so much of a man. Never, she told him, had she been with such a virile stud. Why, the size of him, the hardness: he was awesome. So awesome, she wanted to reward him properly.

Now she was seated on her bare heels between his spread legs, teasing at the thrusting, jerking male flesh with her talented tongue. As though he were a stalk of delicious human sugar cane, she licked her languid way from base to tip.

Over and over again.

Pausing occasionally to murmur, "You like that, darling? Feel good?"

"Y-yes…I…I…but…please…"

"Oh, I know," she whispered, sensing exactly what he wanted her to do next. "Soon, you wicked boy…. Very soon now…."

Finally, when she'd tortured him enough, when she had him so hot and excited he could hardly stand it, she allowed his strong fingers to guide her open mouth down over the bursting head of his blood-filled tumescence. His eyes immediately closed in ecstasy. The rapture was fleeting. After only a few brief seconds of incredible pleasure—not enough to bring him to orgasm—she took her mouth away, lifted her head, tossed her hair back out of her eyes, and smiled evilly at him.

He couldn't speak, he was so undone; he moaned and quivered, helpless, in agony, physically hurting.

"Love me?" she asked, rising onto her knees, raking her nails down his naked chest.

"Yes, God, yes," he gasped. "I love you…. Pleeeease…"

Satisfied she had him so aroused he'd never forget her or this night, she quickly lifted her voluminous skirts and petticoats, beneath which she was naked to the waist. She climbed astride him agilely and, looking directly into his eyes, eased herself slowly down on his gleaming, tongue-wet erection.

"Ahhhhh," he groaned, grabbed handfuls of her bare buttocks, and went to town.

In minutes he was climaxing. She swiftly covered his mouth with her own to stifle his deep groans of ecstasy. The tempest finally passed, and she sagged against him tiredly, her head on his shoulder, a tiny little smile of triumph on her lips.

"Jesus Christ, what are we doing?" He came suddenly to his senses, anxiously urged her up off him. "Someone could walk down here and catch us."

She laughed softly, unfazed. "You didn't seem to mind the danger a minute ago."

He pushed her from him, rose to his feet, looked anxiously about, and grabbed his discarded trousers. "Get dressed, Brandy. We have to get back to the party before we're missed."

"Why? So you can dance with that silly child?" She tickled his chest playfully. "You're wasting your time, Daniel. Mary Ellen Preble has eyes only for Clayton Knight."

Daniel Lawton irritably shoved Brandy Templeton's hand away. Cruelly he said, "Before the summer's over, she'll forget that sullen seamstress's son
exists."

"Perhaps," said Brandy, carefully folding her lace-
trimmed pantalets into a small, neat square. She
reached out, pulled one side of Daniel's dark evening
jacket away from his body, and stuffed the underwear
into an inside breast pocket. And she said, "Before this
night is over, you'll forget that spoiled Mary Ellen Preble exists."

His trousers back on, his hands at his belt buckle,
Daniel Lawton started to smile again. He liked Brandy.
He liked her a lot. She was daring and wild and did
things to him no other girl would consider. After what
they'd just done, it would be fun to go back to the party
and dance amid the crowd, knowing she was naked beneath her petticoats, that the insides of her bare thighs
were sticky with the residue of their hot loving.

Brandy was right.

She probably could make him forget he'd like to get
his hands on the beautiful golden-haired Mary Ellen
Preble. Chances were Mary Ellen was such a baby,
she'd cry and run to Papa if he so much as kissed her.

Daniel raised his hand, cupped Brandy's chin in his
thumb and forefinger. "You know you're the only
woman for me, Brandy."

"You know you're the only girl for me, Mary."

"Well, I can't help it. I was so worried and jealous
when I saw you with her."

Clay and Mary Ellen danced together to the reso-
nant music; the mellow light from a colorful Japanese
lantern spilled down from overhead. He held her prop-

erly in his arms, as a young gentleman was supposed to hold a young lady. Carefully adhering to the rules of propriety, Clay was mindful of decorum. And of her parents keeping a watchful eye on them. He left the correct amount of space between them, but he longed desperately to hold her closer. Much closer. So close he could press his lips to her ear to reassure her, to murmur how much he loved her.

"Mary, dearest Mary," he said, speaking softly so that only she could hear, "you have no need to be jealous of Brandy Templeton. Or of any other girl."

"Then why were you with her? Where were you two going? What would have happened if the music hadn't ended when it did and I came searching for you?"

"I told you, I wasn't *with* Brandy. I was alone. Just relaxing. She came to join me."

"And…?"

"And…nothing. She said she was overwarm and needed a rest from the dancing. That's all."

"That isn't all. She was holding your arm. I saw her. Where did she want you to go?"

Clay felt himself flush, said sheepishly, "To the summerhouse."

"The summerhouse?" Mary Ellen's voice lifted and her perfectly arched brows shot up.

"Shhhh." Clay frowned. "Not so loud."

"But the summerhouse!" she lamented. "That's our spot, yours and mine. You would go there with her?"

"No. No, I wouldn't. And I didn't."

"But you thought about it. You considered going—"

"If I did," he cut in, "it was because you were in Daniel Lawton's arms when Brandy suggested we go down there. You danced four times with Lawton, and you smiled and simpered and allowed him to hold you too close." His silver eyes had turned frosty.

Mary Ellen's feet stopped moving. She quit dancing. She stared at his dark unhappy face and was swamped with overwhelming feelings of love and affection for him. Longing to throw her arms around him and kiss him and keep on kissing him forever, she put her hands atop his shoulders, rose on tiptoe, and whispered into his ear, "I can't stand Daniel Lawton. He's spoiled, arrogant, and boring."

She pulled back a little, looked up at Clay. Unconvinced, he said, "He's also rich, handsome, and educated."

"I don't care if he's—"

"Mary Ellen, the guests are starting to leave now," John Thomas Preble interrupted them. "Mind your manners and come bid them good night."

A half hour later John Thomas Preble closed the heavy front doors. The last of the guests had finally departed. Only Clay remained.

John Thomas turned and said, "Son, it's late. Time you went on home now."

"Yes, sir, Mr. Preble."

"I told Sam to bring the brougham around," said John Thomas. "He'll drive you home."

"Thank you very much, sir."

"Mary Ellen"—her father turned to her—"say good night to Clay and then get on up to bed."

"I will, Papa," she said. And stayed where she was.

"Well, good night, children." John Thomas Preble, yawning sleepily, climbed the stairs to join his wife, who had already retired to their suite.

Neither Clay nor Mary Ellen made a move until they heard the door to the master suite open, then close.

Even then a full thirty seconds elapsed before Mary Ellen tiptoed over to Clay and whispered, "I'll walk you to the carriage."

He nodded.

Outside, a full white moon floated in and out of some high, scattered clouds. Down on the river a steamer sounded its whistle. Katydids and frogs croaked a loud summer chorus. The hot, sultry air had cooled, and a pleasant breeze blew out of the south.

The young in-love pair sauntered slowly toward the waiting carriage, Mary Ellen's golden head on Clay's shoulder, her hand firmly enclosed in his.

Harnessed to the big brougham, the matching blacks snorted and blew. One lifted his hoof and pawed at the pebbled drive. The trappings jingled. Old Sam sat atop the box, his white hair shining in the summer moonlight.

He saw the children approaching the carriage, gave them a wide, toothless grin. Then, when they stood directly below, he thoughtfully turned his head, looked away.

Clay and Mary Ellen smiled. They knew the faithful Preble driver had turned his head so they could steal a good-night kiss.

"Bless his dear old heart," said Mary Ellen, turning to face Clay.

"He's one in a million," said Clay, and wrapped his arms around her.

They kissed there in the moonlight beside the waiting carriage. Once, twice, three times they kissed, until finally Clay tore his burning lips from Mary Ellen's and said raggedly, "I better go."

"I don't want you to go." She sighed, pressing her slender body against his tall, slim frame. "I wish you never had to leave me."

Inhaling deeply, he felt his senses reel, assailed by the faint perfume of her golden-white hair. "Me too, me too," he whispered as his hands glided down her back to settle on her hips.

"You'll come to see me tomorrow?" she asked, and laid her head on his shoulder, her face turned in.

"You know I will."

"I'll have the cooks pack a hamper with party left-overs. We'll go for a picnic."

Clay's heart started to pound. "And a swim?"

"And a swim," she said, and pressed her lips to his tanned throat.

Clay Knight shuddered.

Seven

The picnic hamper sat untouched on the grassy riverbank. A protective red-and-white cloth remained tucked neatly over the specially prepared lunch. The varied delicacies filling the heavy wicker basket held no interest for the young pair, whose only real hunger was for each other.

The minute they left Longwood behind, hurriedly descended the bluffs, and reached their secret concealed cove on the river, Clay dropped the hamper to the grassy bank. He turned to Mary Ellen. His eyes a warm smoky gray, he reached out, curled his tanned fingers around the back of her neck, and drew her to him.

He stepped in closer.

He lowered his head, and his dark face descended slowly to hers. He paused, his mouth hovering a scant inch above her own. Softly, seriously, he said, "From the minute I left you last night I have waited for this *minute.* Kiss me, Mary. Kiss me and make me know you love me as much as I love you."

Mary Ellen's hands lifted, clasped his rib cage. She put out the tip of her tongue and wet her lips. Then she lifted her mouth to his and kissed him. Clay sighed with pleasure when her warm, soft lips settled sweetly on his. His hand wrapped around the nape of her neck, he held her securely to him as she kissed him.

The tip of Mary Ellen's tongue slid slowly, tantalizingly, along the seam of his full lips. He sighed deeply, shifted his weight slightly, and opened his mouth to her. Her tongue penetrated and did all the wonderful teasing, tempting things to the sensitive insides of his mouth he'd taught her.

Clay's heart pounded. His pulse raced. He pulled her closer, bent a knee, and wedged it between her legs. Through the barrier of their clothes, Mary Ellen instinctively rubbed herself against the hardness of his lean thigh.

Clay's hands moved, went to her buttocks. He cupped her bottom, lifted her a little to fit more fully against him, and felt her pelvis immediately start to grind insistently up and down against his leg.

By the time that first long, openmouthed kiss finally ended, both of them were as hot as the blistering June sun.

Out of breath, trembling with emotion, Clay tore his heated lips from hers. His heavy-lidded silver eyes were glazed with passion. His chest was rising and falling rapidly with the forceful pounding of his heart. His tanned throat glistened with perspiration in his open-collared white shirt.

Mary Ellen was just as affected. Her breath was short, her legs were weak. She sagged against Clay, her hands gripping his biceps, her forehead resting against his chin.

When he could speak, Clay said, "There was a time, not so long ago, when it took us hours to get this worked up. Now with just one kiss we're—" He stopped speaking, inhaled with effort.

"I know," she agreed breathlessly. "Clay…oh, Clay."

For an interminable time they stood as they were, just holding each other, weak with passion but fighting the inevitable.

"Let's take a swim," Clay said at last, knowing that a swim would do little good. Nothing could cool his ardor for this beautiful girl he adored. "We need a cooling swim."

"Yes," she said weakly, "a swim's just what we need."

Clay released her. Both took a couple of steps backward, moving away from each other. But neither turned away. They continued to face each other as Mary Ellen's pale fingers went to the tiny buttons going down the center front of her lilac summer dress. Clay's tanned hands went to the buttons of his white shirt. Watching each other closely, they began to undress.

His shirt open, the long tails yanked outside his trousers, Clay paused, bent from the waist, took off his shoes and socks. Her dress open to the waist, Mary Ellen crouched down and removed her shoes and stockings. Then she straightened and smiled at Clay.

Her eyes lingered on the growth of dense black hair covering Clay's dark chest when he shrugged out of his shirt and dropped it carelessly to the ground. Clay stared unblinkingly when Mary Ellen pulled up her full-skirted lilac dress. When it came off over her head, she released it. The colorful garment mushroomed to the grassy bank below.

Clay's hands went to the waistband of his beige cotton trousers. Mary Ellen's nervous fingers went to the tape of her long, lacy petticoats. Clay unbuttoned his fly, shoved his pants to the ground, stepped out of them, and kicked them away. Mary Ellen yanked the tape of her full petticoats, pushed them impatiently to the ground, stepped out of them, and kicked them aside.

Now both were stripped down to their underwear. An awkward moment passed, and Mary Ellen made a move toward the water.

"Wait," Clay said, stopping her. He came to her, placed gentle hands on her bare upper arms, and looked into her dark eyes. "You know I love you, don't you, sweetheart?"

She nodded. "Yes. I know you love me."

"And you trust me?" Again she nodded. He said, "Then let me undress you, Mary. Please."

She smiled nervously. "I am undressed, Clay."

"No, I mean all the way. Take everything off." He held his breath, waited.

Mary Ellen hesitated, swallowed hard, but finally nodded her golden head. And then she stood obediently still while Clay's tanned hands went to the tiny hooks going down the center of her batiste camisole. When the camisole was open to her waist, he slowly pushed it apart and down her arms. And released it. The wispy garment whispered to the grass at their feet.

His eyes caressing her bare, pink-tipped breasts, he found the opening at the waistband of her pantalets. It came undone. He sank to one knee before Mary Ellen and gently urged the lace-trimmed underpants over her hips. When the pantalets plunged downward until they were below her navel, Mary Ellen's breath caught in her throat and she automatically grabbed at the swiftly vanishing underwear. Suddenly shy, uncertain, she was hesitant to let go of the undergarment and of her innate modesty.

"No," Clay scolded gently, "don't stop me, sweetheart. Not now. Move your hands. Let me finish."

Mary Ellen reluctantly moved her hands away. He leaned to her, brushed his warm mouth to the shadowed hollow beneath her left hipbone. Mary Ellen winced, and an involuntary shiver of excitement surged through her near naked body.

The silky jet black hair of his head ruffling against her bare sensitive stomach, Clay said, his lips moving against her pale flesh, "Just this once, Mary. Let me undress you completely. Let me hold you naked in my arms for this one time. That's all. Just once. Then I'll never ask again."

Mary Ellen's dark eyes slid closed and her fingertips danced nervously atop his bare brown shoulders as Clay's hands dragged down the pantalets. She felt the fabric's softness slip over her buttocks, slide down her tensed thighs, fall from her knees to her ankles. Felt Clay's strong fingers encircle her left ankle, lift her foot to free it of the garment. He did the same thing with her right foot.

Mary Ellen didn't dare open her eyes. She was now totally naked. Her face burned like fire, and she suddenly wondered if he would find her ugly. All the breath left her body when, still on his knees before her, Clay's arms came around her and he laid his cheek against her bare belly.

Mary Ellen's eyes flew open. She looked down on the dear dark head bent to her, released a soft whimper of pent-up emotion, grabbed handfuls of his midnight hair, and pressed his handsome face closer.

Once again, for a long silent moment they stayed just as they were. She standing naked in the sunlight, her hands in his hair, her eyes shining with love and excitement. He kneeling before her in his white linen underwear, his hot cheek laid against her flat stomach, the restless flutter of his long thick eyelashes tickling her sensitive flesh.

Young and naive though she was, Mary Ellen knew that right now, right here, this minute, on this sweltering Sunday afternoon, she had measureless power over Clay Knight. For the first time she perceived fully the fierce intensity of his total devotion. With a flash of stunning clarity, she understood that he not only loved and desired her, he idolized her, would do anything for her.

Anything at all.

She knew beyond a doubt that if she commanded him to stay on his knees and worship at her feet, he would do it. She knew as well that if she forbade him to touch her, he would obey. The newfound knowledge filled Mary Ellen with a mixture of great joy and greater fear.

Even naked as she was now, she knew she was as safe as a helpless infant in Clay's care.

If she wanted to be safe.

If that safety were forfeited, if Clay made love to her here by the river today, she would have no one to blame but herself. Clay would never take advantage of her; that's how much he loved her.

As if he knew what was going through her mind, Clay's dark head slowly lifted. He looked up at her, and there was so much love and tenderness shining from the depths of his beautiful silver eyes, she would have given him anything he asked for.

He said softly, "I love you more than anyone or anything on this earth. I want you so much I hurt, but I won't lay a hand on you if you don't want me to."

Trusting him, wanting him, loving him with all her young heart, she said, "Make love to me, Clay."

"Mary. My sweet Mary," he murmured. He cupped her hips with his hands and drew her down to kneel before him.

Clay put his arms around her, gathered her into his close embrace, and kissed her. When their lips separated, he said, "I'm a virgin just as you are, sweetheart."

"I'm glad," she said, and meant it.

"Me, too. But I don't know how to love you the way you deserve to be loved."

"We'll learn together," she told him sweetly, "just as we learned to kiss."

And so they did.

Clay reached around Mary Ellen, tugged the red-and-white tablecloth off the picnic hamper, and spread it out on the grass. They lay down on the cloth. Mary Ellen stretched out on her back, Clay lay on his side, turned to her, his weight supported on an elbow. There in the hot, blinding June sunlight they kissed and touched and murmured sweet words of love.

Neither was quite sure when Clay's white linen underwear came off; all they knew was that it was twice as thrilling to kiss and hold each other close when he was as naked as she.

As hot and excited as he was, Clay was nervous, anxious. More afraid than he'd ever been in his life. He wanted desperately to please Mary, to give her great pleasure, but he wasn't at all comfortable that he knew how. He kissed her, and while his lips were on hers, his dark hand cupped a soft pale breast, his fingertips plucked gently at the budding crest.

As unschooled as Mary to the ways of love, he was

terrified he would hurt her. At the same time he was
so aroused, he felt as if he couldn't wait another moment to take her completely. Cautioning himself to
slow down, to take his time for Mary's sake, he kept
kissing her, caressing her.

Mary Ellen clung to Clay, stirred by his heated
kisses, tingling to the gentle touch of his hands, thrilled
by the heavy hardness pulsing against her bare belly.
She began to undulate against him, and Clay sensed
she was as ready as he.

He lifted his dark head, gazed into her passion-
bright eyes. "Mary, are you…"

"Yes," she whispered. "Oh, yes."

Clay kissed her again. And as he kissed her his hand
swept down over her stomach, raked softly, gently,
through the crisp white-blond curls, and went between
her legs. Mary Ellen's eyes closed when, with only his
middle finger, he touched her. Clay's mouth lifted from
hers, and he watched her beautiful face as he caressed
her, his finger slipping and sliding easily in the silky
wetness flowing from her.

Mary Ellen's back arched. She gasped and squirmed
with pleasure, her eyes shut tightly, her face aflame.
And she wondered if it would feel as good to him if
she touched him the way he was touching her.

Her eyes opened and she looked up at Clay. She
said, "I want to touch you, Clay."

Afraid he would explode in involuntary climax if
she touched him, he said, "No, Mary, I—"

"Yes," she insisted, pushed his hand away, and
rolled to a sitting position. "I want to make you feel
good."

Clay gave in, stretched out on his back, and watched
with in-held breath as Mary shyly wrapped her fingers

around his thrusting masculinity. She held him very gently, as if afraid she would break him. Awed by the feel, the size, of him, she quickly warmed to this new exercise in lovemaking, letting her fingers slide slowly up and down the length of him.

Clay suffered silently in sweet agony.

His heart hammered, and beads of perspiration dotted his lip and hairline and pooled in the hollow of his throat. He wanted to give her ample opportunity to explore and play to her heart's content, but his body couldn't stand it. Abruptly he tore her hand away, rolled up from the ground, and pressed her onto her back.

Anxiously he moved between her pale thighs and urged her legs wider apart. Then, murmuring, "I love you, Mary," he thrust swiftly into her. She winced in shock and pain. He felt the tearing, the tightness, and knew he was hurting her. Yet he couldn't stop, no matter how badly he wanted to.

It was as if the hard, throbbing flesh he'd buried deep inside her had a mind all its own. It completely ignored the tears spilling from Mary's eyes and her obvious torture. It ignored his own silent commands to pull out and inflict no more pain on her. It would *not* listen. Controlling him completely, it kept pounding swiftly, deeply, into her soft wet warmth until a great explosion of heat ended its forceful aggression.

Clay groaned loudly in his ecstasy, and Mary Ellen, watching his dark, contorted face, wondered if she were hurting him.

He collapsed atop her and immediately began telling her how sorry he was he'd hurt her, how he'd make it up to her.

"In time I'll be a better lover," he told her. "I'll learn how to give you the kind of joy you gave to me."

"Lying here in your arms is joy enough," she said, stroking his damp silky hair, his smooth shoulders, his perspiration-streaked back.

When he calmed they went into the water, and Clay carefully, patiently, bathed Mary Ellen, his dark face a study in loving concern. When both were clean and she assured him that there was no lingering pain, they began to play the way they had when they were children.

They raced each other across the sheltered inlet, then dove under the surface and did all sorts of underwater acrobatics. Out in the center of the pool they surfaced, coughing and laughing and spitting water.

Mary Ellen squealed loudly when Clay caught her by her hair as it lay spread out on the water's surface like a shimmering golden fan. She slapped his hand away and twisted free, then lunged forward, put her hands atop his dark head, and dunked him, laughing. He tugged on her waist and drew her under the water with him. He pulled her all the way down to the sandy bottom. And kissed her. Both got water in their mouths.

They shot to the surface and kissed again. Mary Ellen looped her arms around Clay's neck. He drew her slender legs around his waist and clasped his wrists beneath her bottom.

When they got out of the water, they hurried to the spread red-and-white cloth and flung themselves onto their backs. Holding hands, they lay there and let the hot June sun dry their dripping wet bodies.

They stayed all afternoon in their private little hideaway. They sampled the array of foods from the wicker basket, laughing as they fed each other figs and grapes and sugared strawberries. Full and happy, they napped in the sunny peaceful silence of that golden summer day, two beautiful, healthy young animals, naked and unashamed in paradise.

Everything was perfect.

But while they slept the sky above them changed.

Dark clouds formed in the clear blue heavens, and the hot sun disappeared.

Clay awakened with a start as an ominous chill skipped down his naked spine.

"What is it?" Mary Ellen asked, roused by the shuddering of his slim brown body against hers.

Clay didn't answer. Trembling, he wrapped his arms around her extra tightly, feeling strangely uneasy. He was frightened and didn't know why or what of. He crushed Mary Ellen to him as if she might somehow be torn from his arms.

"What is it, Clay?" she asked, feeling his heart race against her bare breasts. "Tell me."

"Nothing," he said. "It's just I love you so much it scares me."

Eight

It arrived the very next day.

Overnight, the dispatch came upriver. Shortly before sunrise on Monday morning, a messenger knocked loudly on the front door of the frame house where Clay and his mother, Anna, lived.

Clay awoke immediately. He lunged out of bed and pulled on his trousers anxiously, his heart hammering in his naked chest. Running a hand through his dark, disheveled hair, he grabbed a shirt and hurried into the parlor.

Anna Knight, tying the sash of her peach dressing robe, was there ahead of him. They exchanged worried looks. She brushed her long braid of hair over her shoulder, drew a breath, and opened the front door.

The messenger nodded, handed her the envelope, and departed. The envelope was addressed to her: Mrs. Anna Tigart Knight. She handed it to her tall son. Clay ripped it open and read aloud:

> Mrs. Knight:
> Regret to inform that your beloved father, Commodore Clayton L. Tigart, died peacefully in his sleep at nine o'clock this evening. Admiral Tigart suffered a fatal...

Clay handed the message to his mother and slowly shook his dark head. The passing of his maternal grandfather was no great tragedy in and of itself. The commodore had reached his eighty-third birthday. The old gentleman had remained alert and independent to the end. He had insisted on staying on in the Pass Christian Seaman's Boarding House he'd called home for the last decade, refusing repeated offers to come to Memphis and live with his only daughter and grandson.

The real tragedy of the old man's death, Clay thought guiltily, was that his own only hope of an appointment to the Naval Academy died with his grandfather.

Tears filling her pale eyes, Anna Knight put a hand on her son's shoulder. "Clay, I'm so sorry. I've prayed every night that Papa would live long enough to help get you an appointment to Annapolis."

"It's all right, Mother," Clay said, patting her hand. "Really it is." He kissed her temple. "You start packing. I'll go down to the levee and see about booking passage on a southbound steamer."

Nodding, she said hopefully, "There's still Professor McDaniels. He'll help you all he can. I know he will. Maybe there's still hope, maybe there's some way you can get into the academy."

"Yes, Mother," he said, heartsick, knowing it would take nothing short of a miracle to realize his long-cherished dream now.

Fortunately Mary Ellen, Clay's other "long-cherished dream," made it easier to bear his anguish over the lost opportunity for an appointment to the academy.

Mary Ellen kissed away the hurt and sympathized and swore she believed that where there was a will, there was always a way. He'd get his appointment. She knew he would. Why, wouldn't Professor McDaniels do everything he could to help? Write letters on Clay's behalf and assure the academy that Clay made the highest marks of anyone in school?

"You'll still get to go to the academy," she told Clay confidently. "I just know you will. It wouldn't be fair if you didn't. Not when you want it above all else."

"*You* are what I want above all else," Clay corrected her. "I can stand it if I don't get to go to Annapolis, so long as I have you."

And it was true.

When Mary was in his arms, nothing else mattered much. And she was in his arms often during that long, sultry summer.

After their initial intimacy, Clay and Mary Ellen could hardly keep their hands off each other. They employed every possible excuse to be alone. And the moment they were alone, they sought the privacy of their secret river cove or the deep dense woods or an old abandoned building. Anywhere they could safely be together. They made love at every possible opportunity, day or night, unable to get enough of each other.

It was the most wonderful summer of their lives.

Even the torture of not being able to touch, to kiss, when in the company of others was strangely enjoyable, exciting for them both. Mary Ellen found it incredibly stirring to steal glances at Clay as he sat in the front parlor of Longwood or at the dining table, talking, making conversation with her parents. Ever polite, he answered her father's many questions about school and his work at the cotton mill. When John Thomas mentioned—and it was not the first time—the possibility of Clay attending the Naval Academy, Clay again confessed that with his grandfather's death he had little chance of gaining an appointment to Annapolis. Purposely, Clay paid Mary Ellen little or no attention.

More than one leisurely evening meal in the candlelit dining room, Mary Ellen watched as Clay's tanned fingers curled caressingly around a crystal tumbler of iced tea and felt a delicious thrill surge through her. His beautiful, artistic hands would be caressing her before the evening ended.

Clay's thoughts were even more dangerous, more immodest, than Mary Ellen's. For that reason he focused on her as infrequently as possible. At times just the sight of her across the dining table, or seated primly on a beige-and-white-striped sofa in the parlor, was enough to conjure up shameful erotic visions. He couldn't forget for a second what she looked like, felt like, beneath her pastel summer dresses. And he could hardly wait to undress her again, didn't think he could stand it if he couldn't make love to her within the hour.

The sexual heat between them was so intense, they knew they had to be extra careful. It was imperative that they behave discreetly at all times.

Not only were they too young to consider marriage, Clay was not yet able to provide for a wife. He cautioned Mary that they would have to wait if they were to have any hope of gaining John Thomas Preble's blessing.

Mary Ellen agreed. But she was certain it was only their ages that would keep her father from saying yes immediately. Clay was not so sure. In subtle, hard-to-pinpoint ways, the blue-blooded Prebles managed to let him know that they would prefer a better match for their aristocratic young daughter.

Clay couldn't blame them. But he hoped that in time he could prove himself worthy of Mary.

For now, they had to keep quiet about their undying love and their plans to marry one day. Had they dared let anyone suspect the truth about their intimacy, they'd surely be torn apart. They couldn't risk that.

So both were extremely cautious. Yet they managed to steal unforgettable moments of bliss in each other's arms. The glorious summer went by far too quickly to suit the young lovers. It would, they knew, be twice as difficult to carry on their secret love affair in the freezing cold of a Tennessee winter.

"But, Father, I don't want to go to St. Agnes." Mary Ellen's tone was emphatic.

It was a sweltering Saturday afternoon near the end of August. She stood in her father's book-lined study, shaking her head, frowning at him.

"You'll change your mind once you're there, dear," he said confidently.

John Thomas Preble sat behind his mahogany desk, leaning back in the burgundy leather chair, arms raised, hands laced behind his head.

"I will not." Mary Ellen was adamant. "I want to stay at Eugene Magevney, where all my friends are, and—"

"You'll make new friends," John Thomas interrupted.

"I don't want new friends. I like the ones I have."

"Now, Mary Ellen…" Julie Preble broke her silence, rose from the long leather couch, and came to her daughter. Putting an arm around Mary Ellen's narrow waist, she said, "We thought you'd be pleased."

"Why? Give me one good reason why I would be pleased."

"Well, the most privileged girls in Tennessee attend St. Agnes Academy for Young Ladies," Julie told her. "Your father and I want the very best for you."

Mary Ellen sighed heavily. "I know you do, Mother. But why must I attend some stuffy old school with a bunch of stuck-up girls?"

"It won't be so terrible," her mother said soothingly. Then: "You're growing up, Mary Ellen. Sixteen already. Time you learn things that aren't taught in public school. St. Agnes turns out some very cultured, poised young ladies."

"Who cares!" Mary Ellen made one last attempt. "Father, please—"

"There will be no more discussion on the subject." John Thomas Preble's hands came unclasped, his arms came down from behind his head. He leaned up to his desk. "When the fall term begins in mid-September, you'll attend St. Agnes." He gestured toward the door. "Now, you may run along, child." He fished a gold-cased watch from his waistcoat, looked at it, and added, "It's after six and I have some work to do. Don't forget, we're due at the Simpsons for dinner at eight sharp."

"Father, you said earlier in the week that I didn't have to go to the Simpsons, remember?"

"Did I?" He looked from Mary Ellen to his wife.

Julie nodded. "You did, John."

"Very well. I guess you don't have to go."

"Thank you, Father." Mary Ellen started from the room.

John Thomas stopped her. "Wait a minute. Is Clay coming over here this evening?"

Mary Ellen turned back. "He said he would."

Her father started to object, caught himself, and

began to smile. "That's nice. You won't have to spend the evening by yourself."

"No," she said. "Clay will keep me company." And she left the study.

Julie remained, closing the door after Mary Ellen. She turned and looked worriedly at her husband.

John Thomas smiled at her. "Come here, pet."

Her skirts rustled faintly as Julie crossed the carpeted study. She reached him; John Thomas took her hand and pulled her onto his lap. "You're worried. You needn't be, my dear."

"John, suppose Mary Ellen continues to fancy herself in love with Clay Knight? What are we to do?"

John Thomas raised a hand, toyed with the cameo brooch pinned to the high stiff collar of his wife's fashionable dress. "Have I ever let you down?"

"No. No, of course not."

"And I never will. I know how to handle Mary Ellen. And I know how to handle Clay Knight, if it should come to that. But I assure you, it won't."

Julie Preble exhaled slowly, wrapped her arms around her husband's neck, and leaned her forehead against his. "Forgive me, John. I suppose I'm behaving like the typical overly protective mother."

"And why shouldn't you?" he said, ever indulgent. "Let me assure you this is one typical overly protective husband who will never let anything or anyone upset his wife." Julie raised her head, looked into his dark eyes. He said, "When the time comes, Mary Ellen will marry a young man who pleases us as well as herself. This I guarantee."

Nine

The warm golden days of summer grudgingly gave way to a chilly early autumn. The leaves of Tennessee's dense timberlands changed their hues to suit the season. Deep emerald greens turned to brilliant golds and russet reds. But the glorious golds and vivid reds were too rare, too beautiful, to last.

They faded quickly into lackluster tans.

As if ashamed of their dismal color, the drab leaves no longer fought to stay alive. Willingly they curled up, became dry and brittle. And drifted lifelessly to the ground.

The elder Prebles supposed that with summer gone, the romance between Mary Ellen and Clay would slowly fade and die as well. Young people could be quite fickle. Often it took nothing more than a bit of separation to work great magic.

Mary Ellen would be attending the St. Agnes Academy for Young Ladies, so she and Clay would no longer be together each day at school. And since Clay was, admittedly, a handsome, likable lad, it wasn't out of the question to imagine he'd catch the eye of a number of his female classmates.

Given a little breathing space without Mary Ellen shadowing him, Clay might find himself attracted to someone else. It wouldn't be surprising if he had a new sweetheart by Christmas. Which would solve a host of problems for everyone.

By Thanksgiving the Prebles were quietly congratulating themselves, assuming that the relationship was already starting to cool. They supposed—and certainly hoped—that the bloom of romance had begun to fade and that their lovely young daughter would soon find someone more suitable.

Someone like Daniel Lawton, the older, highly eligible, university-educated son of extremely wealthy parents who were charter members of Memphis's Old Guard.

While the Prebles were pleased with their ploy to keep Clay and Mary Ellen apart as much as possible, it served only to make the young lovers' time together sweeter and more precious than ever. It was true they didn't see each other as often now. St. Agnes was miles from Eugene Magevney. And when classes were dismissed each afternoon, Clay had to go directly to the cotton office, where he worked until seven each evening.

By the time he got home, cleaned up, had supper, and completed his lessons, it was too late to call on Mary Ellen. Mary Ellen understood. She looked forward eagerly to the weekends, when they could be together.

Clay worked hard, studied hard, and cautiously revived his dream—thanks to his supportive school professor—of an appointment to the Naval Academy.

The young, much-in-love pair continued to carry on what the elder Prebles believed—and Anna Knight prayed—was an innocent courtship that was beginning to chill along with the winter weather.

Christmas came and with it the usual round of gay seasonal parties for Memphis's moneyed upper crust. One such gathering was at the opulent country estate of the James D. Lawtons on Thursday evening, December 23. The Lawtons' handsome son, Daniel, was home for the holidays, so John Thomas Preble insisted Mary Ellen attend the gala.

She didn't want to go. She worried that it would upset Clay if he knew she was at a party with Daniel Lawton. So she decided not to tell him. She wouldn't lie to him. She simply wouldn't mention it.

The evening came, and Mary Ellen reluctantly accompanied her parents to the Lawtons' lavish Christmas party, dreading the affair, wishing she didn't have to go. Wishing she could stay home and Clay could come over and they could lie in front of the fireplace together.

But she couldn't.

And he couldn't.

And they couldn't.

Light and music and laughter spilled out of the imposing Lawton mansion when the heavy cypress door opened and a British butler in full livery ushered the Prebles inside.

Daniel Lawton, attired in dark formal evening wear, stood talking with a circle of gentlemen in the drawing room. He caught sight of a gorgeous blond girl in a long red velvet cape sweeping into the foyer. His fingers tightened on his stemmed glass of champagne and he stopped speaking abruptly, stared.

"Please excuse me," he said momentarily, set his champagne glass atop a passing waiter's tray, and made his way through the crowd. He reached Mary Ellen as she was unhooking the stand-up collar of her flowing red velvet, fur-lined cape.

"May I?" he inquired politely, stepped up directly behind her, and took the covering wrap from her shoulders.

Mary Ellen turned about to face him. Daniel Lawton favored her with a wide, disarming smile, undisguised interest flashing in his green eyes.

It didn't go unnoticed by either the Prebles or the Lawtons that Daniel hardly let Mary Ellen out of his sight all evening. To the chagrin of the other young ladies present, the handsome eligible bachelor made no effort to conceal his attraction to the slender, golden-haired Mary Ellen.

"Let's take a stroll in the back gardens, Miss Preble," Daniel said less than an hour after she'd arrived.

"Don't be absurd," she replied tartly. "It's freezing cold out."

Daniel leaned closer. "I can keep you warm. Come on."

"Certainly not!" She whirled away from him.

Intrigued, enchanted, he spent the entire night attempting to get her alone. Mary Ellen was having none of it, but that wasn't the way it looked to her pleased parents. Nor did it look that way to a particularly unhappy young woman who would gladly have gone a whole lot farther than a walk in the cold with Daniel Lawton.

Green-eyed with jealousy, the voluptuous Brandy Templeton muttered beneath her breath, "I'll fix you, Mary Ellen Preble. I'll tell Clay Knight all about you and Daniel Lawton."

The collar of his dark wool jacket turned up around his freezing ears, his hands stuck deep into his pants pockets, Clay finally reached the pebbled drive of Longwood on that cold Thursday night in December.

He began to smile.

Lights shone from inside, and he was sure a blazing fire burned in the spacious parlor. He could almost feel its welcome warmth, could almost taste a cup of steaming hot cider.

Mary would be surprised to see him.

He rarely came to Longwood during the week. Even now, with school out for Christmas vacation, he had little free time. He was putting in full ten-hour days at the cotton office through the holidays.

But tonight he had felt such a strong yearning to see Mary, he had finally stopped fighting it. He had to see her, to hear her voice, to touch her hand.

His mother had looked up from her sewing and frowned when Clay shot out of his chair and announced—shortly after nine o'clock—that he was going to Mary's.

"Clay, it's late. It isn't a decent hour to call on a proper young lady. Besides, it's too cold for you to be walking so far." Anna smiled then and said patiently, "I know you want to see Mary Ellen. But the weekend's only a couple of days away. Wait and go Saturday. Christmas."

Clay shook his dark head. "I can't, Mother. I have to see her. I have to. You just don't understand."

He went for his coat and was gone before she could say more. Under the lamplight, Anna Knight bent back to her sewing, but her gray eyes were clouded. She was troubled, worried about her son's happiness.

While there was no sweeter, more down-to-earth young girl alive than Mary Ellen Preble, she was nonetheless one of Memphis's elite.

The Prebles were aristocrats.

The Knights were not.

Though nothing had ever been said, Anna couldn't imagine the powerful, protective John Thomas Preble allowing his precious only daughter to marry a boy whose blood ran red, not blue.

Anna shook her head and laid aside the half-finished garment. Tiredly she rose from her chair, crossed the small, spotless parlor, and pulled the curtain away from the front window. She raised a hand, rubbed the condensation from the glass, and looked out.

She saw her son walking fast, his strides long and determined, his dark hair gleaming in the winter moonlight. He was in a great hurry. He wanted to see his sweetheart. *Had* to see his sweetheart. He went around the corner and out of sight.

Anna Knight's eyes closed. She sighed and wearily leaned her forehead against the cold, wet windowpane.

The worried mother remembered what it was like to be desperately in love. All too vividly she recalled the power and urgency of burning passion.

She strongly suspected that when a dead tired young man was willing to walk more than three miles on a bitter cold winter night to see a young woman, he had already learned more than he should about burning passion.

Clay knocked at the front fan-lighted doors and waited.

Blowing on his stiff fingers, he stood on one foot, then the other, so cold that he was shivering.

"Why, Mist' Clay," said the Prebles' smiling butler, Titus, throwing the front door open wide. "Come on in here out of the cold 'fo' you freeze."

"Thanks, Titus." Clay rushed inside. "My respects to Mr. and Mrs. Preble. Is Mary still awake?" He glanced at the grand staircase, shrugged out of his coat, handed it to the butler.

"Miss Mary Ellen awake, sho' 'nuff, but she's not here."

"Not here? It's after nine o'clock. Where is she?"

"She went with her momma and papa to some fancy Christmas party."

"Oh." Clay's face fell; he couldn't hide his disappointment. "Where was the party? Who gave it?"

"Land sakes alive, Mist' Clay," Titus said, grinning. "I can't keep up with all them parties and whatnot. Seems like everybody havin' a party. The Master and Mistress Preble, why, they git so many invitations, can't count 'em all. Sure do get lots o' invites."

"I can imagine."

"They might be home 'fo' long. Why don't you come on back to the kitchen and let Mattie fix you a cup of chocolate."

"I don't think so, Titus." Clay said. "Thanks all the same, but I guess I better get on home." He smiled at Titus and added, "I have to work tomorrow, and six a.m. comes early."

"Don't it, though," said the butler, shaking his gray head in agreement. "Sure come early when it's cold and dark outside."

Coat back on, Clay moved toward the front door. "Tell Mary I came by, will you, Titus?"

"I'll sure tell that child," Titus said. "She be mighty sorry she missed you."

Clay changed his mind. Titus was right. Mary *would* be upset if she knew she'd missed him. So he wouldn't let her know. He wouldn't lie about it. He just wouldn't tell her.

"Titus, never mind." Clay turned to the servant.

"Don't mention it to Mary, all right? Don't tell them I
was here."

"No, suh, Mist' Clay. I won't tell nobody."

Ten

Their winter wraps were spread out on the rough plank floor of the old shuttered gatehouse. The boarded brick gatehouse, almost totally concealed with overgrown vines and thick underbrush, was at the entrance of a weed-choked lane that led nowhere.

The grand house that had once sat at the end of the oak-bordered drive had burned to the ground many years ago. The owners never rebuilt on their remote piece of river property.

Mary Ellen had discovered the place one day when a house servant's pet strayed and she'd volunteered to help with the search. She'd never found the missing dog, but she'd stumbled onto the shuttered gatehouse and promptly claimed it for her own.

Hers and Clay's.

They were there now on this cold gray Sunday afternoon in January. It was their first time alone together since before the Christmas holidays. Clay had splurged for the occasion, hiring a one-horse gig so he could take Mary away from Longwood and out for an afternoon ride. A ride that brought them directly to this secluded place.

Once inside the small dark enclosure, Clay had quickly touched off the paper and kindling in the old brick fireplace. In minutes a small fire had caught and begun to burn. They had lighted the half dozen candles they'd brought along and placed them on the floor, spacing them out evenly so that they made a large circle. They'd stepped into the circle, shrugged out of their winter wraps, and spread the coats on the cold floor.

They looked at each other, then laughed, and immediately fell to their knees and began kissing.

In a matter of minutes they had shed all their clothes, mindless of the forty-five-degree weather. Warmed by passion, they made love there in the flickering candlelight. Afterward they lay on their backs in silence, hearts beating fast.

The fire now blazed brightly in the brick fireplace. The room was toasty, and their bare bodies were bathed in the fire's orange glow. They were cozy and contented.

"Mmmmm." Mary Ellen sighed and turned more fully toward Clay.

She loved to look at Clay's handsome face right after they had made love. He was a study in tranquillity. His heavily lashed eyes were always closed, and his classic features were so totally serene he looked nothing short of angelic. Boyish. Beautiful.

Smiling dreamily, Mary Ellen gazed at his face. And her smile fled. She began to frown, puzzled. Clay's eyes were wide open. He was staring at the rough ceiling overhead. He didn't appear to be wonderfully composed and peaceful. Not at all. His tanned jaw was rigid, his full lips compressed, his brow furrowed.

Mary Ellen raised onto an elbow, shoved her wild blond hair behind an ear, and asked worriedly, "What is it? What's wrong?"

Clay's head turned slowly. His gaze shifted to her. He swallowed with difficulty and finally said, "You know Brandy. Brandy Templeton."

"Yes. Of course. You know very well the Templetons live close to Longwood. Why?" She stared at him.

The pulse throbbed in his tanned throat. "Brandy and her father stopped by the cotton office Christmas Eve." Again he swallowed and folded a hand beneath his head. "She told me she saw you at a Christmas party at the Lawtons." He fell silent, studied Mary Ellen closely.

"Oh, Clay, I…" Mary Ellen laid a hand on his chest. "I should have told you myself, but I didn't…."

"Brandy said you were with Daniel Lawton all evening."

Her mouth rounding in an O of horror, Mary Ellen flipped onto her stomach, put out her hands, and quickly levered herself up. Sitting back on her bare heels, she said firmly, "That's a lie! I ran from Daniel Lawton all night, and Brandy knows it. I did, I swear it. You have to believe me, Clay, you have to."

"I *want* to believe you, Mary."

"Oh, dear God, this is all my fault," Mary Ellen said, tears filling her dark eyes. "I should have told you about the party myself. I didn't want to go. I asked to stay home, but Father insisted."

"And you were never alone with Daniel Lawton?" Clay probed. "You didn't allow him to drive you home from the party or—"

"Good Lord. No! Never! I wouldn't do that, ever!" Mary Ellen swore. "The only thing I'm guilty of is not telling you about the party. It was a mistake." Tears spilled from her eyes. "A big mistake. I didn't want to upset you, that's the only reason I kept it from you."

Agilely, Clay rolled to a sitting position beside her. The tenseness was gone from his face. His cold gray eyes had warmed. He gently curled a hand around the side of her neck, and his thumb stroked the hollow of her throat.

"I understand," he said. "I haven't been totally honest with you, either."

Mary blinked to clear her blurred vision. "You haven't? Is there someone else? Brandy? Have you—"

"No, Mary, not that. You're my girl, I don't want anyone else." He confessed then: "I came to Longwood that night you were gone to the party."

She made a face. "You came? Titus didn't say anything, and you never… Why didn't you tell me?"

"I knew you'd feel bad about my walking there in the cold and finding you gone." Finally he smiled at her. "I didn't want to upset you."

"You didn't want to upset me?" Mary Ellen, too, began to smile. She had wanted to protect Clay. Clay had wanted to protect her.

Clay's hand left her throat, moved to her face. With the pad of his thumb, he tenderly rubbed away the moisture from her tear-wet lower lashes. Mary Ellen threw her arms around his neck and laid her head on his shoulder.

"Oh, Clay," she said, relieved.

"You'd never leave me, would you, Mary?" he said. Before she could answer he tangled his fingers in her unbound hair, drew her head up, and looked directly into her tear-bright eyes. Solemnly he asked, "You couldn't hurt me, could you?"

"Never, my darling, never."

When spring came again to Tennessee and Mary still clung to her schoolgirl crush on Clay Knight, her parents were extremely displeased. But, wisely, neither tried to talk her out of her lingering fondness for Clay. They had spoiled Mary Ellen too much, had allowed her to have her way too long. And they knew their willful daughter too well. Should she learn that they were bitterly opposed to her romance with Clay, hell wouldn't stop her. She would be all the more determined to have him.

There was nothing they could do but bide their time until Mary Ellen broke it off and moved on. Which she would. At least, she'd better.

John Thomas Preble had no intention of allowing his aristocratic daughter to become the wife of a lowly seamstress's son. He had a much more suitable son-in-law in mind and was confident that Mary Ellen would wake up one day and decide she too preferred to spend her life with a handsome young man who was of her own kind. The patrician Daniel Lawton.

But spring turned to summer and Mary Ellen showed no signs of tiring of her sweetheart

Julie Preble stood at a tall window and watched the young couple stroll, hand in hand, toward the summerhouse late one scorching hot July afternoon. She was suddenly beside herself. She could stand it no longer. Something had to be done.

She turned from the window, wringing her hands in despair. "John, you must do something at once!" she said to her husband, almost frantic, her voice shrill. "You must forbid Mary Ellen to see Clayton Knight! This foolishness has to end. We have to put a stop to it this minute."

Calmly, John Thomas Preble rose from his chair, went directly to the rosewood liquor cabinet against the far wall. He took two sparkling brandy snifters from inside the cabinet, unstoppered a carved crystal decanter, and splashed a healthy portion of cognac into the glasses. He went to his wife, handed her a cognac, and encouraged her to drink it straight down. She did. He took the empty glass from her, set it aside, then ushered her over to the long beige-and-white sofa.

At his insistence, she sat down. He sat directly beside her and held out his untouched snifter of brandy. "Drink this one, too, my dear."

Julie Preble took the glass, turned it up, and drained it.

"There, that's better," said her husband. He put an arm around his distraught wife's slender shoulders. "Now I want you to listen to me, Julie. Don't interrupt until I have finished speaking. Will you do that?"

She sighed. "Yes. I'll listen."

"Good, good. I realize, as you do, that we have a highly dangerous situation on our hands, and it's my fault. I accept full responsibility. I confess I thought Mary Ellen would have grown bored with Clay Knight long before now."

"That's not going to happen, John, she's—"

"Please, Julie." He shook his head, silencing her. "Forbidding Mary Ellen to see Clay isn't the way to handle this problem. You know better. If either of us so much as hints to her that we disapprove, we'll lose her for good. I want you to promise me you'll do nothing of the kind."

Sighing, Julie nodded, knowing her husband was right. "I won't say a word."

John Thomas smiled then. He said, "May I remind you, my dear, that I'm a man of considerable influence to whom many a well-placed politician and moneyed comrade owe a personal favor or two." His confident smile broadened. "Leave everything to me, pet. Hold on a while longer. Give me a little more time to set things in motion, call in some favors." He brushed his lips to his wife's pale cheek. "I'll have our impetuous daughter out of harm's way with no one the wiser."

It wasn't his imagination.

He was sure it wasn't.

As the weeks of summer had gone by, the Prebles had become unusually warm and cordial toward him, and Clay couldn't have been more pleased. John Thomas Preble, especially, made him feel at home. The master of Longwood now talked to Clay as an equal, listening with genuine interest to what he had to say.

Clay had never known his own father, had never had a figure of male authority in his life, so he enjoyed John Thomas Preble's company, liked talking with him man to man. He was flattered that John Thomas had begun to discuss anything and everything with him. And he didn't talk down to Clay, didn't treat him like a child.

John Thomas listened attentively when Clay spoke, and he encouraged Clay to confide in him.

Clay felt sure the change had come about because the Prebles realized that he was now a grownup. An intelligent, dependable adult. A responsible man who was deeply in love with Mary Ellen and wanted to marry her one day. Clay was relieved that he could now talk freely with John Thomas Preble. The two spoke often and at length of Clay's burning ambition to attend the Naval Academy at Annapolis.

Thrilled to be fully accepted by the Prebles, a jubilant Clay took Mary Ellen in his arms one summer evening and said, "You know, Mary, I believe your father really does like me."

She laughed at the foolishness of his statement and hugged him. "Well, of course, he does, silly."

Eleven

Clay Knight stepped right into the trap that had been set for him.

Throughout that long steamy summer of '48 John Thomas Preble had cunningly cultivated the unsuspecting Clay. Biding his time, quietly setting in motion his far-reaching, well-laid plans, John Thomas had waited patiently. Then when the time was exactly right, when everything was ready and he had the complete confidence and trust of the guileless young man, he made his move.

The scheme was put in play on a warm Saturday evening in mid-August. Clay arrived early for dinner at Longwood. John Thomas Preble met him at the front door. Smiling broadly, the older man warmly welcomed Clay and guided him directly into the mansion's spacious drawing room.

"Mary Ellen's running a little late," John Thomas said congenially. "You know how females are. Takes them twice as long to dress as it does us men."

"Yes, sir," Clay said, nodding, smiling. "But then it's always well worth the wait, isn't it."

"That it is, son," John Thomas agreed.

He turned and closed the heavy double doors, shutting the two of them inside the lamp-lit parlor. Over his shoulder he said, "As it happens, this is one occasion I'm glad Mary Ellen and her mother are taking so long to get ready."

He turned to face Clay. The warm smile never leaving his face, John Thomas strode straight to the rosewood liquor cabinet and poured fine Kentucky bourbon into a couple of leaded shot glasses. Clay was puzzled when John Thomas held out one of the glasses.

"Have a drink with me, Clayton," he said, and when Clay hesitated, John Thomas urged, "Go ahead. One won't hurt, and the ladies need never know."

"Tonight special, Mr. Preble?"

"It is, Clayton. A very special occasion."

Clay took the bourbon, raised the glass, drank, and made a sour face. John Thomas laughed, then drank down his own whiskey in one long pull. He took both glasses, set them aside.

Acting as if the two were co-conspirators, he winked at Clay, clasped him on the shoulder, and said, "You love my Mary Ellen, don't you, son?"

"I do, sir. With all my heart," replied the well-mannered, handsome eighteen-year-old.

"Good. Good," said John Thomas, acting pleased. He stroked his chin and added thoughtfully, "And I know that the death of your grandfather, Admiral Tigart, greatly lessened your hope of an appointment to the Naval Academy."

Nodding, then looking down at his feet, Clay said, "Yes, that's true. I've had little luck, even with Professor McDaniels's help. I'm afraid I no longer have a chance of—"

"Perhaps you have," John Thomas cut in smoothly. "What would you say if I told you I might be able to get you an appointment to the academy?"

Clay's dark head shot up. His gray eyes widened, and he swallowed convulsively. "You could manage that, sir? You could actually—"

"Let me see what I can do," said John Thomas, beaming now. "I may very well manage to get you that appointment you've been longing for."

"I don't know what to say. It's something I want so badly. It means so much to me that I—"

"I know it does, son. Now it's not a certainty, you understand."

"No, no, of course not," Clay said. "But when? When do you suppose you could find out if—"

"I've done a bit of checking already," John Thomas said, his smile growing wider. Lowering his voice almost to a whisper, he confided, "Actually, I've done a great deal of checking. I've been working at it for months now. I have managed—through an old and dear friend with a great deal of political pull and close ties to the academy—to schedule interviews for you." At the surprised look on Clay's face, John Thomas laughed heartily, then continued, "I've made the traveling arrangements as well. You're to take an eight o'clock steamer to New Orleans tomorrow morning, where you'll board the SS *Caspian* for Baltimore on the eighteenth. I've fixed it with your superiors down at the mill, informed them that you will be gone for two or three weeks."

Thunderstruck, Clay finally said, "Tomorrow morning? You mean it? I actually leave… I can't believe it!" His handsome young face radiated joy as he broke into a wide grin. "How can I ever thank you?"

"No thanks necessary, son." John Thomas again clasped the younger man on the back. "I'm just pleased that I can be of help to you. And to Mary Ellen," he added.

Thrilled, beside himself with excitement, Clay said, "I can't wait to tell Mary!"

"Now, Clay, if I were you, I'd wait until we're sure you're accepted by the Naval Academy." Continuing to smile, John Thomas said, "I know my daughter best. She's spoiled and willful, and it would be better to present her with an actuality than an expectation. And besides, neither of us wants to look foolish in her eyes, now do we?"

Clay's smile slipped a little. "No, but if I'm to be gone for—"

"Leave it to me. I'll take care of Mary Ellen," said John Thomas.

The two men stayed sequestered in the drawing room for the next quarter hour while John Thomas explained to Clay what he could expect upon his arrival in Baltimore. He laid out exactly what would happen. He helpfully instructed Clay on how he was to comport himself in the all-important interviews with the academy's selection board and alerted him to the battery of tests, both oral and written, to which he would be subjected.

Concluding, he said, "Now don't worry about a thing, my boy. I've complete confidence in your ability."

"Thank you so much, Mr. Preble. I'll try very hard to be worthy of your faith in me."

"I know you will. Now remember, when we join the ladies, you must act as if nothing has happened. You'll behave just as always, and when you're alone with Mary Ellen after dinner, not a hint of this academy business. Promise me."

"You have my word."

Clay's mind raced with all the new, exciting plans,

but he took great care to hide his elation at dinner. Terrified he would let the cat out of the bag, he was subdued, said little. He was not the only one. John Thomas Preble was so uncharacteristically quiet, Mary Ellen asked her father if something was wrong. He shook his head and made no reply. She glanced at her mother. Julie lowered her eyes to her dinner plate. Mary Ellen frowned, puzzled, and shrugged her slender shoulders.

When finally the strained meal was over and Clay and Mary Ellen were at last alone down at the summerhouse, he could hardly keep from telling her the wonderful news.

But he had sworn not to.

When she came into his arms and asked, "What's going on, Clayton Knight? Both you and my father are acting very strange. Have you two quarreled? Has he said something to—"

"No. No, of course not."

Skeptical, she said, "What went on at the meeting you and Papa had before I came downstairs. What was that all about?"

Clay smiled nervously. "It wasn't a meeting, Mary. You weren't dressed, so your father kept me company until you came down. That's all."

Mary Ellen's perfectly arched eyebrows lifted suspiciously, but she said no more about it. To Clay's relief. His head filled with splendid visions of the glorious moment when he would return from Baltimore to take her in his arms and tell her of his appointment to Annapolis, Clay drew her close and kissed her.

Sighing, Mary Ellen clung to him, but somewhere back in the far recesses of her mind, she was struck by the notion that he'd had a drink. She could taste it, faint traces of bourbon on his mouth and tongue. She had never known Clay to drink hard liquor. How strange that he would have been drinking tonight.

His kiss grew hotter, deeper, and Mary Ellen forgot the liquor. She forgot about everything except how much she loved him.

Finally Clay tore his burning lips from hers. "I better go," he said. "It's getting late."

"It isn't late. Besides, tomorrow's Sunday. You don't have get up and go down to the mill," Mary Ellen said, her arms clinging to his neck. "Don't go. Don't leave me, Clay."

"I really have to go." He rose to his feet, bringing her up with him.

"Well, I don't see why." She sighed with exasperation. "You'll come over tomorrow?"

Clay looked into her dark, flashing eyes and almost weakened. He wanted to tell her the truth. That he was leaving at eight a.m. tomorrow, bound for Baltimore and Annapolis. That he would be back as soon as possible. That if everything went as he hoped, he would get an appointment to the academy and all their dreams would soon come true.

He thought better of it. He didn't tell her. John Thomas Preble had assured him that he would take care of Mary Ellen, so Clay trusted the older man to give her a plausible explanation for his abrupt departure.

Clay kept the secret he had promised to keep.

"Kiss me good night, Mary," he said softly, bent his dark head, and tenderly kissed her one last time.

He had no idea that he was kissing her good-bye.
Nor did she.

Clay smiled happily when he entered the roomy cabin on the majestic river steamer *Gulfport Belle* shortly after seven Sunday morning. He glanced around the lavishly appointed cabin and whistled through his teeth. After dropping his small valise to the patterned rug, he crossed to a curtained porthole and looked out.

He squinted into the morning sun, anxiously scanning the bluffs above until he focused on the gleaming white mansion of Longwood. His gaze was immediately riveted to a pair of tall second-story windows that he knew were directly beside Mary's bed. He pictured her there asleep, warm and sweet and beautiful.

Yawning, he turned away from the porthole, shrugged out of his suit jacket, and flung himself onto the cabin's soft bed. He stretched out his long legs, folded his arms beneath his head, and lay there dreaming of the day when he and Mary would be sleeping in the same bed.

Lulled by the pleasant thought, Clay closed his eyes and soon drifted into peaceful slumber. He never knew when the *Gulfport Belle* threw off its moorings, backed away from the busy levee, moved cautiously out into the middle of the Mississippi, and headed downstream.

But John Thomas Preble did.

Watching anxiously from just inside the open double doors of his book-lined study, the master of Longwood finally relaxed and began to smile. As the twin paddle wheels of the gingerbread-trimmed *Gulfport Belle* churned up great spumes of water and the big craft maneuvered out onto the river, John Thomas sighed with a mixture of pleasure and relief.

Hands clasped behind his back, eyes locked on the slow-moving white steamer, John Thomas stayed where he was—where he had been for the past hour—

until the riverboat's tall texas deck finally disappeared around a heavily timbered bend in the wide river.

Only then did he turn away.

He dropped onto his tall-backed leather desk chair, clutched the padded arms, and exhaled loudly. His dark eyes beginning to dance with delight, he sat there for a long moment, silently congratulating himself for his cleverness.

Savoring the moment, John Thomas reached for the carved decanter sitting atop his desk and poured himself a stiff drink of bourbon. He drank it down and poured another. The fiery liquor warmed his insides and gave him the necessary nerve to execute the next step of his plan.

The hard part.

John Thomas swiveled his chair about and gave the bell pull a firm yank. Titus appeared almost at once, ready to do his master's bidding.

"Titus, is Miss Mary Ellen awake yet?"

"Yes, suh, Mast' John. She awake. She sent fo' her breakfast to be brought up."

John Thomas nodded. "Tell her I need to see her here in my study."

"Now, Mast' John? 'Fo' she eat her breakfast?"

"Now, Titus." His tone was somber, commanding. "This minute."

"Yes, suh," said the obedient servant, and hurried away.

In minutes John Thomas heard Mary Ellen and Titus out in the corridor, nearing the study. The curious Mary Ellen was questioning Titus, who was saying, "I don' know, Miss Mary Ellen. I don' know, honest."

John Thomas drew a deep, spine-stiffening breath

and rose to his feet. Mary Ellen appeared in the open doorway, her white-blond hair sleep-tangled and tumbling down around her robed shoulders. She was barefoot. She looked like an innocent child of twelve.

"Papa? You wanted to see me?" she asked, her dark eyes wide and questioning.

"Yes. Yes, I did. Come in, sweetheart." Her father beckoned to her. "Come inside and close the door."

Mary Ellen's heartbeat quickened slightly beneath the soft batiste of her pale pink nightgown and matching robe. She stepped inside, closed the door, leaned back against it, and looked at her father.

"Mary Ellen, sweet Mary Ellen," John Thomas said, a woeful expression on his face. "Come here to me, child."

Instantly alarmed, Mary Ellen asked, "What is it, Papa? What's happened?" Anxiously gathering her gown and robe up to her knees, she hurried across the room and moved around her father's massive desk.

John Thomas took her right hand in both of his and said, "It's Clayton Knight, sweetheart."

"Clay?" Mary Ellen murmured, fear causing her heart to race. "Clay's been hurt down at the mill? He's been in an accident and he… No…no…. Today's Sunday. He wouldn't be at the mill, he…" Confused, she fell silent, withdrew her hand from his.

Shaking his head in despair, John Thomas gently clasped Mary Ellen's upper arms and told her, "No. Clay isn't hurt, Mary Ellen. He's gone."

"Gone?" Mary Ellen stared at him, totally baffled. "Gone where? Clay isn't gone. He's coming over in a little while and—"

"No. No, he's not." Her father drew her tenderly into his embrace. "Oh, sweetheart, sweetheart," he said,

stroking the crown of her blond head, "how can I tell
you? What do I say to ease the blow?"

Terrified now, Mary Ellen clung to her protective father and said, "Papa, you're not making sense. I don't
understand. Where is Clay? I must see Clay!"

"Shhhh," her father murmured, "my baby, my child.
You must start forgetting Clayton Knight as soon
as—"

Mary Ellen's head snapped up. She pulled away
from him. "Forget Clay? You're frightening me, Papa.
What has happened? Tell me, please!"

John Thomas looked straight into his daughter's
dark, questioning eyes. "Dearest, I wouldn't hurt you
for the world, you know that, don't you?"

"Yes, yes, but—"

"Darling, you remember Clay came early last evening, before you and your mother came downstairs."
John Thomas drew a tortured breath. "He said he
wanted…no needed…to have a talk with me. I assumed he meant to ask for your hand in marriage, so
I—"

"He didn't?" Mary Ellen interrupted anxiously.

John Thomas shook his head sadly. "No. I learned
to my horror and total surprise that Knight has been…
Oh, God, this is so hard…."

"What? Tell me!" Mary Ellen's young face was
flushed blood red now, and the pulse throbbed madly
in her throat.

"Child, the boy we thought we knew so well is nothing at all like we supposed. Clayton Knight marched
in last night and went straight to the liquor cabinet. He
poured himself a bourbon, downed it, and poured another. Then he said…he…he… I tell you Clayton
Knight is a heartless cad who—"

"No...no.... That's not true...." Stunned, Mary Ellen protested adamantly, "That isn't true!"

"It is true. Clayton Knight has—for years—coldly, cleverly used you, used us all." His face dark with rage, he said, "That boy is an unprincipled, manipulative, obsessively ambitious swine who finally came to me last evening with a diabolical proposal!"

"Dear Lord, this can't be happening! You've gone mad! You don't know what you're saying, you don't, you don't!"

"I do, darling. That callous bastard held up his whiskey glass as if he were proposing a toast to the future, then said to me, and I quote, 'It's time you and I level with each other, Preble. You don't want me for a son-in-law and I'm not thrilled with the notion of having you for a father-in-law. Help me get what I *really* want.' To which I said, 'Good God, man, you mean Mary Ellen is not what you really want?'"

Her eyes as round as saucers, disbelief and hurt flashing from their dark depths, Mary Ellen gasped. "Clay doesn't want me, Papa?"

Again John Thomas shook his head sadly. "That lowly seamstress's son smiled smugly at me and said, 'I've tolerated Mary for years. Get me an appointment to Annapolis and I'll hand your precious daughter back to you.'"

"No.... No...." Mary Ellen shook her head violently, choking on the lump forming in her throat, bright tears stinging her eyes. "No. Clay would never say that. He wouldn't do that. I know he wouldn't. He loves me." Her voice lifted, was shrill. "Clay loves me!"

Her father again put his comforting arms around his distraught daughter and said soothingly, "I'm as shocked as you, sweetheart. Of course, I knew—we both knew—how much he wants to go to the academy. But, my God, I never dreamed he would…" Patting her trembling back, he said, "Mary Ellen, darling, unfortunately those of the lower classes prey on people like us. There's nothing they wouldn't do, nothing."

Mary Ellen sobbed heartbrokenly, "Clay's not like that…. He wouldn't—"

Interrupting, her father said, "Have I ever lied to you?"

Ignoring the question, she said, "If he had said those horrible things, you wouldn't have allowed him to stay and—"

"I did that for your sake. In fact, I commanded Knight to stay for dinner just as if nothing had happened. I made him swear he would say nothing to you about any of it." He hugged her closer to his chest. "I didn't want that black-hearted son of a bitch to be the one to tell you all this."

"No…. No!" she sobbed, refusing to believe. "Clay wouldn't hurt me. He wouldn't have held me in his arms and stayed…."

"He didn't stay long. I heard you come in," said her father. "Didn't he make excuses to leave early?"

Confused, hurt, Mary Ellen thought back to their final moments together. She had tried to get Clay to stay. But he'd gone. For no good reason, he had left her. Had he been anxious to get away from her?

Suddenly she remembered the faint taste of liquor in his kiss. She'd never known him to drink before. Had he needed a drink to propose his ungodly bargain? Had he known, as he kissed her good night, that he was kissing her good-bye?

"I'll ask you again, dear. Have I ever lied to you?" John Thomas said softly.

"No, but—"

"And I never will. There, there, my precious baby girl, your papa will take care of you."

Twelve

John Thomas Preble took a seat in his tall-backed desk chair. He drew his weeping daughter onto his lap and held her while she cried. He rocked her just as he had when she was a child, and he cooed to her and promised he would make everything all right again.

When finally Mary Ellen had cried herself out and was so totally exhausted that she went limp against him, the powerful master of Longwood rose from his chair and carried his pale, heartsick daughter upstairs to her room.

Gently he laid her atop the high, soft featherbed and murmured, "Rest now, dear. Sleep. Sleep, my baby, and when you awaken your papa will have put an end to this terrible nightmare."

Knowing she wouldn't sleep, feeling as if she would never sleep again, Mary Ellen closed her puffy, red-rimmed eyes. She wanted her father to leave. She wanted to be alone. Alone with her grief.

Hoping his beloved child had cried so long and so hard she would soon be dozing peacefully, John Thomas kissed Mary Ellen's smooth forehead, tiptoed from the room, and quietly closed the door.

Outside in the corridor, he exhaled deeply, then went in search of his wife.

"It's done," he told the worried Julie, ushering her into his book-lined library and closing the door. "Clayton Knight's on his way to Baltimore, and in a couple of days you and Mary Ellen will be on your way to New York and then on to England."

"How did she take it, John?" asked his troubled wife.

John Thomas Preble shrugged negligently. "As you would expect a starry-eyed, trusting young girl to take the betrayal of her sweetheart. At the moment Mary Ellen is devastated, but that won't last." He smiled confidently and touched his wife's cheek. "A month from now she will have forgotten all about Clayton Knight." His smile broadened when he added, "She'll be the blushing bride of Daniel Lawton and honeymooning happily in the sunny South of France."

Skeptical, Julie Preble said, "I don't know, John. She's truly fond of Clay. They've been soulmates since they were small children." She paused a moment, then said, "Besides, how can you be sure Daniel Lawton will want to marry Mary Ellen?"

"Now, Julie, you know very well I see Lawton's father regularly at my club. The two of us have often discussed the attractive prospect of our offspring marrying. James Lawton is just as anxious to have Mary Ellen for his daughter-in-law as we are to have young Daniel for our son-in-law."

"I understand that, dear, but what about the children? Daniel's been seeing Brandy Templeton off and on for the past two years, and he might not—"

"I foresee no real problems. Daniel hasn't exactly been *seeing* that Templeton girl in the way you mean. He's been sleeping with her, dear. Lawton Sr. assured me the boy has never had any intention of marrying her." Smiling, he added, "I've caught the way young Lawton looks at our Mary Ellen. He has wanted her since the moment she became a woman. He'll jump at the chance to marry her, mark my words. As for Mary Ellen, after what Knight's done to her, she'll be extremely vulnerable. If Daniel is around—which he will be—she'll naturally turn to him for comfort." John Thomas snapped his fingers loudly and smiled. "Before you know it, she'll be in love again and safely married."

Julie Preble nodded. It made sense. And it was for the best. Of that she was certain. Poor Mary Ellen was suffering now, but she was young. She'd get over Clay Knight. And she would have a much happier life with Daniel Lawton than she'd have ever had with Clay. Clay was a sweet young man, but he could never fit in with their circle of friends. It really wouldn't be fair to poor Clay to subject him to that kind of cruel snobbery.

John Thomas circled his mahogany desk, took a thick packet from the middle drawer. "Here's the itinerary for your trip," he said, handing it to her.

Julie took the packet as John Thomas counted off the items on his fingers. "One, you and Mary Ellen will leave Memphis Tuesday morning. Two, when you reach New York, you will board the Cunard liner SS *Oceana*. Three, when you arrive in London you will check into the Cannaught. Four, a couple of days later the Lawtons show up in London and check into the Cannaught, where they will naturally bump into you and Mary Ellen. Five, after a few days the Lawtons will invite the two of you to board a chartered yacht and accompany them to their villa in Monte Carlo."

"And you will meet us there in Monaco," said Julie.

John Thomas smiled and shook his head. "Just in time to give my beautiful daughter away at her wedding."

Two weeks after a grieving Mary Ellen and Julie Preble stepped onto a steamer in New Orleans for the journey to New York to board an oceangoing vessel, a jubilant Clay Knight stepped off the steamer *Dixie Star* at the Memphis levee.

He was eager to get to Longwood and Mary. He had exciting news to share with her. He could hardly wait to see her lovely face when he told her he had been accepted at Annapolis. His long-held dream had come true! He would be a plebe midshipman in the autumn, and when he graduated from the academy, they would be married. She would one day be the proud wife of a naval Captain!

Valise in hand, Clay hurried down the gangway to the busy wharf. Dodging waiting riverboat passengers and sweating dock workers and huge bales of cotton, he weaved his way through the crowd and eagerly climbed the Chickasaw cliffs.

He ran all the way to Longwood and was so out of breath once he got there, he had to lean for a moment against a tall white porch column to collect himself.

His breath finally regained, he knocked on the front door and waited anxiously, the smile on his face as bright as the afternoon sun. Heart beating fast with anticipation, he hoped it would be Mary who answered the door.

It was Titus who let him in.

"Hello to you, Titus," Clay said cheerily. "Is Mary around?" He automatically looked up the grand staircase, expecting to see her come flying down to greet him.

The old Preble house servant looked grave. Unsmiling, he said, "Mast' Preble waitin' for you in his study, Mist' Clay. If you jes' follow me, please."

Clay's bright smile slipped a little. Nervously he asked, "Mr. Preble is waiting for me? Why is he here at Longwood in the middle of the day?"

Titus gave no reply. Clay followed the uniformed butler down the silent corridor, puzzled, a feeling of uneasiness settling over him. They reached the open study door. Titus left him, turning away quickly, avoiding Clay's eyes.

"Come in, son," came John Thomas Preble's low voice from inside the shadowy study.

Clay felt a hint of a chill skip up his spine. He drew a shallow breath and walked into the booklined study. He squinted in the pervasive dimness. He found it strange that all the curtains were pulled against the afternoon sun and the tall double doors behind John Thomas's massive desk were closed. The room was overwarm, and it was stuffy.

John Thomas Preble was seated behind his mahogany desk. He came slowly to his feet when Clay walked in.

"Clay, Clay, my boy," John Thomas said, his tone clearly revealing that something was wrong.

"Mr. Preble," Clay said, alarmed, "what is it? Are you ill, sir? Has something happened? Why are you shut up here in the shadows?"

"Forgive me for that," John Thomas said wearily. "I guess I was feeling so bad I just—" He stopped speaking.

He sighed, crossed to a set of tall windows, and drew the heavy damask curtains, flooding the room with bright sunlight. It was then Clay saw that the older man's gray-streaked dark hair was badly disheveled, that his lower face was covered with a couple of days' growth of beard. He looked haggard and very tired.

"Oh, God, no," Clay murmured, fear clutching his heart. "Mary? Something's happened to Mary! She's fallen ill. She's been hurt. She's...she's... No, God, no...."

Shaking his head, John Thomas said, "She isn't ill. She hasn't been hurt." He paused. A muscle jumped in his cheek. "But I'm afraid you are going to be badly hurt, son."

Clay stared, dumbfounded, at the older, shorter man. "I don't understand. What are you saying? Where is Mary? Why isn't she—"

"Mary Ellen is gone, Clay," said John Thomas. Gesturing, he added, "You better sit down."

"I'll stand," Clay said firmly. "Where is Mary? When is she coming back?"

"I just don't know how to tell you this," said John Thomas, running both hands through his ruffled, silver-streaked hair. "It's so hard for a father to admit that his only daughter is a...a very foolish, fickle little...heartbreaker."

"Mary? A heartbreaker? What in heaven's name are you talking about?"

"Christ, this is terrible, terrible! Clay, I'm afraid that the impetuous Mary Ellen let no moss grow under her dancing slippers while you were away." John Thomas covered his eyes with a hand, gritted his teeth. "Son, I'm ashamed of my own daughter, so help me God." His hand came down, and he looked Clay squarely in the eye. "As soon as I told Mary Ellen you were to be gone for a couple of weeks, she ups and invites Daniel Lawton over for dinner. Can you believe it? The very first night you were gone, she was…they were… Can you imagine?"

His tight face showing his puzzlement and disbelief, Clay said simply, "No, sir. No, I can't. I *don't* believe it. There must be a reasonable explanation. Mary would never entertain someone else when she's… she's—"

"When she's been sleeping with you for more than a year," the older man interrupted. Smiling sourly then, he added, "Well, neither would I, but there you have it. It's your own fault, Knight. You turned her out at such a tender age, she knows no better. Bedding my baby, you…you—!" He stopped speaking, but his dark eyes flashed with condemnation.

Clay's tanned jaw tightened, and his hands balled into fists at his sides, but he said nothing.

"I'm sorry." John Thomas's expression softened immediately. "I didn't mean to lose my temper, but I'm as upset as you. She's my daughter, she's behaving abominably, so I guess I lashed out at you because I so badly want to blame someone else. Anyone else." Preble moved to a crystal decanter of liquor. Pouring whiskey into a couple of shot glasses, his back to Clay, he said, "Mary Ellen fell right into Lawton's arms, and it must have been love at first kiss. They've sailed to Europe to be married on the French Riviera. They'll honeymoon there in the Lawtons' villa overlooking the Mediterranean."

Clay's tanned face paled, and his heart squeezed so painfully in his chest he was afraid he might pass out. "No. No, that can't be," he said, and his voice sounded hollow, foreign even to himself. "Mary loves me, she wouldn't—"

"Apparently she would." John Thomas turned to face him. "We tried to talk her out of it, but her mind was made up."

Thinking out loud, Clay muttered, "I have to talk to her, to see what really happened. To find out why—"

"That's out of the question, I'm afraid. She's with Daniel Lawton, and they're already inseparable. I realize that Mary Ellen has acted rashly and that you've been hurt by her heartless betrayal. But you'll get over it. You'll get over *her*. You're an intelligent, likable, handsome young man, and there'll be an abundance of beautiful women in a young naval officer's life." Finally John Thomas smiled.

Clay did not.

His very soul exposed, he said sadly, "I don't want an abundance of beautiful women." He began to choke, swallowed hard, fought back the tears that were stinging his gray eyes. "I only want my Mary."

Thirteen

Brokenhearted, a pale wan Mary Ellen Preble spent long hours at the rail of the Cunard line's majestic SS *Oceana* as it slowly crossed the choppy Atlantic. Her white-blond hair blowing wildly about her head, the skirts of her traveling suit pressed against her slender form, she stared sightlessly out at the dark, restless seas and gray, leaden skies.

The long, solitary hours she stood gripping the sea-misted railing were filled with agonies of a kind she had never known existed. She hurt so badly, it was like an intense physical pain from which there was no release. For which there was no balm. She felt as if she couldn't bear the acute suffering one more hour, one more moment.

Tortured beyond endurance, so utterly miserable she felt as if she no longer wanted to live, Mary Ellen kept reviewing the events of the past terrible week. Again and again and again she relived the horror of hearing her father repeat Clay's cruel, damning words, words that kept echoing through her aching head like a hated litany: *I've tolerated Mary for years. Get me an appointment to Annapolis and I'll hand your precious daughter back to you.*

Mary Ellen still could not accept what had happened.

She couldn't understand how she could have been so wrong about Clay. She couldn't believe that the man she loved with all her heart and soul had used her so callously.

She *didn't* believe it. It couldn't be true. It wasn't true. There was some mistake, some explanation for all this. If only she could see him. Talk to him. Straighten it all out. Clay *loved* her. He couldn't hurt her.

Could he?

Maybe he could.

She, better than anyone, knew just how badly he wanted an appointment to the academy. It meant so much to him. Everything. It was everything and she was nothing. *Nothing!* She was but a pawn to be traded for what he really desired. For what really mattered to him.

The strangest, saddest part of the whole affair was that he could have had both. Her parents had loved and trusted Clay, just as she had. They had fully approved of him and would have welcomed him warmly into the family. He was already like a member of the family, so why...why...why?

Round and round in circles she went, one moment believing that it was all some horrid mistake, that Clay loved her and would always love her. The next moment she was convinced that what her father said was true: Clay cared nothing for her and never had. He was, like it or not, heartless, unprincipled, manipulative, and obsessively ambitious.

Agonizing over the hopeless situation would bring on a fresh flood of tears, and she would weep anew. Then the intense crying would finally end, and Mary Ellen's demeanor would become even more frightening to her worried mother. For hours at a time Mary

Ellen would stand unmoving at the ship's railing, stoic and unreachable. Her staring eyes would hardly blink. Her face was devoid of emotion.

Julie Preble was extremely uneasy about her distraught young daughter. She made it a point to keep a close, watchful eye on Mary Ellen, afraid she might do something foolish, might even attempt to leap to her death in the sea. Her heart ached for her suffering child, and she wondered if perhaps she and John Thomas had made a tragic mistake by what they'd done. Suppose Mary Ellen *didn't* get over Clay Knight? Suppose she remained unhappy for the rest of her life?

No. No, that wasn't going to happen. Mary Ellen would be perfectly happy as the wife of Daniel Lawton. She and John Thomas were doing this for Mary Ellen's sake, and one day Mary Ellen would thank them.

Mary Ellen was no better when they reached England.

She wouldn't talk, she hardly ate, she couldn't sleep. No amount of cajoling and humoring could make the heartbroken young girl leave their luxurious Cannaught corner suite.

The worried Julie Preble sighed with relief when she learned that Daniel Lawton and his parents had checked into the hotel.

"Good news, dear," she said brightly, popping unannounced into Mary Ellen's bedroom, "the Lawtons from home are in London! They're right here in the hotel! Isn't that a pleasant surprise?"

Mary Ellen made no reply.

Julie Preble tried again. "They've invited us to join them for dinner, and I—"

"No."

"Now, Mary Ellen. I know you're still not feeling well, but—"

"Not feeling well?" Mary Ellen exploded. "You think that's all there is to this? Poor little Mary Ellen. She isn't feeling well today." Her dark eyes were so cold and mean, it frightened her mother. "Don't you understand that the man I love more than life itself has forsaken me! What would it take to convince you that my world has ended! Can't you grasp the fact that I don't want to live without Clay! Nothing matters to me. Nothing and no one. I don't want to live, Mother, and I *damned* sure don't want to have dinner with the Lawtons! Now, please, please, get out and leave me alone!"

Julie Preble's eyes widened. Her hand lifted, clutched her throat. She felt as if she'd been slapped in the face. Mary Ellen had never before spoken to her like that. Shocked to the roots of her pale hair and more alarmed than ever, the stunned mother was at a loss. She knew better than to say anything more to her nearly hysterical daughter. Trembling with emotion, Julie Preble backed away, then turned and left the room.

Unsure what to do, wondering if she should call for the hotel's physician, Julie sent a frantic telegram to her husband on the floor of the cotton exchange, asking him what she should do. She paced nervously, waiting for an answer.

When the uniformed page told her regretfully that Mr. John Thomas Preble could not be located, the concerned Julie Preble had no choice but to dash off a hurried message to Daniel Lawton. She needed to speak with him in private as soon as possible.

A half hour later Julie sat across the pink damask-draped table from Daniel Lawton in the Cannaught's darkly paneled tea room.

"It isn't going to work, Daniel," she confided in a low, shaky whisper, her fingers playing nervously on the rim of the fragile teacup before her.

Daniel Lawton smiled confidently. "Of course it will work, Mrs. Preble. You're worrying needlessly. You'll see."

"No, no, you don't understand. Mary Ellen is extremely distressed. She loves Clay so much that… that…" She stopped, thinking how that must sound to this handsome young man who hoped soon to marry Mary Ellen. "She's not just upset, she's also very skeptical." Julie shook her head. "John Thomas counted on Mary Ellen taking his word for everything, but she's far too clever to accept all this without question. She's written to Clay, and I'm so afraid—"

"We fully expected that, Mrs. Preble. Of course she's written to Knight. And I'm sure he's written to her as well, if he knows where she is. But all messages sent from either of them to the other will be safely intercepted, thanks to the thorough planning of Mr. Preble. Neither Mary Ellen nor Clay Knight will ever receive a letter or any kind of message from the other." He smiled broadly then.

Julie Preble sighed, looked down at the pink tablecloth. "There's yet another very real problem, Daniel."

"Which is?"

Julie raised her head slowly, looked him in the eye. "Mary Ellen says she will not have dinner with you. Now or ever."

* * *

Mary Ellen continued staunchly to refuse to have anything to do with the blondly handsome Daniel Lawton. But Daniel was very persistent. He wanted Mary Ellen Preble, and this was his chance. She was, at the moment, too weak and unhappy to effectively fight anyone for very long.

Daniel pressed his advantage.

Depressed, sick of the dark rainy London skies, Mary Ellen finally gave in and agreed to a visit at the Lawtons' villa in the South of France.

Aboard a luxurious chartered yacht, she and her mother traveled with the Lawtons to the French Riviera. There they settled comfortably into their hosts' enormous pink cliffside palace high above the sparkling harbor of Monte Carlo.

The huge villa was light and airy, the Mediterranean sun invading every spacious room. The nights were balmy and beautiful. The lights of the city below twinkled like glittering diamonds, and in the harbor magnificent yachts from around the world bobbed on the calm, protected waters.

Inside the opulent villa, a fleet of well-trained servants were on hand to fulfill the smallest wish of any invited guest.

Except one.

When Mary Ellen secretly passed a sealed letter to a houseboy and asked that he see to it the missive was posted, quietly and without delay, the young man smiled and took the letter. The moment he was out of Mary Ellen's sight he delivered the peach parchment envelope to Daniel Lawton's room. Daniel thanked the dutiful servant, took the envelope, and quickly checked the addressee.

Unopened, the letter was tossed into the huge marble hearth, where a small fire blazed purely for aesthetic purposes.

Daniel crossed his arms over his chest and watched, smiling, as the envelope with the small girlish script caught instantly, curled, and turned to ash. Then he went in search of its sweet sender, who obviously needed a strong male shoulder to cry upon.

John Thomas Preble soon joined his wife and daughter at the Lawtons' cliffside villa. The morning after his arrival, John Thomas stood alone on the wide, sunny balcony outside the lavish second-story guest suite he shared with his wife.

Squinting, he gazed down at the two people strolling hand in hand on the sandy beach far, far below. He smiled with satisfaction. His smile broadened when his wife walked up behind him, slipped her arms around his waist, and laid her cheek on his left shoulder.

His hands quickly covering hers, John Thomas said, pleased, "Mary Ellen and Daniel are out for a morning stroll. Soon they'll be taking moonlight strolls as well." He inhaled deeply of the clean, coastal air, loosened his wife's hands from around his waist, and turned to face her. Putting his arms around her, he pulled her to him and said, "Ah, sweet, my little plan has worked perfectly."

"Mmmmm. I hope so," murmured Julie. "Still, it's a long way from a stroll on the beach to a walk down the aisle."

"Not when you're as hurt and defenseless as Mary Ellen." He hugged his wife more closely to him, tucking her pale head beneath his chin. "She'll marry Daniel Lawton within the month."

For a long moment both were silent. Then Julie, her

head resting on her husband's shoulder, said, "God help us if either Mary Ellen or Clay Knight ever find out exactly what we've done."

"Don't fret, they will never learn the truth," he said confidently. "There are only three people who know or will ever know of this deception. You. Me. And Daniel Lawton."

Fourteen

"And do you, Daniel Lawton, take Mary Ellen to be your lawfully wedded wife?"

"I do."

They stood before a robed priest in a small stone chapel on a narrow street in the ancient village of Monaco.

The buoyant bridegroom was tall and handsome in a cutaway and custom-cut pinstripe trousers.

The subdued bride was beautiful in a long, flowing gown of eggshell satin trimmed with thousands of tiny seed pearls. Her white-blond tresses were elaborately dressed atop her head. A shoulder-length veil covered her carefully coiffured hair and pale, pretty face. And effectively concealed the sadness that lingered in her large, dark eyes.

Half dazed, Mary Ellen exchanged vows with Daniel Lawton while the proud parents and a small circle of the Lawtons' European friends looked on. The brief, solemn ceremony pleased the assembled onlookers. Everyone was light-hearted and happy. Everyone but Mary Ellen.

She didn't love Daniel Lawton and knew she never would. But they—mainly Daniel and her father—had finally worn her down. She was tired of the battle. She couldn't fight them all, she no longer had the strength or the will.

The decision they'd all been breathlessly awaiting came after Mary Ellen finally forced herself to accept the cruel fact that Clay didn't love her, had never loved her. He was, she had realized at last, as cold and uncaring as her father said. If he were not, he would have answered her letters, would have attempted to get in touch with her. She had written to him repeatedly, seeking an explanation, asking for the chance to see him, to talk with him.

He never responded.

Still, even now as she stood beside the tall, blond man who was to be her husband, she wondered: If Clay knew that at this very moment she was marrying Daniel Lawton, would it sadden him just a little? Would he feel at least a trace of regret and loss? She hoped so. She hoped he would hurt the way she hurt.

Mary Ellen told herself she hated Clay Knight and she hoped more than anything in the world that the day would come when he got exactly what he deserved.

"I now pronounce you man and wife…." The priest's words jolted Mary Ellen out of her painful reverie. "You may kiss the bride."

Smiling brightly, Daniel turned to Mary Ellen, lifted the veil from her face, and carefully folded it back atop her pearl-encrusted headdress. He clasped her slender shoulders, bent his blond head, and, mindful of his rearing, brushed only a brief, chaste kiss on her lips.

Then he tucked her hand around his bent arm and led her down the narrow aisle and out into the bright October sunlight while the proud parents and invited guests applauded and tossed rice.

A waiting carriage, embellished with ropes of white orchids interwoven with tiny silver bells, whisked the newlyweds up the steep cliffs to the pink villa, where a sumptuous feast awaited. The entire wedding party followed the pair to the cliffside mansion to help them celebrate the grand occasion. The lavish luncheon was served outdoors, and the merry-making began when the first toast was proposed to the handsome pair.

Mary Ellen ate little, but when her new husband handed her a second glass of chilled champagne, she drank thirstily. Daniel smiled, squeezed her narrow waist, and signaled a passing waiter to refill her glass. The revelry lasted for hours, and Mary Ellen continued to sip the bubbly wine throughout the sunny autumn afternoon. She had every intention of being more than a little tipsy when night fell and she was alone with her husband.

When the warm October sun began to slide toward the deep blue Mediterranean, guests began departing.

It had been decided by Daniel and his parents that he and Mary Ellen would honeymoon in the villa. Well before the ceremony, the Lawtons' and the Prebles' luggage had been packed, taken, and stowed on a chartered yacht in the harbor. The elders would spend the night on the yacht and come morning leave the port of Monaco, return to London, and begin the journey home to Tennessee.

Within minutes all the guests had gone. The Lawtons then said their good-byes. They were descending the steps to a waiting carriage when Mary Ellen's mother, tears shining in her eyes, hugged Mary Ellen tightly. She stepped back and dabbed at her eyes with a lace-trimmed handkerchief.

John Thomas took Mary Ellen in his arms, and she

clung to him, trembling. She longed to leave with her parents. It was all she could do to keep from begging her father to take her with him. To take her home. She wanted to go home. Home to Memphis. Home to Longwood.

"I hope you'll be very happy, sweetheart," John Thomas whispered in her ear. He kissed her. "Take good care of her, Daniel," he said then, handing her over to her beaming bridegroom.

"I will, sir," Daniel replied. He put his arm around Mary Ellen, shook John Thomas's hand, and said, "Mary Ellen and I will honeymoon here at the villa for a few weeks, then go to Paris. After that perhaps a trip to the Greek isles and anywhere else my beautiful bride wishes to go." Smiling, he drew Mary Ellen closer. To her father he said, "Don't look for us home for at least six months."

"No hurry," said John Thomas, and ushered his teary-eyed wife out the door and down the steps to the carriage.

Mary Ellen and Daniel were left alone.

It was five-thirty in the afternoon.

Mary Ellen cleared her throat needlessly. "I really should change out of my wedding dress," she said, her hands nervously skimming over the full satin skirts. "I've a lovely new Paris gown that will be perfect for dinner tonight." She started to move away. Daniel stopped her.

"It *is* time you undress," he said, smiling, looking down at her, "but you won't be dressing again. At least not before tomorrow." A strange new light came into his green eyes, and Mary cringed inwardly.

"But Daniel," she said, "the sun's up."

"Well, so am I," he replied, repelling her with his

unexpected crudity. He laid a hand on his straining groin and told her, "It's been half-up all afternoon. Just being with you does it to me."

Before she could protest further, Daniel swept her into his arms and strode directly toward the staircase. Mary Ellen was filled with dread as he determinedly carried her up the stairs. Never once had she entertained the displeasing prospect of having to make love with him in the naked light of day. She had assumed that their first time would be in the covering darkness of midnight.

As they neared the enormous master suite, she knew just how wrong she had been.

Within minutes Mary Ellen, stark naked and so shamed and embarrassed that her face was beet red, lay trapped beneath a nude, panting Daniel while the dying October sunlight streamed into the room and directly across the bed.

She was incensed and disappointed that Daniel had made absolutely no effort to woo and ready her for the act of lovemaking. She was completely shocked by his uncaring behavior. He had been so thoughtful and understanding over the past few terrible weeks. Unfailingly compassionate, he had never pressed her; he had vowed he would never rush her. She had counted on that tolerance and patience now.

But it was missing.

Insensitive to her feelings, Daniel insisted, as soon as they got inside the bedroom, that they hurriedly undress. He stripped down to the skin right there before her, unmindful of her modesty. And he insisted she do the same. When her disrobing had gone too slowly to suit him, he had stepped in to lend a hand. She was mortified when he forcefully yanked down her lace-trimmed satin pantalets.

Once they were naked he drew her to the bed and after only three or four less-than-stirring kisses, he had climbed atop her, fumbled around for a few agonizingly awkward seconds, then given a forceful push and penetrated, despite the obvious fact that her body was not ready to receive him. Deaf to her quick intake of breath and the wince of pain she couldn't suppress, he immediately began to thrust deeply, rapidly.

As he moved atop her now, Mary Ellen felt only disgust and mild discomfort and self-loathing. Her head turned to the side, her gaze was fixed on an ornate gold-and-porcelain clock that rested on the night table beside the bed. Oblivious of her feelings, Daniel drove into her eagerly, and Mary Ellen couldn't help but question his glaring ineptness in the art of lovemaking.

For years she'd heard whispered stories of Daniel Lawton's great appeal and attraction to women. A number of Memphis's prettiest belles were said to be madly in love with him, and some of the city's most sophisticated divorcées and widows were known to have enjoyed dalliances with him. The glamorous Brandy Templeton had never made a secret of her intimacy with Daniel.

He was almost five years older than Clay and had had numerous women, yet he seemingly knew nothing about pleasing a woman. He was a terrible lover, and she was repulsed. There was only one aspect of his lovemaking of which Mary fully approved: the blessed brevity.

The act had hardly begun before it was finished. Her dark, unhappy eyes stayed riveted on the gold-and-porcelain clock, so she knew exactly how long the unpleasant ordeal lasted. From the moment Daniel had

impatiently climbed atop her until he groaned in his
shuddering release took a few seconds less than three
minutes.

Daniel sighed loudly, pulled out of her quickly, and
fell over onto his back, exhausted and satisfied.

Breathing hard but smiling foolishly with pleasure,
he said, "Wasn't that wonderful."

It was more of a statement than a question, so Mary
Ellen felt no need to reply. She turned her head slowly,
looked at him. Already his eyes were closing and his
breath was slowing. She held her own breath, hoping
that he was tired and would fall asleep for a while.

Without opening his eyes, Daniel reached over and
clamped a big hand atop her bare left thigh. She recoiled involuntarily, terrified he might already be wanting her again. But he only patted her and repeated, "Ah,
yes, that was good, darling." His fingers stroked her
thigh. "Let me catch my breath for a minute and we'll
make love again. We'll make love all night long. How
does that sound?"

Mary tensed, sickened by the idea. "Daniel, I really
don't…I…" She fell silent when his spread hand went
limp upon her bare thigh.

She looked hopefully at him and felt a great sense
of relief when she saw that his naked chest had begun
to rise and fall evenly. In seconds he began to snore
softly. Mary Ellen waited until she was certain he had
fallen into a deep slumber. It was only a few short
minutes; it seemed like hours. She carefully lifted his
hand from her thigh, placed it on the bed. Her eyes
never leaving his sleeping face, she scooted away from
him cautiously and rose from the bed.

Her bare feet making no sound on the plush carpet,
she hurried to the spacious bath and dressing room. A

hot bath awaited, prepared for her earlier by one of the servants. Gratefully she stepped into the tub and sank into its warm, soothing depths.

Shivering despite the heat of the water, she raised her knees and wrapped her arms around them. She bit her lip hard, but the tears still came. A knifelike pain stabbed through her naked breast as she recalled Clay's sweet, sensual, satisfying lovemaking. Her body ached for him just as her heart did. She yearned to have his arms around her, his lips on hers.

She was so unhappy, she felt as if she wanted to die. She sat there in the tub, realizing with startling clarity that never again would she be in Clay's arms. Worse, she would be in the arms of the inept lover who was her husband, again and again for years.

Tears of sorrow and regret spilling down her cheeks, Mary Ellen laid her head on her raised knees.

And she wept.

But when finally she stopped crying and raised her aching head, the deep hurt that had shone in her eyes was gone. A peculiar coldness had replaced it, and Mary Ellen vowed silently she would never again cry for Clay Knight. She would stop grieving for the past and look to the future. She had married Daniel Lawton, and she was going to be a good and faithful wife to him.

It wouldn't be that hard, because she no longer loved Clay Knight. She hated him. She hated him as fiercely as she had loved him, and her only prayer was that he would one day suffer the way he had made her suffer.

"Mary Ellen, where are you, dear?" Daniel's sleep-heavy voice came through the open bath door.

"I'll be right with you, darling."

Memphis Appeal
Sunday, October 22, 1848

Miss Mary Ellen Preble and Mr. Daniel Lawton were married abroad on Saturday, October 14th.

The morning ceremony took place in Monaco, where the couple will honeymoon for several months before returning to their Memphis home.

The seventeen-year-old bride is the only daughter of prominent cotton producer John Thomas Preble and his wife, Julie. The twenty-three-year-old bridegroom is the son of...

Clay stopped reading.

His hand reflexively wadded the newspaper article that had been clipped neatly from the society page of the *Memphis Appeal*. He didn't bother to read his mother's accompanying letter.

The crushed clipping gripped tightly in the palm of his hand, Clay pushed back his chair and rose from the small student desk where his books lay open. He crossed the compact, Spartan dormitory room to the window, his teeth clamped together so tightly he felt the pain in his jaw. He stood and stared out at the windswept quadrangle, where uniformed midshipmen rushed to and from their morning classes. His eyes lifted and he gazed sadly out at Chesapeake Bay.

He told himself it didn't matter that Mary had married Daniel Lawton. He didn't care. He had what he'd always wanted. He was here at the Naval Academy, and he was determined to excel. A bright future lay ahead of him.

But despite his firm resolve, tears gathered in his pain-filled gray eyes.

Without Mary, even the long dreamed of appointment to Annapolis didn't mean as much to him. Without her to share in his triumph, the victory was hollow.

Abruptly the painful knowledge that Mary would never again share in his triumphs and tragedies struck him with such force, it weakened him. *His* Mary was another man's wife. Another man's lover. And he would *never* hold her in his arms again.

Mary… His trembling lips formed her name soundlessly. *Oh, Mary.*

Clay's wide shoulders were beginning to shake, and his throat hurt so badly he could hardly swallow. He raised a long arm, placed his hand on the wooden window frame, and laid his tanned face on his forearm.

And he cried.

When at last he stopped and straightened, the tears and the pain were gone from his red-rimmed gray eyes. Replaced by a distinct coldness.

Clay never cried again.

But the coldness in his eyes and in his heart would remain for years to come.

Fifteen

From his very first hours as a lonely plebe at Annapolis, Clay directed all his time and energy to being a model midshipman. The regimen was extremely rigorous. Rugged physical fitness began ten minutes after reveille on his first full day at the "Yard." Before sunup he and the other green plebes assembled for the punishing calisthenics designed to build finely honed brawn. Clay gave it everything he had, eager to strengthen his still boyishly slim body.

His introduction to the sea came on his second day. In a small boat on the Severn River, he learned the rudiments of hull, mast, boom, tiller, and sail. Soon he was practicing the basics of navigation and piloting, the practical uses of charts and navigation, and the importance of command and responsibility.

Clay worked hard and studied hard. Along with celestial navigation, seamanship, ballistics, and cannonry, he became proficient in Greek, Latin, botany, geology, zoology, philosophy, and the great literatures.

A natural athlete, he quickly learned such things as precision drill, immediate obedience to proper commands, and the ability to perform—and to lead—under pressure.

His few free hours were spent mostly alone, either

in his Spartan room at the old stone dormitory or at the academy's vast nautical library. He rarely joined his boisterous classmates on their treks "landward" into the town of Annapolis. And he took severe teasing because of it.

"What's wrong with you, Knight?" a fellow midshipman would ask. "Don't you like women and whiskey?"

"Love 'em both."

"Well, come on, then. It's Saturday night and liberty's already begun. Let's go buy some wild women a drink."

"Not this time."

"Not this time, not this time," they'd all mimic, chuckling, elbowing each other in the ribs. And one of the bunch would inevitably say, "Know what I think about old Tennessee Knight here? I think he's afraid. I believe he's scared to death of women." Loud laughter and then: "How about it, Knight? You scared? That it?"

Clay would just smile at their taunts and let them have their fun. Then he'd turn back to his books as soon as they left on their adventure, uncaring that there wouldn't be another liberty call for a month.

Despite his seeming indifference and continued refusal to their offers of companionship, both his roommates and the other midshipmen liked Clay. They respected him for his tenacity and steely determination. They envied and admired him the total lack of concern he showed when bullying upperclassmen attempted to get his goat and make him lose his temper.

But none of his mates understood him.

Clay Knight seemed older than his years. He was never one of the gang. There was an aura of coolness about him that kept everyone at arm's length. Nobody got close to Clay Knight. He was a true loner with chilly gray eyes and an I-couldn't-care-less-what-you-think manner.

In the early spring of Clay's plebe year at the academy, word came that his mother, Anna Knight, had fallen ill with a serious case of influenza. Given a compassionate leave, Clay returned at once to Memphis.

But he was too late.

His hardworking, uncomplaining mother had passed away the night before his arrival. Only a handful of people attended the graveside services. Clay nodded to a few old friends and acquaintances. But he stood alone before the coffin, his hands clasped before him.

He bowed his dark head. His wintry gaze rested on the plain wooden coffin as he listened to the white-haired pastor speak eloquently about the good, kind woman who was his mother.

When the short service ended, he raised his head slowly. And saw, standing directly across the lowered coffin from him, Mary Ellen Preble Lawton on the arm of her husband, Daniel.

Clay's eyes clashed briefly with Mary Ellen's.

Hers were a defiant, angry black; his, a cold, uncaring gray.

They didn't speak.

She turned away quickly. A muscle spasmed in Clay's tight jaw. His eyes narrowed, and he watched helplessly as Daniel Lawton guided Mary to their waiting carriage. Clay's heart slammed against his ribs. He wanted to run after Mary, to call out to her that she couldn't go home with Lawton. She couldn't; she belonged to him!

Into his mind flashed that cold Sunday afternoon in January when they'd driven out to the deserted gatehouse on the old abandoned estate. They'd lain naked on their coats in a circle of lighted candles and made sweet love. Afterward he'd asked her, "You couldn't hurt me, could you?"

Never, my darling, never. That was what she had said, and her beautiful dark eyes had shone with what he had believed to be love. *Never, my darling, never.*

His chest tightened. He swallowed hard. He stood there unmoving until everyone had gone.

Then he plucked the fragrant white carnation from his uniform lapel, stepped forward, and placed it on his mother's coffin. "Good-bye, Mother," he said softly, his eyes filled with tears. He blinked them away, raised his dark head, stepped back, looked around, and added, "And good-bye, Memphis."

He turned and walked away.

Clay went straight to the levee and boarded a river steamer, vowing never to come back home again.

Mary Ellen returned to the huge Lawton mansion with her husband. Longing to be alone, she held her tongue when Daniel followed her up the grand staircase to their suite.

"I thought I'd lie down for a while," she announced, hoping he would give her an hour of privacy.

"Sounds like a very good idea," he replied, that telling grin she'd learned to recognize coming to his lips.

They went inside their suite. "Daniel, please…" She tried to keep her voice low, level. "I have a faint headache, and—"

"Yes, and I know what caused your 'faint headache.'" He took off his dark suit jacket and loosened his gray silk cravat.

Calmly removing her dark brown velvet bonnet, Mary Ellen said, "I have no idea what you mean."

"Don't you? Then let me clarify. Clay Knight. Knight's the source of your headache, isn't he? You saw him again, and you want—"

"Don't," she interrupted. "Don't be absurd." She smoothed her hair where the bonnet had ruffled it.

Daniel came to her, took hold of her upper arms. "You're *my* wife, Mary Ellen. Mine. You're to remember that." He pulled her close. "I know how to make you remember. I know how to get that seamstress's son out of your head."

He forcefully drew her up on her toes and kissed her hard. In minutes he had her undressed and in their big four-poster. Mary Ellen closed her eyes when he made the move to climb atop her, but she opened them again as soon as he'd thrust into her.

She focused on the white porcelain clock that sat on the mantel across the room. And she started the countdown. The countdown to the three minutes it would take Daniel to climax. The practice had become a habit, a habit about which she felt guilty.

But then she felt guilty most of the time. Guilty that she had married Daniel Lawton when she didn't love him. Guilty that she hadn't learned to love him, hadn't even grown fond of him. Consumed with guilt, she had tried in the very beginning to be a good wife, to lose herself in his lovemaking. It hadn't worked. So she had quickly fallen into the practice of counting down to three minutes, when it would mercifully end.

But today Mary Ellen lost count when unbidden came the vivid recollection of a cold February day when she and Clay had slipped down to the summerhouse and he had kissed her for the very first time. She could still feel the smoothness of his lips on hers, the warmth of his breath against her cheek. It was the sweetest, most innocent of kisses, and to this day she could remember exactly how it felt.

After they had kissed several times, Clay said, "Don't *ever* kiss anybody else, Mary. I couldn't stand it if you did. You belong to my heart. No other lips must kiss you but mine, no other arms must hold you but mine."

"Ahhhhh," Daniel groaned loudly in his ecstasy.

In the spring of 1852 Clayton Terrell Knight graduated from the Naval Academy at Annapolis at the very top of his class. He planned to make the military his life-long career just as his maternal grandfather, Admiral Clayton L. Tigart, the commodore, had before him.

Clay promptly volunteered to be sent completely across America to the Western Station. But even at remote frontier ports of call, he managed to attract the attention of his Pacific Fleet superiors. And he managed to attract the attention of the fair sex as well.

At twenty-two Clay was already a strikingly handsome man. The long hours of exercise coupled with his healthy appetite had changed the way he looked. He had been a tall, gangly boy when he'd first arrived at the academy. Upon leaving it, he was a lean, well-built man with wide sculpted shoulders, a drum-tight abdomen, and strong, lightly muscled legs. His face, like his body, had changed in his years at Annapolis. All traces of the youthful openness and childish enthusiasm were gone. His classic boyish features had hardened into those of a slightly cynical, self-assured man.

Clay's brooding good looks turned heads wherever

he went, and he never wanted for female companionship. He was a dark, seductive figure with strangely hypnotic silver-gray eyes that instantly set hearts aflutter. His very presence stirred shameful thoughts and secret longings in the bosoms of respectable women, young and old.

A sensual man by nature, Ensign Clay Knight was perfectly willing to enjoy the feminine charms so unselfishly offered to him. At every officers' dance or outside social event, Clay had a beautiful woman on his arm. The woman understood, in advance, that she would also share his bed later in the evening.

Didn't tradition say, "Forces ashore must treat forces afloat"?

Through an ever-changing parade of beautiful women, Clay remained unreachable. He never promised love or commitment, never pretended an emotion he didn't feel. He had become a cold, aloof man whose heart was permanently scarred. To Clay Knight, women were a mere convenience, a troublesome necessity, a series of warm, willing bodies to help him make it through the long, lonely nights.

Knowing all this, the women still made themselves readily available. His heart was cold, but his body was hot, and he knew how to use it. His dark animal beauty instantly aroused their sexual hunger. And he had learned, through the passing of the years and the passing parade of women, any number of techniques to give a voracious lover the ultimate in sexual pleasure.

So when a woman was in his arms, when he was skillfully, if dispassionately, making love to her as no other man ever had, the grateful woman forgot that he would never really be hers. He was hers for now, and she gladly immersed herself in the exquisite joy he gave her.

Still, despite his complete honesty before taking them to bed, many of the dazzled women fell madly in love with Clay. It was to their sorrow. His love—and his hatred—for Mary Ellen Preble Lawton never cooled, never diminished, never let him go.

It was much the same with Mary Ellen.

She was the envied wife of one of the richest, most handsome gentlemen in the entire Southland, but never a single day went by that she didn't think about Clay Knight. She never stopped hating him. She blamed him for all her unhappiness. Her empty, loveless marriage was his fault. Had she not been so totally devastated by his cruel, sudden jilting, she would *never* have married Daniel.

Regretting her rash, foolish actions ever since, Mary Ellen remembered how hurt and confused she had been at the time. And how she'd been pushed from all sides into the relationship with Daniel. How she had finally given in one balmy night in Monte Carlo and said yes. She'd been so tired of fighting everyone, especially her father. As soon as he had joined them on the Riviera, her father had begun insisting she come to her senses and marry Daniel. Finally she had given in.

Now she existed in a state of perennial apathy. Her days were spent in resignation and regret in the lavish upstairs suite of rooms she'd come to think of as her silk-walled prison. Her nights were spent in the prison's four-poster with a man whose touch neither excited nor repelled her. It did nothing to her, one way or the other.

Night after night Mary Ellen lay lifeless beneath the amorous Daniel, sadly remembering the thrilling touch of the heartless man she hated, loved, couldn't live without. Totally unaware of what was going through her mind, Daniel never failed to attain a deep, seemingly satisfying climax.

But for her it never happened.

Her body—and her heart—were permanently anesthetized.

Sixteen

Before they celebrated their second anniversary, Daniel Lawton had begun staying out late many evenings. Mary Ellen was not surprised, nor did she blame him. She hadn't been the adoring wife, had never shown him the love and affection that were his due. If their marriage was less than perfect—which it certainly was—she was the one responsible.

Daniel made up elaborate stories, explaining that it was absolutely necessary that he stay out till all hours. It was business. She knew better. It was monkey business. Daniel wasn't a very convincing liar. She knew exactly where he had been.

Everyone in Memphis was aware of Antole's, the fancy sporting house that catered to the city's moneyed patricians. Years ago she had heard house servants whisper that many of the city's most illustrious citizens, including Daniel's distinguished white-haired father, had on occasion been a patron. Apparently Daniel had now joined the ranks of his father and those other aristocratic gentlemen who spent evenings at the famed brothel.

She suspected that he'd also resumed an intimate relationship with his former lover, Brandy Templeton Fowler. Brandy was a newlywed herself, but her marriage to a wealthy middle-aged real estate magnate from New Orleans hadn't changed her. And she'd always had a weakness for Daniel.

More than one midnight Mary Ellen was awakened by the late arrival of her husband, the scent of perfume that wasn't her fragrance clinging to his fine clothes. And occasionally when he got undressed she saw scratch marks on his back.

Mary Ellen never confronted him. She never asked him where he had been. She never complained that he was neglecting her. She never so much as hinted that she thought he was being unfaithful to her.

She didn't particularly care. Truth to tell, she welcomed his absence at bedtime. It was a relief to be left alone. She was more than willing to allow Brandy or some high-paid fancy lady to stand in for her. Or *lie* in for her, she thought with wicked satisfaction.

Secretly, shamefully, Mary Ellen was glad Daniel was expending some of his sexual energy away from home. Away from her. She was equally glad that Daniel at least had the decency not to touch her on the nights when he had been with another woman.

Evenings when he stayed at home, Mary Ellen continued dutifully to share his bed without complaint because Daniel desperately wanted a son. She hadn't given him anything else. Surely she could give him a son who would love him as she did not.

But months, then years, passed and Mary Ellen did not conceive.

"It's your fault," Daniel accused her one morning when he learned that once again Mary Ellen was not pregnant. "There must be something wrong with you or you'd have conceived a long time ago."

Mary Ellen calmly sat down at her dressing table

and began to brush her hair. "I'm sorry, Daniel. Truly I am."

"Well, so am I." He paced back and forth behind her. "Dammit all, a wife's supposed to give her husband children. All our friends are talking about us. They're saying I can't father a child."

"That's your imagination," she told him evenly. "Our friends wouldn't be so unkind."

"Well, maybe they're not saying it, but they're thinking it."

"Perhaps they are right," Mary Ellen said. "You've insisted I see the doctor, which I have done repeatedly. He says there is nothing wrong, no reason why I shouldn't get pregnant. Have you considered the fact that it might be you who—"

"I?" he interrupted, incredulous. He stopped his pacing and came to stand directly behind her. "My dear," he said arrogantly, crossing his arms over his chest and meeting her eyes in the mirror, "let me assure you that I am more than capable of producing an heir." He began to smile then. A slow, sly grin spread over his smug face, and Mary Ellen strongly suspected he had living proof of that boast.

She said nothing, just nodded and continued to brush her hair.

"It's all right," he told her finally, his arms coming uncrossed. "We'll just have to try harder. We'll make love more often." He gave her shoulders a squeeze, turned, and crossed the room. At the door he paused and said, "If it is possible for you to conceive, I *will* make you pregnant."

Daniel tried.

So did Mary Ellen.

But after a half dozen years of an empty, loveless

marriage, the couple still remained childless. Daniel finally gave up on Mary Ellen making him a father. In his frustration and disappointment he accused her of not wanting his child.

"You think you're so very clever, my dear, but I'm not fooled," he said one winter evening when he'd had too much brandy. "You don't really want a child. You don't want *my* child. You never did."

"That isn't true, Daniel. I have done everything I can to give you a child."

"I don't believe you. Not for a minute," he said, slurring his words. "You want to know what I really think? I think that all these years you've been practicing some secret effective procedure to keep from conceiving."

"We've been over this before," Mary Ellen said wearily. "I've told you, I know of no secret method. You must believe me."

But no amount of denying such an absurdity convinced Daniel. He was sure there could be no other explanation.

The failing marriage finally came to an end in the early summer of 1857. On a warm sunny day in late May, Daniel returned from a week-long business trip down to Mobile. It was the third time he had been to Alabama in the past three months.

Daniel found Mary Ellen alone in the rose garden at the south side of the Lawton mansion. Curled up on a settee of white wrought-iron lace, she was so engrossed in her book by Jane Austen, she was unaware of his presence. So he stood for a long moment and observed her quietly.

Her white-blond hair was dressed atop her bent head, exposing the graceful curve of her neck. The summer dress she wore was a pale shade of pink organza, the exact hue of the delicate roses covering the tall bush directly behind her. Her full skirts and lacy petticoats spilled down onto the manicured grass at her slippered feet.

One side of the dress's low bodice had fallen down to reveal her pale bare shoulder. Her skin looked like fine porcelain, and when she breathed the swell of her breasts strained against the fallen bodice.

Daniel's breath caught in his chest.

Mary Ellen Preble Lawton was the loveliest woman he had ever seen, and even now, after nine years as her husband, the mere sight of her filled him with desire. It was as if he had never touched her, never had her. Sometimes he wondered if he ever had. And knew, deep in his heart, that he had not.

Yes, she had lain naked in his arms night after night, but he had never really had her. She had never given herself to him. Since their honeymoon night in Monaco, she had indifferently allowed him the use of her beautiful body because he was her husband. But she had never really responded.

She did her duty.

But she always remained detached and unemotional even when they were intimate. She held back her love and fire, wouldn't give it to him. It had been that way throughout their marriage.

He knew the reason. Had known from the beginning. The beautiful, angelic-faced girl he had married in Monaco had been desperately in love with Clayton Knight.

As he studied her now, Daniel wondered if, after all these years, she was still in love with Knight.

"Mary Ellen…" He spoke her name at last. She looked up.

"Daniel," she said, closing the book on the red silk marker. "I didn't know you were home. When did you get back?"

He didn't answer her question. He said, "I've something to tell you."

"Please," she said, indicating the settee, "come and join me."

Daniel walked over, dropped down beside her, and without preamble told his beautiful twenty-six-year-old wife that he had fallen in love with a pretty seventeen-year-old Alabama belle he'd met while at Mobile's Mardi Gras last February.

"I want a divorce immediately, Mary Ellen," he said. "I'm going to marry the sweet young girl who loves me as you never did."

Mary Ellen agreed without argument. She said, "I sincerely wish you every happiness, Daniel, and I hope she will be able to give you the son I couldn't."

Daniel's fair face colored, and Mary realized that the seventeen-year-old was already pregnant with his child.

"Then, congratulations," she said, smiling, and reached out to touch his cheek. Then she rose from the settee and started to walk away.

"Mary Ellen, wait." He stopped her. She turned back, looked at him. "There's...there is something I must tell you. Something you ought to...something you have a right to know...and...I..." He stopped speaking.

"Yes, Daniel?" Her well-arched eyebrows lifted questioningly. "What is it?"

Daniel started to say something, hesitated. He didn't reply. The oath he had sworn to years ago came back to haunt him. He had promised John Thomas Preble that no matter what happened, he would *never* disclose to Mary Ellen, or to anyone else, the scheme they had jointly implemented to break up Mary Ellen's romance with Clay Knight. And he feared John Thomas Preble.

Daniel shook his blond head. It didn't matter anyhow. It was too late to undo the deed. Too late to change all that had happened.

"Nothing," he said finally. "It was nothing."

Mary Ellen and Daniel quickly divorced.

The day the decree was final, Daniel married his pregnant Alabama sweetheart. The newlyweds didn't go on a honeymoon. Instead, less than an hour after the civil ceremony, they hurried to the Shelby County Hospital. The bride was in labor.

At midnight she gave birth to Daniel Lawton's first child.

A healthy nine-pound boy.

Mary Ellen had, as soon as Daniel asked her for a divorce, returned to the Preble mansion to live with her parents. On the day the divorce became final and Daniel remarried, she took back her maiden name.

She was again a Preble, and her powerful father's name and position in the community kept the young divorcée from being ostracized by polite society. The only daughter of John Thomas Preble would continue to be accepted by the city's elite.

So once she was legally Mary Ellen Preble again, her parents expected her to start accompanying them to the many gala balls and elegant parties to which they were invited.

But Mary Ellen never attended the many social activities so favored by the Prebles. And she staunchly refused dinner invitations from a number of the city's eligible bachelors and widowers. She suspected their main interest in her stemmed from the fact that she was a divorced woman and therefore more likely to be passionate and loose moraled than if she had never been married.

Her parents were disappointed that she refused all invitations. So were a host of would-be suitors. Mary Ellen was more beautiful now than she'd been at seventeen, and the fact that she was a divorcée certainly added to her appeal. Polish and grace had replaced childish enthusiasm and wide-eyed innocence. She was a woman now, and with her fair blond looks and her somewhat sulky poise, she was a powerfully seductive challenge to many a hopeful male.

Mary Ellen gave none of them the time of day, which only made her more attractive. She was totally unattainable, therefore incredibly alluring. She was, to the chagrin of the other eager local beauties, the most sought after female in all Memphis.

A year passed.

Then two.

And still Mary Ellen preferred to stay close to the comfortable refuge of Longwood. Her parents were concerned. It wasn't right for a woman so young and pretty to never go anywhere or see anyone.

They planned a trip abroad. They insisted she go with them to England for the summer season. She wouldn't. She stayed behind at Longwood.

Worried about their reclusive daughter, the Prebles acknowledged they might have made a terrible mistake by sending Clay Knight away all those years ago. And they wondered if they should, even at this late date, admit their error.

"Maybe we should tell Mary Ellen the truth, John," Julie Preble said as they strolled on the deck of the SS *Ambassador* while she crossed the rough Atlantic.

"Perhaps you're right," John Thomas mused aloud. "I suppose she has a right to know, even if she hates us for what we did." He recoiled at such an unacceptable possibility. "God, all I was trying to do was ensure her happiness, but—"

"I know, dear," said his wife. "I know. Mary Ellen will understand if we tell her."

"I don't know," he said, leading Julie over to the ship's railing. Shaking his graying head worriedly, he said, "We misjudged her then. We could be misjudging her now if we assume that she'll forgive us." His dark eyes were somber.

Julie Preble laid a gentle hand on her husband's arm. "Dearest, that is a chance we must take. Mary Ellen has been miserable for far too long. She never learned to love Daniel as we had hoped. Neither of them was happy. Their marriage was a terrible sham."

"Yes, it was, and I—"

"My contacts with ties to the academy tell me Clay Knight has never married. Maybe it's not too late for…" Her words trailed off. She fell silent.

John Thomas patted her hand. "When we get back home this fall, we'll have a long talk with Mary Ellen. We'll tell her the truth. Confess everything." He drew a long, deep breath of the salt air and added, "If she wants to try to get in touch with Ensign Knight, I'll do everything in my power to help her. To help them both."

"Yes," agreed Julie Preble. "We'll tell her just as soon as we get back home."

Seventeen

Mary passed the summer in lonely solitude at Longwood. In mid-October, when the leaves began to fall and the humid air began to cool ever so slightly, she assembled the many servants together. She instructed them to begin readying the mansion and the grounds for the return of her parents.

They were due back in Memphis in three weeks.

Across the ocean on that very same October day, Julie Preble was dressing for their last evening in London. Come morning, they would start the voyage home to America. John Thomas was already dressed and waiting impatiently in the parlor of their opulent Savoy hotel suite.

Dapper in black evening clothes, he whistled softly as he poured himself a drink. He felt lighthearted and happy. Their long stay abroad had been a mixture of pleasure and business. He had met with his European cotton buyers and assuaged their fears about the talk of a possible war between the states. It would never happen, he assured them. Preble cotton would continue to flow uninterrupted to their markets or his name was not John Thomas Preble!

Now John Thomas was more than a little eager to go home. Glass in hand, he went to the foyer for his long black evening cape and silk top hat. Returning to the parlor, he finished his drink and set the glass aside, deciding against a second. He fished a gold-cased watch from the pocket of his white waistcoat, checked it, and smiled.

Julie was running late, as usual.

"Better hurry, darling," he called through the open bedroom door. "We're already a quarter of an hour late."

John Thomas turned his head and listened, expecting to hear her cultured voice calmly telling him that she wasn't quite ready; she would be out in just a moment.

Several seconds passed and Julie didn't answer. John Thomas shook his head and called to her again. When she still didn't answer, he grew mildly alarmed.

"Julie, is something wrong? Are you having trouble with some pesky hooks? I'll be glad to be of service." No reply. Only silence. "Julie? Julie? Answer me!"

Beginning to frown, John Thomas tossed his evening cape and silk top hat on a sofa and started for the bedroom. He reached the door and looked about anxiously. His wife wasn't seated at the mirrored vanity table. She wasn't behind the dressing screen.

He advanced into the room, looking about, his heart beginning to pound.

Then he saw her.

She was on the far side of the bed. Frightened, he hurried to her. Her new taffeta ball gown half on, half off, she was on her knees, one hand clutching the bed's brocade counterpane, the other at her throat.

Her eyes were filled with fear, she was struggling to say his name. But blood came instead of sound.

"God in heaven!" her terrified husband swore, and fell to his knees beside her. "Julie, Julie!"

The hotel's physician arrived minutes after John Thomas rang frantically for help. Still dressed in her bloodied Paris gown, an unconscious Julie Preble was taken at once to St. Mary's Hospital a few short blocks away.

But they couldn't save her. She hemorrhaged to death from a perforated ulcer.

John Thomas Preble was devastated.

He took his beloved wife home for burial, then went into seclusion in his Memphis mansion. He refused to leave Longwood. He wouldn't see old friends who came to call. He spent long hours alone in the upstairs suite he had shared with his wife, clutching a piece of Julie's jewelry or staring at a faded photograph of her.

He wouldn't let the servants touch anything that had belonged to her. He roared like a wounded lion when Mary Ellen suggested he at least allow them to take Julie's clothes away. For days at a time he stayed sequestered in the suite, carefully fingering strands of silky golden hair that clung to Julie's hairbrush.

He was prostrate with grief—so lost in his own misery, he didn't remember that he and Julie had planned to tell Mary Ellen what had really happened with Clay Knight more than a decade ago.

Mary Ellen was deeply concerned about John Thomas. She had lost her mother; she was afraid she was losing her father as well. She was fearful he would literally grieve himself to death.

Weeks passed and he got no better.

Christmas came and went, with no change in the depth of his mourning. Winter turned to spring, with John Thomas Preble still immersed in sorrow. Summer settled in with its sticky, oppressive heat, and the brooding master of Longwood stayed shut up in the stuffy upstairs shrine, his shirt soaked with perspiration, his dark eyes dead.

John Thomas had lost all interest in his vast cotton empire. Profits had declined steadily. The Preble fortune had begun to dwindle away. Slaves were sold to neighbors. Rich fertile fields went unplanted.

Mary Ellen expressed her growing concern to her father. She attempted to shock him out of his grief by telling him they were going to end up ruined financially if he didn't take hold and intervene. She warned him about the possibility of a war between the states. If it happened, a Union blockade would likely keep all cotton from reaching the lucrative European markets. He'd better wake up! He'd better ship as much cotton abroad as possible right now so they wouldn't be left destitute.

But John Thomas Preble was unreachable.

Eighteen

On the rolling decks of the southbound navy screw sloop *Water Witch,* a tall, solitary figure stood on the bow in the late night darkness. Dressed for the frigid temperatures of the open sea in winter, the lean officer wore dark woolen trousers, a high-necked pullover sweater, a heavy woolen seaman's jacket, and a black watch cap.

The winds ruffled locks of the blue-black hair escaping his watch cap and pressed his dark trousers against his hard thighs and long legs. His feet were braced apart in the stance adapted by seamen who often stand on the pitching decks of a moving ship.

His balance perfect despite the rough seas, he withdrew a thin brown cigar and match from his lips, struck the match with his thumbnail, then cupped his hands around the tiny flame while he puffed the smoke to life.

Captain Clay Knight drew deeply on his cigar. Orange sparks blew around his head and dissipated quickly in the strong north winds.

This cold dark night was, Captain Knight reflected, but one of hundreds like it that he had spent on the heaving deck of a moving ship. He had been at sea when winter storms had struck with full, dangerous fury. He remembered ropes and halyards sheathed with ice and the crew suffering from frostbite and bitter debilitating cold. He recalled winds so strong that he had to shout to be heard above the roar of the waves, and the motion of the ship was so great it seemed as if she were racing when she was only rising and lowering with the giant waves, making no forward progress.

He remembered the hauling of ropes that bit into his raw hands and the chopping of ice and fighting the elements and the heavy darkness that came far too early on those short, leaden days. He remembered so many cold, lonely nights he had spent on the deck of a ship far, far from shore.

Yet never, it seemed, far enough.

Since his graduation from Annapolis a dozen years ago, Captain Knight had been at sea for months at a stretch and had dropped anchor in many a foreign port. From the beginning he had volunteered for any campaign he heard of that would take him a great distance from America's shores, as if the more miles he put between himself and Memphis, Tennessee, the less he would think of Mary Ellen Preble Lawton.

In September of 1852, just three months after graduation, he'd been one of a handful of stripers who'd graduated to the fleet to be sent with a hundred marines on the gunship *Jamestown* down to Buenos Aires, Argentina, to protect Americans living there.

In June of 1853 he'd been sent out on an expedition aboard the *Brinkley* to chart the Pacific islands from the Aleutians to Japan. Called back to shore duty in San Francisco after nine months, he was immediately shipped out as third mate aboard the *Bryson* to Shanghai in April of 1854.

He was with a landing party of ninety men under Commander John Kelly of the frigate *Wichita*, which joined a British naval detachment to drive out the Chinese forces threatening the foreign concessions at Shanghai.

In 1855 it was consular duty in Hong Kong, then later that same year the Fiji islands. In 1856 he led a small landing party from the sloop *Decatur,* who helped the settlers of Seattle, Washington, repel an attack by a thousand hostile Indians.

He spent the majority of 1857 in the States, lecturing at Annapolis, and near the end of the year was promoted to the rank of full Lieutenant.

In 1858 he was down in Paraguay as second officer aboard the gunship *Freedom* and at the mouth of the Congo in 1859.

Now, in early January of 1861, newly commissioned Captain Clay Knight was ten days out of the Norfolk navy yard, where the *Water Witch* had had a complete refit. Bound for his Western Station—the port of San Francisco—the voyage would take him down around the Cape.

It was a long journey, and they would make at least four stops along the way, the first and longest at the tropical seaside city of Rio de Janeiro. The crew was already looking forward to liberty in the warm Brazilian port.

Smoking alone in the darkness on that cold January night, Captain Clay Knight continued to reflect on all the years he'd spent at sea and all the places he'd seen and all the women he'd had. He shook his dark head, and his full lips slowly turned up into a self-mocking grin.

Through all the years and all the places and all the women, he had never managed to totally forget Mary. There had been times, brief and far apart, when his vision of her had dimmed. Times when he had trouble remembering exactly what she looked like, what her voice sounded like, what it felt like to have her arms around him.

Then, like a bolt out of the blue, some long forgotten memory would rise up to torture him. And there she'd be before him, her image so vivid, so real, his fingers ached to touch her. He could almost taste the sweetness of her kisses, could almost feel the warmth of her slender body moving against his own.

Captain Clay Knight finally threw back his dark head and laughed at himself as he stood alone on the bow of the *Water Witch*. Serious trouble was looming on America's horizon. His nation was on the brink of a civil war. A war that would cost untold lives, maybe his own. Yet here he was thinking about Mary Ellen Preble Lawton.

Thank God no one—especially Mary—knew what a sentimental fool he was.

His laughter soon stopped and his firm jaw tightened. His gray eyes narrowed as he flicked his smoked-down cigar into the sea.

If his love had never fully died, neither had his hatred. It was the only thing that had saved him. Anytime he wistfully remembered Mary as being an honest, sweet, loving girl, he quickly reminded himself that she had proven to be none of those things.

She was, in fact, a deceitful, cruel, incredibly cold woman who hadn't thought twice about stepping on his heart. He was glad he would never see the beautiful bitch again.

Nineteen

It was nearing sunset when the glittering jewel of Brazil's long Atlantic coast came up on the starboard bow of the *Water Witch*. Spectacular Rio de Janeiro seemed to have washed in with the tide. It was a stunning sight: the sandy beaches and graceful valleys and hillsides of tropical mountains.

To the sea-weary sailors of the *Water Witch*, Rio looked like a breathtakingly beautiful woman with arms outstretched, seductively beckoning them to come to her.

The *Witch* steamed into Guanabara Bay as the lights of the magical city twinkled on along the sugary white beaches and purple hills above. With a sure hand and a keen eye, the pilot guided the *Witch* cautiously toward its berth in the harbor where dozens of other ships, great and small, were moored.

She slid slowly in between a tacky brown tug and an impressive white-hulled clipper. When the yawl line was tossed to the wharf and the anchor lowered, the *Witch* was berthed at approximately the same site where the first Portuguese sailors had landed more than three hundred fifty years before.

There had been no one to welcome those Portuguese sailors of old, but down on the docks on this warm February evening, a swarm of smiling, waving *Cariocas*—mostly female—were eager to show the American sailors their beloved city. A city that throbbed with excitement and sensuality twenty-four hours a day.

The crew of the *Witch,* freshly shaven and neatly uniformed, shouted and waved madly to the pretty women below, so anxious to step onto Brazilian soil they could hardly contain themselves. Their blood up, they felt as if they couldn't wait another minute to get off the ship and explore the many delights of the seaside tropical paradise.

One of their number would have to wait.

Captain Clay Knight was almost as eager as the others to enjoy the pleasures of Rio. Too long without a woman, he fully intended—before the evening ended—to lose himself for a few hours in the arms of a warm and willing Brazilian beauty.

But first he had a duty to perform.

He was to be one of the honored guests at a welcoming party given by retired naval Captain John D. Willingham, an old-timer who had served under Clay's grandfather in the War of 1812. The aging Captain Willingham had married a wealthy Rio heiress and made Rio de Janeiro his home after leaving the service.

Clay was due at the Willinghams in an hour.

Presently he stood apart from the boisterous crew, a pair of field glasses swinging from his neck. His eyes and his interest were on the gleaming white clipper moored next to the *Water Witch.* Clay knew that the impressive white ship was not a naval vessel.

It was, he supposed, the private oceangoing craft of some incredibly rich Brazilian. A lover of beautiful ships, Clay was fascinated with the tall white clipper.

He studied the magnificent vessel from stem to stern, raised his field glasses, and searched its teak deck for passengers. He saw no one. He smiled when he read the ship's name painted boldly in big blue script letters on the pristine white bow: *Açúcar.*

Açúcar, Clay knew, meant sugar in Portuguese. He made a face. What kind of man would name his ship Sugar?

Starting to grin, he lowered the glasses but continued to examine the craft until the sun had totally disappeared behind Rio's towering hills and he had to get dressed and go.

It was summertime in Rio de Janeiro, so Captain Clay Knight was in immaculate crisp summer whites and ceremonial sword when he stepped onto the ancient wharf. He walked wharfside beneath the bowsprits of giant ships lining the harbor, their bare spars towering into the rapidly darkening sky.

The long wooden levee was crowded on this warm early evening. Portuguese longshoremen were grouped together at various spots along the wharf, kneeling around dice games, waiting to be called to work.

Shifty-eyed men lounged against brick-fronted warehouses, eyeing passersby, procuring for the side street bagnios that catered to deep-water seamen.

Clay shook his head almost imperceptibly when they made a move to approach him. They backed away.

He soon left the wharf behind, crossed busy Avenida Presidente Vargas, and hailed a taxi. When he was settled comfortably on the worn leather seat, the open taxi began its ascent up the steep, winding hillside roads of Rio.

His long arm resting along the seat top, his dark head turning this way, then that, Clay admired the stunning combination of topography that was Rio: dark blue seas studded with rocky islands and tumbling wooded mountains and expanses of stark gray rock that surrounded the city.

Rio on a summer's night such as this was powerfully seductive. The sights and sounds and smells stirred the senses, and Clay was anxious to leave Captain Willingham's even before he arrived.

It was straight up eight when the smartly uniformed Captain Clay Knight, his billed cap tucked under his arm, rang the bell at a hilltop house with incredible vistas of the lighted city and harbor below.

The heavy carved door swung open, and a breathtakingly beautiful young girl with white-blond hair and huge dark eyes stood before him.

"Don't tell me," she said, smiling brightly. "You're Captain Clay Knight." She put out her hand. "I'm Jo Anna Willingham, John D. Willingham's granddaughter. I'm here visiting from New Orleans, and I insist you sit by me at dinner!"

"I'd be honored," Clay said when he was able to speak. His gray eyes darkened to a deep, warm charcoal.

"I told them you would be," said the slender blond charmer. After taking his arm, she led him into the noisy drawing room, where guests stood about talking and sipping chilled wine.

The affair was an informal gathering of thirty people, of whom the majority of the gentlemen were either naval officers of the line or retired old salts. Clay was one of four bachelors present. An equal number of unattached young ladies were there to make sure the bachelors felt welcome.

The outgoing Jo Anna Willingham took her responsibility seriously. She meant to personally see to it that the darkly handsome Captain Clay Knight felt right at home.

In a roomful of military men the conversation turned naturally to the storm brewing back in the states. The aging Captain Willingham said, "If South Carolina seceded from the Union back on December twentieth, then other Southern states would have likely followed by now. Or they soon will. I see no way around it. The South will be fighting the North before summer, mark my words."

At these words, Willingham's wife of forty years spoke up and said, "Now, Captain, you promised you'd not get off on the subject of war until at least after dinner."

"So I did, my dear." He smiled sheepishly at her, then said, "We'll continue this talk later, gentlemen."

When the leisurely meal was finally finished, the silver-haired host suggested the ladies retire to the parlor while the gentlemen join him in his library for fine Havana cigars and Napoleon brandy and further discussion of the imminent war between the states.

His dauntless granddaughter said, "Sorry, Grandfather, but I promised Captain Knight I'd show him your famous flower gardens." She cut her dark eyes at Clay flirtatiously and gave him a saucy smile.

"Why, child, it's nighttime," said John D. Willingham. "The Captain can't appreciate my prize blooms in the darkness."

"There's a full moon," Jo Anna reminded him. She took Clay's arm and guided him from the dining room while the remaining three single ladies cast looks of envy after them.

Clay would have preferred not to go out into the

moonlight with this irrepressible young beauty who so reminded him of the woman it had taken him a dozen years to get over. Her hair was the same white-blond shade, and she wore it loose and long as Mary had when she was a young girl. Her eyes were large and dark and expressive. Her nubile body was tall and slender, with gentle, tempting curves.

Just like Mary's.

Clay wanted her instantly.

He wanted this beautiful replica of the young Mary as he'd not wanted a woman in years. He could hardly keep from drawing her into his arms and quieting her charming girlish chatter with his lips.

Her hand curled around his arm, Jo Anna Willingham strolled through the flower-filled grounds alongside Captain Knight, flirting with him, purposely pressing her breasts against his arm as she pointed out the varieties of sweetly blooming flowers her grandfather grew here in this exotic coastal Eden.

Abruptly Jo Anna stopped talking, stopped walking. From a heavily laden bush she plucked a perfect snow white orchid. She presented it to Clay.

"Take this to remember me by, Captain." Clay smiled and took the orchid. Jo Anna stepped closer, put her arms around his neck. "And take this as well."

She rose up on tiptoe and kissed him full on the mouth. Clay's arms immediately went around her and he kissed her with a fierce urgency that instantly communicated itself to her. Flattered and thrilled, she eagerly pressed herself against his tall, hard frame and sighed her approval when his hands possessively clasped her hips to draw her closer, then slipped down to cup the twin cheeks of her bottom.

Jo Anna Willingham had never been kissed like

this. Short of breath, hot and cold at once, she tingled from head to toe. She clung to Clay while he kissed her deeply, urgently, and she hoped he was feeling the same scary excitement she felt.

He was.

And then some.

But abruptly Clay tore his burning lips from hers, clasped her bare upper arms, and set her back from him so roughly her head rocked on her shoulders.

"Jesus Christ!" he muttered.

"What is it?" asked the baffled Jo Anna Willingham. "Are you angry with me? Have I done something wrong?"

"No, I have," he said in self-disgust. "You're only a child and I shouldn't… I'm sorry, I… You'd best go in."

"I don't want to go in, Captain. I'm no child. I'm eighteen, and I want to stay here with you."

"You're going in," he said, and took her arm to lead her forcefully into the house.

No sooner were they back inside than Clay made his apologies to his host and hostess, explaining that he was tired from the long voyage and felt he had best make an early evening of it.

"You'll come again, won't you, Captain?" said his gregarious host. "Mrs. Willingham and I enjoy entertaining you young military men from the States."

"Thank you, sir," Clay said noncommittally.

He glanced at Jo Anna and saw the bright tears of confusion shining in her dark, questioning eyes. He felt a sharp pang of guilt. He had kissed her, wanted to make love to her, but only because she reminded him of Mary. He had no choice: He left her there wondering what she had done wrong.

Clay hurried down the stone steps of the steeply terraced lawn, taking them two at a time. When he reached the white wall bordering the Willingham property, he anxiously let himself out the gate. Then he turned to look back up at the house on the hill.

Exhaling heavily with relief, he opened his hand and let the perfect white orchid drop to the ground.

His earlier light mood gone, Captain Clay Knight put his billed naval hat on his head and headed down toward the string of brightly lighted saloons lining Ipanema Beach.

Twenty

" . . . And I don't feel it's fair to subject my wife and daughter to the danger," said Pres Templeton, the Prebles' closest neighbor, whose mansion was less than a quarter mile down along the bluffs from Longwood. "I've sold the house to a nice young couple from Nashville. William and Leah Thompson. The wife's a cousin of Andrew Johnson's. Well-bred, genteel people. Fine folks, fine folks."

"So you'll be leaving Memphis, Pres?" said John Thomas.

The two men were in John Thomas's book-lined study on a frigid afternoon in early January. Mary Ellen was delighted that her father had finally agreed to come down and visit with his old friend and neighbor.

For the past few weeks, John Thomas had begun coming downstairs occasionally. And when he did not, he requested that the *Memphis Appeal* be put on his breakfast tray. Mary Ellen knew the reason for the change. Rumors of impending war had piqued his interest as nothing had since Julie's death.

But today was the first time he had agreed to entertain a visiting guest.

Hovering anxiously just outside the study door, Mary Ellen heard Pres Templeton say, "If war does come—and it looks to be inevitable—I can't allow my womenfolk to stay here in harm's way."

"Well, why don't you send them away and stay here yourself?" John Thomas's voice had regained some of its former strength and authority.

Pres Templeton hemmed and hawed and finally said, "I wanted to do that, I surely did. But Mrs. Templeton wouldn't hear of it. She insists I go to Europe with them. You know Brandy's such a spirited handful, her mama can't handle her alone."

"For God's sake, Pres," said John Thomas, "your daughter is how old? Twenty-eight? Thirty?"

"Brandy's thirty-two, but she—"

"And she's been married twice, as I recall."

"Yes, and both of her husbands were no-good scoundrels who treated her badly and made her unhappy," said Pres Templeton. "Brandy's...well...very vulnerable. She's like a child, really. We have to keep a close protective eye on her."

Eavesdropping, Mary Ellen smiled at such an absurd statement. Brandy Templeton was about as vulnerable as a serpent, and there was nothing childlike about her. She'd been a woman by the time she was thirteen or fourteen, and a cunning, dangerous one at that. Half the ladies in Memphis would heave a great sigh of relief if Brandy Templeton left town. The two "no-good" scoundrels her father spoke of had both been fine, fantastically wealthy gentlemen and had settled very generous sums on Brandy to free themselves from their miserable marriages.

There really was nothing like a parent's love.

Pres Templeton left after a half hour, and Mary Ellen expected her father to go straight back upstairs. Instead he joined her in the parlor and said, "Mary

Ellen, would you ask Titus to have the brougham
brought around. I think I'll go into town for a while,
see what they're saying on the streets." He rubbed his
chin thoughtfully. "I wouldn't be surprised to hear
more Southern states are seceding from the Union."
His dark eyes shone with a hint of their old liveliness.

"Why don't you ask Titus yourself," Mary Ellen
suggested, knowing how hurt old Titus was because his
despondent master had hardly spoken to him in more
than a year.

"I'll do that," John Thomas said, nodding. He went
into the corridor and called out, "Titus, where are you?
I need your help!"

Grinning from ear to ear, the graying Titus was
there in the blink of an eye. "Yes, suh, Mast' Preble.
What you be needin'? I sho' get it for you."

John Thomas smiled at the devoted old servant,
who, he suddenly realized, was beginning to shrink
from his years-long battle with chronic arthritis. John
Thomas put a hand on Titus's thin, stooped shoulder
and said, "Could you please see to it that the brougham
is brought around. I'd like to go into town."

Bobbing his gray head eagerly, Titus said, "I do
that right now." He turned to leave.

John Thomas stopped him. "Titus."

"Yes, suh?" His eyes were big, questioning.

"I'm sorry for… I've been a…" John Thomas
cleared his throat. "I honestly don't know what I'd
ever do without you."

Titus chuckled happily. "You never gonna' have to
find out, Mast' Preble."

His silver-gray eyes cold, his dark face set in hard
lines, Captain Clay Knight drank alone at the bar in a

rowdy Rio outdoor cafe. He turned up the shot glass, drained it. It was the fifth one he'd downed.

He was attempting to get drunk. Very drunk. He had every intention of drinking himself into a stupor. Morose, his mood so black he was oblivious of what went on around him, Clay motioned for another drink. The smiling barkeep poured him the sixth shot of whiskey and started to move away. Clay reached out and caught the man's arm.

"Leave the bottle," he ordered.

The barkeep shrugged and left the half-full bottle. Clay wrapped his long fingers around it possessively.

Idly he wondered how many shots of straight bourbon whiskey it would take to make him so drunk that he would immediately fall into a dreamless sleep when he got back to the *Witch*. It would be an interesting experiment.

Pondering the subject, Clay looked around with indifference. The cafe was full of laughing, drinking people, and more than half were women. But he saw no one with whom he'd care to share a drink, much less a bed. He sighed and took another drink. His first night in Rio was proving to be very disappointing.

Clay spent another hour drinking at the bar. Then, finally, half drunk, totally bored, and bone tired, he left the noisy outdoor gin palace.

Alone.

Yawning, he made his way back toward the harbor and the *Water Witch*.

Head hung, hands in his white trousers pockets, he was not paying attention when he stepped into the wide Avenida Rio Branco—and was very nearly run down by a fast-moving white carriage pulled by a matched pair of huge sprinting whites.

The driver shouted a warning and hauled up on the reins. The terrified horses whinnied and reared; their forelegs pawed wildly at the air, their hind legs danced in the dirt a few short feet from the startled Clay. Clay whirled away seconds before the horses' front hooves came down with deadly striking force.

"Beware, sailor!" the shaken driver shouted.

Before Clay could reply, the door of the covered carriage opened and from inside the darkened interior came a woman's low, sultry voice.

"Won't you allow me to drive you to your ship, Captain?" she said in unaccented English. "It's the very least I can do after almost killing you."

Unsmiling, Clay stooped and picked up his billed hat. He dusted the dirt from its flat crown and cast another look at the open door of the carriage. He was mildly curious about the woman inside, wondering if her looks fit her husky voice. Unhurriedly, he walked toward the carriage, asking the fates for only one favor: that she *not* have blond hair.

Clay climbed into the shadowy carriage, stepped across the seated woman, and sat beside her. She immediately tapped the ceiling, and the carriage began to move. Clay tossed his hat on the empty seat opposite, reached up, and turned on the coach lamp above his head.

And he began to smile.

The woman beside him had an excess of dark lustrous hair dressed elaborately atop her head. She had an even greater excess of full, tawny breasts spilling from the tight bodice of her low-cut summer evening gown. The generous size of her beautiful bosom was further accentuated by the smallness of her waist. Clay was sure he could span it easily with his hands and was already hoping he'd get the chance.

He couldn't be certain about the size of her hips since she was seated, but he'd bet a month's pay that they were appealingly wide and that she had a pair of firm tawny-skinned thighs beneath her long skirts and crinolines.

"Do I pass muster, Captain?" she said, smiling at him.

"Forgive me. I was staring rudely, wasn't I?" he said, then smiled. "You more than pass muster, Miss…"

"Mrs.," she corrected, and laughed gaily when a flash of disappointment darkened his smoky eyes. "Mrs. Dawn Richards Campango. My friends back home in America call me Richy." She laughed then, a low, lusty sound that made Clay's belly tighten with a quick rush of desire.

"It's quite late for you to be out alone in Rio, Mrs. Campango. Why isn't your husband with you?"

"Because he's six feet under," she said flippantly. "The poor old dear expired five years, leaving me all alone. Isn't that terribly sad, Captain?"

"Breaks my heart," Clay said, smiling once more.

Again she laughed, and Clay laughed with her.

She turned slightly on the plush white velvet seat and boldly laid a gloved hand on his knee. She said, "Are you due back at your ship, or will you join me for a nightcap, Captain… Captain…?"

"Knight," he said. "Clay Knight. I'd love to join you for a nightcap, Mrs. Campango."

She put out the tip of her tongue and licked her ruby red lips. Then her emerald eyes flashed naughtily as she slowly slid her white-gloved hand up his trousered thigh. "Wonderful," she said. "I've been saving a bottle of hundred-year-old brandy for just such an occasion." She lowered her long, thick lashes seductively and added, "I've been saving myself as well, Captain." Her lashes lifted and she looked into his eyes. "Just for you."

Clay's chest expanded against his snug-fitting uniform blouse. He could hardly wait to get to her place.

"Her place" turned out to be the magnificent white clipper moored next to the *Water Witch*.

As the dark-haired Dawn Campango led him up the long gangway, Clay told her about admiring her sleek vessel earlier in the evening.

"I know," she said. "I saw you. From the portal of my boudoir I admired you admiring the *Açúcar*." She laughed gaily then and informed him, "I'm American, as you can probably tell, but my late husband was Brazilian and he named this craft for me. Raul always said I was 'sweet as sugar,' which, of course, I am."

When they stepped onto the teak deck of the *Açúcar*, Dawn Campango took Clay's arm and said, "Now come let me show you around."

She led him straight through the grand salon and into the enormous master suite. At the very center of the room was a circular bed, where gold-and-coral sheets of silk were turned down for the night. The ceiling was lined with gold-and-coral silk damask, and directly over the round bed was a huge mirrored starburst. On one of the wood-paneled walls hung the stained-glass likeness of a naked goddess.

When Dawn saw his eyes were focused on the stained-glass goddess, she said, "She's me."

"Oh, really?" He frowned in mock skepticism. "How can I be sure?"

She smiled. "You'll see. Very soon you'll see."

Laughing, she removed her gloves and tossed them

onto a marble-topped table. She went to a dark wood cabinet, opened it, and withdrew a bottle of cognac. While she splashed the aged brandy into a couple of crystal snifters, she said, "Now you know all about me, Captain. Tell me about yourself. Where's your home?"

Clay shrugged wide shoulders. "I was born and raised in Memphis, Tennessee, but the sea's my home."

"Mmmmm. And is there a sweet-faced little wife waiting patiently back in Tennessee?" She handed him a snifter of brandy, then touched her own to his. The glasses clinked. They drank.

"No. I never married. Will never marry."

"I see." Dawn Campango liked his answer. She swayed closer, seductively licking the brandy from her ruby red lips as she raised a hand and withdrew the gem-encrusted pins holding her heavy dark hair atop her head. Freed of its restraints, the lustrous locks spilled around her bare, tawny shoulders.

The brandy and the woman warming his blood, Clay reached out slowly and wrapped a thick portion of her unbound hair around his hand. A muscle leaping in his jaw, he forced her head back, bent, and kissed her tempting red lips.

But then he told her candidly, just as he told every woman to whom he was about to make love for the first time, "Mrs. Campango, you're a very beautiful woman, and I want you. But if you're looking for love and commitment, you've got the wrong sailor." His hand staying tangled in her hair, he turned his head and leisurely drained the last of his brandy, giving her the opportunity to think it over.

Dawn Campango drank the last of her own brandy, lowered her hand, and let the empty crystal snifter drop to the Persian rug below. She put her arms around

Clay's neck and, smiling, said, "You are not my first naval Captain, Captain." She moved closer, pressed her full, soft breasts against his chest, bent a knee, rubbed it against his groin. "Keep your heart; it's your body I'm after."

Clay grinned at her. "My kind of woman. What are we waiting for?"

In seconds they had shed all their clothes and stood naked amid the discarded garments, eagerly kissing and touching. His hot lips never leaving hers, Clay drew Dawn Campango to the round bed and fell backward onto it, bringing her down with him. Delighting in the cool caress of soft silky sheets against his bare back and the warm weight of the woman's big-nippled breasts against his chest, Clay sighed with pleasure.

His lean, dark hands moved over her voluptuous body, breasts and waist and hips; his mouth was hot along her throat and ear. Dawn lifted her face for his kiss and met his tongue with her own, attacking and retreating as her hunger, like his, flamed brighter.

She wedged a hand between their bodies and took hold of his throbbing erection, rubbed the bursting tip back and forth across her bare belly, then up and down her pulsing mound. Clay let her have her way. She was not the first aggressive woman he'd had, but she was certainly one of the hottest.

He spread his legs wider apart when she rose up on her knees between them, her hand enclosing his jerking tumescence, her emerald eyes wild with passion. When she climbed astride his hips and eagerly impaled herself upon him, Clay settled his hands on her hips and flipped them over agilely, reversing their positions.

When the throbbing length of him was buried deep

inside her, the highly aroused Dawn Campango looked directly into Clay's gray eyes and murmured huskily, "I am the wild untamable sea in a storm and you are the Captain of a mighty craft being tossed about by my raging waves. I am highly dangerous to all seagoing craft, and only the most capable of Captains can keep his precious vessel riding in me." Her eyes catlike and wicked, she warned, "Be careful you don't capsize and crash to your death."

With that she made the first deep rolling thrust of her hips, tipping her powerful pelvis upward and setting Clay's heart to thundering.

Clay played the naughty nautical game with heated enthusiasm. He derived wave after wave of pleasure as the battling, boiling sea surged up and down against him, attempting to dislodge him and at the same time suck him under.

Dawn Campango would rock violently against him, clench him tightly, attempt to swallow him up with the strength of her hips and firm thighs. Then she would go totally slack, loosening her pinioning thighs, pushing to expel him from her slick, slippery warmth.

There was never any danger of Clay losing the stormy battle. She was a hazardous turbulent sea, but he was a cunning and accomplished Captain who could deftly steer his powerful vessel in the most perilous of straits.

The fierce storm continued with the two of them rolling and arching and plunging and rising until they were slippery with perspiration and their shared carnal excitement was at a fever pitch. At last they exploded in spine-melting release and the sea cried out loudly in her ecstasy while the conquering Captain groaned in his hard-won triumph.

The winded Captain fell over atop the mastered sea, and she sprinkled kisses of gratitude over his dark, sweat-streaked face. Clay sighed with satisfaction and couldn't believe his right ear when Dawn Campango whispered into it, "Now let's change places. You be the wild sea and I'll be the Captain."

Twenty-One

The war cloud that had appeared on the horizon in the late 1850s now hovered ominously over the nation. The hotly debated issue of states' rights was a powder keg that could blow at any minute. Alabama, Georgia, and other states had followed South Carolina in seceding from the Union, and in early February the Confederacy was formed in Montgomery, Alabama. Mississippi's Jefferson Davis was chosen to be president of the provisional government of the Confederate states.

The mood of Memphis that cold winter of 1861 was tense, anxious, uncertain.

Fear and unrest were prevalent across the Southland. Moreover, Memphis was plagued with an added dilemma. It was a city divided. There were those—mainly landholders and slave owners—who railed loudly against the North's economic stranglehold on the South and vowed heatedly they would *never* allow the arrogant Yankees to dictate how the Southerners should conduct their lives. They would fight to the last breath if necessary.

Others—mainly men who owned neither land nor slaves—were just as passionate in their belief that individual financial interests should be put aside for the good of the country. If war came, they swore adamantly, they would throw all their weight behind the Union.

Arguments and fistfights broke out daily on the crowded streets of Memphis as citizens divided into two different camps, much as the country itself was divided.

Of those who believed the meddling Yankees needed to be taught a lesson, none was more fervent than John Thomas Preble. Mary Ellen was glad that her father had finally cast off the debilitating lethargy of grief, but now she worried that if war came, he would foolishly think he should fight.

She expressed her concerns to Leah Thompson, the likable Nashville native who, along with her big, strapping husband, William, and their four children, now lived next door in the mansion they'd bought from the fleeing Pres Templeton.

Mary Ellen liked all the Thompsons immediately. Leah was a friendly, good-natured, plain-looking woman of thirty-eight who genuinely cared about people, loved her new Mississippi River bluffside home, doted on her four healthy, happy children, and clearly adored her big, rugged redheaded husband, William.

Mary Ellen quickly learned that she could confide in Leah and never worry that her confidences might be betrayed. The two women shared secrets and insights and sometimes fears.

On a chilly afternoon in February, Mary Ellen grabbed a woolen shawl, swirled it around her shoulders, and walked down River Road to the old Templeton estate to visit Leah Thompson.

"I'm really worried about Papa," she told the older woman as soon as she was inside the warm, fire-lit parlor. "He's gone out to Martin's horse farm to buy a mount of great speed and stamina."

Leah looked puzzled. "Your father's an experienced horseman, Mary Ellen. I'm sure he can safely handle a speedy mount."

"Leah, I know him. He's hunting a horse to ride into battle."

Leah Thompson laughed at such an absurd notion. "I wouldn't worry all that much if I were you. Even if we go to war, the Confederacy surely won't be needing men Mr. Preble's age. Besides, William says the war won't last long and we're sure to be victorious. He says the Southern leadership is far superior to the Union's because most of the nation's finest officers are Southerners. I'm sure they'll all elect to go with their native Southern states." She smiled confidently. "Think of all the fine men from the South who went to West Point and the Naval Academy at…"

Mary Ellen's thoughts immediately flashed to Clay Knight. When war came, would he resign his commission and come home to fight for the South? Or would his loyalty lie with the Union?

"…and would probably be an easy victory," Leah Thompson concluded.

"Yes, yes, I'm sure you're right," Mary Ellen said distractedly. Then: "I'd best get back and see if Papa's home yet."

On a cool April afternoon, Mary Ellen was at the cotton office with her father when a dispatch rider thundered down Front Street, shouting, "Beauregard's fired on Fort Sumter! The general demanded surrender of the fort, and President Lincoln has issued a proclamation calling for volunteers to fight for the Union. We're at war!"

As soon as he heard Virginia, the old Dominion, had cast her lot with the Confederacy, John Thomas Preble formed and armed a company of Shelby County's best and called them the Bluff City Grays. He saddled up his newly purchased roan stallion and led his Bluff City Grays north to join Lee's army.

Mary Ellen stood on the front veranda of Longwood and watched them ride away.

The saber his grandfather Preble had wielded against the British in the Revolutionary War was strapped to John Thomas's waist, its long blade gleaming in the bright Tennessee sunshine. His shoulders were erect, his bearing proudly military.

Riding at the front of his troop, John Thomas Preble turned in the saddle and waved merrily to his daughter.

The years had magically slipped away. He no longer resembled the broken, gray-haired fifty-eight-year-old man who'd buried himself in his suite for so long. He looked like a dashing young blade off to do battle for his beloved homeland.

Mary Ellen bit her lip.

Tears filled her eyes as she stood on the wide veranda of Longwood and watched until her father had ridden completely out of sight. She felt a definite chill despite the warmth of the sun. An awful sense of loneliness swept over her, and she was shaken by a strong premonition that she would never see her father again.

Mary Ellen swallowed hard, turned, and went back inside the silent mansion.

In June the state of Tennessee held a referendum and, despite some strong Union sentiment, ratified the Ordinance of Secession. Tennessee was proclaimed a Confederate state, the very last one to secede.

In late July, three months after he had ridden away, word came that John Thomas Preble had been killed. He had lost his life in the First Bull Run, the initial major battle of the war.

Mary Ellen was left alone.

There was no time for the luxury of grieving.

The Preble fortune, on the wane well before the war, was materially reduced by the events dividing the nation. The Union naval blockade had destroyed the British cotton market. Mary Ellen realized she was in deep financial trouble when outstanding loans were called in. Little cotton had been planted on the vast out-lying plantations that spring. By late summer most of the slaves had run away.

The war raged on into early autumn, with no end in sight. Reports of a shocking number of casualties reached Memphis, and by Christmastime there was hardly a family who hadn't lost a son, father, brother, or sweetheart.

The sound of marching feet and the roll of drums became a constant, as did the moans and screams of the wounded and dying who'd been brought from the battlefields to the Shelby County Hospital, where Mary Ellen was a volunteer. Determined to do her part for the Cause, she tirelessly tended soldiers who'd been maimed and crippled. Her face bending over a poor, suffering soul was the last thing many of them saw this side of heaven.

The war moved closer to home when Grant's army met General Albert Sidney Johnson at Pittsburg Landing less than a hundred miles east of Memphis. The Battle of Shiloh ensued, and the Tennessee River ran red with the blood of the Confederacy's finest young men.

Later that same month, New Orleans fell into enemy hands when the city surrendered to Flag Officer David Farragut. It was the greatest blow the Confederacy had suffered. And Mary Ellen, along with the rest of the Bluff City, was terrified that the Yankees would come right on up the Mississippi to Memphis.

The Yankees came, but not upriver from New Orleans.

They came downriver from the North.

In May Captain James Montgomery led his Confederate River Defense Fleet in an attack on Union gunboats and mortar schooners that were bombarding Tennessee's Fort Pillow. Montgomery and his men tried valiantly to turn back the advancing Federals.

But the Rebel fleet lost the battle.

Hammered by the fire of Union vessels on the Mississippi, the Confederate forces were forced to evacuate Fort Pillow.

Fort Pillow was the last fortification above Memphis, Tennessee.

Memphis braced for the worst.

The worst came on the hot, muggy early morning of June 6. Messengers quickly spread the word through the sleeping city that the Yankee ironclads had been spotted on the Mississippi a few short miles upriver from Memphis. Citizens leapt out of bed and streamed down to the river bluffs.

Mary Ellen, Leah Thompson, and the four Thompson children watched as the Federal gunboats and rams approached Memphis. Just as the full red ball of the sun rose above the horizon, the first Federal ram, *Queen of the West,* steamed ominously into view.

A pair of powerful field glasses raised to her dark eyes, Mary Ellen focused on the approaching steel

YOUR PARTICIPATION IS REQUESTED!

Dear Reader,

Since you are a lover of fiction – we would like to get to know you!

Inside you will find a short Reader's Survey. Sharing your answers with us will help our editorial staff understand who you are and what activities you enjoy.

To thank you for your participation, we would like to send you 2 books and a gift – **ABSOLUTELY FREE**!

Enjoy your gifts with our appreciation,

Pam Powers

SEE INSIDE FOR READER'S SURVEY

HOW TO VALIDATE YOUR

EDITOR'S FREE THANK YOU GIFTS!

1. Complete the survey on the right.

2. Send back the completed card and you'll get 2 brand-new Romance novels and a gift. These books have a combined cover price of $11.98 or more in the U.S. and $13.98 or more in Canada, but they are yours to keep absolutely FREE!

3. There's no catch. You're under no obligation to buy anything. We charge nothing—ZERO—for your first shipment. And you don't have to make any minimum number of purchases—not even one!

4. The fact is, thousands of readers enjoy receiving their books by mail from The Reader Service. They enjoy the convenience of home delivery…they like getting the best new novels at discount prices BEFORE they're available in stores… and they love their *Heart to Heart* subscriber newsletter featuring author news, special book offers, book reviews and much more!

5. We hope that after receiving your free books you'll want to remain a subscriber. But the choice is yours—to continue or cancel, anytime at all! So why not take us up on our invitation, with no risk of any kind. You'll be glad you did!

YOURS FREE!
We'll send you a fabulous surprise gift absolutely FREE, simply for accepting our no-risk offer!

YOUR READER'S SURVEY
"THANK YOU" FREE GIFTS INCLUDE:

▶ Two BRAND-NEW Romance Novels
▶ A lovely surprise gift

The Reader Service — Here's How It Works:

Accepting your 2 free books and gift places you under no obligation to buy anything. You may keep the books and gift and return the shipping statement marked "cancel." If you do not cancel, about a month later we'll send you 3 additional books and bill you just $4.99 each in the U.S., or $5.49 each in Canada, plus 25¢ shipping & handling per book and applicable taxes if any.* That's the complete price and — compared to cover prices starting from $5.99 each in the U.S. and $6.99 each in Canada — it's quite a bargain! You may cancel at any time, but if you choose to continue, every month we'll send you 3 more books, which you may either purchase at the discount price or return to us and cancel your subscription.

*Terms and prices subject to change without notice. Sales tax applicable in N.Y. Canadian residents will be charged applicable provincial taxes and GST.

ram. And on a tall, dark Union officer—framed against the pink of the dawn sky—standing alone on the hurricane deck. The confident stance, the supreme air of command, were not all that attracted Mary Ellen's attention. There was something else. Something that caused an involuntary shiver to surge through her slender body. Something was eerily familiar about the Yankee naval commander.

Then he moved. He sprang forward agilely and brought down his right arm with swift military authority.

In a second the Federal gunboats opened their batteries. Captain James Montgomery's Confederate flotilla—outmanned and outgunned—swiftly launched a bold attack, and at dawn Battle of Memphis was under way.

The morning was perfectly clear and perfectly still, but the reports of guns on both sides were heavy and rapid. Within minutes a heavy wall of smoke had formed on the river, and Mary Ellen could see only the flashes of the guns.

She blinked and squinted through the field glasses as the guns boomed and men shouted commands and citizens of Memphis prayed for victory.

But the Federal resources far exceeded those of the Confederates, and within two hours the Rebel flotilla had been completely disabled. Only one of the eight Confederate vessels escaped the fiercely fought river battle.

Now completely unprotected, Memphis surrendered.

At noon Commodore Charles H. Davis's Union fleet was able to make its way on downriver toward Vicksburg, where he would link up with Farragut, who was heading north from New Orleans.

But not all of Davis's fleet would be going south with him to Vicksburg.

The gunboat and three companies of fleet marines were to secure the Union's prize: Memphis, Tennessee. The surrendered city of Memphis was to be immediately occupied by Union troops under the command of a brilliant young naval Captain in whom Commodore Davis had total confidence.

By evening blue-jacketed Union sailors were swarming over the city, and that night Mary Ellen took with her to bed the painful knowledge that the victorious Federals had captured her hometown and were now in control of the city.

Memphis—the metropolis of the American Nile— had fallen to the Yankees!

She couldn't believe it. Didn't want to believe it. For the first time in her life she was afraid in her own home. She'd never thought about such things before, but now she wondered how safe she was in the big empty mansion with only the old cook, Mattie, and the aged, arthritic Titus.

The other servants had gone months ago. Those who hadn't run away had been sent to the homes of more prosperous citizens. Mary Ellen would have sent Mattie and Titus, but no one wanted the helpless old couple who, after years of caring for the Prebles, now had to be cared for by her.

Sleep was a long time coming that night.

When Mary Ellen awakened to a new day and hurried to Shelby County Hospital, she was incensed that the streets of Memphis were filled with Yankee sailors.

And she was horrified to see, atop the five-story post office, the Stars and Stripes fluttering in the gentle morning breeze.

She stopped and stared in disbelief.

Shaking her head, Mary Ellen moved on dazedly. On Adams Street, a block from Shelby County Hospital, Mary Ellen was stunned to see blue-uniformed Yankees streaming up the old Wheatley mansion's steps and into the house as if they belonged there. Transfixed she watched in horror for several long moments.

And as she watched, she was being watched.

From inside the Wheatley mansion's spacious front parlor, a tall, dark Union naval officer leaned a muscular shoulder against a wooden window frame and looked out. His narrowed eyes as cold as ice, his hard, handsome face totally devoid of expression, the officer unblinkingly studied the slender blond woman standing directly across the street.

The dark, lean Captain was the officer who had led the steel ram of the conquering Federal fleet into Memphis. The Captain was now in command of all occupying naval forces. At ease in a position of authority, the respected commander discharged his duties with decisive proficiency and still had time to monitor Mary Ellen's every move.

The Captain knew each time she left Longwood. The Captain knew where she went and what she did and when she returned home. The Captain even knew the exact minute when she blew out the lamp beside her bed each night.

Twenty-Two

Mary Ellen now had a new worry, that the Yankees might occupy Longwood. The prospect of such an occurrence filled her with dread.

Days passed, and she held her breath each time she saw a blue-jacketed man near her home. Many of the city's mansions had been swiftly taken over by the occupying forces. Mary Ellen was terrified that they would move in and destroy her beloved home.

A full week went by, and Mary Ellen began to breathe a little easier. She told herself there was an abundance of large, comfortable houses in Memphis; maybe the hated conquerors would have no need of hers. Thank heaven. She could think of nothing worse than seeing those arrogant, blue-uniformed Yankees lounging around on the rosewood furniture in her parlor!

Mary Ellen hated the sight of them filling the city streets; hated passing by them on her way to the hospital each morning; hated the lecherous looks they cast her way.

Even when there was not a single Union sailor or soldier in sight, there were times when—for no logical reason—she felt the wispy hair at the nape of her neck rise, as if one of the Yankees had his eyes on her.

As if he were following her. Examining her. Watching her.

Abruptly she'd stop and look around anxiously, expecting to catch some blue-uniformed sailor or soldier staring insolently at her. But she'd see no one. She assumed it was her raw nerves getting the best of her. She was so edgy, she was imagining things.

Finally Mary Ellen began to relax a little. A couple of weeks went by with no Yankees setting foot on Longwood's overgrown grounds. Apparently she was being spared. She didn't know why, but whatever the reason she was grateful and relieved.

The despised Yankees continued to cast longing glances her way when she walked to and from the hospital, but none had really bothered her. For a host of reasons she continued to have trouble sleeping, but her sense of security had partially returned.

Still, she knew very well it was unsafe for a woman to be out alone after dark in the Union-occupied city, and she hadn't dared tempt fate.

Until one sweltering hot June evening when she could stand the heat and the loneliness no longer. She recklessly left the safety of Longwood, wandered down to the river, and encountered the naked naval Captain.

Part Two

Twenty-Three

"Clay Knight," Mary Ellen murmured again.

"Yes."

That was all he said.

Then a long silence as the pair stood motionless in the moonlight. His tanned fingers gripping her fragile wrist, Captain Clay Knight, commander of Memphis's occupying Federal naval forces, held Mary Ellen Preble close against his tall, wet body and looked directly into her eyes.

Mary Ellen stared up at the dark, formidable figure and was instantly swamped with conflicting emotions. Anger and attraction caused her temples to pound, her eyes to sting with unshed tears.

Clay. Clay Knight.

The sweet-faced boy who used her heart for a stepping-stone to a vainglorious military career was now this cruel-looking Union naval Captain. Closely examining the darkly handsome face that with the years had hardened into roughly chiseled lines, Mary Ellen realized she had almost forgotten how much she'd once loved him.

How much she hated him.

Clay looked into Mary's wide, dark eyes as similar emotions swept through his tall, naked frame.

Nan Ryan

Mary. Mary Preble.

The spoiled, pretty young girl who had used her charms to frivolously break his heart was now this haughty, highly desirable woman. Her closeness instantly rekindled a kind of passion and pain that made his bare belly contract, his knees go weak.

His gaze shifted, touched the radiant white-blond hair now silvered by the moonlight, then slid appraisingly over the perfect features of her beautiful face, before finally settling on the tempting, full-lipped mouth.

God, he had nearly forgotten how much he had once loved her.

How much he hated her.

The spell was broken when finally Captain Knight spoke.

In a low, rich baritone, he said, "Surely you must realize, Mrs. Lawton, that it is unsafe for you to be out alone at night."

Mary Ellen quickly replied. "I am no longer Mrs. Lawton. I'm Mary Ellen Preble, and it was perfectly safe until you and your horde of heathens got here." Again she tried to free her wrist from his grasp. "Let go of me!" she commanded, confused and trembling with mixed feelings.

Captain Knight held her fast.

He took the wadded greenbacks from her clenched fingers and calmly stuffed them inside the bodice of her low-necked summer dress.

His warm, wet hand against the rising swell of her breasts, he said, "Accept this as partial payment for lodging, Mary Preble." He removed his hand. "As commander of all occupying naval forces, I have chosen your home, Longwood, to be my headquarters for as long as I'm stationed in Memphis. You can expect me at noon tomorrow."

Mary Ellen was horrified. "No!" she shouted, shaking her head. "No, I don't want you there. I forbid it!"

"You misunderstand. I'm not asking for permissions, I'm informing you of my intent."

"And I'm informing you that I'll *never* allow you to set foot inside Longwood!"

"I'll be there at noon tomorrow," he repeated calmly.

"Why? Why my home?" she asked angrily, struggling against him. "There are dozens of large mansions in Memphis."

"Yes, I know," he said. "As you may recall, I once— a long time ago—lived here."

"Take one of the finer homes for your headquarters!"

"I was always partial to Longwood," he said. "I'm sure I'll be quite comfortable there." The merest shadow of mockery flickered around his hard mouth.

Mary Ellen saw it, and her anger rose. "Is there no end to your cruelty?"

"I had an excellent teacher," was his puzzling reply, and his cold silver eyes were starkly pale in the darkness of his face.

He moved back slightly, revealing his wet, hair-covered chest, powerful shoulders, and swelling biceps.

He said, "Unless you want your modesty shocked, you'd better hurry back home. I'm ready to get dressed now."

Afraid he would carelessly expose his nakedness, Mary Ellen anxiously reached out and clasped his slippery upper arms. "Don't you dare move until I've turned around!"

Mary Ellen pushed him away and spun about all in one swift, fluid motion. She immediately lifted her long skirts and sped across the damp sandbar as if she were fleeing from Satan himself.

Clay made no move to get dressed. He stood there naked in the moonlight, watching Mary race madly across the wet sand, her loose white-blond hair dancing around her slender shoulders, her skirts swaying with her rapid movements.

That she was anxious to get away from him was more than evident, but that didn't particularly bother Captain Knight. He would occupy her home whether she liked it or not; her feelings were of no real importance to him.

He started to stoop and pick up his discarded clothing, then changed his mind as a thought struck him. When he had come up on Mary, she had been barefoot. Which meant she had left her shoes and stockings on the riverbank. She would have to retrieve them.

Idly he wondered. When she stopped to pick up her shoes, would she look back at him?

All at once every muscle in his lean body tensed and he found himself hardly daring to breathe. He didn't move, didn't blink. He watched and waited, speculating. Would she look back? He found himself hoping she would, even as he told himself he didn't care.

You will turn and look at me, Mary, he commanded silently. *You can't keep from it. You will turn. You will look back.*

At last Mary Ellen scampered off the long sandbar and stepped onto the riverbank. She had gone but a few steps when she bent and snatched up her shoes. She straightened but didn't immediately hurry on up the path. She hesitated. For some insane reason she was tempted to look back. But she couldn't do that. She wouldn't.

She sucked her bottom lip behind her teeth and told herself she'd be worse than Lot's wife in the Bible if she turned and looked back. Why on earth would she even want to look at him, anyway? She didn't! Lord, no. Besides, the Yankee naval Captain had likely gotten dressed and was gone. He wouldn't still be just standing there, for heaven's sake.

And since he wouldn't, what difference did it make if she looked back?

Mary Ellen couldn't help herself.

Slowly she turned and looked back.

The tall, dark Union officer stood there just as she had left him, naked and unmoving in the moonlight. Mary Ellen gasped, whipped around, and anxiously ascended the river cliffs, her heart hammering.

Out of breath when she reached the safety of Longwood, she hurried inside the double fan-lighted doors and threw the bolt lock against intruders. Exhaling with exertion and relief, she climbed the stairs to her room and nervously undressed in a shaft of moonlight.

Troubled, Mary Ellen lay awake in her bed, wondering if Captain Knight actually meant to occupy Longwood. Could he be that cruel and insensitive? Hadn't he hurt her enough all those years ago? Did he wish to exact even more pain from her?

Mary Ellen cursed his name and vowed she would never let him come inside her house. Or her heart. Thinking it over, she told herself he probably had no intention of occupying Longwood. He had wanted only to frighten her. To devil her. Surely he wouldn't show up.

But she knew he would.

Mary Ellen couldn't sleep. She tossed restlessly, worried and upset. Each time she closed her eyes, visions of the dark, naked, very masculine Captain Knight loomed before her. Dawn was not far off when finally she fell asleep.

But even then she found no rest, no peace. She thrashed about, moaning and whimpering, frightened by the dark, disturbing dreams that dominated her fitful, uneasy slumber.

As the noon hour approached, an exhausted, anxious Mary Ellen stood alone on the wide gallery of Longwood. One of her father's ancient heavy dueling pistols gripped tightly in her right hand, she waited and watched.

At straight up twelve o'clock, she saw Captain Knight coming up the pebbled drive of Longwood. Bareheaded, his blue-black hair glittering in the sunlight, he was unarguably dashing in his dark blue naval uniform. Brass stars decorated his stiff, stand-up collar, yellow Captain's stripes pulled on his firm biceps, and a double row of shiny brash buttons marched down his broad chest. A bright yellow sash was tied around his trim waist, securing the gleaming saber that rested against his dark blue-trousered thigh.

He was astride a spirited, high-stepping stallion whose sleek, shimmering coat was as black as his rider's midnight hair. Man and beast were perfectly matched; both were sleekly handsome, incredibly graceful, and very likely dangerous.

Following several paces behind their mounted commander, a column of armed, blue-coated men marched determinedly up the drive toward the big bluffside mansion.

Her heart pounding with emotion, her pale hand gripping the pistol at her side, Mary Ellen Preble stood alone on the wide front gallery and watched as the Yankees moved steadily closer.

She despised them, each and every one. But it was their dark, arrogant commander she hated most of all.

Mary Ellen took a long, deep breath and lifted her chin proudly as Captain Knight dismounted just beyond the front lawn. Dropping the long leather reins to the ground, he spoke softly to the black stallion, put his troops at ease, then turned and let himself in the heavy wrought-iron front gate.

Mary Ellen stiffened.

She felt short of breath as he entered the estate's grounds, which were badly overgrown with dying vines.

The brass buttons on his chest catching the noonday sun, he advanced up the flagstone walk as if he belonged there. When he reached the steps of the shaded gallery where Mary Ellen waited, he stopped.

He put a booted foot on the first step, rested his hand on the hilt of his gleaming saber, looked directly at her, and said in a low, even voice. "I told you I would be here at noon, and so I am."

"And I told you I would never allow you to set foot inside Longwood." She clamped her jaw down and lifted the heavy dueling pistol. Holding it in both hands, she pointed it directly at Captain Knight.

He didn't flinch or make a move.

"Are you meaning to shoot me, Mary?"

"If necessary," she told him, dark eyes flashing dangerously. "Take one more step and I'll pull the trigger."

"I suppose I should be frightened," he said, the relaxed attitude of his tall, lean body indicating he wasn't. "But you can't kill a dead man," he said, and leisurely climbed the remaining steps.

"Get back!" she warned, the gun growing heavier in her shaking hands. "I'll shoot you, so help me I will!"

"What are you waiting for?" he asked in a low, even voice as he moved forward until he stood directly before her, filling the entire scope of her vision.

Finally he was so close that the wavering silver barrel of Mary Ellen's raised pistol was pressed to his chest.

He said, "That's not quite the right spot."

And he helpfully shifted slightly so that the barrel was directly over his heart. If she pulled the trigger, it would kill him instantly.

He knew it.

She knew it.

Mary Ellen battled with her conscience. She was frightened by the strength of her desire to actually shoot this hard-faced Yankee Captain whom she had hated for the last dozen years. It would be so easy simply to squeeze the trigger and end his life as he had ended hers when she was a young, trusting girl.

Mary Ellen looked into his pale gray eyes and saw not the slightest hint of fear. She was baffled by his strange behavior. It was as if he didn't care whether he lived or died. And what had he meant when he'd said you couldn't kill a dead man?

She understood nothing about this tall, intimidating man. There was not a trace left of the boyish countenance of the young, sweet Clay Knight from her childhood. At thirty-two his features had hardened and sharpened into harshly chiseled lines. Even his lips were different, still sensual but strangely firm, as if the beautiful mouth had been touched by bitterness.

He was a stranger. She did not know him.

Still, it was no use. She couldn't shoot him.

She gave up without a struggle when he unceremoniously lifted a hand and relieved her of the pistol. He studied the firearm, then studied her face.

He warned softly, "This old pistol is dangerous, Mary. It's likely to blow up in your face." He stuck it inside his yellow waist sash. "Now, it's up to you. You can make this easy or hard. It's of no difference to me. Either way, I'm occupying Longwood."

Beaten, she attempted to sound as unemotional as he when she said, "What would you do, Captain, if I objected? If I refused to get out of your way? I couldn't kill you. Could you kill me?" He made no reply. "Would you? Would you take out your own pistol and shoot me? Would you cut me in half with your shining saber?" Her chin lifted a little higher, and defiance flashed from her large, dark eyes.

With the easy command of a man used to exercising authority, he said, "Such drastic measures won't be necessary. You *will* obey my orders." With the speed and litheness of a cat, he moved around her, was now between her and the front door. "Now which is it to be? Shall I take peaceful possession of the premises? Or must it be a sad surrender after a bitter battle you cannot win?"

Mary Ellen looked into his calm gray eyes and knew he meant exactly what he said. She could fight him, but it would do no good. He was bigger and stronger than she. She preferred to keep a small portion of her dignity.

"I cannot keep you out of my home, Captain Knight," she said flatly. Then passion stirred anew in her dark eyes when she added, "But I promise you that when the war is over and the South has won, you will personally pay for this."

Twenty-Four

Captain Clay Knight occupied Longwood.

Mary Ellen was heartsick as the tall Yankee Captain and a dozen of his handpicked men took up residence in the river bluff mansion.

She had no choice but to stand helplessly by in the marble-floored foyer as blue-coated men swept inside her home. They quickly fanned out through all the downstairs rooms, examining their new quarters, jovially calling out to each other. Mary Ellen gritted her teeth as they poured into the high-ceilinged drawing room and picked up valuable art objects and ran rough hands over the fine furniture. In the white-and-gold music room they banged on the out-of-tune rosewood piano and plucked at the strings of the gold harp.

It was torture, but she forced herself to keep silent. She stood there in the foyer, saying not a word, shaking her head in despair as the uninvited guests roamed about at will.

But when a powerfully built sailor came out of the parlor and glanced meaningfully up the grand staircase to the second-floor landing, her hand went to her throat and she could keep quiet no longer.

"No!" she warned, then immediately softened her

request. "Please, no," she pleaded gently, "not up there.... Don't...."

Her heart sank when, ignoring her, he brushed breezily past her and went straight toward the stairs. There was nothing she could do to stop him. She watched powerlessly as he placed a big, heavy boot on the first carpeted step of the stairs.

And she jumped, startled, when a low, deep voice from directly behind said, "Don't do it, Boatswain Mills."

The burly sailor stopped where he was, didn't take another step. Mary Ellen turned about.

Captain Knight stood beside her, his attention directed to the big man standing at the base of the stairs.

"The second floor of this mansion is off-limits," he said in a soft, low voice that nonetheless conveyed command. "You and your mates are *not* to go topside. Whether I am here or away, you are never to be on the second floor. Do I make myself clear?"

"Aye-aye, sir," said the chastened sailor, and sheepishly came away from the staircase.

Mary Ellen experienced a small measure of relief.

It didn't last.

While he had ordered his men never to go upstairs, the conquering Captain Knight took the second-floor master suite for his own. Over Mary Ellen's loud objections.

"No! Not here," Mary Ellen said, frantically following him from the suite's luxurious sitting room into the elegant boudoir.

"*Here* will do nicely," he said, turning around and around in the spacious bedroom, where gigantic gold-leaf framed mirrors gracing all four walls reflected his every move. He laid a tanned hand on the huge four-poster's mattress, tested its softness, and shook his dark head approvingly. "I'm sure I'll be quite comfortable *here.*"

"Have you no decency?" Mary Ellen said, glaring at him. "This was my parents' suite."

Not bothering to look at her, he said coldly, "They no longer need it. I do. It now belongs to me. It is mine for as long as I'm in Memphis." His gaze shifted from the four-poster to Mary Ellen. "And you, Mary? Still have the same room?" He lifted a hand, rubbed his firm chin thoughtfully. "Let's see, that means you'll be right across the hall from me."

"You heartless, insolent bastard!" she snapped, whirled about, and left the room in tears.

A long, tense summer had begun for Mary Ellen Preble.

Mary Ellen hurried down the stairs and stormed out of the house. She went straight to the hospital, glad she had somewhere to go to get away from the infuriating Captain Knight.

She threw herself into the work of caring for the sick and wounded, determined she'd not give the bullying Yankee Captain another thought. Within minutes she was so busy she hardly noticed the hours ticking away. There was precious little time to think of anything save the terrible tasks at hand.

But when her back ached dully from lifting and lowering sick patients and she was so exhausted she could hardly put one foot before the other, Mary Ellen glanced out a window and saw with dismay that the summer sun was going down.

She was instantly alarmed.

She had to get home at once. As tired as she was, Mary Ellen walked at a brisk pace all the way to Longwood, propelled along by a rising sense of unease.

There was a house full of unwelcome, unruly Union sailors at Longwood, and only one could be trusted. The Captain's aide, Ensign Johnny Briggs, was a freckle-faced, red-haired young man with a sweet smile and good manners. The others were animals. She was alone and unprotected with a bunch of big, rough men.

As threatening as they were, Mary Ellen realized she was far more afraid of Captain Knight than she was of his men. He was a cold, uncaring man. He took what he wanted, when he wanted.

A man like that was dangerous.

As she climbed the front steps of Longwood, Mary Ellen paid no mind to the half dozen uniformed men lounging about on the gallery. She knew at a glance that their Captain was not among them.

Mary Ellen let herself in and made her way straight through the house to the kitchen. She pushed open the swinging kitchen door and stopped short.

Captain Knight, his knees spread wide, his shirt carelessly open down his dark chest, lolled lazily on one of the straight-backed chairs, smoking a cigar and enchanting a captive audience of two. Mattie, the old black cook, stood at the wood stove, pouring him a fresh cup of coffee. And old Titus, his eyes twinkling, his mouth fixed in a permanent wide grin, sat at the table, listening attentively as the Captain told of his adventures on the high seas. He fell silent when he caught sight of Mary Ellen.

Without a word she turned and left them looking after her. She was furious with her servants. It was one thing to accept and make the best of this enemy occupation, quite another to coddle and cozy up to the intrusive Yankee commander!

Dark eyes snapping with outrage, Mary Ellen hurriedly climbed the stairs to her room. She'd go to bed hungry rather than risk not being locked safely inside when the hated Captain Knight came upstairs. She rushed into the shadowy bedroom, threw the bolt, leaned back against the locked door, and sighed wearily.

She was hot and tired and hungry.

She crossed the dim room, lighted the coal-oil lamp by her bed, took the oyster-shell combs from her heavy hair, and let it fall around her shoulders. Then she started stripping off her hot, soiled clothing. She kicked off her shoes, sat down, and rolled her cotton stockings down her aching legs. She rose to her feet, unbuttoned her green poplin dress, pulled it up over her head, and released it. She yanked at the tape of her wilted petticoats, shoved them impatiently to the floor, and stepped out of them.

Sighing with exhaustion, she undid the hooks going down the center of her white camisole, shrugged her slender shoulders, and let the undergarment slide down her arms. Her thumbs were in the waistband of her pantalets when the knock came at the door.

Mary Ellen flinched and threw her arms across her bare breasts. She stood there frozen, afraid to answer, afraid not to. If she didn't answer, surely he would go away. She kept silent.

Again the knock, prodding her into action.

"Go away! You hear me? You get away from that door this minute!"

"Miz Mary Ellen," came old Titus's thin, frightened voice, "don' make me go 'way. Mattie tol' me to bring up your supper and not be comin' back down till you took it."

Mary Ellen exhaled loudly with relief and exasperation. "Give me a minute, Titus."

She snatched the blue silk wrapper lying across the foot of her bed and hurriedly drew it up her arms. She tied the sash tightly at her waist, pulled the lapels together, pushed her wild, unbound hair behind her ears, and opened the door halfway.

The old black butler stood there with a cloth-covered tray in his arthritic hands and a somber look on his face.

"Is somethin' wrong, Miz Mary Ellen?" he asked innocently, his eyes big, his wrinkled chin starting to tremble.

His question struck Mary Ellen as funny. Hysterically funny. Here she was, nearly destitute and alone. The South was at war. Memphis had fallen to the Federals. The Yankees had occupied Longwood. The conquering commandant was the heartless lover of her youth. Her own servants were treating the Captain like visiting royalty. And Titus—sweet, dear old Titus—wondered if anything was wrong.

Mary Ellen began to laugh.

She couldn't help herself. Her nerves were raw, and she was so physically exhausted she was on the verge of hysterics. She started laughing and couldn't stop, startling the old servant, frightening him half to death.

She leaned for support against the solid door frame and laughed, unable to speak, unable to tell Titus what was so funny. Tears filled her eyes, so she closed them. Wildly she shook her head back and forth. Her eyes tightly shut, the tangled white-blond hair hiding her hot face. Mary Ellen continued to lean against the door frame and laugh until her stomach hurt. She clutched it with both hands.

She was out of control and knew it. She laughed until she was so weak she could hardly stand and felt almost physically ill.

Finally she began to calm a little. Coughing, gasping for breath, she raised her head and slowly opened her eyes. She lifted her hands and shoved her wild hair off her face. She blinked once, twice, to clear her tear-blurred vision.

And almost had a heart attack.

Titus was gone.

In his place stood the tall, dark Captain Knight with the tray balanced on the palm of his hand.

The laughter immediately choked off in her throat, and Mary Ellen involuntarily trembled under his cool, brazen scrutiny. His pale silver eyes were not on her flushed face. They were on her breasts. Mary Ellen suddenly realized that with her violent shaking laughter the lapels of her blue silk robe had parted to expose her bare bosom.

Frantically she pulled the slippery lapels together over her naked breasts, hoping he hadn't seen too much.

As if he read her mind, he said, "Only that which can be seen in your most daring of ball gowns."

Their eyes clashed then. His cold, calm, assessing. Hers hot, angry, mortified.

He said, "Your dinner, madam."

He held out the tray. She refused to take it.

"Shall I bring it inside, then?"

Her hand shot out and slammed against his dark chest where the shirt was open. Her palm flattened in the crisp black hair covering the hard, sculpted muscle. Pushing against him with all her might, she said, "I'd starve to death first!"

"Then take the tray."

"I will not," she said, her hand steadily applying pressure to his chest.

"You're behaving like a child."

"I'll behave any way I choose. This is *my* home, Captain!"

He said nothing more, but raised a dark eyebrow and pointedly lowered his glance to the pale hand on his dark chest. Mary Ellen's gaze followed his, and she frowned with distaste when she saw her fingers entwined in his curly black chest hair. She yanked her hand away as if it were burned.

"Stay away from me!" she hissed, stepped back inside, slammed the door in his face, and leaned against it as if to hold him out physically.

Through the door he said, "I'll leave the tray here. You may get hungry before the night is over."

Her cold hands, trembling body, and hot cheek pressed flush against the solid door, Mary Ellen said nothing. Just prayed that he would go away and leave her alone. She stayed there for several long minutes, her heart beating fast, her breath coming in short, hurting gasps. She was afraid. Afraid of him. Afraid of the dark allure he held for her.

Finally she moved away. Her shoulders slumping with fatigue and emotion, she sat down wearily on the armless rocker.

She was still as hot and tired and hungry as ever and now upset as well. She wanted to cry.

It was only his first night under her roof, and already the cool, compelling Captain Knight had her off guard, confused, embarrassed, mixed up, and…attracted?

This dark, disturbing stranger who had occupied her home was not the sweet, good-natured Clay of her youth. Captain Knight was handsome, suave, confident, and menacing.

His low voice still had that gentle Tennessee twang, but he now spoke with a slow, measured calm. The beautiful gray eyes that had once shone with such warmth and boyish enthusiasm were very different. Now those chilly silver eyes—eyes that never missed anything—were shadowed, predatory, fearless. But it was the mouth that had changed most of all. Lips that had been soft, sweet, and sensual were now firmly sculpted, touched with cynicism, and threateningly provocative.

His was such a strong masculine presence, it was impossible to ignore. The sight of him bothered her in a terrifying way. It wasn't just his dark good looks. It was the strangely appealing, icy air of command combined with an underlying, carefully leashed sensuality.

Mary Ellen shuddered and automatically pulled the lapels of her silk robe tighter, feeling her nipples tighten involuntarily. Instinctively she knew that beneath the steel exterior of the unemotional Captain Knight lurked a hotblooded, highly passionate male. And his threatening sexual presence unnerved her.

Mary Ellen was achingly aware that the disturbing Captain Knight was, this very minute, just across the hall. Was he awake or asleep? she wondered. Dressed or undressed? In bed or out?

Captain Knight's close proximity caused gooseflesh to pop out on Mary Ellen's arms. Ashamed and terrified of the unwanted feelings he stirred in her, she got up from the rocker, crossed the room, and checked the door to make sure it was locked.

She closed her eyes in an attempt to shut out the handsome, hawklike face and forced herself to remember the kind of man he was.

Unfeeling. Ruthless. Cruel.

She hated him. She hated him and would always hate him. The day would never come when she'd forgive him for what he had done to her.

Across the hall on that warm evening, the object of Mary Ellen's undying hatred lay stretched out naked atop the wide featherbed, smoking in the darkness. It was a hot, muggy Memphis night, and the Captain was uncomfortably warm.

The sticky heat made him miserable. He felt as if he couldn't get a breath, and his long, lean body was covered with a fine sheen of perspiration.

But it was heat of a different kind that most vexed him. He couldn't forget that Mary was just across the hall, and the knowledge tortured him.

At the mere sight of her standing there in her blue silk wrapper, laughing, he'd felt a wave of the old pleasure and passion wash over him. She wasn't a girl any longer; she was all woman. The tomboyish awkwardness of youth had vanished. She moved with a natural feline grace and managed, even in the sweltering heat, to look generally cool, unruffled, and demure.

She didn't look demure in the blue silk robe. She looked warm and soft and desirable. What a sight she made with her magnificent mane of white-blond hair falling about her lovely face. As she'd laughed, the slick silk of her robe had hugged hips that were lush, feminine, rounded. Best of all was the fleeting glimpse he'd had of a soft pink nipple when her robe's lapels had parted. His hands had ached to reach out and slip his fingers inside the robe.

Captain Knight took a long drag from his cigar.

No woman had so stirred him. He'd been all over

the world, and he'd had his pick of beautiful, exotic women. But none had made his blood run thick and hot as Mary did.

Damn her.

Damn her to hell.

She was a beautiful viper who'd stung him badly once. He wouldn't let it happen again.

But that didn't mean he couldn't avail himself of her charms. She was available to him whether she realized it or not. He'd caught the guarded glances she cast his way; had noted the mixture of fear and fire in the depths of her dark, passionate eyes.

If she didn't know the full meaning of it, he did. He excited her. Not that she cared for him; she didn't. No more than he cared for her. But hers was a fiery, sensual nature, and she was a divorced woman who probably missed the comfort and pleasure of connubial bliss.

She was no longer the spoiled, impetuous girl, and he damned sure was not the gullible, worshiping boy. He was a man and she was a woman. Physically he wanted her and she wanted him. It was that elemental.

It looked as if he would be stuck here in Memphis for weeks, perhaps months. His stay would be made infinitely more pleasant if she shared his bed. In his jaded view she was but another spoil of war, another comfort to be enjoyed while he was here, like the spacious mansion, and the home cooking, and the enormous featherbed on which he lay.

Clay crushed out his cigar in a crystal ashtray. He took a corner of the silky top sheet and blotted away the moisture from his hair-covered chest. And he gritted his even white teeth and wrapped the sheet around the hard, straining tumescence jerking on his belly.

Cursing the sleeping blond beauty responsible, he vowed that the next time it happened she would be held accountable.

Twenty-Five

Each day Mary Ellen dreaded seeing the sun go down.

Each night she lay awake in her bed, tensely aware that she and the Yankee Captain were all alone on the silent second floor of the old mansion. She half expected him to beat on her door in the middle of the night, demanding that she let him in.

It never happened.

Night after night passed uneventfully. Soon Mary Ellen began to feel foolish that she had supposed he might behave so rashly. He had certainly done nothing to make her think he'd even want to get inside her bedroom. He was, whenever she bumped into him, coldly polite, nothing more. He never tried to detain her, never made any attempt to get her alone. He hardly acknowledged her presence. Often his icy silver eyes would flick to her, then quickly dismiss her, as if she weren't there.

To her chagrin, the enigmatic Captain was unfailingly kind and patient with the old cook and butler. It was evident that they were as fond of him as if he were still the likable young boy who had spent so much time at Longwood.

She couldn't fault them. Neither Titus nor Mattie knew what had really happened all those years ago.

They had been told nothing. Now they were old and childlike. She would say nothing to them.

Surprisingly enough, or perhaps not so surprisingly, the old black couple were not the only ones who showed absolutely no aversion to Captain Knight. The news that he was in command of the naval occupying forces had spread quickly. So had the news that he had commandeered Longwood.

The pro-Union *Press Scimitar* even did a favorable "Hail the Conquering Hero" piece in its Sunday edition.

It rankled Mary Ellen when old female acquaintances, stopping by the hospital with baskets of food and bandages, asked about the Yankee Captain with an accusing gleam in their eyes.

On a brief afternoon visit to the home of her friend Leah Thompson, Mary Ellen learned that Leah had heard gossip about the dark, handsome naval Captain.

"What? What are they saying, Leah?" Mary Ellen asked, a worried expression on her face.

"Now, Mary Ellen, don't look so troubled," said Leah. "No one is talking about you. They know you can't help it that the Captain commandeered Longwood for his headquarters." Leah inclined her head toward the back of the house. "Isn't my home full of them, as well as dozens of other Memphis mansions up and down River Road? And all along Adams Avenue, too. They've moved into Isaac Kirkland's big pink granite palace and James Lee's mansion and even the old Massey house. There's hardly a fine home in Memphis that hasn't been taken over by the Federals, and Betsy Graham told me they've fanned out and moved into some of the outlying plantations and country estates where...where...well, now, not all the estates. I understand the Lawtons have been spared and—"

Mary Ellen cut in. "Leah, you were going to tell me about—"

"I guess you heard," Leah went on as if Mary Ellen hadn't spoken. "Daniel Lawton didn't join the Confederate Army. No, sir, that able-bodied millionaire's son has been right here at home all this time. Some whisper that Lawton Sr. might have ties to the North. I don't know about that, but I do know the Lawtons are living like royalty while the South suffers. How long's it been since you were able to get your hands on a pound of coffee? Cindy Smallwood said Daniel's wife's expecting again. That makes four, or is it five? I can't keep up with—"

"Leah…" Mary Ellen gently tried again.

"Well, anyway, you can't take two steps in this town without tripping over a blue-belly. I'll tell you one thing: If my William wasn't down in Vicksburg fighting with the Rebs, these Yankees wouldn't be sleeping in his bed. He'd sweep them all out like a—"

"Leah, Leah, please," Mary Ellen interrupted again, knowing her friend was such a talker that she'd go on forever if not stopped. "What have you heard about Captain Knight?"

"Oh, yes, the Captain. I got off the subject," said Leah, smiling. "Where was I?" She frowned thoughtfully, then her eyes lighted as she remembered. "I know what I was going to say. I was going to tell you that if anything, you're an object of envy, Mary Ellen. Some of our lonely ladies would gladly overlook the fact that the handsome officer wears the wrong color uniform. He'd be more than welcome in their parlors." Leah smiled wickedly and added, "And I suspect a few of those ladies would like to see Captain Knight *out* of that blue uniform, if you know what I mean." She laughed heartily.

"Leah Ruth Thompson!" Mary Ellen scolded.

Mary Ellen's face reddened, and she was inexplicably annoyed with Leah. She found nothing humorous about a bunch of silly women lusting after the Captain.

"Oh, don't act so shocked," Leah said, and continued to laugh. "You've got to admit the Captain's a handsome devil, and I'll bet he knows his way around the bedroom."

"I have to go," Mary Ellen said, springing to her feet.

"Go?" Leah stopped laughing and rose, too. "You just got here."

"I like to get home before dark." She went to the door.

Leah followed. "What is it, Mary Ellen? What's the real story here? You've said you and Captain Knight were good friends when you were young. Childhood sweethearts. But you never told me what happened. Did he—"

"I married another man," Mary Ellen said, forcing a smile to her face. "That's what happened. Nothing more."

Leah touched Mary Ellen's arm. "You can't fool me, Mary Ellen Preble. There's something between you two, isn't there? Tell the truth. Aren't you attracted to him? Aren't you just a little bit afraid of the conquering Captain Knight?"

"No. No, I'm not afraid of the Captain."

But she was.

Mary Ellen thought about it as she walked back home. She *was* afraid of him. Afraid of the effect he had on her. There was something about him that filled the hot June air with a crackling electric tension. When he was in the house it was like being caged with a sleek black panther that might spring any second and devour his startled prey.

She could tell when he entered a room well before she caught sight of him. She could sense when he was near her; the blood ran a little faster through her veins. When she heard his deep, compelling voice out in the hall, her heart skipped several beats. When he looked at her with those icy silver eyes, she felt heat rise in her cheeks. When his lean, long-fingered dark hand absently rubbed his blue trousered leg, she felt the touch on her own tingling thigh. When he was present, her clothes felt too tight for her body and it was hard to get a deep breath.

Yes, she was afraid of him. This new, commanding Clay frightened her in a way she had never been frightened before.

She was terrified of him.

But weeks went by and Captain Knight continued to pay her little or no attention. While some of his men covertly cast covetous glances her way now and again, their aloof commander took no notice of her.

It was as if she didn't exist.

Mary Ellen began to let down her guard. Sleep, though still difficult, came a bit more easily.

She was finally able to get some much needed rest in her own home.

Until she awakened in the middle of a sweltering, moonless Memphis night, hot and thirsty.

Her throat was parched. She felt as if she'd been trekking across the vast Sahara Desert at high noon. She got out of bed, felt her way in the darkness to the marble-topped chest of drawers, and eagerly picked up the china water pitcher.

Mary Ellen shook the pitcher in disbelief and frowned. It was empty. She turned it up to a glass, hoping there was at least enough water for one small sip. There wasn't a single drop.

"The devil!" she said aloud.

Irritated, she set down the empty pitcher and glanced toward the clock, but she couldn't see it, much less read the time. The room was far too dark. No moon at all.

Mary Ellen stood there in the thick darkness and listened for sounds from below. She heard nothing. Evidently it was very late or perhaps even early morning. Longwood was dark, silent, sleeping.

She *had* to have a drink.

It would, she felt sure, be safe to slip out of her room and down the back stairs to the kitchen. She was familiar enough with the old house; she needn't light a lamp and risk awakening anyone. She'd feel her way along in the darkness. Nothing to it. She'd hurry down to the kitchen, have a nice, cooling drink of water, and be back upstairs in her room before anyone knew she was out of bed.

Mary Ellen went back to the bed, felt around for her blue silk wrapper. She pulled it on over her thin blue cotton nightgown and drew her long, loose hair up outside the robe. Tying the sash, she cautiously made her way across the dark bedroom. Quietly she opened the door and slipped out into the pitch black hallway. Barefoot, she tiptoed a few tentative steps in the inky blackness and stopped short.

In the hot darkness she saw the tiny orange pinpoint glow of a lighted cigar. She froze as the tip of the cigar burned hotter, glowed brighter, moved closer.

Anxiously Mary Ellen began backing away,

bumped into a hall table, and was trapped. A perspiring, bare-chested Captain Knight loomed before her, the lower half of his hard, handsome face faintly illuminated in the cigar's tiny circle of light.

He said nothing, but he took the cigar from his mouth, reached around her, and crushed it out in an ashtray on the table. A little gasp of fear escaping her lips, Mary Ellen pushed on his naked chest and attempted to whirl away from him. But an arm of iron encircled her waist and he swept her tightly against his tall, lean body. She trembled. She blinked and squinted, but she couldn't see him. Could only feel the heat of his body, the warmth of his breath on her face.

"Don't do it," she murmured weakly.

"I have to," he said, and his hot, hard mouth captured hers in a long, penetrating kiss.

When finally his lips released hers, Mary Ellen found herself sagging weakly against him, her flushed cheek pressed against the granite muscles of his slippery naked chest.

She closed her eyes, inhaled deeply of his clean masculine scent, her heart and her body in a tumult. But she managed to make a biting remark.

"You got your Annapolis appointment by making love to me. Wasn't that enough for you, Captain Knight?"

His long fingers tangled in her hair, the Captain urged her head up off his chest. "Quite enough, thank you," he said, meaning to hurt her, which he did. "And you, Mary? You got what you wanted as well?"

Preble pride fashioned her swift reply. "Of course I did. Yes! I most certainly did." She wanted desperately to hurt him as he had hurt her. "I always get what I want," she boasted, her head thrown back, straining desperately to get a glimpse of him.

She never saw, in the thick darkness enveloping them, the fleeting expression of pain that crossed his handsome face.

It was gone in an instant, and he said coldly, "And the divorce? Did you discover that a forbidden dalliance with the son of a seamstress was more to your liking than making love with your rich, aristocratic husband?"

"You vile, vulgar bastard!" she said, struggling against him. "I hate you, Captain Knight! With all my heart and soul I hate you, and I shall go on hating you until there is no breath left in my body!"

"Hate away, my sweet," he said coolly as he tightened his grip on her hair and his lips slowly descended to hers, "because I intend to kiss all the breath out of your body."

Twenty-Six

He bent his dark head and again kissed Mary Ellen forcefully, his hot mouth almost brutal on her open lips. He felt her whole body stiffen against him and realized she was afraid of him.

He didn't care.

His mouth stayed fused with hers as she tried frantically to free herself from his embrace. He refused to release her. He shifted their positions, pressing her back against the wall, trapping her with his leanly muscled body.

And he kept on kissing her.

Moaning her protests, Mary Ellen attempted to turn her head from side to side to tear her lips from his. But his strong fingers were tangled in her hair and he held her fast, forcing her head back.

And he kept on kissing her.

Overwhelmed by his fiery aggression, Mary Ellen tried desperately to save herself. She beat frantically on his bare back and shoulders with her clenched fists and whimpered her outrage at the forced assault on her senses. But the invasive, blazing kiss continued.

And continued.

It was a deep, intrusive kiss of such blatant intimacy, Mary Ellen felt its effects in the shock waves rocketing through her body. Her nipples began to peak, and a gentle throbbing started between her legs as his powerful, probing kiss awakened her long sleeping passions. Her entire body tingled as a thousand new electrifying sensations swamped her.

Her swelling breasts were crushed to his sweat-slick torso, the crisp damp hair of his chest tantalizingly abrasive to her aching nipples straining the thin fabric of her nightclothes. Pressed flush against him, she responded involuntarily when his wet, sleek tongue plunged deeply into her mouth, leaving nothing inside untouched, untasted, untried.

Mary Ellen's head was spinning, her heart pounding furiously. She was both apprehensive and appalled at what was happening to her. She so wanted to be repelled by his kiss, to despise his touch. But it was impossible. She hadn't felt like this since the last time he had held her, kissed her. No, that wasn't true, either.

She had *never* felt like this.

She remembered only an innocent boy's sweet, gentle kisses. This was a jaded man's probing, urgent caresses, and she couldn't resist him. Still she tried, knowing what would surely happen if she did not.

Mary Ellen continued to fight her fierce attraction to this dark, dangerous man who held her so tightly in his strong arms. Shocked and excited by such raw masculine power and passion, she felt panicky. Felt as if she were smothering, but deliciously so. Each brazen thrust of his tongue, every strong pull of his lips, the growing pressure of his arm around her waist, drew her more fully into him.

This dark, erotic seducer whom she could not even see was practically swallowing her up in his bold, burning kiss, as if starved for the taste of her. Mary

Ellen couldn't help herself; she melted under the fierce persuasion of the handsome Captain's drugging kisses.

Her fists stopped raining impotent blows on his bare back and muscular shoulders. She quit struggling so furiously. Her body stopped thrusting and wrenching against his in a futile attempt to get away from him. The long dazzling kisses, the animal heat and granite hardness of his well-honed body, the blessed cover of the encompassing darkness—all combined to work their provocative magic on the weakened Mary Ellen.

Somewhere far back in her still functioning brain a warning was flashing that she was in imminent danger of losing herself to this mysterious man. She should fight doggedly on or risk dire, far-reaching consequences.

But at the moment she didn't want to listen to reason or warnings. She didn't want to think. She wanted only to feel. Finally Mary Ellen sighed softly in acquiescence, wrapped her weak, weary arms around his neck, and dissolved in his embrace.

The experienced Captain Knight knew the exact second of her surrender. And it *was* surrender. She didn't know it yet, but he did. He knew as well that this surrender was total.

She was now his.

Under different circumstances he would have immediately slowed the pace of his seduction. Skilled and generally sensitive even with the most wanton of women, he would have taken the opportunity to start over at the beginning. To woo and win her with whispered words and tender kisses and gentle caresses.

But the tension between them had built for too long; his hunger for her was too great.

Captain Knight's passion swiftly eclipsed Mary

Ellen's, and his blood turned to liquid fire in his veins. Ruled only by blinding desire, he could barely keep from tearing the nightclothes from her warm, desirable body and taking her right there on the floor.

He continued to conquer her with amorous kisses, and when his heated mouth finally freed hers, Mary Ellen tried one last time to save herself.

"Let me go," she whispered breathlessly, her head falling back against the wall, her heart drumming a rapid, uneven cadence.

Her answer was a wet-hot kiss to the sensitive side of her throat and a firm, decisive tug of the sash at her waist.

"No…please…" she murmured as he swept the blue robe from her body in one swift, fluid movement, leaving her defenseless in her thin damp cotton nightgown.

The touch of his fingers as he unbuttoned the gown's high-throated bodice made Mary Ellen's senses reel. She tried to say no, but she choked on the word. Her pulses leapt wildly with the warmth of his breath on her shoulder. Her exposed flesh trembled, and she moaned when his fiery lips pressed a kiss to the curve of her neck and shoulder.

She winced when his hand slipped inside the opened gown and closed warmly over her swelling left breast. His thumb rubbing back and forth over the tightening crest brought a gasp of pleasure, and he quickly covered her mouth with his own in a searing kiss. Her lips opened ardently under his as her passions flamed.

Mary Ellen stood there in the inky darkness of Longwood's upstairs corridor, eagerly kissing Captain Knight as he plucked teasingly, tormentingly, at her diamond-hard nipple with all five fingers. It felt good to her, so incredibly good that she hoped he would never stop.

His lips left hers, but his hand continued to fondle her bare breast, to toy with the nipple. She felt him shift against her, and she blinked owlishly. But she could see nothing in the darkness, so she let out a little whimper of shocked wonder when his heated lips closed around her right nipple through the soft fabric of her blue nightgown.

"Captain." She sighed. "Cap…oh…Captain Knight."

Her head came away from the wall, and she bowed it slowly. Her unbound hair fell forward, spilling around her flushed, hot face. Her hand lifted, touched his wide, slick shoulder, moved up, and cupped the back of his dark head.

He tongued her peaking nipple through the wet, clinging cotton until it was pebble hard and throbbing, feeling as if it were on fire.

"Please…oh, yes…pleasssse," she whispered in the darkness, and her slender fingers tangled in the silky jet black hair at the back of his head.

The obliging Captain opened his lips and covered both nipple and gown and sucked forcefully. Mary Ellen's fingers tightened in his hair, and she pressed him close, closer. Almost frantic with joy, she suddenly wished more than anything in the world that she could see him.

She knew he was down on one knee. Knew one strong hand was anchored at her waist, the other still stimulating her naked left breast. She could imagine how he looked kneeling there before her, with his wide, sensual mouth clamped on her breast, his beautiful silver eyes closed, the long raven lashes sweeping down on his dark, high cheekbones.

Oh, if she could only see him.

Mary Ellen could see nothing. She could only feel.

She could feel the wet heat of his mouth enclosing her throbbing right nipple while his lean brown hand toyed with her left. She drew a sharp intake of air when his mouth abruptly lifted from her. He swept away the fabric, but when his mouth came back to her, it settled on her left breast. He playfully nipped and licked and sucked on the nipple while his fingers stroked the kiss-wet right breast.

The hot, dark night was also a very still and quiet one. No sigh of winds. No settling of the house. No shouts from the river below. The mansion was totally silent. Mary Ellen could hear nothing but the sound of his hungry sucking, and it was powerfully erotic. She shivered with bliss and bent forward a little, at the same time clasping the back of his head to draw him closer.

Abruptly he allowed the hard, wet nipple out of his mouth, and his fevered lips pressed kisses to her delicate ribs. Mary Ellen felt his hands tugging the opened gown down her shoulders and arms. She helpfully drew her hands free of the sleeves, and when the gown settled on her flaring hips, she placed anxious fingers atop his wide, bare shoulders.

She closed her eyes and sighed when he kissed her waist, her quivering stomach, and, pushing the gown down with his hot face, dipped his tongue into the small indentation of her navel. She made no move to stop him when he lifted his face, gave the snagged gown a firm yank, and lowered it over her hips. She felt it whisper down her bare legs to the floor, felt his fingers enclose her ankle to lift her left foot free.

He didn't bother freeing the right foot. His hot face

returned to her bared flesh, and his sure hands clutched her hips. Mary Ellen sighed and squirmed as his burning lips sprinkled kisses over her tingling stomach, tracing the prominent hipbones with his tongue, licking at the thin line of wispy white-blond hair going down from her navel.

He caressed her dimpled knees and firm thighs and fluttering belly, his lips tasting and his tongue stroking until she was so aroused she couldn't stand still. Her entire body ignited with the most incredible heat, and she felt as if she couldn't tolerate the sweet joy for another second. Naked and breathless, she was on fire, swept away on a rising tide of passion. All pretense of wanting him to stop was gone. She'd die if he stopped. She couldn't stand it if he were to leave her like this. She needed—had to have—what he alone could give her.

Yearning for the blessed release his strange yet familiar body promised, Mary Ellen felt a sob of pain and pleasure building deep within her, and every tensed muscle in her body cried out for him to help her, to save her, to give it to her.

Yet when she felt his hot face nuzzle in the white-blond curls between her trembling thighs, Mary Ellen gasped in surprise and pushed on his wide, perspiring shoulders.

"No!" she murmured anxiously, beginning to struggle once more. She felt his firm hand nudging her legs apart and his fiery breath on the inside of her thigh. Then his teeth were nipping her gently, his heated lips were kissing her. She was aghast. "Don't… No… you…must…stop," she whispered breathlessly.

But he didn't.

Shocking her, thrilling her, his tongue swept the

crisp white-blond coils out of his way and his heated mouth covered the throbbing, ultrasensitive tiny nubbin of slick female flesh where her blazing desire was centered.

A stunned sob broke from Mary Ellen's throat, and her first impulse was to push him away violently. Before she could try, his tongue touched her there in that most feminine of spots, and her whole body shuddered with shock and pleasure.

His hands filled with the twin cheeks of her bare bottom, Captain Knight pressed his feverish face to her and gently, expertly, stroked her with his tongue. Mary Ellen was instantly dazzled by the hot, loving mouth pressed between her parted legs. She had never known such wild ecstasy. She whipped her head from side to side and pressed her perspiring palms flat back against the wall, her rubbery knees bending slightly of their own accord.

Suddenly grateful for the heavy velvet darkness of night that covered both her shame and her splendor, she eagerly allowed him to love her in this unorthodox fashion, wondering at him, wondering at herself—but not really caring if they were behaving indecently. Mary Ellen panted for breath as his face sank closer, deeper, sweeter, until he was buried in her. She was so totally aroused by his searing mouth, she didn't care if it was right or wrong. She cared only that this dark, handsome man kneeling between her legs in the stygian darkness was licking, lapping, loving her, and it was as wonderful as it was wicked.

Her body was on fire, aflame. She was wild with passion. All inhibition was gone. She was a greedy sexual female animal demanding the ultimate ecstasy from her mate.

Mary Ellen grabbed her dark lover's hair and pressed her burning pelvis to his masterful mouth, every heated part of her body screaming, begging him for release.

The Captain gave it to her.

His tongue expertly stroked her throbbing flesh until Mary Ellen was totally engulfed in the searing wet heat. No longer in control of her own body or mind, she trusted him to liberate her from this wonderful pain/pleasure gripping her. Never in her life had she felt as she felt now. Never once in all the years she had been married had her husband made love to her this way. Never before had she surrendered so completely to the blinding joy of such raw, uninhibited sex.

She wished it would last forever.

She wished it would end this very second.

Clinging to his dark hair, Mary Ellen tossed her head wildly and moaned and sighed and urged him on until she felt the first frightening beginnings of her coming orgasm. She flung a hand up to her mouth and bit viciously at the backs of her knuckles to keep from crying out. Wave after terrifying wave of blinding ecstasy washed over her, and Mary Ellen was rocked to the tips of her bare toes by the great explosions buffeting her heated body.

As the climax went on and on, Mary Ellen looked down on the dark man she could not see and blessed him silently for keeping his hot, healing mouth fused to her until her wild, wonderful climax was completed. Finally it ended with a potent explosion of heat, and Mary Ellen clasped his hair and frantically pulled his face up away from her, unable to stand one more second of such incredible ecstasy.

Then she slumped limply against him, her bent knees

buckling beneath her. The Captain's strong hands kept her from falling. He rose to his feet, swept her up into his arms, and carried her across the hall to the master suite. His suite. Inside he kicked the door shut behind them, carried her straight through the suite to the bedroom.

Lamps burned brightly on either side of the enormous mahogany four-poster, and Mary Ellen closed her eyes against their intrusive light.

Captain Knight laid her in the very center of the soft mattress. Her pale, slender body limp with luxurious satiation, her eyes closed, Mary Ellen sighed lazily in total relaxation. Basking in the sweet afterglow of fabulous fulfillment, she felt herself already slipping toward sweet, dreamless slumber.

But Captain Knight had other ideas.

He hurriedly stripped off his trousers and climbed naked into bed beside the sated, lethargic Mary Ellen. Mary Ellen felt his lips on hers, and he kissed her. She tasted herself on his mouth and was appalled.

Her sleepy dark eyes came open.

The Captain's hot silver gaze was on her flushed face. His lean brown hand touched her thigh.

"Now," he said, "I will make love to you."

Twenty-Seven

Totally sated, Mary Ellen knew she couldn't possibly respond to any further lovemaking.

"No…no, I can't," she whispered.

"Yes, you can," he told her, his voice deep, melodious, his gleaming gray eyes penetrating hers.

"You don't understand," she said softly, too weak to move, "I can't… I won't…"

He smiled, his warming charcoal eyes half closed. He lay on his side next to her, his weight supported on an elbow. "I have," he said confidently, "methods to meet your resistance."

His hand slid down her pale thigh, closed around the back of her knee. He turned her to face him, drew her leg up over his hip, and placed it around his back. His hand then cupped her bare bottom, and he pressed her pelvis close to his straining erection.

Mary Ellen's breath caught when it touched her lower belly. He shifted their positions slightly, and she felt the awesome heat and hardness of him throbbing in her open thighs, pressing against the white-blond curls still damp from his burning kisses.

"Kiss me," he commanded softly.

Feebly she shook her head, licked her dry lips.

Unruffled, he looked at her with those compelling

hot-cold eyes and began the slow, rolling movements
of his hips, emulating penetration and copulation. His
spread fingers on her buttocks kept her pressed to the
marble hardness of his blood-filled tumescence. Her
warmth made his erection surge and pulsate against
her. He had her positioned so intimately against him,
it was impossible for her to maintain her state of sleepy
repose.

To Mary Ellen's surprise, she began to feel stirrings
of new desire as he rocked rhythmically against her.
Hardly realizing she was doing it, she started the slow,
sensual grinding of her pelvis against him, finding his
rhythm, her warming groin offering a heated haven for
the heavy male flesh pulsating against her.

"Kiss me, Mary," he commanded again, and this
time she sighed and slipped a caressing hand across his
sweat-dampened chest, up over his slick shoulder, and
around the back of his neck.

She lifted her lips to his and kissed him. It began as
a slow-building, sensual kiss. Her mouth played with
his, her tongue tracing his smooth, warm lips, sucking
his bottom lip into her mouth, then sliding her tongue
between his open white teeth.

He took charge then. He kissed her with hunger
and passion, and as they kissed, he drew her even
closer to him, making her intensely aware of the esca-
lating heat and full arousal of his lean body.

His mouth feasting on hers in a long, languorous
kiss, he moved his lean hand to the cleft in her buttocks. His long dark fingers slipped between, and he
touched her with studied gentleness. She didn't jump,
she didn't jerk, she sighed into his mouth. So the tips
of his fore- and middle fingers began caressing her,
teasing her, readying her for lovemaking.

Her eyes now closed, her mouth and body pressed to his, Mary Ellen couldn't believe what was happening to her. Here she was hot again. Hotter even than she had been out in the hall. So hot she knew she'd do anything he asked, anything he wanted.

His lips still covering hers, Clay turned onto his back, bringing Mary Ellen with him, placing her atop his long, lean body. He drew her bent knees up on either side of his rib cage so that she was spread open against him. His hands came up to sweep her long loose hair back off her face as they continued to kiss hotly, anxiously. He felt the weight of her naked breasts against his chest, felt the diamond-hard nipples digging into his flesh.

Feeling as if he couldn't wait one more second to be inside her, he held back for her sake. He allowed her to remain there draped atop him, kissing him, moving seductively, knowing she was growing increasingly excited.

At last Mary Ellen tore her burning lips from his and of her own accord rose to a sitting position astride him. She looked at him with an expression that said, "I'm ready, please, please make love to me," and she waited breathlessly. Waited for him to reach for her, lay her over onto her back, and then take her.

He didn't do it.

Looking straight into her passion-glazed dark eyes, he said, "It's yours, Mary. You want it?"

"Y-yes," she breathed. "Oh, yes. Now. Right now."

"Then take it," he said.

A half frown came to her flushed face, and she started to move off him. "No." He stopped her. "Stay as you are."

"But I thought—"

"Make love to me like this."

She looked puzzled. "Like this? I don't know—"

"Rise up onto your knees," he instructed calmly, and she obeyed. "Now take me in your hand."

Exhaling loudly, Mary Ellen wrapped her fingers around his hard, throbbing flesh and smiled foolishly, dreamily, when he jerked involuntarily in her warm grip. She glanced at him.

"Go ahead," he said, and his low, deep voice was a caress.

Biting her lip with concentration, Mary Ellen slowly, carefully guided the rocket-shaped tip of his tumescence into the wet heat between her parted legs. Her hand continuing to hold him, she raised questioning eyes to his once more.

"Now just ease down on me," he said. "Take your time. No hurry. Don't force it. Relax and get comfortable with it."

He watched, fascinated, as she slowly, gently, lowered herself onto his throbbing masculinity. His heartbeat quickened. A vein throbbed on his forehead. The muscles in his buttocks clenched. And then a last...

White-blond curls met raven black. Tight wet heat gripped hard, pulsing flesh. And incredible pleasure spread through his long, lean body as Mary Ellen impaled herself upon him.

At first he let her set the pace. She moved tentatively, slowly, unsure of herself, as if afraid of hurting one of them or both. But oh, what an erotic vision she made, seated naked astride him, her glorious hair spilling around her lovely face and shoulders, her breasts swaying with the motion of her undulating hips.

The control he had exercised since their first burning kiss in the corridor was rapidly slipping away. He couldn't stand it much longer. He closed his eyes against her wanton blond beauty and silently recited the words of an old navy song in an effort to hold on, to keep his full erection, to wait for her to climax before he let himself go.

The sweet agony was too great; she made him too hot. Hotter than any woman he'd ever had.

The Captain opened his eyes, settled his hands on her hips, and took charge, his pelvis surging up to meet the thrust and roll of her hips, speeding the rhythm, driving deeper, giving her everything he had. To his delight, she stayed with him, bucking and thrusting, giving as good as she got, reaching for her own release.

For a few unbelievable minutes they mated like wild animals, savage in their quest, keening and screeching, clawing and clasping, their joined bodies moving so rapidly, so violently, they rocked the enormous mahogany bed. When they climaxed together, Mary Ellen cried out in her ecstasy while Clay shuddered and groaned loudly, the tendons in his neck standing out in bold relief, his face contorted as if in great pain.

The last small shudders of pleasure still tingling through her body, Mary Ellen collapsed tiredly atop him. Her tangled blond hair covering her face and his, she lay there panting for breath, too weak to move, too sated to care. His own breath labored, he silently stroked her hair, her satiny back.

Mary Ellen soon fell asleep.

The Captain left her where she was for a while, continuing to hold her, to stroke the white-blond hair, the pale satiny flesh, as he wondered at Mary's seeming naiveté. He was certain she was a virgin to the kind of lovemaking they had engaged in out in the darkened corridor. She was shocked; he could tell. Instinctively he knew that no man had ever done that to her.

Then later, here in the bed as she sat astride him, he had found it necessary to let her get comfortable with a favored position that oddly enough seemed totally foreign to her. Watching her through half-closed eyes, he had wondered again at her innocence.

Mary was no maiden.

She was a divorced woman who'd been married for years. He found it surprising—shocking, even—that she knew so little about lovemaking. Stories of Daniel Lawton's many conquests had circulated around Memphis long before Mary married him. Surely Lawton was an experienced, knowledgeable lover. So why, Clay wondered idly, hadn't the rich, blond aristocrat been more intimate with his own beautiful wife?

He sighed heavily.

It made no difference to him. He didn't care what kind of relationship they'd had. Or not had. His only interest was his own relationship with Mary. A purely sexual relationship. That's all he wanted from her, with her. Her warm, willing body next to his. This pale, slender, beautiful body whose feminine charms he fully intended to enjoy until he tired of her.

Carefully he moved Mary off his chest, laying her on her back beside him. She never awakened, just sighed in her sleep and snuggled down into the softness of the mattress. Clay reached up and turned out the bedside lamp. He left the other one burning, too sleepy to get up.

He yawned, turned Mary onto her side, drew her soft, naked body back against his own, and went to sleep.

* * *

Long before the first gray tinges of light appeared in the east, Mary Ellen awakened. Her eyes opened slowly. She was confused and disoriented. But for only a second.

She was, she realized quickly, lying naked in the arms of the despised Captain Knight in the middle of her parents' big featherbed. She was on her side, backed up against him. His arm was around her, his hand cupping her breasts. His breath was warm on her neck, the crisp hair of his chest tickled her back, and his firm thighs cradled her bare bottom.

Mary Ellen's heart pounded.

She squeezed her eyes shut and held her breath, terrified he might be awake. She lay very still for what seemed an eternity until she was finally sure he was asleep.

Only then did she open her eyes and cautiously move the Captain's cradling hand from her breast. She lifted his heavy arm from around her waist, placing it gently on his hard thigh. Slowly, carefully, she disengaged herself from him and scooted away, her bottom lip caught between her teeth.

She paused when she'd managed to put a foot of space between them, then turned onto her stomach and ventured a look at his face. His eyes were closed, the long dark lashes resting on his tanned cheeks. He moved in his sleep, and Mary Ellen flinched. He turned onto his back and flung a long arm above his dark head. His breathing remained slow and even, and his chest rose and fell rhythmically.

Mary Ellen exhaled softly with relief and again started scooting on her stomach toward the edge of the mattress. It was a long scoot on this specially built bed, which measured seven and a half feet wide. She was terrified she would never make it without awakening the Captain.

Her wary eyes stayed on him the entire time.

Harsh reality set in as she looked at him lying there naked, so dark and hairy and masculine against the rumpled snowy white sheets. Dear Lord, what kind of fool was she? What had possessed her? How could she have done such an unforgivably stupid thing?

She couldn't believe it. She had fallen right into bed with the cold, heartless cad who had used her to realize his own ambitions. She had been lying here naked all night in the arms of the man who'd broken her heart. She had made love with the cruel bastard who had jilted her when he'd attained his only real goal: an appointment to the Naval Academy.

Mary Ellen finally reached the edge of the bed. She turned, sat up, threw her legs over, and stepped onto the deep, plush carpet.

Overcome with anger, guilt, and regret, Mary Ellen burned with humiliation. She was appalled and shamed by what she had done. Backing away from the bed, she caught sight of herself in the huge French gold-framed mirrors and was further shamed. Her eyes went back to the bed. Staring at the dark man sleeping peacefully there, Mary Ellen cringed at the vivid recollection of their abandoned intimacy.

Hand over her mouth, brows knit with misery, she backed out of the bedroom, turned, and hurried through the dim sitting room, opened the door, and peered about cautiously.

She saw no one.

She tiptoed out into the dark, silent corridor, anxiously gathered up her discarded nightclothes, and hurried into her own bedroom. Once inside she leaned back against the door, her eyes shut, her heart drumming, and vowed she would never let Captain Knight compromise her again.

Twenty-Eight

Mary Ellen pushed away from the door, felt her way across her darkened bedroom, and—with shaking hand—lighted a lamp beside her bed. She looked at the clock on the mantel.

Four-thirty.

No use going back to bed. She wouldn't be able to sleep. Sighing with despair, Mary Ellen turned slowly and glanced at herself in the free-standing pier glass. Frowning, she moved closer, staring at the strange refection. Her pale hair was a wild mass of tangles falling into her face and around her bare shoulders. She raised her hands and pushed the disheveled tresses back and ventured closer to the tall mirror.

She stopped a few feet away.

And shuddered.

She hardly recognized the naked woman staring back at her. It was obvious what this wanton had been up to during the hot, dark hours of the night. Pale, bare breasts were still pinkened and sensitive from a lover's heated kisses, and a small bruise decorated the inside of an ivory thigh. An unfamiliar soreness between her legs was a constant physical reminder of the dark Captain's total possession.

Tears stung Mary Ellen's eyes as mortification and

regret engulfed her. She hated herself for what she'd done. For what she had allowed him to do. And she hated the arrogant, amorous Captain Knight for stripping her of her dignity.

His scent was all over her body, and she suddenly felt so dirty and unclean that she couldn't stand it.

Mary Ellen turned from the mirror, snatched up the blue silk robe, and shoved her arms inside. She went to the bell pull beside the bed and yanked on it frantically. She tied the robe's sash, then paced and fidgeted. Five minutes passed. She returned to the bell pull, tugged on it again, then waited impatiently. Pacing once more, she felt as if she were going to jump out of her skin.

Her soiled, dirtied skin.

She flew across the room in answer to the soft knock on her door. Blinking sleepily in confusion, old Titus stood there yawning and scratching his gray head. Mary Ellen grabbed his arm and pulled him inside.

"You're to heat some water," she told him anxiously, "and bring it right up here."

"Miz Mary Ellen," he protested, "it ain't ebben five o'clock in the mornin', and I'se—"

"Titus Preble, you get down those stairs right now and heat some water! You hear me? I need a bath and I need it now."

Her tone and the wild look in her dark eyes kept him from saying anything more. The old house servant bobbed his head and went to do her bidding, but he was puzzled by her odd behavior, her uncharacteristic flash of anger. And he wondered at her change of habits. What was she doing up so early? And why was she ordering up a bath? Rarely did the young mistress of

Longwood have a bath in the morning. She unfailingly bathed each night. He wondered what had gotten into her. But he wasn't about to ask her. No, sirree.
Wasn't none of his business. Let her bathe in the middle of the night if that's what she wanted.

Still, he muttered to himself as he heated the water
and then struggled to get it up the back stairs.

Perspiring, out of breath, he finally delivered the hot
water. Mary Ellen took one look at him and was immediately repentant. She was sorry that in her anger
and guilt she had awakened Titus and yelled at him.
Sorry she had ordered him to haul the water upstairs.
He wasn't able, hadn't been in years.

"Titus," she said apologetically, taking the heavy
pail from him, "I'll do it. You go on back to bed. I'm
sorry I woke you. Forgive me for being so selfish."

Blinking, the old retainer turned and left, more puzzled than ever.

As soon as he was gone, Mary Ellen stripped and
poured the pail of steaming water into her tub. She
scrubbed herself so vigorously her pale skin turned
rosy. She soaped herself from head to toe, determined
to wash away any lingering vestiges of Captain Knight.

When her body was as clean as a newborn babe's, she
rose from the tub, toweled herself dry, and began to dress
hurriedly, anxious to be gone from Longwood before
anyone—namely the Yankee naval commander—awakened.

It was a little past dawn when Mary Ellen cautiously
opened her door and slipped out into the corridor.
Glancing automatically at the closed door of the master suite, she felt a chill skip up her spine. But she offered silent thanks that the door was closed, the suite's
occupant apparently still asleep inside.

Mary Ellen flew down the back stairs and out into the early June morning. She was out of sight of the mansion before she finally drew an easy breath. She inhaled deeply of the cool moist air as faint pink rays of the rising sun colored a bank of low-lying clouds.

Mary Ellen hurried to leave River Road behind, then slowed her pace as she neared town. At this early hour most of Memphis was still sleeping. The streets were almost deserted, not a single blue-coated Yankee in sight. It was so still she could hear the birds singing in the highest branches of the dogwood trees.

Mary Ellen reached Front Street.

She walked slowly down Cotton Row, pausing a moment before the frosted-glass windows that read "Preble Cotton Company." The doors were closed and padlocked. No one was inside. No activity took place there anymore. There was no furious trading and selling inside the shuttered offices. No big contracts to purchase tons of the precious "white gold" that had put her hometown on the map.

Mary Ellen sighed sadly and moved on down Front Street, turning east when she reached Adams Avenue. A block up Adams she passed Saint Peter's Catholic Church, feeling as though she should slip inside and say a prayer for forgiveness. She strolled past all the fine Adams Avenue mansions, pausing when she reached the old lace-embellished Wheatley house across from Shelby County Hospital.

All the big, beautiful mansions had been occupied by the Federals. But now, at dawn, with everything still and quite, none of the enemy soldiers were in sight. It was as if the horrible war had never happened. As though the Yankees had never set foot in her beloved Memphis and it had all been a bad dream and now she had awakened.

Oh, if only it were just a dream. If only none of it had ever really happened. If only the Union navy had never conquered the Queen City on the Bluffs. If only the compelling Captain Knight had never occupied Longwood. If only he had never…if she had never…if they had never…

Mary Ellen reached the three-story Shelby County Hospital.

"Why, Mary Ellen Preble, what are you doing here at this ungodly hour?" asked a weary surgeon in a bloodstained white coat, lounging on the hospital's front steps. "What's the matter? Couldn't you sleep?"

Mary Ellen felt herself flush and hoped her terrible guilt wasn't written all over her face. Nervously she smiled at the physician and said, "I? What about you? You were here when I left late yesterday. Did you stay all night?"

Rolling his stiff, tired shoulders, he nodded his sandy head. Then, rising slowly to his feet, he smiled, took Mary Ellen's arm, and said, "I'm glad to see you, Mary Ellen. We're so short-handed that I—".

"And that's exactly why I'm here," she said as he ushered her inside.

"Good girl. I've got a ward full of patients who keep hollering to have their bandages changed."

"Leave it to Nurse Mary Ellen, Doctor Neal."

Mary Ellen was hard at work when the summer sun rose fully. She was grateful she had something to do, something to keep herself occupied.

Still, as busy as she was, Mary Ellen was distracted. No matter how many wounds she cleaned and bandaged, no matter how many bed baths she gave, no matter how many letters she wrote home to wives and sweethearts for weak, wounded soldiers, she never managed to fully forget about the dark, handsome, able-bodied man at Longwood.

At midmorning she was hurrying down the long hospital corridor with fresh linens when unbidden came the vivid vision of the naked Captain Knight on his back with her bucking wildly astride him.

Mary Ellen stumbled and nearly fell.

Later, as she fed steaming hot broth to a patient whose arms were bandaged up to his shoulders, her mind flashed back to the silent upstairs corridor of Longwood and to what Captain Knight had done to her in the hot, inky darkness.

"Hey, watch it!" cried the startled patient, and Mary Ellen was horrified to see that she had spilled broth down the front of his pajamas.

"Oh, my goodness," she said, setting aside the bowl of broth and dabbing anxiously at the spilled liquid. "Have I burned you? Are you hurt?"

"Naw, I'm okay."

"I'm so sorry, how clumsy of me."

"Something bothering you today, Miz Preble?"

"No. No, not a thing."

Mary Ellen continued to be plagued with the shaming memories she'd rather have forgotten. She *would* forget, she told herself. She would *not* think of it again. But as the day drew to a close she thought of little else, and she dreaded going back to Longwood.

She didn't leave at the usual hour. She stayed on at the hospital, purposely waiting until the summer sun was setting before she started home. Finally she could put it off no longer.

Her shoulders and back aching, exhausted from a long hot day at the crowded clinic and last night's sleeplessness, Mary Ellen said her goodnights and walked out into the gathering dusk. She went wearily down the front steps.

And stopped short.

She blinked and squinted in the fading light. She saw, across the street, a solitary Union officer mounted atop a coal black stallion. Twilight was settling in, but she recognized the Yankee Captain by the set of his wide shoulders, the distinctive tilt of his dark head.

Waves of anxiety and shame immediately washed over her. She looked about frantically. There was no avenue of escape. No way she could get past him.

Mary Ellen gritted her teeth. Then she squared her tired, slender shoulders, lifted her hot, wilted skirts, and, pretending she had no idea he was there, set out down the street.

Captain Knight gently kneed his black stallion, and the big beast slowly moved forward. Ignoring her tormentor, Mary Ellen marched haughtily down the wooden sidewalk. The hint of an amused smile on his lips, the mounted Captain rode down the street beside her. Looking neither to the left nor to the right, Mary Ellen continued on her merry way.

Seething silently, she proceeded down the street until Captain Knight turned his horse directly into her path, blocking the sidewalk.

Mary Ellen was forced to stop.

Dark eyes flashing with fury, she looked up at the mounted man and angrily ordered him to get out of her way. Captain Knight swung down out of the saddle.

His silver eyes as cold as ice, he said, "When will you learn that it is dangerous for you to be out alone at night?" He inclined his dark head toward the end of the block, where a gathering of Union soldiers was growing. "You'd do well to believe it. See all those soldiers? They are lonely men, far from home. You're asking for trouble."

Mary Ellen snapped, "The only danger I'm in is in my own home!" Her jaw rigid, she stepped around him and the big black stallion and again headed off at a fast, determined pace.

For a long moment Captain Knight stood there in the deepening dusk, watching her. He shook his dark head and his eyes narrowed. What a haughty little hypocrite she was. Last night, when there had been no risk of being found out, she'd been his willing and eager lover. Now, it seemed, she preferred to forget that it had happened. Well, he wasn't going to let her forget.

A faint smile again touching his lips, Clay Knight decided that for as long as he remained in Memphis, Tennessee, the mansion and its mistress were his. And he would continue to occupy both.

Leading his stallion and keeping his distance, the Captain followed Mary Ellen to make sure she got home safely. He stopped at Longwood's front gate, watched in wry amusement as she lifted her long skirts and flew up the steps. She disappeared through the tall fan-lighted doors with flashing flounce of white petticoats.

Once inside the house, Mary Ellen stopped in the kitchen only long enough to prepare a quick, cold supper on a tray. She carried it upstairs, hurried into her room, and locked the bedroom door. She tensed every time she heard the smallest noise, afraid it was the Captain climbing the stairs.

An hour passed. Two.

Exhausted, Mary Ellen went to bed. But she didn't go to sleep. Lying there alone in the hot darkness, she was tortured by the knowledge that Captain Knight either was—or would soon be—just across the hall. His close proximity presented both a nagging threat and a powerful temptation.

Much as she hated to admit it, last night's lovemaking had been thrilling beyond belief. So incredibly exciting, it was impossible to forget. And equally impossible not to yearn for more of the same.

Impossible not to consider that all she would have to do to experience such glorious ecstasy again would be to get out of bed, cross the hall, and slip into his suite. She seriously doubted that he would turn her down. Was almost certain he would take her in his arms and make languid, lustful love to her.

Mary Ellen turned over impatiently, looked at the windows beside her bed to make sure they were open to catch any breeze off the river. They were. But it was close and hot in her room. Not a breath of air stirred the curtains, and she felt moisture collecting in the valley between her breasts and at the backs of her knees.

She kicked the top sheet to the foot of the bed, pulled the bodice of her nightgown away from her heated flesh, and blew down inside. It didn't help.

She sighed.

And she pictured the Captain lying naked in the darkness just across the hall. Pictured the thick raven black hair ruffling on the white pillow. The hard, handsome face with its cruel, sensual mouth. The corded artery that throbbed on the tanned column of his throat. The bare brown shoulders that were wide and well muscled. The strong brown hands resting against the whiteness of the sheets. The chest with its mat of curling black hair. The drum-tight abdomen. The boyishly slim hips. The long, lean-muscled legs.

Her breath growing short, her top lip beaded with perspiration, Mary Ellen got out of bed. Irritably she unbuttoned her white nightgown. Blaming the hot gown for her discomfort, she drew it up over her head and off. She blotted the perspiration from her slender body with the garment, then dropped it to the rug.

Naked, she crawled back into bed.

But she was no cooler than before.

She tossed and turned, telling herself she did *not* want the Captain. She didn't want to go to him. She didn't want him to come to her. She wanted to forget last night had ever happened.

She *would* forget.

Punching her pillow, Mary Ellen murmured, "Damn you, Captain Knight! Damn you to hell! It'll be a cold day in July before I let you touch me again."

Twenty-Nine

While the bloody War Between the States raged across the Southland, a different kind of war raged in the big white mansion on the bluffs of the Mississippi River.

Mary Ellen valiantly battled her involuntary attraction to Captain Knight and his overpowering maleness. But with little success. In a totally different way he was every bit as captivating to her as when he was a young boy. There was now a cold dignity about him, an unshakable strength that was incredibly appealing.

He was so very handsome, and he had the look and manner of a man who was used to getting his way. He was all potent virility, all hard muscle and masculine planes and angles. His presence was so strong, so compelling, Mary Ellen could sense his closeness before she saw him. She could feel with a kind of electrifying thrill the pressure of his silver-gray eyes upon her.

Still, she reminded herself often that this tall, commanding Union officer was—and always had been—a ruthless man who had no aversion to breaking promises and hearts for his own personal gain.

For his part, Captain Knight made no attempt to temper his appetite for the beautiful blond aristocrat who had jilted him to run off to London with the wealthy, worthless Daniel Lawton.

Captain Knight wanted her and made no bones about it. He was a man of strong animal hungers, but he didn't regard his passion as having anything to do with love. He was impatient to have Mary back in his arms, back in his bed, but never back in his heart.

A capable officer at ease in a position of authority, Knight was confident he could conquer the beautiful Mary Preble. Her unconditional surrender was imminent; he would see to it. In pursuit of that goal, he altered his schedule, his regular routine. He managed frequently to get in Mary's way. And under her skin. And when he caught her alone, the determined Captain turned up the heat.

There was no safe place for her to hide.

One Sunday afternoon Mary Ellen, bored and restless, weary of being shut up in her bedroom, ventured downstairs. She glanced cautiously into the spacious dining room that Captain Knight had set up as his main command post. She'd come to think of it as the War Room, and she knew that when the Yankee Captain was there with his men, discussing strategy and going over the battlefield maps spread out on the long dining table, he was completely engrossed.

The Captain now stood on the far side of the long table. He was leaning over, tapping a spot on a spread map with one long forefinger while speaking in a low, deep voice to the uniformed men gathered around the dining table.

He didn't look up.

Comfortable that neither the Captain nor any of his men had seen her, Mary Ellen tiptoed away. She hurried into her father's study, chose a leather-bound book from the shelves, and started to go back upstairs. But she stopped and considered the fact that Captain Knight was totally absorbed in the business of war, was unlikely to leave the dining room for several hours.

Mary Ellen hurried out the back door, skipped down the steps, crossed the north lawn, and moved past the marble-faced sundial to the vine-covered summer-house on the lower terrace.

She sat down on one of the long white matching settees that faced each other, sighed with the simple joy of being outdoors on a beautiful summer day, opened her book, and began to read *Pride and Prejudice*.

But before she had finished a full page she felt the hot, muggy air come alive with that unmistakable electricity. She knew, before she looked up, that Captain Knight was somewhere close.

A shadow fell across the entrance of the latticed gazebo. Mary Ellen felt a tremor of excitement, felt her pulse quicken. She slowly raised her head. The tall dark Captain stood there looking down at her, unsmiling.

He ducked his head, stepped inside, dropped down onto the settee opposite her. He took the book from her hands and laid it aside.

"Just what do you think you're doing?" she asked irritably, commanding her heartbeat to slow, her hands not to shake.

"Just this," he said. With a swiftness that caught her off guard, he reached out, wrapped his long fingers around the backs of her knees through her full skirts, and drew her forward to the edge of the settee.

"Will you please—" Her breath caught when he bent his dark head and placed a warm, open-lipped kiss to the pale flesh exposed in the unbuttoned lace-trimmed collar of her summer dress. Mary Ellen winced and forcefully pushed him away. She leapt up, but he caught her skirt, trapped her.

Her dark eyes flashing black fire, she slapped at his hand and said, "Either you let me go this minute or I'll scream."

"No, you won't," he said with that cool, infuriating confidence, and drew her down onto his right knee, wrapping a long arm around her waist.

"I will, so help me," she threatened, pushing on his broad chest, struggling to free herself.

"Go ahead," he challenged, took her chin in his hand, turned her face toward his, and kissed the sensitive side of her throat.

"Please. Don't," she said, some of the venom going out of her tone. "I mean it. Stop it."

The Captain didn't stop.

His lips continued to kiss a hot path up to her ear, and his hand released her chin, moved down, settled gently, caressingly, on her breast.

His even white teeth worrying her dainty earlobe, he whispered, "I want to undress you and make love to you here in the summerhouse, Mary."

"You are insane," she managed, a little breathlessly, brushing his hand from her breast. "If you think for one minute that I—"

The sentence was never finished. He silenced her with his lips, and as much as Mary Ellen tried not to respond to his passion, she didn't quite succeed. His devastating kiss disarmed her, and the first thing she knew, the Captain had lifted her feet up into the settee, settled her more comfortably in his arms, and flipped her skirts and petticoats up over her stockinged legs. And his hand was stroking her thigh directly above her blue satin garter.

When he began deftly to unbutton her bodice, Mary Ellen finally came to her senses.

Blinking and shaking her blond head, she said, "No...we can't...I won't...I have to get back to the house!"

"Then be still," the Captain ordered, and looking directly into her dark, flashing eyes, he leisurely rebuttoned her bodice and lowered her raised skirts. "Now you may go, Mary."

She jumped up off his knee and glared at him when he caught her wrist. "I want you, Mary," he said, the deep timbre of his voice sending tingling chills up her spine. "And I will have you. I'll make love to you in ways you can't even imagine."

"You filthy, depraved beast, I will not listen to—"

"You want it as well, Mary. I know you do. Come to me tonight. Come and I'll be waiting."

She clawed at the firm fingers imprisoning her wrist and told him adamantly, "You'll have a long wait, Captain!"

"Maybe." He shrugged negligently. "Maybe not nearly as long as you think."

"Oh!" She wrenched free of his grasp and whirled away. She could hear his easy laughter as she ran across the lawn to the house. It was the first time she had heard the stony-faced Captain Knight laugh, and he was laughing at her! Well, let him laugh. She'd be the one laughing when he waited in vain for her tonight!

Mary Ellen kept to her room for the rest of the day. When night came she listened, straining, tensed. Finally, shortly after nine o'clock, she heard the door across the hall open, then close. And she smiled wickedly to herself. The restless Yankee Captain had *never* retired this early before. She knew the reason he did so tonight. He actually had the unmitigated gall to expect her to come across the hall and submissively climb into bed with him. The arrogant bastard.

Mary Ellen felt almost light-hearted as she undressed for bed. The egotistical Captain Knight was waiting for her, and he could go right on waiting till hell froze over!

He had laughed derisively when she'd run from the summerhouse, but he wasn't laughing now.

She was.

Mary Ellen felt as if she had won a very important battle of wills. The insolent Captain Knight supposed that she was so foolish and so weak and so helplessly attracted to him that he need do nothing more than snap his long brown fingers and she would come running. What a laugh! She could go for the rest of her life without his ever touching her again, and she fully intended to do just that.

Mary Ellen smiled as she blew out the lamp and got into the bed. It was great fun knowing that she was the one who had had the last laugh.

Her triumph didn't last long.

Mary Ellen stepped out into the corridor early the next morning and came face-to-face with the handsome, immaculate, uniformed Captain Knight. He was leaning against the wall just outside her door, long arms crossed over his broad chest, one black-booted foot raised and crossed over the other.

"Mornin', Mary," he said as casually as if it were an everyday occurrence. Thunderstruck, she stared openmouthed as he uncrossed his arms and pushed away from the wall. With the speed of a striking serpent, he swept her up into his arms.

His dark face descending to hers, he said, "r... you're one of those women who prefers making love in the morning."

Before she could answer, his lips captured hers in an overpowering kiss of such fierce heat and passion, her knees buckled. Her whimpering protests were barely audible beneath his covering, conquering mouth. Quick as a wink he maneuvered her back inside her bedroom and closed the door behind them.

The determined Captain Knight kept kissing Mary Ellen, and he held her so close to his tall, hard frame that she felt the shiny brass buttons of his uniform blouse digging into her tender breasts. A trousered knee was wedged between her legs, leaving Mary Ellen achingly aware of the hard muscle and bone pressing the folds of her full skirts against her groin.

The mouth covering hers was too capable, too captivating; the body crushed against hers was too virile, too blatantly male. Mary Ellen stopped struggling in his arms and clung to him. His lips finally released hers, he raised his head and looked into her dark eyes.

"Make love to me now," he said softly, persuasively, "before you go to the hospital."

"Don't be absurd," she managed, but with little conviction.

"Is it? I don't think so. And I don't believe you think so, either."

She studied his smug handsome face, and a small measure of her innate good sense returned. "What you mean is you don't believe I *think* at all. Isn't that it?" She began to pull from his embrace. "What happened the other night was a mistake. A terrible mistake for which I take full responsibility. But I guarantee you it will not happen again."

"It will, Mary. You know it. I know it."

She pulled completely away from him, and her dark eyes narrowed. "No, it will not. You vainly suppose that all you need do is touch me and I'm rendered incapable of intelligent thought." Her ire was rising swiftly, steadily. She put her hands on her hips, smiled sanguinely, and, hoping to sting him, said, "You've forgotten who you're dealing with, Captain Knight. While your questionable charm may work wonders on an occasional female, may I remind you its effects are short-lived on me." Her smile widened as she drove her point home. "Why, I once went right from your arms into Daniel Lawton's without giving you a second thought!"

Mary Ellen hoped to see at least a fleeting flicker of pain cross his handsome face. But she was disappointed. His expression never changed. His silver-gray eyes maintained their usual calm. To her dismay he just smiled at her, reached out, and toyed with the decorative piping on her sleeve as if he hadn't heard a word she said.

Angered, Mary Ellen brushed his hand away, pushed past him, and stormed from the room, saying over her shoulder, "Stay away from me!"

Thirty

The chase continued.

The able aggressor was coolly resolute, and he was also imaginative and resourceful. Tactically trained, he was ever careful. He did not attract the attention of anyone other than the beautiful opponent he meant to capture and conquer. He kept his moving target always in sight, never allowing her to stray too far outside the realm of his reach.

The anxious quarry was fully aware she was being shadowed. Nobody's fool, she was well aware of her pursuer's clever strategy and took extra precautions not to be caught anywhere alone if at all possible. She could do nothing about his watching her incessantly, but she could and would foil his plans to pounce on her when no one was looking.

And the chase continued.

Captain Clay Knight pursued Mary Ellen with a cold determination that both frightened and flattered her. He had her so effectively fenced in, she couldn't possibly escape. He was everywhere at once, watching her, taunting her, waiting for her to fall into his arms.

Despite all her best efforts to keep the Captain from

catching her alone, he was ingenious at devising methods of doing just that.

He single-handedly surrounded her.

And when he had her alone, he kissed her until her head spun, embraced her until she was weak in his arms, and told her in low, caressing tones all the shockingly intimate things he meant to do to her. He spoke graphically of all the ways he would make love to her.

Appalled, Mary Ellen swore repeatedly she didn't want to hear his disgusting talk, would not listen to such lewd language. But she found—guiltily—that it was incredibly arousing to hear the strikingly handsome Captain promise her forbidden erotic pleasures she could never have even imagined.

His animal appeal was too potent. She had been lonely for too long. As the hot summer days—and hotter summer nights—marched listlessly by, Mary Ellen knew she was weakening, knew she couldn't fight him much longer.

So did the Captain.

He sensed when her capitulation was at hand and planned accordingly.

On a sticky hot evening in early July, Mary Ellen, arriving home later than usual, saw no blue-coated men on the grounds of Longwood. Curiously, none were lounging about on the front gallery. Nor were there any inside the quiet mansion. She circled through the drawing room, moved on through the dining hall War Room, and went into the kitchen.

Not a single Yankee in sight.

Mary Ellen smiled.

Longwood was deserted.

If they were off on some kind of maneuver or contraband exercise, that meant their menacing commander was also absent from Longwood. Which afforded her a few hours of blessed peace.

Titus and Mattie were not in the kitchen. Mary Ellen started to call out to the old servants, then changed her mind. No hurry. She had all evening to see about dinner and a bath. First she'd go to her room and get out of her hot stockings and petticoats.

Back out in the marble-floored corridor, Mary Ellen looked up the grand staircase and saw that old Titus had lighted the frosted globe wall sconces leading up to the second floor. She blessed him silently for remembering. He'd been awfully forgetful of late.

The summer twilight was turning to full darkness as Mary Ellen languidly climbed the stairs. How pleasant it was not to be in a rush. What a luxury not to feel as if she had to get quickly inside the safety of her room.

Mary Ellen reached the second-floor landing, and her brief sense of well-being vanished.

Captain Knight, looking oh so threatening and darkly appealing in a pair of neatly pressed white uniform trousers—and nothing else—stood just outside the open door of the master suite.

In the muted light from the wall sconce above his head, he was a study in light and shadow. Black and white. White trousers. White teeth. White towel draped around his neck. Black hair. Black silk robe over his arm. And through the white trousers, under which he obviously wore no underwear, the thick blue-black hair of his groin was a shadowy reminder of his virility.

Mary Ellen looked at him silently.

The harshly handsome face. The beautifully configured body. Captain Knight was surely one of nature's most perfect works, and she could have spent the rest of her life doing nothing but admiring his extraordinary masculine beauty.

At the same time, she resented him for being so irresistibly handsome. Damn him for being so gorgeous! Why should he possess a body so splendid she was constantly tempted to run her hands over the beautifully carved planes and angles?

Wishing to high heaven he were not so physically flawless and dangerously fascinating, Mary Ellen purposely kept her features composed. She gazed at him impassively without speaking. Until he held out his hand to her.

Sarcastically she said, "What do you want from me, Captain Knight?"

Unsmiling, he said, "Isn't it obvious?"

"No, I mean besides that. What are you after this time? Surely just making love to me isn't your main goal. Now, when I was a girl you wanted—"

"Your body is all I want, Mary," he cut in smoothly. "Nothing more, believe me."

"Well, how very flattering," she said bitingly. "And you suppose I'll just hand myself over for your... your...use."

"It works both ways. You seem to be temporarily without a lover, so—"

"I don't take lovers!" she snapped defensively.

"No? When did you change? As I recall, you took Daniel Lawton for your lover the minute my back was turned."

"Your back wasn't turned, Captain!" she said angrily. "It was gone!"

"Ah, well, I'm here now and so are you."

Bristling, she said, "I do not have lovers!"

"All the more reason for us to—shall we say—accommodate each other. We're both available, convenient, and no one ever need know."

"You vile, low bastard," she said acidly, "I really do hate you, do you know that?"

Unruffled, he replied, "So you've mentioned. But then how we feel about each other has little to do with lovemaking, wouldn't you agree?" He stepped closer. "Don't fight it any longer, Mary. What's the use?"

What was the use? she wondered wearily. She hated him, but still she wanted him. Why couldn't she be as detached and sophisticated and blasé as he about having a brief affair? Why not enjoy a few nights of forbidden ecstasy in a world that now offered little joy?

After all, it would only be her body he toyed with, not her heart.

The Captain read the indecision in her expressive dark eyes and again lifted his hand, extended it to her.

"No," Mary Ellen said, barely above a whisper, knowing as well as he did that she really meant yes.

"Mary," he said quietly in his most even, self-assured voice. "Come to me, Mary."

Still she hesitated.

If she took his outstretched hand and went inside his suite, she would be spending the rest of her nights with him for as long as he wanted her. Until he tired of her and tossed her aside as he'd done once before.

But, Lord, she was so very tired of fighting her intense attraction for this coldhearted, hotblooded man. His chilling indifference could inflict great pain. But his warm touch could afford unbelievable ecstasy.

"Give me your hand, Mary," he commanded, his voice remaining low, soft.

Mary Ellen laid her fingers atop his warm palm and said inanely, "I...I...need a bath."

"I know," he said, and gently drew her to him. "And I'm going to give you one."

Thirty-One

And so he did.

The bare-chested, white-trousered Captain ushered Mary Ellen into the master suite and locked the heavy door behind them. His hand enclosing hers warmly, he led her through the shadowy sitting room to the bedroom and dressing room/bath beyond. In the marble-walled bath lighted only by tall white candles in gleaming silver candlesticks, the white marble tub was brim full with steaming water and rich perfumed suds.

"My lady's bath awaits," he said, and tossed the black silk robe on a long velvet chaise.

He slid the white towel from his neck, looped it around Mary Ellen's waist, and pulled her to him. He sat down on a tufted velvet vanity stool. With the towel he reeled in the unresisting Mary Ellen to stand between his spread knees, facing him.

He released the towel, let it drop to the plush white rug.

With the easy deftness of a man who had undressed his share of beautiful women, the Captain leisurely disrobed Mary Ellen, refusing to let her help. As he removed each article of clothing, he kissed the pale flesh he'd exposed. And as he undressed her and kissed her, he told her he'd do everything he could to make the evening a pleasant one for her

Mary Ellen had no reason to doubt him. The cruel things they had said to each other were forgotten as she surrendered to the sensual pleasure this man so effortlessly provided.

When she was totally naked, Mary Ellen made a move toward the waiting tub and he said, "No, wait, Mary. Just for a moment."

Mary Ellen felt the heat of his silver gaze as he held her at arm's length and studied her intensely as if she were some interesting work of art.

The man staring fixedly at her was thinking that the Almighty had surely fashioned no more perfect female than the one standing before him. At least physically. Mary was tall for a woman, but she wasn't large. She was appealingly slender, and the long, clean lines of her pale body spoke of both strength and grace. Her breasts were not heavy, but pleasingly full and well shaped, the nipples still the shy pink hue of a young virgin's. The arch of her hips was ideal in their sheer physical beauty, and while neither hips nor pelvis was wide and generous like those of some of her more voluptuous sisters, she was clearly fashioned for fucking.

He knew how perfectly their bodies fit together, remembered with vivid clarity how tight she was, how sweet and hot. Recalling the smallness, the snugness, of her gripping him, he was struck by the idea that she'd have a hard time delivering a child.

The senseless thought was gone as soon as it came, and Captain Knight rose to his feet, gently cupped Mary Ellen's face with his hands, and kissed her. Then he lifted her up into his arms and carried her to the tub. Mary Ellen clung to his neck as he leaned down, dipped his fingers to check the water's temperature, then lowered her slowly into the sudsy depths.

"Mmmmmm." She sighed with pleasure and leaned her head back against the tub's small cushioning pillow. "Wonderful," she murmured.

Standing above, looking down at her, he said, "Stay just as you are; I'll be right back."

Nodding, Mary Ellen closed her eyes, felt her tense, tired muscles starting to relax beneath the surface of the hot, bubbly water.

When he returned from the bedroom, Mary Ellen's eyes were closed and she was almost dozing. He spoke her name softly. She opened her eyes and looked up at him. He held a clean white washcloth in one hand, a couple of white towels in the other. She lifted her arm, reached for the washcloth.

"Allow me," he said, and laying aside the towels, he knelt beside the tub.

Supposing he must surely be teasing, she nonetheless said, "No, I... Really, no... I can—"

"Shhh," the Captain warned as he dipped the cloth into the water and reached for the new bar of perfumed soap.

Mary Ellen lunged up anxiously when he pressed the soapy cloth to the base of her throat. But she sank back against the tub rim's cushioning pillow when his lips covered hers and he whispered into her mouth, "Mind me now, Mary."

In no mood to argue, Mary Ellen minded him. She was as submissive as a small child being bathed by a parent. But she was no child and he was no parent, and soon she was experiencing the most memorable bath of her entire life.

He started with her shoulders, then had her sit forward while he washed her slender back. It was wonderfully sensuous to have him guide the soapy cloth gently up and down her spine as if she were made of priceless porcelain. Mary Ellen bent her head, put her face on her raised knees, and sighed with the enjoyment of it. When her back was clean and fragrant from the perfumed soap, he instructed her to raise her head and lean back again.

She did.

And she felt her face flush with heat when his strong brown hand generously soaped her slippery breasts. The wet nipples instantly became taut under his gentle touch and hot silver gaze. He reached in the tub, scooped up rich bubbles, and deposited them on her tingling nipples. Then he bent his dark head and blew them away.

He bathed every inch of her body, touching her in ways that thrilled and excited her. And when she sighed and gasped and arched up to meet his cloth-covered hand, he looked at her with those smoldering slate eyes and asked, "Does that feel good? Is this better? Or this?"

By the time the erotic exercise in cleansing was over, Mary Ellen was so aroused, she could hardly wait for him to make love to her. She was sure he felt the same because his dark, naked chest was rising and falling heavily and the fabric of his crisp white trousers strained across his swollen groin.

When he drew her up out of the tub and began toweling her off, Mary Ellen trembled with rising anticipation. When she was dry at last, he picked up the black silk robe from the chaise and held it out for her. Her back to him, she slipped her arms into the long sleeves, then sighed and leaned back against him while he reached around her and tied the robe's sash at her waist. He turned her to face him, rolled up the sleeves over her hands, and pulled the slick lapels together over her naked breasts.

His attention shifted to her hair, which was twisted into a severe knot at the back of her head. He reached up and, seemingly in no particular hurry, slipped the pins from the tresses and watched, fascinated, as they spilled down around her black-robed shoulders. He combed his fingers through the long pale hair, lifted a lock, and pressed it to his nose and mouth, inhaling deeply.

"I washed it last night," Mary Ellen said anxiously, "but it's been so hot today that—"

"Smells good," he reassured her, lifted his dark head, and drew the lock of hair down to his naked chest, tickling his flat brown nipple with the wispy white ends before he released it.

He then took her into the bedroom, and Mary Ellen looked about in stunned surprise. The only illumination in the large room was romantic candlelight. The French gold-framed mirrors reflected the tiny flames from dozens of tall white candles in ornate candelabra. On the floor before the cold marble fireplace, a snowy white damask tablecloth was spread on the plush wool rug. Champagne was chilling in a silver bucket, and a pair of sparkling crystal flutes awaited the splash of the cold bubbly.

A crystal vase at one corner of the white cloth held a fragrant bouquet of velvety ivory roses. A tempting spread had been laid out on porcelain dishes; cheeses and cold meats and breads and nuts and figs. Plump purple grapes spilled from a silver bowl, and an array of sweet confections graced a porcelain platter.

Mary Ellen was both pleased and perplexed.

She was pleased that he had gone to so much trouble to make the evening a special one, but perplexed that he obviously intended them to dine before making love. The stimulating bath had left her weak with wanting. It wasn't for food that she hungered.

"I thought we'd have a little repast first," he said, and Mary Ellen had no choice but to agree.

They sat on the rug beside the spread feast. The Captain poured the chilled champagne and handed a glass to Mary Ellen. They nibbled on nuts and figs, then dined on the cheeses and meats and breads. On another occasion Mary Ellen would have relished these delicious delicacies, foods she hadn't tasted in ages. But not now.

It seemed to Mary Ellen that the meal lasted forever, and she wondered at him. He ate slowly, leisurely, as if in no hurry at all. Surely he knew that he had awakened her passions with the arousing bath; that she was excited, would stay excited until he made love to her.

Wearing only his oversize black silk robe, Mary Ellen was seated on the soft rug with her slender legs curled to one side, sipping her champagne and gazing at him, feeling as if she couldn't stand it one more minute. That she would die if he didn't take her straight to bed.

She wasn't sure what was most responsible for keeping her so aroused. The lingering effects of the bath. Or the chilled champagne lowering her inhibitions. Or the provocative touch of the slick black silk on her naked flesh. Or the sight of him stretched out on his side, weight supported on an elbow, a knee bent and raised, his awesome erection straining the white fabric of his tight trousers.

As if he had read her mind, he rolled into a sitting position, reached for the sash of the robe, and gave it a gentle but decisive tug.

"If you're too warm," he said, "why not take off the robe."

Her breath caught. Any second now he would strip it from her body, carry her to the bed, and make love to her.

He didn't.

He took a long swallow of champagne, looked at her with hooded gray eyes, languidly pushed the opened robe apart so that she was naked to his scrutinizing gaze. Then, to her surprised dismay, he stretched back out on his side, reached over, and plucked a purple grape from the silver bowl.

Mary Ellen thought she would explode.

The dark man calmly eating grapes knew the state she was in. He knew very well that she was so hot and eager, she could hardly stand it. So was he. But he made her wait, made himself wait. He had a reason. He wanted her to be so hot, to want him so much, that when finally he took her, she'd agree to be his for as long as he was at Longwood.

So, ignoring his aching groin, his thick hot blood, he bided his time. He offered her the various rich pastries, telling her how good they were, insisting she sample some of each. He fed her the sweet confections, then leaned over and licked the powdered sugar from her lips.

He poured her more champagne. He plied her with the chilled wine until she was light-headed and tipsy.

And hotter than ever.

All her inhibitions washed away in the chilled champagne and hot bath, Mary Ellen melted against him when finally he eased the black silk robe from her shoulders and down her arms. He kissed her. While his lips moved warmly on hers, his hand caressed her breasts, teased the stinging nipples.

Their lips finally separated, but his hand stayed on her tingling flesh. The candlelight reflected in the depths of his smoky eyes, he looked at her, unblinking, and said, "Mary, rise up onto your knees."

Without questioning him, she rose to her knees, knelt there naked before him. His hand swept over her ribs, stroked her contracting stomach. Mary Ellen's breath came out in a rush, her eyes closed, and she heard him say, "Sit back on your heels, Mary."

Eyes still closed, she sighed and eased back onto her bare heels. His hands went to her knees; gently he urged them apart, spreading them. Mary Ellen trembled when his hand went between her parted legs, touched her in that spot where she burned so hot.

"Open your eyes, Mary," he commanded softly.

She opened her eyes, looked at him. His fingers caressed her while he gazed into her dark eyes. Then, abruptly, his hand left her flesh, and he lifted it up before her face, showed her his glistening dark fingers. He said, "See how ready you are for me."

"Yes," she whispered, on fire, hurting, praying he'd lift her into his powerful arms and carry her to the bed.

"You're hot and wet."

"Mmmmm," she murmured, licking her dry lips.

"Say it, Mary."

Mary Ellen shook her head, turned it away. He caught her chin, turned her face back to his.

"Say it. Say 'I'm hot and wet and ready for you, my Captain.'"

Mary Ellen looked into his icy-hot charcoal eyes and knew she'd say anything, do anything. Her words coming out in a rush, she said, "I'm hot and wet and ready for you, my Captain." She paused, held her breath, then pleaded, "Please...please..."

"Yes, baby," he said, and in an instant he swept the dishes out of the way and Mary Ellen found herself lying flat on her back on the damask tablecloth.

"The bed," she murmured.

"No," he told her, anxiously peeling off his tight white trousers, "here. Here on the floor where we can see better."

"See?" she asked breathlessly.

"In the mirrors. Look, Mary," he urged, parting her long, slender legs and moving between, "everywhere you look you see the two of us naked."

Mary Ellen turned her head to the side, glanced directly at one of the many tall, gold-framed mirrors. There they were, naked on the floor in the flickering candlelight. Entranced, she watched boldly as her dark lover lowered his lean body to hers. She flung her arms above her head and stared in wonder as his gleaming brown body met, then became a part of hers.

It was shocking.

It was beautiful.

It was highly erotic.

"Now look into my eyes," he instructed, and Mary Ellen, sighing, turned her head and looked at him.

His handsome face loomed just above hers, the candlelight casting shadows beneath the high, slanting cheekbones. The muscles in his wide, sleek shoulders bulged as he balanced his weight on stiffened arms and stared fixedly down at her.

Nan Ryan

He had eased into her as she'd watched, and now he flexed his firm buttocks and implanted himself more deeply, causing her to gasp and clasp his rigid biceps.

"Feel me, Mary," he said, expecting no answer. "This is all of me you need, but you need this. Say you need this."

"I do," she admitted, so dazzled, so aroused, she would have said anything, done anything. "I need this."

"You need this from me?"

"Yes, yes, from you. You and nobody else."

He began the slow, sensuous movements of loving as he told her, "You'll deny me no longer. You'll share my bed whenever I want you. When I come upstairs each night, I'll come to you and you'll be waiting. You will no longer lock your door against me."

"No, never," she whispered, feeling him fill and stretch her. "I won't lock my door."

"There are no locks that can keep me out of your room or out of your body, Mary. Do you understand?"

Nodding, she sighed with the ecstasy of having him moving inside her and with the excitement of seeing their blended naked bodies from every angle in the spacious, candlelit bedroom. Reflected in the many mirrors were dozens of hims and hers, and all of them moved together so perfectly, so provocatively.

All the naked hims were so dark, so masculine, so masterful. All the bare hers were so pale, so feminine, so receptive. It was like watching an entire group of exquisitely beautiful men and women making love, and the seductive sight of it made the hot blood race through Mary Ellen's veins.

Burying himself deeply within her, the Captain again asked, "Do you understand?"

Her pelvis rising to meet the driving thrust of his,

she said breathlessly, "I understand. There will be no locks between us."

She moaned with rising pleasure and added in a whisper, "And you will love me like this every night. Every night."

"I will," he whispered, and kissed her.

Thirty-Two

After a night of unforgettable lovemaking before the gold-framed mirrors, Mary Ellen awakened in the big mahogany four-poster bed alone.

The high, hot sun streaming in through the open French doors reached the oversize four-poster and fell across her face. The morning light was so strong, it shone through her closed eyelids.

Her sleepy eyes opened and she turned her head slowly. The pillow was empty beside her, but it still bore the indentation of Captain Knight's dark head. Mary Ellen sat up, pushed her tousled hair from her eyes, and saw her naked reflection in the French gold-framed mirrors.

She immediately reached for the covering sheet as her face pinkened and she recalled how brazenly she had watched herself in the mirrors making love with Captain Knight. Her bare stomach fluttered at the recollection, and her face flushed with embarrassment.

But she no longer kidded herself that she was sorry it had happened. If he were here right now, she'd gladly get back down on the floor with him. She'd make love to him all day if he wanted her.

It shamed her to realize what a wanton she was with him, but the days of denying it were over. She'd made her decision last night, and she wouldn't change her mind now, even in the harsh light of day. Right or wrong, foolish or wise, she couldn't resist him physically. Didn't really want to resist him.

And what difference did it make? She was no longer a trusting young girl who could be easily hurt. She was a grown woman and wise enough to realize that no matter how ardent his lovemaking, he cared nothing for her. As he had so coldly pointed out, she was available and convenient.

Well, so was he. So why not sleep with him for the sole purpose of the pure carnal joy it gave her?

Mary Ellen smiled sadly at the irony of it. Her husband had once loved her, yet she'd derived absolutely no pleasure from his inept lovemaking. Captain Knight cared nothing for her, but his skilled lovemaking lifted her to the heights of erotic bliss.

Lord, life was impossible.

Mary Ellen threw off the sheet and got out of bed. Yawning, she went into the marble bath where the Captain had undressed her last night. She gathered her discarded clothes and returned to the bedroom. She saw his black silk robe lying on the rug beside the white damask tablecloth.

Mary Ellen slipped on the robe and, clothes in hand, walked barefoot through the silent sitting room, opened the door, and peered out cautiously. She hurried across the empty hall and into her room.

"You're late, Mary Ellen." The white-uniformed head nurse, Miss Stevens, looked up when Mary Ellen hurried through the front door of the Shelby County Hospital.

"I know, I'm sorry," Mary Ellen apologized.

"Is everything all right?" asked the nurse. "Are you feeling well?"

"Yes, I... I'm fine. I just overslept."

The stocky, middle-aged nurse looked her up and down, then said, "You've been working too hard, child. You look tired and pale this morning." She laid a plump hand across Mary Ellen's brow. "I believe you're running a slight fever."

I am feverish, Mary Ellen thought guiltily, but not the kind you're talking about. "No, I'm sure I don't have any temperature." She smiled at the frowning woman who was a nurse twenty-four hours a day. "It's hot as blazes out there, Miss Stevens, and I forgot my bonnet. A bit too much sun, that's all."

"Well, you take care now, you hear?"

"I will," Mary Ellen said, smiling, "and I promise not to be late again."

As she went about her usual hospital duties, Mary Ellen found herself counting the hours until it was time to go home. The terrible truth was, she was looking forward eagerly to being back in Captain Knight's arms, could hardly wait until bedtime.

When finally the long hot day had passed and she walked tiredly up the front steps of Longwood, she found herself looking about anxiously for the tall, dark Captain. She spotted him in the War Room with a couple of his men. One was the red-haired Ensign Briggs. The three were standing, and she could tell by their conversation that the meeting was coming to a close. The Captain glanced up. She was sure he saw her.

Her heart fluttering, she decided she'd make it a point to be close by when he came out of the War Room. She was more than a little curious to see how he would behave.

Mary Ellen went out into the marble-floored foyer and picked up the messages left in the silver note basket on the lower shelf of the petticoat mirror. The messages had been there for a couple of days and she'd read them before, but the Captain wouldn't know that.

Momentarily the freckle-faced Ensign Briggs and the other sailor came into the corridor. Both smiled at her, nodded, then went outdoors. A long minute passed. And then all at once she felt that unmistakable electrical charge in the air when the darkly handsome Captain was close to her.

Acting as if she had no idea he was there, Mary Ellen dropped the messages into the basket and turned around as he walked into the foyer. His chilly gray eyes touched her, then dismissed her. She might have been a total stranger. He said nothing to her, didn't so much as acknowledge her presence.

He went directly to the mahogany coat tree, pulled his white uniform jacket from the top peg, slung it over his shoulder, and went out the fan-lighted door.

Stunned, Mary Ellen stood there and watched him walk unhurriedly across the shaded gallery and descend the front steps into the summer sunlight. He paused then, unhurriedly drew on the white uniform blouse. He strolled down the front walk and stepped through the gate just as a groom led his saddled black stallion around.

The Captain took the long leather reins but did not mount immediately. He stood for a time leaning against the huge black stallion, a long arm thrown over the creature's saddled back, talking with the youthful blond sailor.

Mary Ellen had eyes only for the Captain. His wide shoulders strained the white uniform blouse, and his blue-black hair gleamed in the late afternoon sunlight. He said something, then threw back his handsome head and laughed. Then he nodded to the shorter man, looped the leather reins over the stallion's sleek neck, and swung agilely up into the saddle.

Mary Ellen stood and watched as he cantered down the pebbled drive and out onto River Road. She turned from the door, feeling empty and confused and miserable. No one else was around, yet he had said nothing to her. Hadn't even spoken or smiled and acted as if he knew who she was. He had ignored her. Cut her cold.

And he had ridden away from Longwood at the hour when she usually returned to the mansion. He was freshly shaved and wearing his summer white dress uniform. A strategy session at the Gayoso House with General C. C. Washburn, perhaps?

But if that were the case, where was his trim black naval dispatch case?

Dear Lord, he had already tired of her. That was it. He had bent her to his will, had coaxed her into unconditional surrender, and that was what he'd really wanted. He had stripped her of all decency and decorum. Had persuaded her to say things and do things that were shocking and shameful. He had encouraged her to cast off all inhibitions and behave scandalously with him. And now the insensitive son of a bitch was through with her!

Mary Ellen stormed up the stairs and into her room. She paced edgily back and forth, fuming and imagining the worst. She supposed the easily bored Captain had gone out in search of fresh female companionship. Or perhaps he had an arranged engagement. He'd surely met any number of women since arriving in Memphis, plus all those he'd known as a boy.

Leah Thompson had said the ladies of the gentry were atwitter over the darkly handsome Captain Knight. Mary Ellen ground her teeth. She knew it was true. Knew he'd have little trouble finding a woman—or women—quite eager and willing to entertain him in their parlors.

And in their bedrooms.

Angry, tense, Mary Ellen left her room, went back down the stairs. She stuck her head in the kitchen and told the old servants not to fix her any dinner. She wasn't hungry. She was going to walk down to the old Templeton place and visit with her friend Leah Thompson.

Mattie just nodded, but old Titus shook his head worriedly. "Now, Miz Mary Ellen, I wouldn't do that if I was you."

"You're not me," she said crisply.

"Night's comin' on," he told her, "and you know that the Cap'n don' like you bein' out by yo'self after dark."

"I don't give a fig what the Captain likes," she said irritably. "I go where I please, when I please, Titus Preble!"

"Yes'm," he said, but he hobbled after her when she left the kitchen, mumbling about how she shouldn't be out traipsing around and she was gonna get herself in a whole lot of trouble if she wasn't careful.

Knowing he meant well, Mary Ellen paused at the front door. She came back to the bossy old servant and put her arm around him. "Titus...dear, sweet Titus, I'm not a little girl anymore." She smiled and gave his stooped shoulders an affectionate squeeze. "Please don't worry. Nothing's going to happen to me."

Thirty-Three

It was after nine o'clock when Mary Ellen started home from Leah Thompson's. Admittedly she was a little nervous. The city and riverfront were swarming with Yankees and Northern merchant riffraff.

When she'd gone less than a hundred yards, Mary Ellen saw a group of mounted Union soldiers riding toward her. Apprehensive, she started to turn back, return to Leah's. But it was too late.

The soldiers reached her, and Mary Ellen felt her heart beating in her throat. They shouted and whistled, and one leaned down from the saddle and asked if she'd like to take a little ride in the woods with him. She made no reply, didn't look up, kept walking at a brisk determined pace down River Road. Finally the soldiers rode on, laughing and calling out to each other.

But Mary Ellen felt a great measure of relief when she reached the front gate of Longwood.

The coxswain on guard rested the stock of his rifle on the gravel drive with one hand and opened the iron gate for her with the other.

Going up the walk, she saw several sailors lolling about on the front gallery, as usual. Mary Ellen pointedly ignored them. Her chin lifted defiantly, she stepped around a long-legged young man sprawled out on the top porch step. As regally as possible, she crossed the wide gallery and went into the silent house. She hadn't so much as glanced at any of the men, but she knew that their Captain was not among their number.

Her jaw hardened as she crossed the marble foyer and started up the grand staircase.

Likely the Captain wouldn't be returning to Longwood before sunup. Mary Ellen bristled at the thought of him lying naked in bed somewhere in the city with a pretty young girl. Or a lonely widow. Or even a wayward wife. Worse, the lady in question might very well be one of her own friends or acquaintances.

Sickened by the thought, Mary Ellen went inside her darkened room, closed the door, and leaned back against it. After a moment she sighed heavily and pushed away. She moved to the marble-topped dresser, lifted the globe of the coal-oil lamp, and lighted the wick. Soft mellow light filled the white-and-yellow bedroom. Mary Ellen replaced the glass globe, turned, and saw him.

And her hand flew up to her mouth.

Captain Knight lay naked in her bed.

Sleeping.

Stretched out on his back in the middle of the soft mattress, he looked very large and dark and out of place amid the frothy, feminine white-and-yellow lace bed hangings and lace-trimmed white pillows and matching white sheets.

Venturing closer, her hand coming down from her mouth, Mary Ellen stared at him. Cautiously she studied every shadowed plane of his hard, handsome face. The firm, chiseled features and long raven eyelashes and straight, well-shaped nose and cruelly sensual mouth. She examined every inch of the lean, bare body

that had once been so familiar, was now so strange, just
as he was strange.

He was a stranger.

A dark, erotic stranger was in her bed, and he looked
menacing even in sleep. He didn't appear totally relaxed and boyishly vulnerable. Not at all. There was a
coiled tension about his well-honed body, as if at any
second he could be fully awake and highly dangerous.

Mary Ellen's assessing gaze touched the wide-mus-
cled shoulders, the broad, hair-covered chest, and slid
lower to the corded ribs and drum-tight belly. Finally
she came to the part of his anatomy that had so easily
proved to her that she was no lady.

Mary Ellen's face grew warm as she stared unblinkingly at the flaccid male flesh at rest amid the dense,
curly blue-black hair of his groin. She trembled at the
recollection of what that innocent-looking organ could
do to her when it was fully erect.

Mary Ellen's dark eyes widened with disbelief, her
gaze riveted on the sleeping member, when the soft,
limp flesh began to rise and stiffen. Her mouth rounding into an O of surprise and amazement, she continued to stare helplessly while it lifted to life before her
marveling eyes.

"If you can do that with just a look," came that
deep, baritone voice, "imagine what will happen when
you touch it."

Mary Ellen's head snapped up. He was wide awake
and staring at her accusingly. Stammering, she said,
"I...I didn't...know you—"

"Come here," he cut in smoothly, continuing to lie
there on his back while his erection swelled. Mary
Ellen went to the bed. He patted the mattress beside
him. "Sit down, Mary."

Mary Ellen sank to the edge of the mattress, facing him. He lifted a hand, curled long fingers around her upper arm, and drew her down to him. He kissed her, his lips warm from slumber and wonderfully smooth against her mouth. He parted her lips with his tongue and swiftly deepened the kiss.

When finally their lips separated and Mary Ellen sat back up, he looked into her dark eyes, took her hand in his, and slowly guided it across his chest, over his belly, to his pulsing tumescence. He released her hand.

"Love me," he said coaxingly, and reached up to unbutton her bodice.

"I will," she promised, entranced.

Mary Ellen's slender fingers wrapped around him cautiously. She touched him gently, she stroked him up and down, she toyed with the jerking head, licking her forefinger and drawing a wet circle around the smooth tip's tiny opening.

"Oh, God, baby...baby." He groaned, breathing heavily. Finally he ordered, "Stop. Please, Mary."

"Shhh," she murmured, and continued to caress and tease and drive him half crazy with desire.

A vein pulsing on his dark forehead, the Captain lunged up momentarily, tore her hand from him, and drew her down on the bed.

Too aroused to waste precious time undressing her, he swept her full skirts up to her waist, swiftly removed her lace-trimmed pantalets, and moved between her shapely legs.

A foolish little smile of guilty pleasure crossed her face as Mary Ellen drew a quick breath and arched up against him as he thrust deeply into her. Her sharp nails punished his hard biceps as she pulled him to her eagerly. Then her hands slid beneath his muscled arms, and she clutched at his corded ribs.

Mary Ellen looked up at his handsome face as he plunged deeply into her, then slowly pulled almost all the way out, leaving only the glistening tip inside.

"No," she whimpered in protest, her nails biting into the smooth flesh of his clefted back.

"No, what?" he murmured huskily, poised there above, withholding that which she most desired. "Tell me what you want."

"You…you…know…" she gasped, pressing him closer, frantically clasping his hips, attempting to draw him back into her.

"It has a name," he told her brazenly. "Say it and it's yours."

Both excited and agitated, Mary Ellen frowned up at him, frantic to have him back inside her, reluctant to say such a word.

He read the reservation in her expressive dark eyes. She wanted it badly, but she hesitated to say it. He was determined to hear it. The Captain leaned down and kissed Mary Ellen passionately; then, trailing his lips across her flushed face, he whispered in her ear.

"No. No, I can't," she argued as he rose back up above her.

"You can. I know you can," he coaxed softly. "For me. Just for me."

On fire, in desperate need, Mary Ellen finally relented. Looking directly into his burning charcoal eyes, she said, "Captain, give me your cock!"

He gave it to her.

All of it.

She sighed with the sweet wonder of it.

And as they moved together in hurried, heated excitement, Mary Ellen wondered at herself and at him. They were shamelessly reckless and impetuous, behaving more like animals than civilized human beings. She had spoken a word aloud she'd never dreamed she would hear a man say, much less say herself.

And here she was, fully clothed save for her pantalets—she even had on her shoes and cotton stockings—making passionate love with this totally naked Yankee Captain in her lace-hung white-and-yellow girlhood bed while the lamp across the room washed over them and the bedroom door remained unlocked.

And it was pure heaven.

Much later that night, when the door was locked securely and the lamp had been extinguished and the two of them were naked in the midnight darkness of her room, Mary Ellen was curled comfortably against the Captain. She lay on her side, backed up to him, the crisp hair of his chest pleasantly tickling her back, his hard, hair-dusted thighs cradling her bare bottom. His long arm was around her, his hand cupping her breasts gently.

She could tell by his deep, even breathing that he was asleep.

She sighed.

She liked lying in his arms while he slept. She could almost forget—as he slumbered so peacefully and held her so possessively close—that he was a cold, cruel man who was manipulating her, exploiting her for his own greedy sexual pleasure.

Tears sprang to Mary Ellen's eyes as she recalled what a sweet, good-hearted boy he had been when they were children. Clay Knight had never been able

to inflict pain on anyone or anything. And when he un-
wittingly hurt somebody, he suffered more than his
victim.

A tear slipped from Mary Ellen's eye, splashed onto
her bare shoulder.

No matter how many times she'd gone over it, no matter how many times she had told herself she must face
the facts, she still found it impossible to believe that the
love of her youth had *never* loved her. Now here he was,
back. He was in her bed. He made exquisite love to her.

And still he didn't love her.

Mary Ellen blinked away her tears.

She couldn't pretend that she had never loved him.
She had. She had loved him with all her young heart.
She had never loved anyone else; would never love
anyone else. But she loved him no longer. She loved
no one. The Captain was not the only one whose heart
was made of ice. She could be just as indifferent, just
as unemotional, as he.

It didn't matter that he made love to her with only
his body, because she did the very same thing.

Satisfied that their heated couplings were inconse-
quential, Mary Ellen soon fell asleep.

When she awakened shortly after sunup, she was
surprised to see that he was still in bed with her. Supposing he was asleep, she carefully removed his encircling arm, scooted away, and rose to her knees.

"Come back here," he said, and his hands gripped
her waist, drew her down, and pulled her onto her side,
returning her to her former position against him.

"The sun's coming up," she warned. "The house
will be stirring."

"Let it stir," he said in a sleep-heavy voice, and his
dark hand moved over her.

The lean fingers spread on her bare, quivering belly and slipped down through the triangle of white-blond curls to touch and tease the tiny bud of her desire.

Mary Ellen's breath came out in a rush, and she wiggled and squirmed and sighed when she felt his powerful erection pulsating against the cleft in her bare buttocks.

"Ohhh," she murmured anxiously, involuntarily opening her legs and arching her back to afford him entrance. "Ohhhh, yes, yes." She gasped when she felt the hard, heavy flesh move between her legs and push cautiously up into her.

"Am I hurting you?" he asked, his breath hot and ragged on the nape of her neck.

"N-no…" she managed, "but I don't know how… I've never…"

"I'll show you, baby," he whispered, pressing heated kisses to her ivory shoulders. "Relax against me," he advised. "Let me do all the work. I'll go slowly, gently, until you're…" He thrust a little farther into her as she sighed and settled against him.

His strong but gentle hands guided her movements. He pressed her hips down on him as he thrust up into her. As promised, he was easy with her, pushing cautiously—inch by slow inch—until the full, throbbing length of him was buried in her.

"You all right, Mary?" he asked solicitously.

"Yes," she whispered, "I…yes…" she murmured, but she trembled in his embrace.

So he waited, lay there for a time, unmoving, letting her get comfortable with the position, with the feel of him taking her from behind.

One of his hands went between her legs, the other fondled her swelling breasts. Those skilled, eager dark hands labored at further arousing his pale, unsure lover. They worked wonders on her. Lost in the building ecstasy, Mary Ellen began to move seductively against him, and the Captain immediately found and matched her slow, sensual rhythm.

Their bodies joined, their hearts hammering, they moved slowly, perfectly together, the pleasure increasing steadily. At last their movements speeded up, and they surged and met in growing splendor while the strong rays of the rising summer sun spilled into the room and bathed their joined bodies with a warm pink light.

"Ohhhh, Cap... Oh!" Mary gasped as the first wave of her coming climax washed over her.

"Yes, baby, I know. Let it come," he encouraged hoarsely, knowing his own wrenching climax was close.

In seconds they were in the throes of blinding ecstasy, the incredible tremors of pleasure gripping them, buffeting them, casting them about as if they were a couple of children's spineless rag dolls. The spasms were so intense, so prolonged, Mary Ellen cried out again and again in her carnal joy as he held her tightly, staying with her, making sure she got as much as she wanted. Then he groaned in his own deep satisfaction.

When finally the extended orgasm had passed, two limp, perspiring lovers sagged into the soft mattress, their bodies still joined, their racing hearts beginning to slow to a more normal beat.

Sated and feeling wonderfully lazy, Mary Ellen wished they didn't have to get up. She wished they could lie there like this while the sun climbed high into the cloudless sky, reached its zenith, started down again, finally sank below the western horizon, and night settled over them.

The Captain stirred behind her. She felt him pull out of her and sit up. He leaned down, kissed the arch of her hip, and, trailing kisses down to her bent knee, bit her playfully and said, "Meet me in the master suite tonight at seven."

She hugged her pillow and purred, then argued, "The summer sun's still up at seven."

"Yes," he said, "I know."

"All right," she said, giving in happily.

"And Mary…"

"Yes?"

"Don't let me catch you going out alone at night ever again!"

Thirty-Four

Mary Ellen and the Captain carried on a torrid affair that rivaled the blistering heat of the hot Tennessee summer. Upstairs in the privacy of Longwood's large second floor, the pair repeatedly made love in the master suite before the French gold-framed mirrors. And in the master suite's spacious dressing room. In the roomy marble-walled bath. In the bath's marble tub. In Mary Ellen's white-and-yellow bedroom. In every single guest room. And even—a time or two—right out in the wide upstairs corridor.

They were insatiable.

Anytime one of them caught the other upstairs, a heated session of lovemaking ensued. Mary Ellen no longer made any pretense of not wanting him as much as he wanted her. She couldn't get enough. She surrendered willingly, again and again, to the burning passion he evoked. Succumbed enthusiastically, despite his curious insistence—every time they came together—on making certain she clearly understood that the fever-hot lovemaking meant nothing to him.

She meant nothing to him.

His unkind words hurt, cut her to the quick. She hated him for his cruelty, but she responded in kind. She assured him passionately that they were of the same mind. It was a relationship of convenience, grounded solely on physical, not emotional, need. So he needn't concern himself that she might learn to care for him. That would *never* happen. The *only* thing she wanted from him was just what he was giving her.

Nothing more.

When they were not upstairs making love, they might have been strangers. Whether alone or in the company of others, they never acknowledged each other. They never talked. They never dined together. They never went out together. Neither paid the other any attention.

They were lovers by night, enemies by day.

Until, curiously, Captain Knight abruptly stopped pursuing Mary Ellen. The first time it happened, Mary Ellen was at a complete loss. Around nine on a rainy August night, she had glimpsed the uniformed Captain smoking alone in her father's study.

When she walked by, he had glanced up. She knew he saw her. So Mary Ellen had gone straight up to bed to wait for him, leaving her bedroom door wide open.

She'd bathed, brushed out her long hair, and slipped into a never-before-worn champagne satin nightgown left over from her trousseau.

Impatient to be in the Captain's arms, she paced restlessly about, moving back and forth between her white-and-yellow bedroom and the mirrored master suite. She was in the wide upstairs hall when finally she caught sight of him. He stepped into the downstairs corridor and approached the grand staircase. He paused for a moment with a hand on the polished railing, a booted foot on the bottom step.

Then he started up the stairs.

Smiling, Mary Ellen shivered with anticipation and

hurried back into her room. She leapt up onto the turned-down bed and positioned herself provocatively against a bunch of lace-trimmed pillows piled up against the headboard. She wet her lips and smoothed her flowing blond hair back off her face. She eased the long satin shirt of her champagne nightgown up her pale thighs and eased one side of the low-cut lace bodice off her shoulder.

Anxiously she waited.

And waited.

Long minutes passed, and Captain Knight didn't walk through her bedroom door. Finally Mary Ellen got out of bed. She went out into the hall. The door of the master suite was now closed.

Mary Ellen moved swiftly to the closed door and lifted her hand, then lowered it without knocking. Baffled and incensed, she turned and went back to her own room, slamming the door.

The affair had ended.

It was over.

And Mary Ellen was relieved. She was sick of feeling guilty, dirty, as if she were as immoral as one of the paid strumpets down at Antole's. The dark, sensual Captain had brought out the very worst in her. She had been his convenient prostitute, engaging in any and every shameful act he suggested.

She was glad it was finally over.

She was also puzzled.

Mary Ellen saw less and less of Captain Knight. Suddenly he was rarely at Longwood. He left the mansion each evening before sunset, and he didn't return until late at night. Days passed without Mary Ellen even seeing him. And, perversely, that bothered her.

Night after sweltering night she lay awake in her lonely bed, imagining the handsome Captain in the arms of another woman. She tormented herself by wondering who had captured his fleeting attention. And she tortured herself by envisioning him doing to some other woman all the delightfully forbidden things he'd done to her.

Mary Ellen reminded herself repeatedly that she didn't care what he did or with whom. What difference did it make? None. None whatsoever. She was grateful he'd finally gone elsewhere in search of diversion. He had tired of her? Well, she had tired of him, too!

Mary Ellen was in just such a mood one hot August evening when she decided she'd walk down River Road to the old Templeton mansion and visit Leah Thompson. It was nearing sunset. Huge black clouds that had been boiling up in the summer sky all afternoon were now threatening rain.

But Mary Ellen chose to ignore the possibility of rain as well as the stern warnings of Captain Knight.

Don't let me catch you going out alone at night ever again! That was what he had said the night she'd found him sleeping in her bed.

"Well, don't worry, Captain. You won't catch me," she said aloud now as she came out of her room. "How could you when you're never here!"

Mary Ellen skipped down the stairs and plucked a pink parasol from the umbrella stand in the foyer. Disregarding the usual looks of inquiry and interest she drew from the sailors filling her parlor and front porch, she left.

Once at the Templeton mansion with the ever-cheerful Leah and her four spirited children, Mary Ellen immediately began to feel better. Leah had received a long letter from her husband, William, in Vicksburg, so she was in an exceptionally good mood. It rubbed off on Mary Ellen. Her sagging spirits lifting, she was soon laughing and enjoying herself. Leah cut a freshly baked chocolate cake and loudly cursed the Yankees because there was no coffee to go with it.

Mary Ellen, Leah, and the children gathered around the kitchen table just as a flash of heat lightning struck close by. Leah squealed and jumped. All four of her children giggled and teased her about being an old scaredy-cat.

With an echoing boom of thunder the rain started, coming out of the south, and Leah ordered everyone—including Mary Ellen—to start shutting windows. Laughing, they all raced about closing windows as the rain became a deluge, pouring down in blinding sheets. The windows closed, they returned to the kitchen. Gathered around the table, they enjoyed the chocolate cake as the torrential rains beat down loudly on the steep roof and lashed the lush river bluffs below.

The rain, coupled with the pleasure of being with the friendly, fun-loving Thompsons, caused Mary Ellen to stay longer than intended. It was after ten when finally she said she'd better leave, should have left an hour ago.

Even then Leah followed her to the door, saying, "You can't walk home in the rain. Stay and I'll send these wild Indian children of mine off to bed so we can talk."

"The rain's almost stopped," Mary Ellen told her. "I really need to get home. When you write William, tell him he's in my prayers. And thanks so much for the cake and the company."

"Anytime. You be careful now."

"I will."

Mary Ellen opened the pink parasol and stepped out into the gently falling rain. She walked rapidly, eager to reach the security of home. Blinking, peering ahead into the misty darkness, she saw no one on the road and credited the summer storm. Even the Yankees had enough sense to get in out of the rain.

Mary Ellen had gone less than a hundred yards down River Road when a drunken Union soldier leapt out of the bushes and grabbed her. The pink parasol flew out of her hand and she screamed in shocked surprise. The Yankee's large hand swiftly clamped over her mouth, and Mary Ellen felt herself being dragged backward into the rain-drenched trees and wet undergrowth.

She was roughly slammed down onto her back and temporarily lost her breath. Gasping, fighting for air, she regained her lost breath as the powerfully built soldier crawled atop her. Mary Ellen kicked and bit him and thrashed about, but she couldn't escape. Trapped beneath his huge, heavy body, she struggled impotently to rise. Frantic, she screamed and pleaded with him and knew it would do no good. She whipped her head about so violently her hair came undone, fell into her frightened face.

She wanted to die when the sweating, grunting drunk braced a muscular arm across her shoulders and chest and shoved up her skirts. Raindrops pelted her face as his big hand slid roughly up her thigh. She shuddered when he tore her pantalets and she felt the rain peppering her bared flesh. The big man began unbuttoning his uniform trousers, and Mary Ellen felt bile rise in her throat. The arm across her chest lifted. He grabbed her unbound hair and lowered his ugly face to hers.

Unable to move, Mary Ellen closed her eyes in horror as her heart tried to beat its way out of her chest. Body tensed, bracing for the pain to come, she was saved from a fate worse than death when the soldier's heavy weight abruptly left her. His blunt fingers pulled painfully at her tangled hair and then released it.

Mary Ellen's frightened eyes opened to see Captain Knight above her in the rain, his hand gripping the drunk's collar, pulling the grunting beast off her. Then the brutal slam of the Captain's fist against the man's startled face sounded like a pistol shot. The swift, powerful force of the blow knocked the soldier out cold, and Mary Ellen whimpered in stunned relief.

She was sitting up, smoothing down her damp, dirty skirts, when the Captain pulled her to her feet and put his arms around her.

"Are you all right?" he asked anxiously, his shaky voice betraying the depth of his concern. "Mary, did he hurt you?...Did he...?"

"No," she murmured, trembling like a leaf in the wind. She clung to him, burying her face in the curve of his neck and shoulder while the gentle rain pelted them. "No, you got here in time, Clay. Oh, Clay, Clay," she said, then choked, crying now.

"I've got you," he whispered against her wet, tangled hair, realizing that she had called him Clay instead of Captain. She hadn't called him Clay since they were children. "I've got you, Mary. No one can hurt you now. Shhh, don't cry. Shhh."

The tall Captain stood there in the falling rain, holding Mary Ellen close, comforting her, soothing her, murmuring her name over and over again in a tone of voice she hadn't heard before.

The moment of tenderness passed.

Captain Knight set her back and scowled at her, a muscle spasming his cheek. Nobody else on earth could give him such a scare. Damn her for frightening him so badly.

Mary Ellen stood before him, shivering with emotion. She looked young and vulnerable and incredibly desirable. Her face was wet with rain and tears, her hair dirty and tangled, her dress damp and clinging to her slender, shaking body.

Tense, angry, Captain Knight whistled for his well-trained black stallion, and the big beast came to him immediately. The Captain turned to the horse and swiftly unstrapped his rolled-up black slicker from behind the cantle. He shook out the slicker, draped it around Mary Ellen's shoulders, and drew her to him.

He raised a hand, swept a damp, dirty lock of hair from her cheek, and spontaneously lowered his mouth to her wet, trembling lips.

But he caught himself in time. He was an inch away from kissing her when he abruptly came to his senses, raised his dark head. Teeth gritted, he lifted Mary Ellen into the saddle. His silver eyes narrowed, he cast one quick glance at the unconscious soldier, vowing he'd deal with the drunken bastard later. He turned away angrily, leaving the soldier lying in the rain.

The Captain swung up behind Mary Ellen. He was stiff and silent as they rode to Longwood in the falling rain. But Mary Ellen was so grateful he had saved her and so happy to be enclosed inside his strong arms, she sighed and leaned back against his hard chest, laying her damp head on his shoulder.

She stole glances at his rain-wet profile outlined against the night sky, some features clearly defined, the others in deep shadow. His raven hair was wet and plastered to his well-shaped head, and diamond beads of rain clung to his long, sweeping eyelashes.

He looked like a dark god to her, and Mary Ellen could hardly wait to get home to Longwood. If what he was feeling was anything like what she was feeling, he would take her straight upstairs to his suite. Together they would strip and bathe away the rain and the dirt, and then they would get into that seven-and-a-half-foot-wide mahogany bed and make love while the rain peppered the balcony outside the open French doors.

As they rode up the pebbled drive of Longwood, Mary Ellen smiled contentedly.

But she blinked in disbelief when the Captain remained mounted, plucked her from the stallion's back, and deposited her at the front gate.

Then, without so much as a by-your-leave, he wheeled the big stallion about and rode off into the rainy night.

Thirty-Five

Captain Knight rode away from Longwood the minute he'd lowered Mary to her feet. It was one of the hardest things he had ever done. It took all his strong will and practiced self-control to leave her standing in the rain.

But he had to do it.

His dark face set, his gray eyes narrowed, Captain Knight dug his heels into the black stallion's flanks. The surprised creature neighed loudly but immediately went into a ground-eating gallop. Gravel crunched and flew beneath the black's striking hooves as he carried his troubled master swiftly down the pebbled drive.

The Captain had forced himself to stay away from Mary.

He had stopped making love to her when he found himself starting to fall in love with her all over again. He couldn't let that happen. He wouldn't. She wouldn't get a second crack at him. Not this boy.

At River Road the determined Captain turned his mount toward South Memphis. His blood up, wanting Mary, wanting to *not* want Mary, he headed for the city's most famous brothel.

He had not yet paid a visit to the plush sporting

house, but he'd heard from fellow officers that the women were extraordinarily beautiful and more than competent at their craft.

That was what he needed.

That was *all* he needed.

One beautiful woman was like another. He'd learned years ago that they were all the same. There was virtually no difference in any of them.

Including Mary Preble.

It wasn't Mary he wanted, it was a woman. Any woman. As long as she was beautiful. A night in the arms of a beautiful woman and this nagging tension would leave him.

When he reached the imposing three-story structure on the southern outskirts of the city, Captain Knight dismounted and tossed the reins to a waiting groom. He glanced about curiously. Fine carriages were parked around the lighted establishment, most with liveried drivers waiting patiently beside them. The house was doing a brisk business on this rainy August night.

Captain Knight climbed the red-brick mansion's stone steps, lifted the brass door knocker, rapped it a couple of times, then waited. He brushed raindrops from the shoulders of his white uniform blouse, withdrew a handkerchief from an inside pocket, and blotted the moisture from his dark face.

A smiling, red-jacketed butler opened the heavy oak front door. The Captain went inside and was directed to a spacious, richly carpeted parlor. The elegant room was filled with a mixture of uniformed officers and expensively dressed civilians and gorgeous, lushly gowned women.

White-jacketed waiters passed through the crowd,

serving stemmed glasses of chilled champagne. And in the far corner of the room, a smiling black man in evening clothes played a mellow love song on a square rosewood piano.

Captain Knight stood in the arched doorway, looking around leisurely, when an elegantly gowned, plump middle-aged woman stepped up beside him and took his arm. She greeted him warmly and scolded him teasingly for waiting so long to pay a call.

"Where have you been, Captain Knight?" she asked.

"You have me at a disadvantage," he said politely.

"Belle. Belle Leyland, Captain Knight," the buxom madam introduced herself, her fleshy cheeks dimpling. "My girls have seen you in town and they're most eager to entertain you."

He smiled and, spotting an extremely tall, incredibly glamorous redhead in a shimmering silver evening gown standing beside the massive piano, said decisively, "That one." He inclined his dark head. "The lady in silver."

The dimpling madam told him titteringly, "You've made a good choice, Captain. Her name's Lita, and she's only been with me a few weeks. Came here from New Orleans and she—"

"I'll want her for the entire night," he interrupted the madam's monologue. "And I want her now."

"Ah, our handsome Captain is most eager. Lita will be delighted." The madam motioned to the leggy Lita, and the large, luscious redhead crossed the crowded room. She wore nothing beneath the shimmering silver gown, and as she walked unhurriedly toward him, her unfettered breasts bounced appealingly and the shiny silver fabric pulled across her stomach and hips.

The statuesque Lita reached them, laid a red-nailed hand on the Captain's damp uniform blouse, and smiled at him seductively. At six feet she was almost as tall as he, and her body was as white and as soft as his was dark and hard. Her flaming red hair framed a beautiful face with large green eyes and a wide, red mouth.

Surely this exotic Amazon could make him forget the slender, pale-haired mistress of Longwood.

"Forgive my appearance, Lita," he said, sliding a long arm around her waist. "I was caught in the rain."

Her emerald eyes aglow, she said, "Why, you look good enough to eat, *mon Capitaine.*"

He laughed, and the leggy Lita took his arm and ushered him up the carpeted stairs. The pair had started down the long upstairs corridor when a tall, richly dressed gentleman with mussed blond hair and bleary eyes exited one of the many bedrooms.

The blond man looked up, and his gaze clashed with the Captain's.

"Knight," he said, stepping in front of them, "Clay Knight!"

Nodding almost imperceptibly, Captain Knight responded coolly, "Hello, Lawton."

Half drunk, Daniel Lawton gave the red-haired Lita an apologetic smile and said to the Captain, "Can I have a word with you, Knight?"

Captain Knight's hand possessive on the redhead's bare arm, he said, "Anytime, Lawton. Naval headquarters are open daily. Now, if you'll excuse us…"

"No, wait," said Daniel Lawton, a degree of urgency in his voice. "Give me five minutes. Please, it's important. There's something I want to get off my chest."

The redhead squeezed the Captain's muscular arm, indicated a closed door, and said, "I'll be waiting for you, Captain. Hurry."

Captain Knight watched her walk away. He was irritated and anxious to be rid of Daniel Lawton. But he reluctantly allowed the half-drunk man to guide him down the long hall and outside onto a small balcony. When they stepped out into the rain, the Captain's irritation grew.

"What's on your mind, Lawton?" he asked impatiently.

"Mary Ellen," said Daniel.

The expression on Captain Knight's face changed quickly. The rain and the redhead forgotten, he listened attentively while the slightly inebriated Daniel Lawton confessed what had really happened all those years ago.

Speaking rapidly, as if more than anxious to tell it, Daniel began, "One afternoon in the late spring of forty-eight, John Thomas Preble asked me to come down to the Cotton Company for a talk. I had no idea what was on his mind until I got there." Daniel inhaled heavily, shook his blond head, and continued. "He shut his office door and said, 'Daniel, my boy, how would you like to marry my beautiful daughter, Mary Ellen?' Now I admit that I had always wanted Mary Ellen, but I knew it was out of the question because she loved you. John Thomas said you weren't good enough for his daughter, that he was going to get you out of the way, and then Mary Ellen would fall right into my arms."

Daniel Lawton stood there in the gently falling rain, telling how John Thomas Preble had so cunningly, cleverly planned everything down to the last detail and had successfully manipulated all of them.

"As soon as Preble sent you off to Baltimore for those academy entrance interviews, he told Mary Ellen you had jilted her. Said you didn't want her, didn't love her and never had. Said you'd used her to get what you really wanted—an appointment to Annapolis."

His dark face impassive, Clay listened as Daniel Lawton continued, relating how the badly hurt, grieving Mary Ellen had been sent to Europe and then coerced into marriage. Daniel talked and talked, explaining everything, leaving out nothing.

He told Captain Clay Knight that Mary Ellen's father had lied to her, just as he had to Clay. He swore that she was totally innocent and ignorant of all the wrongdoing.

The rain and the gravity of his confession sobering him, Daniel Lawton related the whole sordid story to the tall, dark man whose sweetheart he had stolen. He admitted to being a willing party to John Thomas Preble's ruse and said that the heartbroken Mary Ellen had never loved him, that their marriage had been a charade from the very beginning.

Finally convinced Lawton was telling the truth, Captain Knight said, "Why? Why are you telling me this now?"

Daniel Lawton said sadly, truthfully, "I'm not much of a man, Knight. I've never worked a day in my life. I'm aimless and lazy. I'm a lousy husband and an indifferent father. I'm a drunk and a womanizer. And a coward as well. Bought my way out of serving in the war." He sighed wearily then and admitted candidly, "I'd like to do one thing in my life that I can feel good about."

Captain Knight left the brothel immediately.

He rode even faster going back to Longwood than

when he'd left. Laughing in the rain, his heart pounding with excitement, he raced happily home to Mary.

Once there he climbed the stairs anxiously, taking them two at a time, and went straight to Mary's door. He lifted a dark hand, then lowered it without knocking.

Tempted as he was, he knew he would have to wait. If he asked her to let him in, she'd suppose he wanted only to make love to her. He stood outside her door for a long, agonizing time. And finally turned and walked away.

Inside, Mary Ellen had heard his approach. She had sensed he was standing outside her door. Wondering what kept him from knocking, wishing he had, glad he hadn't, she sagged to her knees and leaned her cheek against the door.

He crossed the hall to the master suite, closing the door quietly behind him. He shrugged out of his damp uniform jacket and lighted a cigar. In the shadowy sitting room he smoked and paced restlessly. As he walked back and forth, back and forth, doubts and worry set in to take the edge off his exhilaration.

The newly learned truth, as sweet as it was to know, changed little. Too much time had passed. Too much had happened.

Who was he to suppose that Mary might still care for him? She didn't. She had told him as much many times. And even if that were not completely true, if she had cared just a little, he had managed to kill any lasting love she'd had for him.

He closed his eyes in pain, recalling how he had treated Mary since occupying Longwood. He had been cruel and mean and had shown her no respect. He had coldly seduced her and then used her as though she were one of the women down at Antole's.

Ashamed, heartsick, he came to the sad conclusion that it would do no good to tell Mary the truth about what had happened when they were children in love.

It was too late.

Much too late.

Thirty-Six

At noon the next day Mary Ellen was at the Shelby County Hospital, giving a wounded Confederate soldier a bed bath, when another volunteer came into the ward, hunting for her.

Mary Ellen apologized to her patient, stuck her head around the white privacy screen, and said, "Right here. What is it, Amanda?"

"There's a gentleman downstairs saying he must speak to you at once," the young woman said. Mary Ellen's heartbeat quickened instantly. "I'll take over here," Amanda Clark told her. "You go down, Mary Ellen. Go on."

"Thanks." Mary Ellen turned back, patted the patient's shoulder, smiled at him, and said, "Amanda will take good care of you."

Mary Ellen hastily washed her hands and took off her soiled white apron. She smoothed her hair, anxiously tucked loosened strands under the neatly plaited braid wound around the crown of her head. She eagerly fled the stifling hot ward and hurried down the stairs, automatically looking about for Captain Knight.

Daniel Lawton stepped forward.

Mary Ellen was both surprised and disappointed.

Daniel took her arm and said, "Mary Ellen, I must talk with you."

"Daniel, I'm very busy and—"

"Please," he said, and guided her out the front door and down the steps.

"What's this all about?" she asked, annoyed.

Pleading with her to keep quiet and listen to what he'd come to say, Daniel told her.

Everything.

Speechless, Mary Ellen stared at the man who had once been her husband as he stood there in August sunshine and confessed to a terrible deception. He told Mary Ellen, just as he had told Clay, exactly what had happened. Stunned, Mary Ellen listened in silence, her lips parted, her dark eyes wide with shock and disbelief.

"Your father told you Knight didn't love you, that he'd heartlessly used you to get an appointment to the Naval Academy. At the same time he told Knight that you were foolish and fickle and fell into my arms the minute he was gone."

"No. No," Mary Ellen murmured, shaking her head as if to clear it.

"Knight was as heartbroken as you were, Mary Ellen."

"But if that were true, then…why…why didn't he at least try to get in touch with me and—"

"He did. He wrote letters just as you did, but all were intercepted and destroyed."

"You mean Clay never received any of my—"

"No. Not a one."

"Dear God!" Mary Ellen exclaimed. "Clay thought that I…all this time he…he…" She swallowed hard, then asked, "Why? Why would Papa do such a horrible thing?"

"He wanted the best for you, Mary Ellen. He thought Knight was beneath you, that you deserved better." He smiled then, sheepishly, sadly. "So he called on me." Daniel shrugged and hung his head.

"Why did you agree?" she asked, half dazed by what he had told her.

Daniel raised his blond head. "Because I wanted you so badly I didn't care how I got you so long as you were mine." He exhaled heavily, then said, "But you were never mine, you were always Clay Knight's."

"Yes," she said wistfully, "I was."

"I'm sorry, Mary Ellen. You may not believe me, but it's the truth. I told Knight about this yesterday, but then I got to worrying. I was afraid he might not say anything to you. He might think it was too late. He might leave again with you never knowing. So I came here to tell you myself."

Mary Ellen nodded, the realization of what this could mean beginning to fully dawn on her. Daniel continued to talk, to explain and clarify anything that might still be a mystery, to tell her he was sure Clay had suffered as much as she had. When he was finished, Mary Ellen was smiling, hope causing her heart to beat erratically.

She impetuously threw her arms around the astonished Daniel Lawton's neck and hugged him. "Oh, Daniel, thank you, thank you so much!"

"You mean you don't hate me?"

"Hate you? I don't hate anyone," Mary Ellen said happily. "I love everyone alive!"

Mary Ellen ran all the way home. Out of breath, a stitch in her left side, she hurried up the mansion's front steps, shouting Clay's name. She ran through the big house calling to him, startling old Titus from his noontime nap.

He grinned and pointed. "The Cap'n is down at the stable with his—"

Mary Ellen was out the back door before Titus could finish his sentence. Skirts lifted, she sprinted across the terraced north lawn as the sun reached its zenith. She flew past the old sundial and the white summerhouse. Breathing so hard her lungs burned, she raced around the silent carriage house. The long run had jarred loose her neatly plaited hair; it had fallen down, and the long braid was bouncing off her back.

Holding her aching side, her heart pounding in her ears, the badly winded Mary Ellen finally stepped into the open door of the small, shadowy barn. Shirtless, his back to her, Clay was currying his black stallion.

Swallowing with difficulty, her hand on her racing heart, Mary Ellen softly spoke his name. "Clay."

The currying brush poised in his hand, he turned around slowly and saw the look in her eyes. His dark face brightened, and he broke into a wide grin.

"You know," he said, and it was a statement, not a question.

"Everything!" she assured him. "Daniel told me."

Mary Ellen pulled the door shut as Clay dropped the brush and opened his arms wide in invitation. She ran to him eagerly, and then they were in each other's arms, saying "I love you, I love you!" between anxious kisses.

Passions flared immediately.

"Clay, darling," Mary Ellen said breathlessly, "let's go up to the house—"

"It's too far, sweetheart," he murmured against her throat.

They couldn't wait. Kissing hotly and whispering endearments, they sagged to their knees on the straw-strewn floor. Kneeling there in bands of bright August sunlight slicing through the stable's weathered plank walls, they anxiously undressed each other.

When they were naked Clay sank back on his bare heels, spread his knees, and reached for Mary Ellen. She came to him breathlessly, climbing astride his hard thighs. Both watched and sighed as she clutched his wide shoulders and impaled herself upon him. His hands gripping her flared hips, Clay bent his dark head and kissed her bare breasts while he plunged into her. Her arms wrapped around his neck, Mary Ellen gasped with pleasure, her head thrown back, a smile of pure joy on her fevered face.

The pair made hurried, heated love there on the straw-covered floor while Clay's indignant black stallion danced about nervously, whinnying, snorting, and tossing its great head.

The lovers ignored him.

They climaxed quickly, and afterward Clay rose to his knees, bringing Mary Ellen with him. A strong supporting hand beneath her buttocks, his body still a part of hers, he put out a stiffened arm and lowered her gently to the straw, following her down.

For a long moment he lay silently atop her while she sighed and stretched in sweet contentment, her eyes closed, her arms draped around his neck, a hand idly stroking the silky black hair at the back of his head.

Finally Clay kissed her ear and said, "Marry me, Mary Preble."

Mary Ellen's dreamy dark eyes opened. Her arms fell heavily to her sides as she smiled and said, "I'll marry you, Clay Knight. When?"

"Today."

"Yes!" she said excitedly. "Let's get dressed and—"

"Wait, sweetheart," he said, and Mary Ellen felt him stir inside her.

Clay rose up over her, a wicked smile on his full lips. Surprised but pleased, Mary Ellen lay there smiling up at him while he swelled and surged inside her. He began to move his pelvis seekingly and sliding strongly into her. Wholly erect again, he penetrated to his full length, and Mary Ellen sighed and wrapped her slender arms around his neck, her long legs around his back.

This time they made love more leisurely, but just as lustily, as if each had been long starved for the other and must feast yet again. They looked into each other's eyes as they moved together sensuously, their souls as well as their bodies mating.

Now of the same mind, heart, and body, the deeply-in-love pair communicated perfectly without speaking. Silently they agreed to prolong the pleasure. To extend the ecstasy. To delay the delivery.

It was sweet, sweet agony.

Incredibly exciting to maintain their heated level of passion without ending it in swift orgasm. Mary Ellen bit the inside of her lip in an effort to keep from climaxing and heard his gentle words of praise wash over her.

"Yes, baby, that's good. So good. Hold back for just a while longer. Keep loving me, sweetheart."

Mary Ellen listened and heeded this magnificent man who was to be her husband and who had taught her all she knew about love and lovemaking. She thrilled to the sure knowledge that he would continue to teach her through the long, happy years to come.

Proud of herself for already learning a small measure of control, Mary Ellen moved erotically with her adored lover, but in carefully reined-in splendor. They played and pleasured each other there on the straw in the shafts of sunlight while the excited stallion reared and whinnied, threatening to kick down the walls around them.

At last neither could wait any longer.

"Now, darling," Mary Ellen gasped.

"Yes, baby," Clay murmured hoarsely.

The delayed release was frightening in its intensity, and Mary Ellen viciously bit Clay's sweat-slick shoulder to keep from screaming while he groaned and spasmed wildly against her.

When finally it had passed, when they lay limp and perspiring in the straw, Clay raised his dark head, smiled down at Mary Ellen, and said, "Jesus, honey, that was so good it scared the hell out of me."

"Scared you?" Mary Ellen said. "I thought I was dying!"

And they began to laugh. Clay fell over onto his back beside Mary Ellen, and they lay there laughing deliriously for several minutes.

Finally they calmed, and Mary Ellen said, a smile in her voice, "Now about that marriage proposal, Clayton Terrell Knight... Was that just passion speaking, or does it still stand?"

Grinning, Clay rose onto an elbow, looked down at her. He picked a piece of straw from the frazzled blond braid lying over her shoulder, and the smile abruptly left his handsome face. Solemnly he said, "I love you, Mary Preble, with all my heart and soul."

"Oh, Clay, did you miss me as I missed you?"

"Every day was a year."

"For me, too," she said honestly.

"I never stopped loving you, Mary, not for a min-

ute. You'll never know how very sorry I am for all the
cruel things I've said and done to you since I came
back. It's no excuse, but I was badly hurt and I wanted
to hurt you. Forgive me, Mary, even if I don't deserve
it. I'm sorry, I swear I am. Marry me, sweetheart. Let
me make it up to you. Tell me you'll be my wife and
I promise to love you and cherish you for the rest of
our lives."

"Oh, Clay," Mary Ellen said, tears of happiness filling her dark eyes. "All I've ever wanted was to be your
wife. I love you so much. I thought I'd die without
you."

"I know, Mary, I know," he said softly. "Don't cry,
sweetheart. No more tears."

She blinked away the tears, smiled, and said, "Do
you remember what you said to me in the summerhouse the first time you ever kissed me?"

Clay smiled and shook his dark head.

Then he repeated the words he'd said so long ago.
"You're mine, for now and always. You belong to my
heart. No other lips must kiss you but mine, no other
arms must hold you but mine." He paused, grinned
devilishly, and asked, just as he'd asked that cold February day, "Do you understand?"

"I do," she said as she'd said then, thrilled and flattered that he could remember verbatim the words he'd
said to her that day. "Oh, I do. Now please, Clay. Kiss
me the way you kissed me that day."

He leaned down, gently pressed his closed lips to
hers, and said against her mouth, "We'll get married
today and catch up on all the years we lost. What do
you say, sweetheart?"

"Yes! Yes! Yes!"

Thirty-Seven

At five o'clock that same afternoon, Mary Ellen Preble finally became the bride of Captain Clayton Terrell Knight. The handsome pair stood at the altar in the old Asbury Chapel while a distinguished, gray-haired Union naval chaplain read the rites.

Suffused sunlight spilling through the tall stained-glass windows fell on the pair, illuminating them softly, giving them an almost mystical appearance. It was as if they'd been touched by the angels.

The slender, pale-skinned bride looked unusually young and beautiful in a simple low-necked summer dress of lilac dotted swiss. Her white-blond hair, freshly shampooed and shimmering with healthy life, was swept atop her and secured with a tortoise-shell comb. In her hand she held a well-thumbed white leather Bible, atop which lay a lace-doilied nosegay of fragrant hothouse flowers.

The tall, dark groom looked remarkably boyish and handsome in his starched summer whites. Medals decorated his broad chest, and the blouse's double row of brass buttons glittered in the mellow light. A wide sash circled his trim waist. His heavy ceremonial sword rested against his white-trousered thigh, and snowy white gloves were tucked in the sash.

On Mary Ellen's left stood the tall, plain Leah Thompson. The smiling matron of honor held a bouquet of pink roses in her hands. On Clay's right stood the young, freckle-faced Ensign Johnny Briggs. The beaming best man clutched a plain gold wedding band in the palm of his white-gloved hand.

Few witnesses sat on the hard hickory pews of the dim chapel. Old Titus was there, dabbing at his watery eyes. Mattie, in her best Sunday bonnet, was beside him. Leah Thompson's well-scrubbed children—lectured thoroughly by their momma to keep quiet and behave themselves—gazed at the pair solemnly exchanging vows.

When Clay slipped the gold wedding band on the third finger of Mary Ellen's left hand, she looked into his beautiful silver eyes and saw a mist of tears shining there. Her full heart instantly swelled with such a surge of compassionate love, she could hardly breathe. Never in all the years she'd known him had she seen her beloved Clay cry.

Tears of happiness spilled freely down her own cheeks. Her slim fingers clasped his lean dark hand when Clay spoke quietly, in his most even, self-assured voice, repeating the wedding vows.

"Until death do us part," he concluded.

And for one fleeting second Mary Ellen's complete happiness was marred by a frightening thought. Suddenly she was acutely aware of the never-before-considered possibility that her husband could be killed in the continuing war!

The fear was gone as quickly as it had come when the chaplain announced that Clay could kiss the bride and she was anxiously swept into the security of her husband's strong arms.

The assembled guests waved and tossed rice as the pair hurried up the aisle of the chapel and out into the hot Tennessee sunshine. A large gathering of the sailors in Captain Knight's command greeted them with laughter and shouts and whistles.

Smiling and nodding to his troops, the Captain hurriedly handed his beautiful bride up into a waiting carriage and climbed in beside her. The pair held hands and laughed on the ride south to the hotel; the clatter of tin cans and old shoes tied to the rear of the carriage loudly announced their approach.

People on the street turned to look and point. Familiar faces peered curiously at the passing coach, and Mary Ellen and Clay knew that by nightfall the entire city would know of the afternoon nuptials and all Memphis would be abuzz with speculation and gossip.

Neither cared.

At the elegant old Gayoso House, Memphis's finest, they were immediately shown to a suite that had been readied for their arrival. The big hotel was no longer open to guests; it had been taken over completely by Union troops. But Captain Knight, as commander of all naval occupying forces, had only to issue the command and a luxurious top-floor corner suite was immediately vacated and made ready for the couple's wedding night.

The Gayoso House was one of the city's and the South's greatest buildings. The stately two-hundred-fifty-room hotel had its own waterworks, gasworks for gaslighting, bakeries, wine cellar, sewer and drainage system, and, of course, indoor plumbing. It was the perfect place for a happy, if brief, honeymoon.

After the sumptuous five-course wedding supper served in the elegant sitting room of the corner suite,

the newlyweds stripped and, ignoring the huge marble tub with its silver faucets, made use of the hotel's
hot shower. A novelty boasted only by the Gayoso
House, the marble-walled shower was roomy enough
for two. Especially when those two preferred to stand
so close their bare, slippery bodies touched and they
couldn't keep their hands off each other.

Happy as they'd never been before in their lives,
Mary Ellen and Clay laughed and sang and soaped
each other in the steamy shower. Finally the laughter
waned away to smiles. The loud singing softened and
died out. Only the sensuous soaping continued. Then
that too slowed and ceased as the soap fell forgotten
to the floor and they stood under the strong spray of
water, kissing, touching, sighing.

"I'm not sure this will work, darling," Mary Ellen
said skeptically, blinking to see him through the thick
vapor as Clay pressed her back against the slick marble wall, his straining masculinity pulsing against her
bare, wet belly.

"Trust me, Mrs. Knight," he said, then bent to kiss
her hotly, his tongue sliding into her mouth, tasting,
questing, his hands sweeping over her sleek, bare body.

As he kissed her Clay drew her arms up around his
neck and put his hands to her narrow waist. Feasting
on her open lips with sensuous relish, he urged her up
onto tiptoe. Then, with the greatest of ease, he lifted
her slightly up off the wet shower floor.

His burning lips finally left hers and his hand slid
down her left thigh. His lean fingers curled around the
back of her knee and eased her leg up. Getting only
glimpses of his handsome face through the impenetrable mist, Mary Ellen clung to his neck while he hooked
her bent leg over his arm. Mary Ellen sighed when

Clay bent his knees, crouched down, and with his free hand, guided himself up into her.

"Ohhhhh, Clay," she murmured, her arms wrapped around his neck, her head pressed back against the shower wall.

"Told you," he whispered, and began the slow, erotic movements of loving.

By nature a sensual woman, Mary Ellen instantly loved this new method of mating. How unconventional, how incredibly thrilling, to make love standing up! Especially standing up in a marble shower so hot she could hardly breathe and so steamy she could barely see the brand-new husband who was doing such wonderful things to her.

Mary breathed through her mouth and clasped handfuls of Clay's wet raven hair while he held her fast and drove slowly, gently, into her.

Transported, Mary Ellen, smiling foolishly, said, "Clay…"

"What, sweetheart?"

"How much do you suppose it would cost us to install a shower at Longwood?"

Clay grinned, leaned down, and kissed her open lips. Then he flexed his hard buttocks and increased the length of his stroke, letting himself sink fully into her, his granite hardness piercing her velvet softness.

The naked newlyweds stood in the steamy hot shower, making steamy hot love. And it was wonderful. Everything about it. The billowing clouds of mists swirling about them, one second concealing them from one another, the next revealing them to each other. The wetness of their bodies, causing them to slip and slide so seductively together, up and down and back and forth.

And in and out. The moist, enveloping heat raising

their temperatures, flushing their faces, and making them so weak they could hardly stand.

It was out-of-this-world wonderful, and when their simultaneous climax came, neither made any attempt to muffle their cries and whimpers and moans and shouts and groans of ecstasy.

The last tremors finally subsiding, Mary Ellen sagged back against the shower wall, her eyes closed, too spent to move.

"Baby, you okay?" asked her worried husband.

Her eyes opened and she smiled at him. She said, "If you want me clean again, you'll have to see to it yourself. I haven't the energy."

Clay laughed, kissed her, and said, "Sweetheart, it will be my pleasure."

He took her arm, gently drew her forward to stand under the strong, peppering spray. He stepped behind her, urged her back against his tall, supporting frame, and washed away all traces of their lovemaking—first from her body, then from his own. When both were as clean and fresh as newborn babes, Clay led his light-headed wife out of the shower and dried them both with half a dozen white towels.

Thanking him, Mary Ellen reached for the satin nightgown and lace-trimmed negligee she'd packed so carefully.

Clay laughed and said, "You won't need that."

Mary Ellen clutched it to her, suddenly shy about her nudity. "Please, Clay," she said, looking and sounding like a little girl, "I'd feel better with it on."

He saw she meant it, so he said, "Then put it on, baby." He reached out, touched her cheek affectionately, and told her, "I'll give you a little privacy while I put on my pants."

"Thank you, darling."

"You're very welcome," he said, thinking that she was surely the cutest and sweetest of women. Over his shoulder he said, "When you're dressed come on out and we'll watch the sun set."

"I'd like that."

"I like *you*."

Smiling as he left her, Clay found it utterly enchanting that she was suddenly modest and self-conscious. After having just been about as intimate as two people could possibly be, all at once she was uncomfortable with her nakedness, and his.

In the bedroom Clay stepped into his white trousers and buttoned them over his brown belly as he walked into the sitting room. He stood before a tall open window and looked out at the timbered Tennessee countryside as the hot August sun set across the Mississippi River. He sighed, and his bare chest expanded with a happiness almost too great to bear as he gazed contentedly at the lush land that was his home.

Abruptly he shuddered, as if someone had walked across his grave. He rarely considered his mortality, but now he was struck by the very real possibility that he might be killed in the war.

It went right out of his head when his beautiful bride silently entered the sitting room, stepped up behind him, wrapped her arms around his bare torso, and laid her cheek on his back.

"I love you," she whispered, and brushed a kiss to his smooth olive flesh. "If I live to be a hundred, or if I die tomorrow, I could never possibly be any happier than I am right here, right now with you."

Clay swallowed hard, and Mary Ellen felt his chest and stomach muscles tightening, rippling as he said,

"Mary, you can't imagine how many times I've dreamed of the two of us being here like this." He gently withdrew her hands from around his waist and turned to face her. "Not a single day went by that I didn't think of you, want you, love you."

"I know, my darling," Mary Ellen said. "It was the same for me." She reached up, touched his lean jaw with loving fingers, and said, "Promise you'll never leave me again."

Clay exhaled heavily, settled his hands on her narrow waist, and said, "I can't promise you that, Mary Ellen. But I do promise to love you for the rest of my life."

"And I you," she said, leaning into him, laying her cheek to his naked chest.

"Now what about that sunset," Clay said, smiling. He set her back, crossed the room, and dragged a long camel-backed sofa up to the windows.

He extended his hand to the couch, and Mary Ellen sat down. Clay dropped down beside her, smiled, and undid the tiny hooks at the throat of her lace-trimmed negligee. He swept the frothy fabric apart to reveal the shimmering beige satin nightgown beneath.

"God, you're beautiful," he said, awed. "And you're mine. I still can't believe."

"Believe it," she said.

He leaned down, pressed a kiss to the bare swell of her breast, then, catching Mary Ellen totally off guard, he dropped his head into her lap, turned about, and stretched his long body out on the sofa.

Laughing softly, Mary Ellen lifted a hand and with her fingers slowly, caressingly, traced the line of his strong features, touched the blue-black hair of his temples, then the place where it curled so appealingly around his ears.

"Have you ever known total peace?" she asked him.

His silver eyes closing, the long lashes sweeping down over his tanned cheeks, he said, "Not until now."

They fell silent then. Mary Ellen continued to stroke Clay's face, his hair, his wide shoulders, as the last blood red rays of the dying Tennessee sun washed over them.

She smiled with amused pleasure when she realized her lusty bridegroom had fallen asleep. In slumber his face had lost its hardness. In repose his beautifully chiseled features were again those of the sweet young boy she had fallen in love with when she was a girl. He might have been eighteen, not thirty-two.

Mary Ellen never considered waking Clay. She sat there cradling his dark head, enjoying the sweetness of the moment. Her lips turned up into a smile of pleasure as she thought to herself that a man would never have understood it, but to a woman this sweet sexless interlude was every bit as enjoyable as the ecstasy in the shower.

With the dark head of her sleeping husband, the only man she'd ever loved, resting in her lap, Mary Ellen Preble Knight silently ordered time to stand still.

Thirty-Eight

Time stood still.

A moment carved out of eternity.

Mary Ellen felt a sense of serene contentment as she sat there in the fading summer light, studying the noble contours of her husband's head and face.

Her bliss far exceeded imagination's fondest dreams.

She was so completely happy, she was afraid it might actually be a dream. A beautiful, longed-for dream that would vanish when she awakened.

Mary Ellen closed her eyes and took a long, slow breath. Praying this was no dream, that her beloved Clay was really here and really hers, she waited several long seconds. Then, almost fearfully, she opened her dark, hopeful eyes.

And immediately laughed with girlish delight.

Clay was wide awake and smiling impishly at her. He lifted a leanly muscled arm, hooked a hand around the back of her neck, and said in a deep, low voice, "From now on I want your face to be the first thing I see when I awaken. Think you can manage that?"

"I'll do my very best," she promised smilingly, leaned down, and kissed him.

By unspoken mutual consent, the couple migrated

to the bedroom and the big comfortable bed. While twilight deepened into darkness, they made slow, sweet, married love. Then they lay there and held hands and cuddled and laughed and talked and planned and dreamed until late in the night. And they promised each other they would spend every anniversary in this same room. This same bed.

Finally both were so tired and sleepy that they had no choice but to allow their perfect wedding day to come to an end. Sighing softly, Mary Ellen drifted toward dreamless slumber, finding comforting solidity in the hard breast muscles her sleepy head rested upon.

When she awakened the next morning, she opened her eyes to see Clay beaming down at her. She trembled in delight. And felt a quickening excitement when he drew her against him. His hand swept over her with a new tenderness, the lean fingers softly caressing.

"Good morning, my love," he said, and kissed her.

And the good morning became an even better one.

At noon the newlyweds checked out of the Gayoso House and went home. Home to Longwood. The family home was now just that again: the family home. As his wedding gift to Mary Ellen, Clay had moved his naval command to the long-vacant Alexander mansion on Madison. All the uniformed men who had occupied Longwood were gone. The newlyweds had the house to themselves.

And there followed an Indian summer of Tennessee pleasures—swimming in the river, swinging in the summerhouse, playing the piano and singing, card games in the study, and croquet games on the terraced lawn. They sipped iced lemonade on the shaded gallery and took rides through the woods on Clay's big black stallion and strolled, hand in hand, down the city streets, window shopping leisurely.

They bought a watermelon and ate the juicy slices out on the back gallery. They lay on their backs out by the old sundial and studied the stars at night. They read poetry together. They took long walks along the river bluffs at sunset. They danced on the upstairs balcony at midnight.

They embraced life fully, finding magic in the simplest of joys as long as they were together.

The brief hours they spent apart were sheer agony. But the reunions were sweet indeed. Mary Ellen still had her volunteer duties at Shelby County Hospital, and Clay had his continuing military responsibilities. But both managed to spend less time than usual at their respective tasks. More than one sunny noon Clay left the Madison Street headquarters to come by the clinic, where the pair shared a picnic lunch of bread and cheese and cold roast beef on the shaded hospital grounds.

And he was unfailingly there to meet her at day's end. Sometimes they went straight home to Longwood. Other times they dined at one of Memphis's many restaurants, the crowded eating establishments thriving in the wartime economy as never before.

Clay and Mary Ellen refused to think past the precious golden hours in which they happily found themselves.

They lived every minute to the fullest, as carefree as two irresponsible kids. Indulging themselves at every opportunity, they behaved like happy children, doing all the things they used to do together.

The war did not exist.

Life was heaven on earth.

Thirty-Nine

The weather stayed warm and balmy right on into October, but the telltale signs of autumn were beginning to appear. The leaves on the great white oaks and elms were changing color and falling to the ground. The hot sun already seemed to come from another direction; its light was not quite so brilliant, its sting not quite so harsh.

And, of course, there was the river.

The old Mississippi changed with the seasons.

On the long, hot summer days of July and August, the wide river was a bright golden hue and it hummed and rippled with myriad insects skimming its smooth surface. As the summer sun set each evening, the river turned to gleaming copper for a brief time, then to a bright blood red as the sun sank behind its western banks.

Now as autumn settled over the lush timberlands, millions of multicolored leaves drifted lazily down the long, wide waterway. Too soon, patterns of lacy ice would form along the banks as both the nights and the river turned cold and dark, proclaiming that winter had come to western Tennessee.

While neither spoke of their inevitable parting, both Mary Ellen and Clay sensed that he wouldn't be at

Longwood to celebrate their first Christmas as man and
wife. Clay was surprised he'd been in Memphis as
long as he had. The federally ruled river city was secured and peaceful; the smuggling was contained.
There was no further need for him to remain. Any day
orders could come for his departure and return to battle.

But he said nothing to Mary.

When November came to the Queen City on the
Bluffs and chill winds blew from out of the north,
Mary Ellen seemed to blossom like a flower in the
springtime. Her dark eyes glittered with an inner
light, and touches of color brightened her pale
cheeks.

Clay wondered if it were his imagination, or was his
bride growing lovelier and happier with every passing
day.

He had no idea that the added glow, the shining
eyes, were due to a wonderful secret Mary Ellen was
keeping. She strongly suspected that she was pregnant, but she was not going to tell her husband until
she was absolutely certain.

The first week of November Mary Ellen quietly
made an appointment to see Dr. Cain, the intrepid
white-haired physician she worked alongside at the
hospital. It was a cold, rainy Tuesday when the doctor
confirmed her suspicions, and then for Mary Ellen the
sun was shining everywhere.

"You are indeed pregnant, Mrs. Knight," said the el-
derly physician. "You can expect your child around the
first of June."

"Oh, Dr. Cain," Mary Ellen said happily, "thank
you so much!"

The aging doctor smiled at the beaming young

woman. "Don't thank me, thank that husband of yours." And he chuckled at his little joke.

"I'll do that," said Mary Ellen.

"Must have got pregnant on your wedding night," the doctor mused aloud, counting on his fingers, and Mary Ellen felt herself blushing.

"So it would seem," she said. She leapt up from her chair and started to leave the doctor's small, cluttered office on the ground floor of the Shelby County Hospital, but he stopped her.

"Wait, Mary Ellen. Sit back down and let's talk awhile."

Nodding, smiling, Mary Ellen sat down, but she couldn't sit still. Hands clasped and twisting in her lap, ankles together and toes tapping on the floor, she said, "Heavens, there's so much for me to learn, isn't there? I've never been around an infant in my life and I... I... What is it, Dr. Cain? Why are you frowning?"

"Was I? I didn't realize it." He leaned up to his desk, took off his spectacles, and said, "Mary Ellen, I'm not trying to worry you, but it's my duty as your physician to tell you that you are likely to have a very difficult time delivering a child. Some women are built for childbirth, others are not."

Now Mary Ellen was frowning. "You're not saying that I can't have—"

"No, No. Nothing like that. I'm just telling you that when your time comes, you may have to endure a great deal of suffering and—"

"Is that all?" Mary Ellen brightened again. She came to her feet and said, "I figure I can take as much pain as the next woman, Doctor. Or man, for that matter." Her dark eyes glittered with excitement, and she added, "Don't you worry. I promise not to behave like a spoiled, frightened child."

"I know you won't," said the doctor, "but just you be sure and send somebody for me as soon as your first labor pains begin."

"I will, Dr. Cain. I'm already looking forward to our engagement on that happy day!"

Mary Ellen was also looking forward to telling Clay that they were going to have a child.

Finally the day ended. Mary Ellen anxiously drew on her long wool winter cape, pulled the hood over her head, and stepped out expectantly into the gently falling rain.

The youthful Ensign Johnny Briggs stepped forward immediately. "Afternoon, Mrs. Knight," he said, smiling sunnily at her. "Captain Knight is temporarily tied up, so he asked that I drive you home." He inclined his head toward the waiting carriage.

"Why, thank you, Ensign Briggs," Mary Ellen said. Her disappointment at not being able to immediately tell Clay her news vanished as she realized this way would be better. Much better. She could tell him when they were alone, and he would surely be as happy as she, and he'd have the opportunity—and the privacy—to show it.

Despite the dark skies and dreary rain, Mary Ellen smiled all the way to Longwood. Once there she handed her rain-spattered cape to the faithful Titus and asked the old servant where she could find her husband.

"In the study," he said, and Mary Ellen was in such a hurry to see Clay that she didn't notice the troubled look in Titus's eyes.

But when she stepped through the open door and

into the warm, firelit study and saw Clay's handsome face, she knew. She felt a premonitory twinge of terror and knew that what she had been dreading for weeks had happened. The inescapable event she'd been pushing to the back of her mind had come to pass.

Clay was leaving.

Clay caught sight of Mary Ellen standing by the study door. His dark, set face softened immediately and he came to his feet. He circled the massive desk as Mary Ellen entered the room. She rushed to him. He took her in his arms. Stroking her pale hair, Clay drew her against him.

Mary Ellen experienced a sinking sensation, a heavy feeling of loss, and she wanted to shout at him not to speak, not to tell her what she knew he meant to tell her. He couldn't leave her, she wouldn't let him. She was going to have his child, and she needed him. Their child needed him.

Mary Ellen said nothing, just inhaled deeply of the clean, male scent that was uniquely his.

His lips moving against her temple, Clay said, "My love, I'm leaving Memphis."

Her arms tightening around him, she clung to him as though she would never let him go. "Where?"

"Mississippi. I've been ordered aboard the ironclad *Cairo,* on the Yazoo River down in Mississippi."

"When?" she said, her voice barely above a whisper.

Clay raised his hands, cupped her cheeks, and turned her face up to his. "Tonight."

Hanging on to her composure by a brittle slender thread, Mary Ellen said bravely, "I'll help you pack."

"It's done," he said. "Everything's ready."

"Oh. Well, then—"

"Before I go," he interrupted, "make love to me one last time, sweetheart."

Mary Ellen tried to smile, failed. "It will be my pleasure, Captain Knight."

Hand in hand the married lovers climbed the stairs to the master suite. In the suite's mirrored bedroom, a fire blazed brightly in the marble fireplace. No other lights burned. The heavy damask curtains were drawn against the winter rains peppering the glass windowpanes. The spacious room was warm and cheerful and cozy.

The world with all its problems was shut outside, could not intrude.

Her news of the baby kept locked safely in her heart so that her departing husband would not worry, Mary Ellen climbed naked atop their big featherbed. Her loving eyes fastened on the dark man coming to her, Mary Ellen not only opened her arms and legs to him, she opened her heart and soul as well.

Their firelit images reflected in the gold-trimmed mirrors lining the walls, Clay came eagerly into Mary Ellen and murmured, "This heart of mine never changed and will never change. You have a hold on me that neither time nor separation can ever remove. Always remember that, Mary. The only one I have ever loved is you."

When they left the suite the rain had turned to a cold, light mist, but the sky remained low and leaden.

At the base of the stairs, Clay said, "I don't want you coming down to the levee with me, Mary."

She smiled at him. "Afraid I might cry and embarrass you?"

"No," he said, and grinned boyishly. "Afraid I might."

"Let me walk you to your horse."

He nodded, draped her hooded cape around her shoulders, then drew on his heavy woolen navy greatcoat. Titus stepped into the foyer as they were starting to leave. Clay shook hands with him and, laying a gentle arm over the stooped servant's thin shoulders, said, "Titus, I want to ask a very big favor of you."

"You jes' name it, Cap'n."

"Look after Mary for me."

"I sho' will," Titus promised, bobbing his white head. "And you look after yo'self, you hear."

"I'll do that. Good-bye, old friend."

Clay took Mary Ellen's arm and ushered her out the fan-lighted door, telling her as they crossed the chilly, rainswept veranda that he was moving a couple of his men back into Longwood to guard her.

"Johnny Briggs you know," he said. "And you've seen Ensign Dave Graybill many times around Longwood, a big, shy, light-haired man with a mouth full of teeth." Nodding, Mary Ellen listened as Clay told her, "They're good men, both. You need anything, you let Ensign Briggs know. I'll be sending you my navy pay, but if you run short, I've an account at Memphis National on Front Street. Draw as much as you need." They reached the front gate, went through. "Is there anything I've forgotten?"

"No," she assured him. "You've thought of everything."

They walked up to his waiting saddled stallion. The big black whickered and shook his head, sensing that they were off on a journey.

"Just a minute," Clay said to the stallion, then asked Mary Ellen. "Is there anything you need to tell me?"

Yes! she wanted to scream. *Yes, I need to tell you that I'm going to have your baby!*

"No, nothing. I'll be fine. Don't worry about me, please."

"Then kiss me," he said, and swept her into his arms.

Mary Ellen kissed him with all the love in her heart, then stood back while he mounted the excited black stallion. When Clay was seated in the saddle, she stepped close again, raised a loving hand, and laid it on her husband's blue-trousered thigh.

Captain Clay Knight looked down at the woman he had loved since he was a child, and his heart squeezed with the pain of leaving her again.

"Always remember, Mary," he said softly, "you belong to my heart. I love you, my darling, and I'll come back to you."

Tears filling her eyes, Mary Ellen smiled up at him bravely and replied, "Stay safe, my dear. Promise me you'll stay alive."

"I promise," he said, leaned down from his horse to kiss her good-bye, then righted himself and was gone.

Forty

Mary Ellen stood in the misting rain and watched as her husband rode away. When Clay reached the end of the pebbled drive and turned the big black onto River Road, she told herself she'd go back inside.

But she didn't.

She stayed as she was until horse and rider became a tiny speck in the distance and then finally disappeared.

Still she didn't go inside.

The warm cape's hood sheltering her blond head, she simply moved to a better vantage point on the bluffs. Wishing to high heaven she'd had enough gumption to bring her powerful field glasses with her, Mary Ellen jumped, startled, when old Titus, wearing his well-worn winter coat, called out to her.

Frowning, Mary Ellen turned to see the stooped old man, who now walked with a cane, coming toward her, his progress slow and tortured. But he was smiling when he lifted up the field glasses for her to see.

Mary Ellen laughed and ran to meet him. "Titus, you read my mind! Thank you so much."

He turned over the field glasses, but of course he then began to scold her. Shaking a bony, gnarled finger in her face, the old servant said, "Only reason I bring you them glasses is so you'd take a good look, then come on inside where you belong."

"I will, I promise," she said, and patted his shoulder.

Titus didn't leave. Already starting to exercise the authority vested in him by the departing Clay, he said, "The Cap'n tol' me to look after you, and I mean to do it, missy. You not back in that house in the next few minutes, I'll see about cutting me a long willow switch. Sting yo' legs right good, is what I'll do. Yes, I will. Uh-huh."

Mary Ellen didn't laugh, although the vision of poor old crippled Titus out in the rain, cutting a long willow switch, was more than a little comical. Even more comical was the idea of him "stinging her legs right good" with that switch. The gentle old man had never laid a hand on anybody in his entire life.

Mary Ellen said, "I'll be a good girl, I promise. Just let me stay until I can get a glimpse of Clay when he reaches the levee."

Acting exasperated, Titus nodded his white head and informed her, "That boy be a-boardin' the *Andrew Jackson* for the trip downriver. The Yankees commandeered that old sidewheeler to transport their troops."

"Why, Titus Preble!" Mary Ellen was honestly surprised. "Clay didn't mention which vessel he'd be taking down to Mississippi. You're a wealth of knowledge."

"I know lots o' things," he said, pulling his coat's collar higher around his cold ears. "Always have." He turned and limped away, leaning on his cane, muttering to himself. "Not that anybody ebber listens to me, no, suh, don't pay no attention when I talk, but they sho' ought to, and besides…"

Smiling fondly after the dear old man, Mary Ellen turned back to the river, lifted the field glasses, and, looking northward, anxiously searched the crowded levee below.

She swept over the long rows of other craft moored at the landing; trading scows, timber rafts, barges, fishing boats, steam-driven tugs, and other steamers.

At last she found and focused on the *Andrew Jackson.*

Unwavering, her chilled hands held the powerful field glasses to her eyes and she stared almost unblinkingly until she caught sight of Clay. Her hands shook involuntarily then, and the heavy glasses bobbled and blurred her vision.

"Thunderation!" she said aloud, annoyed with herself.

She quickly regained control and leveled the glasses on the tall, dark officer leading a spirited black stallion up the steamer's long gangplank.

Mary Ellen's raised glasses never left Clay.

As soon as he stepped on the decks, a boatswain came forward to meet him. Clay shrugged out of his heavy greatcoat and turned over the coat, his grip, and the stallion to the seaman. The sailor led the black out of focus, and only Clay was in sight.

The riverboat's engines started up, shooting plumes of steam high into the rain-heavy air. The twin paddle wheels immediately began to churn up water, and the bell clanged loudly as the steamer backed slowly away from the levee.

Clay lithely climbed the companionway to the hurricane deck as the *Andrew Jackson* headed for the middle of the wide river. He nodded to the keen-eyed pilot in the glassed wheelhouse, then continued to climb up to the texas deck.

While the last gray light of the cold, rainy November evening began to fade fast, the southbound steamer—running lights now ablaze—reached the point in the river directly below Longwood.

Framed perfectly in her raised field glasses, Captain Clay Knight, in full blue dress uniform, was alone on the tall texas deck. A solitary figure in the gloom, he stood as unmoving as a statue at the white gingerbread railing. His rain-wet face was turned up to the bluffs, the cold November winds tossing locks of his blue-black hair about his head.

A lump starting to form in her throat, Mary Ellen thought as she watched her husband being carried slowly downriver that the old Mississippi had brought him back to her on a hot June night and now the river was taking him away from her on a cold November evening.

Clay. Her lips formed his name silently. *Oh, Clay, please come back to me.*

To Mary Ellen's delight and astonishment, the tall dark man to whom she soundlessly spoke raised his hand and waved. He could see her! He knew she was here, and he was waving to her.

Laughing and crying at once, Mary Ellen shot her arm up into the air and waved madly to him. Through the powerful glasses trained on him, she saw his handsome face break into a wide, boyish grin. She puckered her lips, touched them to her fingers, and tossed him a kiss. He followed suit, raising both hands to his lips, kissing them, and then flinging his long arms out wide and high.

Then he was gone.

Swallowed up in the fog and the mist and the night. In seconds the *Andrew Jackson* itself was no longer visible on the dark, murky river.

Mary Ellen lowered the heavy glasses. She shivered with the cold and with fear.

He was gone.

Clay was gone.

And he might never come back.

There had been no war for Mary Ellen as long as Clay was at Longwood with her. But now that he was gone, the war was paramount on her mind. She read the *Memphis Appeal* voraciously and any other newspaper she could get her hands on. She checked daily with Ensign Johnny Briggs to see what he had learned of the battles being waged across the South, both on land and on water.

Her heart froze with fear when, shortly before Christmas, word reached Memphis that the *Cairo,* the Federal ironclad Clay was on, had been sunk by a mine December 12 in the Yazoo River. There were casualties, but it was not yet known who and how many had perished.

Mary Ellen spent the worst week of her life awaiting further word. When at last the dispatch arrived at Memphis's Union headquarters, young Ensign Briggs quickly brought Mary Ellen the good news. The Captain's name was not among the *Cairo*'s dead or wounded.

Some days later Mary Ellen received a brief letter from Clay assuring her he was unhurt and would stay that way. He was on his way to Arkansas, where he would join Rear Admiral David Porter's fleet.

She was not to worry.

Mary Ellen lowered the letter, shaking her head.

She was not to worry? Worry was all she did. Like thousands of other wives, mothers, sisters, and sweethearts, she worried constantly about the safety of the man she loved.

With Clay in the war, Mary Ellen's duties at the hospital took on new meaning. Anytime she bent to comfort some poor suffering soul, she imagined Clay lying there, wounded and helpless, and compassion swelled in her breast. Worrying that she might not have always been as tender and caring as she could have been, Mary Ellen redoubled her efforts to give the injured, dying men as much attention and kindness as any brave war hero deserved.

To those she tended, it mattered not that she was the wife of a Union naval officer. The infirm men she patiently watched over with grace and sympathy cared only that her pretty face above their own offered a ray of sunshine in a world of darkness. And that her gentle hands on their pain-racked bodies brought a blessed degree of comfort.

Mary Ellen worked extra hard and extra long hours, knowing soon she wouldn't be able to help out at all. The waistbands of her winter dresses were already growing uncomfortably tight, and Dr. Cain had warned her that the stress and strain of working at the hospital was too hard on an expectant mother.

New Year's was Mary Ellen's last day at the clinic. Four months pregnant, she knew it was time to retire to the privacy of Longwood to await the birth of her baby.

Without her duties at Shelby County Hospital to keep her occupied, time hung heavily on her hands. It was the longest, loneliest winter of her life. Each day she prayed a letter would come from Clay, but he wrote infrequently. She'd received only a half dozen letters since he'd been gone, and those she read over and over again.

The winter weather matched Mary Ellen's gloomy mood. Day in, day out, it was cold and gray, and one ice storm after another blanketed the river city during the months of January and February. Great patches of ice formed on the cold, dark Mississippi, and the banks were frozen solid. Mary Ellen felt as if she were in prison, and if it hadn't been for Leah coming often to check on her and cheer her up, she was sure she would have lost her sanity.

Mary Ellen shivered alone in the big mahogany bed each night, wishing Clay were there with her, wondering where he was and if he was cold and hungry and tired and dirty and...hurt? She forced the possibility from her mind. Clay wasn't hurt. He wasn't going to be hurt.

Dear God, don't let him be hurt!

Spring finally came to Tennessee, and nobody was happier to see it than the pregnant, lonely Mary Ellen Preble Knight. Even with the warmer weather, she couldn't go anywhere, because as Titus none-too-gently pointed out, fine ladies did not go out in public in her condition.

"Yo momma'd roll over her grave if'n she thought you was gonna be a-parading down the streets of Memphis lookin' like you do now."

"Titus, I've no intention of 'parading down the streets of Memphis,'" she told him, a hand pressed to her aching back. "But would it shock the gentry if I sit on my own front gallery?"

"Might want to wait till the sun goes down," he said thoughtfully. "Not many folks passing by then."

"I am *not* waiting for sunset," she said, then stormed out the front fan-lighted doors and eased herself down onto a rocking chair.

She sighed and looked wistfully down the pebbled drive. One day she'd see Clay come riding up the drive, and she'd run out to meet him with their child in her arms. Mary Ellen smiled, envisioning it, and placed a protective hand atop her rounded belly.

On that sunny May afternoon Mary Ellen rocked alone on the wide gallery while out on the lawn brilliant butterflies darted from flower to flower and a balmy breeze stirred wisps of hair at her temples and the sweet scent of honeysuckle wafted up from trellises on the north side of the mansion.

She fell to daydreaming of the happy years stretching before her here at Longwood with Clay and their children. Lulled by the quiet and the dream, Mary Ellen dozed.

She'd slept but a few minutes before she was awakened by the drum of horses' hooves on the pebbled drive. Mary Ellen blinked and focused. Ensign Briggs dismounted and let himself in the front gate.

Mary Ellen held her breath. She remained seated as the red-haired young sailor hurried up the front walk. When he got closer, she could tell by his expression that he wasn't bringing bad news. So she relaxed a little and smiled at him.

He had come to tell her that a dispatch had just arrived at Memphis's Union headquarters. On the eighteenth of May, Admiral Porter had sent six gunboats upriver to support Grant's army in the operations east of Vicksburg.

The gunboats were under the command of Captain Clayton Terrell Knight.

Forty-One

Morning, May 21, 1863

Captain Clay Knight shivered as he stood in the bright sunshine on the bow of the squadron's lead gunboat, *Cincinnati*. Despite the warmth of the May Mississippi sun, he felt a chill and his hands shook slightly as he nervously took a cigar from his uniform pocket, stuck it between his lips, and lighted it.

Drawing the smoke deep into his lungs, Clay wondered at himself. He had never known fear before. Never. Not when he was a brand-new striper and he'd been sent down to Buenos Aires to protect endangered Americans. Not when he'd helped drive the Chinese bandits out of Shanghai. Not even when he'd been called on to fight a thousand hostile Indians in Seattle, Washington.

Fear had always been a stranger to him.

Until now.

His gray eyes narrowed against the glare of the sunlight reflecting off the river, Clay was forced to admit to himself that he was afraid.

In an hour this gunboat on which he stood would reach Vicksburg and the Confederates' well-equipped navy yard. And then it would begin. In sixty minutes he would be going into battle. A battle that for him could end only in one of two ways. Either the river city of Vicksburg would fall to the Union.

Or he would be killed in the line of duty.

There were no other alternatives.

His orders were quite clear: to meet and bombard the enemy from the Mississippi River at Vicksburg while Grant's army engaged the Confederates on land. Both navy and army were to remain until the vital city fell, no matter how long that might take.

Clay knew Southerners.

Vicksburg wouldn't give up without a long, bloody fight.

The citizens as well as the soldiers protecting their city knew that if Vicksburg fell to the Union, the Confederacy would be cut in half. And for them the war might well be lost.

Smoke from the cigar clamped between his teeth drifting up into his eyes, Clay patted the left breast pocket of his blue uniform blouse. A neatly folded letter inside a sealed envelope rested there, next to his heart. A letter to Mary. He'd felt compelled to write the letter in the long, sleepless hours of the previous night.

Unable to shake off a nagging premonition that something was going to happen to him, he'd gotten out of bed and written the brief message to his wife. The letter sealed, the envelope addressed, he had put it inside his uniform pocket and would carry it on his person throughout the upcoming battle.

If he was struck by enemy fire, the letter would be found on him and, he trusted, sent directly on to Mary.

Clay flicked away his smoked-down cigar, thinking with bitter irony that the reason he'd never been afraid before was that he hadn't cared all that much whether he lived or died. It was indifference that had made him courageous.

Now he cared.

Now he had Mary, and he wanted to live so badly that he knew he was probably much more likely to die.

Soon there was no more time for contemplation.

The Confederate naval yard was swiftly coming up on the starboard side of the gunboat *Cincinnati,* and Captain Clay Knight ordered the crew to immediately man their battle stations.

His body tensed, his alert gray eyes riveted to the riverbanks, Captain Knight issued the order to hold all fire until he gave the signal. The gunboat slid around the curving, timbered bank. The Captain brought down his right arm, and the shelling began.

And never stopped.

Attempts to take Vicksburg by storm failed, just as Clay had suspected. Grant's army settled down for a long siege, and Porter's naval squadron was active throughout the operation. The well-armed Union gunboats poured more than two thousand shells into the river city in the first six days. They drew sporadic fire from the Rebel batteries on the bluffs but suffered little damage.

"Surely they can't take much more of this, Captain," said one of the sweating gunners as the sun began to set on the sixth day and the river was quiet for a brief, welcome interlude.

"You don't know these stubborn Southerners," said Clay. "We may be here for weeks. They'll hold out until—"

The sentence was never finished.

All at once the batteries on the bluff blazed to life,

and the *Cincinnati*'s starboard cannons immediately answered the assault. The ensuing battle was fierce. The river was aglow with gunfire, and the thunderous boom of cannon and shell was deafening. Thick black smoke billowed into the air, blinding the gunners and filling the lungs of the sailors at their battle stations. The eerie shouts and screams of the shrapnel wounded and dying rose from unseen men enveloped in the thick, blinding smoke.

Standing his ground firmly, Captain Knight shouted clear, precise orders, ignoring his watering eyes and burning throat. All traces of his former fear now vanished in the heat of battle, the cool-headed Annapolis-trained naval officer calmly displayed his ability to perform—and to lead—under pressure.

Captain Knight was shouting an order when a single Rebel shell pierced the gunboat's forward ammunition magazine. The *Cincinnati*'s explosion lit up the night sky as bright as day.

"Mary," Clay murmured as the dark waters of the Mississippi closed over his head and filled his shrapnel-lacerated lungs.

"Clay!" Mary Ellen screamed, and bolted upright in her bed. "No! No! Clay!"

Heart beating so fast and so forcefully she clutched her breast in pain, Mary Ellen trembled violently in the midnight darkness of that warm May night. Her palms clammy, her face covered with a sheen of perspiration, she was gripped with terror from the too real nightmare that had awakened her.

Tears streamed down her cheeks as she struggled in vain to get up. Almost nine full months pregnant, she was clumsy and all but immobile. Her jerky, awkward movements awakened the child sleeping inside her. The baby began to kick viciously, and Mary Ellen held her swollen stomach and cried uncontrollably, unable to move to the mattress's edge to swing her legs over.

She heard the knock on the door but was crying too hard to answer. The door opened slowly. A lamp wavered and moved, and through her tears Mary Ellen saw old Titus limping toward her.

"Child, what is it?" he asked anxiously, his eyes round with fear. "The baby? Is the baby—"

"No, no," she sobbed. "It's Clay. Clay's been killed, I know he has! Titus, Clay is dead! Clay is dead!"

"No sech of a thing," said Titus. He set the lamp on the night table and came to the bed.

"What is it?" Mattie called as she hurried into the room, tying the sash of her robe.

"Oh, Mattie," Mary Ellen wailed, "Clay's been killed, I know he has. I saw it all in a dream, and it was so real I know—"

"Shhhh," said Titus, absently patting her hand where it rested atop her domelike belly. "You're gwine hurt yo'self and that child you're carryin' if you're not careful."

"I must get up! Help me get out of bed," Mary Ellen pleaded.

Now at the bed, Mattie elbowed Titus out of the way, leaned over, and took the sobbing Mary Ellen in her fleshy arms. Resting her cheek atop Mary Ellen's blond head, she murmured, "Ain't nothin' but a bad dream, child, that's all it was. You just lay back down and relax. Soon you'll go back to sleep."

"No, I can't! Something terrible has happened," whimpered Mary Ellen. "I saw, I tell you. I saw the whole thing. Oh, God, I saw Clay—"

"No, you didn't," Mattie interrupted, motioning to Titus to help her ease Mary Ellen back down on the pillows. "What you saw was a nasty ol' nightmare. Don't mean nothin'. Not a thing."

Unconvinced, Mary Ellen continued to weep as the two old servants fussed over her and assured her repeatedly that everything was fine. If anything had happened to the Captain, they would have heard about it. Hadn't that young Ensign Briggs told her just this afternoon that there hadn't been a single one of those Yankee gunboats sunk down in Vicksburg? Not a one.

"I'll sit here with you till you fall back to sleep," promised Mattie.

"I was gonna do that," the protective Titus promptly informed the cook.

"Ain't a bit of need of us both stayin'," Mattie told him. Then she pointed. "Go get me a washcloth. This poor child's burning up."

Muttering, Titus limped into the white marble bath and came back with a washcloth and china basin of cool water. Mattie took it from him immediately and, standing beside the bed, blotted Mary Ellen's shiny forehead and bathed her tear-streaked cheeks. She pressed the cool cloth to Mary Ellen's throat, reached inside the open-throated nightgown, and bathed her shoulders and the tops of her swollen breasts. She hummed as she worked, and then in a low, soothing voice she began to sing an old spiritual that had been a favorite of Mary Ellen's when she was a child.

Mary Ellen finally stopped jerking. Her sobs became quieter, then died away.

Mattie smiled and said, "Now jes' close your eyes, my sweet baby, and forget that mean ol' nightmare."

And she repeated, "I'll stay right here with you till you fall back to sleep."

Not to be outdone, Titus took one of Mary Ellen's hands in his gnarled fingers and, leaning close, said, "I'll be stayin', too, Miz Mary Ellen. Yes, I will. Sit right here beside the bed till you goes back to sleep."

Seated side by side on two chairs they had laboriously pulled up close to the bed, Mattie and Titus were soon sound asleep.

But Mary Ellen wasn't.

She didn't close her eyes for the rest of the night.

Forty-Two

I read only sunshine....

The words were etched on the face of the old marble sundial on Longwood's lower terrace.

For thirty-four years the sundial had worked perfectly. Since the beautiful spring day in 1829 when John Thomas Preble had supervised as it was anchored carefully on the estate's northern lawn, the shadow of the sundial's brass hand had moved slowly, surely around the flat marble face.

But on the twenty-seventh day of May, 1863, the sundial abruptly stopped.

Mary Ellen, tired from her sleepless night and shaken from the dream she feared was prophetic, stood at the broken sundial late the next afternoon. The hot May sun beat down on her uncovered head, but she felt strangely cold, as if she stood in deep, impenetrable shadow.

Her trembling fingers traced the letters deeply carved on the sundial's marble face. *I read only sunshine....* Worriedly, Mary Ellen wondered. Had the sundial stopped because there would be no more sunshine at Longwood?

As Mary Ellen stood at the broken sundial, the damning dispatch arrived at Memphis Union Naval Headquarters. The bulletin concluded:

Lieutenant Theodore Davidson of the gunboat *Lexington* saw the explosion. A Rebel shore battery hit the *Cincinnati* in the forward ammunition magazine, and she went down with all hands onboard. No known survivors.

Mary Ellen remained dry-eyed and stoic as the nervous Johnny Briggs stood in Longwood's spacious drawing room at sunset and gave her the bad news. When he had told her all he knew of the sunk *Cincinnati,* Mary Ellen thanked him and asked that he please let her know immediately if and when there was any further news.

Then she politely excused herself.

Waving away her protective servants, Mary Ellen slowly ascended the stairs. In the privacy of the master suite, she stood at the foot of the oversize mahogany bed she had shared with Clay, remembering the nights they had made love there. One hand on her stomach, the other gripping the bed's tall carved footpost, she smiled wistfully, thinking that one of those wonderful nights in this big bed with Clay had started the new life inside her.

Tears filled her dark eyes.

She hadn't told Clay she was pregnant. At the time, she'd felt sure she was doing the right thing. She hadn't wanted him distracted and worried about her. But not telling him had been a mistake. Now it was too late. She had let her husband die without ever knowing she was carrying his child.

"Clay, my love, I'm so sorry," she murmured sadly.

Too exhausted to stand any longer, Mary Ellen, clinging to the solid bedpost, slowly sank to the carpeted floor at the foot of the bed. She laid her weary head against the footboard, sat down flat, and wept uncontrollably.

She was still there when her friend Leah Thompson, summoned by the worried Titus, arrived. Leah hurried straight up the stairs, knocked, and went inside without waiting for a reply.

The older woman rushed across the room, sank to her knees beside the sobbing Mary Ellen, and put comforting arms around her. The two friends stayed there on the floor for a long time, talking, praying, crying together. It was Leah who finally convinced the distraught Mary Ellen that she had to get some rest.

"Won't you let me help you get undressed and into bed?" she asked gently.

Before Mary Ellen could reply, another knock came on the bedroom door and the white-haired Dr. Cain came in, carrying his black bag and issuing orders.

"You're going to bed immediately, Mary Ellen Knight," he said in a tone that brooked no argument. "Mrs. Thompson, help me get her up and I'll check her while you get her a nightgown. Mary Ellen, I'll give you something to help you sleep, and I mean for you to take it. You must think of your child. If you don't take care of yourself, you…you…" His lecturing words trailed away, and in a kind, fatherly tone he said, "Child, I heard. I'm so sorry, but you mustn't give up hope. It's way too soon to suppose that…that…" He stopped speaking, cleared his throat needlessly, then turned away and rummaged through his black bag.

Dr. Cain gave Mary Ellen a mild sedative, and by the time he and Leah Thompson left the suite, Mary Ellen was sound asleep.

The doctor touched Leah's arm, stopped her when

they were out in the upstairs corridor. "Mrs. Thompson," he said, speaking in a low, soft voice, "I am worried about Mary Ellen. She's not as strong as she should be, and now this terrible blow will make matters worse."

"What are you saying, Dr. Cain? Is Mary Ellen's unborn child in danger?"

Brow deeply furrowed, he nodded his white head. "Mary Ellen's in danger as well, I'm afraid. She's going to have a difficult time delivering the child, and she's already weak to start with. If she isn't careful…" He shrugged, shook his head, and exhaled.

"Dear Lord," murmured Leah, shocked. "I never considered—"

"Emotions affect health as much as anything," the doctor cut in. "This news about the Captain couldn't have come at a worse time."

Leah nodded sadly, then asked, "What can I do, Doctor?"

"Help Mary Ellen's servants see to it she eats properly and gets plenty of rest. I want her to have as much strength as possible when the time comes."

"I'll do everything I can," Leah said worriedly. "And promise you'll send for me when she goes into labor."

"I was counting on you," said Dr. Cain.

The long days of torture dragged by with no definitive word on Clay. It was rumored that some of the men on the ill-fated gunboat had survived the explosion and were now being held prisoner by the Confederates. But it was not a certainty, and no names of survivors had been supplied.

Mary Ellen went about in a daze of despair, and no one was more concerned than the soft-hearted Titus.

"Now, Miz Mary Ellen, they exchange prisoners every week," he said time and again. "If them Rebs is holdin' the Cap'n, they may might jes' trade him for one of their own any day. I 'spect that's what'll happen…yes, I do."

Leah Thompson also tried to cheer up the grieving Mary Ellen. She was at Longwood almost constantly, pleading with Mary Ellen to eat the nutritious meals Mattie prepared and to take long, restful afternoon naps. But try as she might, Mary Ellen could hardly force herself to eat, and she found it almost impossible to sleep at night, much less in the daytime.

Distraught, Mary Ellen grew drawn and pale, her dark eyes hollow and clouded with grief. Her strength was slowly ebbing away at a time when she most needed it.

The sweltering summer weather didn't help.

The sticky heat of June descended like a swarm of locusts on the Bluff City. The days were long, sunny, and almost unbearably hot. The nights were still, muggy, and too warm. For a troubled young woman who was nine full months pregnant, the sultry heat was sheer hell.

On the fifth of June—several days past her due date—a letter arrived for Mary. Ensign Briggs delivered the letter to Longwood at sunset. The ensign stood in the foyer as Mary Ellen slowly descended the stairs. She looked so weak and pale, he was reluctant to give her the letter he had tucked inside his uniform pocket. The envelope was stained with drops of blood, and Ensign Briggs had recognized Captain Clay Knight's distinctive handwriting.

"Mrs. Knight," Briggs said, greeting her.

"Ensign Briggs," she acknowledged, her dark eyes questioning. "Have you come to…to…"

Halfway down the stairs, Mary Ellen stopped speaking as a wrenching pain slammed through her body, taking her breath away.

"Mrs. Knight!" shouted Ensign Briggs, and raced up the stairs.

He swept Mary Ellen into his arms and carried her up the stairs, shouting over his shoulder for her servants. As soon as Titus and Mattie were with her, Ensign Briggs told them he'd go for the doctor. He left the room and raced back down the stairs. The letter still in his uniform pocket, the frightened ensign sprinted down the front walk and out the gate, then ran all the way to the Shelby County Hospital.

Dr. Cain was at Longwood within a half hour. Leah Thompson wasn't far behind.

The two of them were still there eighteen hours later. The doctor's fears had become a reality. A badly weakened Mary Ellen endured hour after hour of debilitating pain as her long labor continued through the still, sticky hours of the hot June night. The suffering Mary Ellen murmured Clay's name over and over as she and her baby slipped closer and closer toward death.

Titus and Mattie hovered just outside the suite, crying and telling each other that Mary Ellen and the baby would be all right. Everything was going to be all right.

Sunrise finally came, but no baby.

As noon approached Mary Ellen's pain-dulled eyes registered her unspoken distress. She was not afraid for herself, but she was worried about her baby.

"Please, Dr. Cain," she pleaded, so weak she could hardly speak, "don't let my baby die. Please, don't… Oooh!…" Another tearing pain came, and Mary Ellen bit the inside of her bottom lip until it bled.

"Scream if you want to, child," said the doctor. Then he lied: "You're doing fine, Mary Ellen. Just fine."

Leah looked at him from across the bed, where she stood bathing Mary Ellen's perspiring, ashen face. Leah read the concern in the doctor's eyes and knew that if Mary Ellen didn't deliver the child soon, it would be too late for them both.

The torture continued through the hottest part of the day. Shortly after noon, black clouds boiled up in the summer sky. Heat lightning flashed, and booming thunder rattled the windows of the mansion.

A torrential rain began and didn't let up.

Nor did Mary Ellen's pain.

But finally, at three o'clock on that hot, rainy sixth of June—a year to the day since Clay's return to Memphis—the exhausted Mary Ellen gave birth to a perfect, healthy baby boy.

Out in the hallway, Titus and Mattie heard the infant's cry above the rain and hugged each other. Mattie sent Titus down to the kitchen to brew some hot tea while she went inside and to clean up the newborn.

When the old cook laid the crying infant in his tired mother's weak arms, Mary Ellen kissed his downy head and said, "Welcome to the world, Clayton Terrell Knight, Junior."

His tiny fists opening and closing, Clay Junior snagged a lock of his mother's loose, tangled hair and opened his eyes.

Tears that were a mixture of joy and sadness immediately sprang to Mary Ellen's dark eyes, and she cooed to the baby, "If only your father could see you."

As soon as her baby had been fed, Mary Ellen fell into a dreamless sleep of total exhaustion, and the baby, full and slumbering peacefully, was taken from her, placed in the waiting lace-trimmed bassinet beside the bed.

Mother and child slept as the violent afternoon thunderstorm changed to a slow, steady rain.

Mary Ellen awakened later that rainy afternoon.

When she opened her eyes, she saw two Clays. The officer and the infant. Both were asleep. Both were beautiful. Both were hers!

Captain Clay Knight, in black boots, blue uniform trousers, and a white shirt open down his chest, revealing his bandaged ribs, sat sprawled on a chair beside the bed, his dark head resting against the chair's tall back, his eyes closed in slumber.

Mary Ellen stared at him as though he were an apparition from a long-remembered dream.

Twenty-four-hour-old Clayton Knight, Junior, in the white cotton nightshirt handmade by his loving mother, rested trustingly against his father's broad chest, his downy head cradled in the crook of Clay's muscular right arm.

Her happiness now complete, Mary Ellen gazed silently in awed wonder at the sleeping pair.

The elder Clay awakened.

His beautiful silver-gray eyes opened and he smiled at Mary. Then, for a long moment, there was gentle silence between them. Clay moved, and his son awakened. The tiny infant opened his blue eyes and looked up unfocused at his father.

Smiling, Clay Senior looked from his son to his wife and asked, "Are you both just a dream that will vanish if I blink?"

"I was about to ask you that." Smiling happily now, Mary Ellen lifted her arms to him and said, "Come here and I'll show you how real we are."

Clay rose from the chair, carefully handed Mary Ellen the tiny baby boy, then laid his open hand against her pale cheek and said, "Why, sweetheart? Why didn't you tell me before I left?"

"I didn't want you worrying about me, about us."

Clay kissed her tenderly.

Pushing aside his shirt to gently touch his bandaged stomach, she said, "Clay, Clay, I thought you had been killed. I was so worried and… Are you badly hurt, my love?"

"No," he assured her, making light of it. "A flesh wound. It's nothing."

"Then kiss me again, Captain," Mary Ellen said, her dark eyes shining. "Kiss all the breath out of my body."

Grinning boyishly, recalling the night he'd said that to her, Clay leaned down and started to comply, but the baby wailed his outrage.

His parents looked at each other, laughed, and turned their full attention on their precious baby son.

Outside, the rain had stopped.

The sun was shining again, bright and hot.

Down on the terraced lawn, the old marble-faced sundial read the sunshine.

And it began to work perfectly once more.

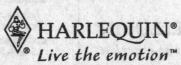

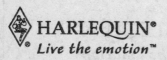

COLLECTION

Nothing is what it seems...

SMOKESCREEN

An exciting NEW anthology featuring
talented Silhouette Bombshell® authors...

Doranna Durgin
Meredith Fletcher
Vicki Hinze

Three women with remarkable abilities...

Three explosive situations that
only they can defuse...

Three riveting new stories that you will love!

Where love comes alive™

**Bonus Features,
including:**

Author Interview

Sneak Peek

and Fearless Females

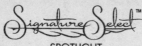

If you enjoyed what you just read,
then we've got an offer you can't resist!

Take 2 bestselling novels FREE!
Plus get a FREE surprise gift!

THE F❂RTUNES OF TEXAS:™
Reunion

The price of privilege. The power of family.

**Your favorite family returns
in a twelve-book collection with a
new story every month starting this June.**

$1.⁰⁰ OFF

the purchase of *Cowboy at Midnight*
by *USA TODAY*
bestselling author Ann Major.

RETAILER: Harlequin Enterprises Ltd. will pay the face value of this coupon plus 8 cents if submitted by the customer for this specified product only. Any other use constitutes fraud. Coupon is nonassignable. Void if taxed, prohibited or restricted by law. Void if copied. Consumer must pay any government taxes. Mail to Harlequin Enterprises Ltd., P.O. Box 880478, El Paso, TX 88588-0478, U.S.A. Cash value 1/100 cents. Limit one coupon per customer. Valid in the U.S. only. Coupon expires July 30, 2005. Redeemable at participating retail outlets in the U.S. only.

FTRCUS

**Visit Silhouette Books at
www.eHarlequin.com**

©2005 Harlequin Enterprises Ltd

Silhouette®
Where love comes alive™

THE FORTUNES OF TEXAS: Reunion

The price of privilege. The power of family.

**Your favorite family returns
in a twelve-book collection with a
new story every month starting this June.**

$1.⁰⁰ OFF

the purchase of *Cowboy at Midnight*
by *USA TODAY*
bestselling author Ann Major.

RETAILER: Harlequin Enterprises Ltd. will pay the face value of this coupon plus 10.25 cents if submitted by the customer for this specified product only. Any other use constitutes fraud. Coupon is nonassignable. Void if taxed, prohibited or restricted by law. Void if copied. Consumer must pay any government taxes. Mail to Harlequin Enterprises Ltd., P.O. Box 3000, Saint John, New Brunswick E2L 4L3, Canada. Coupon expires July 30, 2005. Redeemable at participating retail outlets in Canada only. Limit one coupon per customer.

FTRCCN

```
52605954
```

**Visit Silhouette Books
at www.eHarlequin.com**

©2005 Harlequin Enterprises Ltd

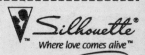

Silhouette®
Where love comes alive™